Waltham Forest Libraries

Please return this item by the last date stamped. The loan may be renewed unless required by another customer.

June 2014		

Need to renew your books?
http://www.walthamforest.gov.uk/libraries or
Dial 0333 370 4700 for Callpoint – our 24/7 automated telephone renewal line. You will need your library card number and your PIN. If you do not know your PIN, contact your local library.

VOYA

'Houck's moving depiction of the love between Lily and Amon is memorable'

Publishers Weekly

D1325292

ALSO BY COLLEEN HOUCK

The Reawakened series
Reawakened
Recreated
Reignited
Reunited

The Tiger's Curse series
Tiger's Promise
Tiger's Curse
Tiger's Quest
Tiger's Voyage
Tiger's Destiny
Tiger's Dream

COLLEEN HOUCK

REUNITED

HODDER

First published in Great Britain in 2019 by Hodder & Stoughton
An Hachette UK company

1

Copyright © Colleen Houck 2017

The right of Colleen Houck to be identified as the Author of the Work has been
asserted by her in accordance with the Copyright, Designs and Patents Act 1988.

Jacket art copyright © Chris Saunders 2017

All rights reserved. No part of this publication may be reproduced, stored
in a retrieval system, or transmitted, in any form or by any means without
·the prior written permission of the publisher, nor be otherwise circulated
in any form of binding or cover other than that in which it is published and
without a similar condition being imposed on the subsequent purchaser.

All characters in this publication are fictitious and any resemblance
to real persons, living or dead, is purely coincidental.

A CIP catalogue record for this title is available from the British Library

B format ISBN 978 1 473 69363 0
eBook ISBN 978 1 473 69362 3

Printed and bound in Great Britain by Clays Ltd, Elcograf S.p.A.

Hodder & Stoughton policy is to use papers that are natural, renewable
and recyclable products and made from wood grown in sustainable
forests. The logging and manufacturing processes are expected to
conform to the environmental regulations of the country of origin.

Hodder & Stoughton Ltd
Carmelite House
50 Victoria Embankment
London EC4Y 0DZ

www.hodder.co.uk

For Aidan, Lex, and Ashley

I gave you a love of Looney Tunes.
But you've given me much more.

Waltham Forest Libraries	
904 000 00645833	
Askews & Holts	04-Jun-2019
TEE	£7.99
6050950	H

The Snare of Love

With snare in hand I hide me,

I wait and will not stir;

The beauteous birds of Araby

Are perfumed all with myrrh—

Oh, all the birds of Araby,

That down to Egypt come,

Have wings that waft the fragrance

Of sweetly smelling gum!

I would that, when I snare them,

Together we could be,

I would that when I hear them

Alone I were with thee.

If thou wilt come, my dear one,

When birds are snared above,

I'll take thee and I'll keep thee

Within the snare of love.

—From *Egyptian Myth and Legend*
by Donald Mackenzie

PROLOGUE

Entombed

"It begins."

"Yes, Master. The chains that bind you are weakening."

"It was foolish of them to think that this prison would hold me indefinitely."

Seth had despaired of ever escaping. But then a spark found him. A human, an ordinary man, discovered a scroll, long forgotten, that held a spell powerful enough to draw a thread from the dark tapestry that fell like a curtain over his mind.

The spell caused a tiny change. A chip in a wall of cement. Seth took hold of a dark thread very carefully and pulled. As he did, his mind's eye connected to that of the mortal, and he imbued him with power. But the mortal proved weak, easily defeated by the Sons of Egypt.

Then a new voice called to him. She was isolated. She was mis-understood. She wielded power. Seth whispered to her mind. Made promises. Told her the things she longed to hear. And she was his. He strengthened her until she was able to escape the bonds that kept her tied to the netherworld and brought her into his own prison instead.

Draining her stored energies, his frame filled to bursting, and in the blackness of the obelisk he sucked in the first breath he'd taken in centuries. Time and space rippled, and then the wall fractured. A bolt of lightning shot through the fabric of space.

Sliding his hands around the split edges, he used his power to open the gap wider, and the walls fell away, fading until he could no longer sense them. One by one, the stars appeared. Nebulas swirled before him in clouds of cerulean, amber, and magenta.

The stars brightened, and he knew they whispered of his escape, but it didn't matter now.

He knew what he had to do.

Once, he thought Isis was to be his counterpart. But thanks to the woman currently hanging on to his arm, her form a black fluttering cloud barely able to hold itself together, he knew there was another one destined to be his.

She was beautiful. She was powerful. She was untouchable. An adder stone clothed in flesh. Because of that, it would be difficult to find her. But there was one who held her heart. Who, even now, clutched it in his undead hands. And Seth knew exactly where to find him.

1

Pancakes and Papyrus

Nana's rooster crowed, the sound of his cry too jarring for me to ignore. I rolled over and licked my lips, which for some reason felt swollen and numb. My mouth was particularly dry. I groaned as I shifted beneath the sheets, tugging them over my head to block out the piercing beams of daylight. The light was an intruder—an unwelcome visitor disturbing the dark tomb where I slumbered peacefully.

There was an awareness tickling the back of my mind, but I doggedly ignored it. Unfortunately, whatever it was had sunk in its claws and wouldn't be pushed aside so easily. What was it that I couldn't remember? And why did I feel like I'd lost a boxing match? My head hurt. I longed for a cold drink of water and a bottle of aspirin, but I just didn't have the energy in my limbs to seek what I wanted.

The clattering of pots and pans told me I wouldn't be able to lounge in bed much longer. Nana was going to call for me soon. Bossy needed to be milked, and there were eggs to gather. My feet hit the cold wooden floor, and as I slid to the edge of the bed my hands shook. I had the sudden feeling that I was in danger.

When I stood, my knees buckled, and I quickly sat back down. Gasping, I took hold of my grandmother's quilt, my fingers tightening into fists that clutched the fragile fabric as fiercely as I would a life preserver. A cold sheen of sweat glistened on my arms. I couldn't catch my breath. Horrors filled my mind: Death. Blood. Destruction. Evil.

Was it a dream? If it was, it was the most vivid nightmare I'd ever had.

"Lilypad?" my nana's voice called. "You up yet, hon?"

"Yeah," I answered, my voice quavering as I rubbed my trembling limbs vigorously. "I'll be out soon."

I attempted to shake off the nightmare as best I could and dressed in a faded pair of overalls, a comfortable T-shirt, and thick socks. By the time I headed out to the barn, the sun had fully risen above the horizon. It perched in the cerulean sky, beaming down on me like an all-too-knowing eye. The light painted the thin clouds above in shades of rose and dusty orange. As I walked the well-worn path, the golden sunshine warming my shoulders and the fragrant air tickling my nose with the scent of Nana's flower garden, I felt like all should be right with the world. And yet I knew it wasn't. The gilded setting struck me as false, and I sensed evil things hiding in the shadows. *Something's definitely rotten in the state of Iowa.*

Settling onto the wooden stool beside Bossy, I thought I had never in my life been so tired. It was more than physical exhaustion. Deep inside I felt battered, drained—like my soul was one of Nana's wet towels, wrung of water and thrown carelessly on a line to dry. Pieces of me skittered around in the breeze, and it was only a matter of time until a gust of wind blew hard enough to send me flipping into the dust. Reaching up to pat Bossy's flank, I let out a breath I didn't know I was holding. The sound of streaming milk was soon pinging against the side of the metal bucket.

What kind of incomprehensible human ritual are you engaged in now? an irritated voice said.

I squealed and staggered up from my seat, accidentally kicking over the milk bucket and my wooden stool in the process.

It's called milking a cow, ya flea-bitten feline.

Naturally, I assumed as much. But such an act is beneath us. And for your information, we don't have fleas.

"Who's there?" I called out, spinning around. I picked up a pitchfork and kicked open a stall, looking for intruders. "My nana has a shotgun," I warned, a statement I never thought I'd ever have to utter. "Trust me. You don't want to get on her bad side."

Why doesn't she know who we are? questioned a voice with an Irish accent.

I don't know. Perhaps there is something wrong with her mind. Lily, we are inside you, the initially irritated voice said.

"What?" I pressed my hands against the sides of my head and crouched down. *Maybe I'm still dreaming,* I thought. *Either that or I'm going insane. Have I finally cracked under the pressure of getting ready for college? I'm now imagining voices. That can't be a good thing.*

You're not imagining us, darlin'.

Yes. We're as real as that too-fat-to-run, very mouthwatering creature you were trying to milk. Milk is not nearly as satisfying as red, raw meat, just so you know.

An image of sinking my teeth into the body of a creature filled my mind. Steaming blood filled my mouth as I licked my chops.

I screamed, falling into the small pile of hay I'd broken apart to feed the cow.

Fantastic. You broke 'er.

One as powerful as Lily doesn't just break.

Shows what you know.

I've been with Lily longer. I think I know her well enough to know what she can handle.

Obviously, she can't handle this. Can't you feel her disconnect? It's like her mind is floatin' above us. Before she was as wrapped around us as a chicken guardin' her eggs. Now she's gone and flown the coop, leavin' us trapped in our little shells waitin' on some fox to scoop us up for breakfast.

I am one of Isis's chosen. An African cat destined to fight in great battles with teeth and claw. I am not a chicken egg.

Well, without Lily, we're just as powerless. When the mama hen dies, her chicks die, too.

Lily is not dead.

Near enough.

I lay there, the prickly straw poking my neck and back as I listened. Was I dead? And all this some kind of special hell reserved just for me? The macabre thought made me want to bury myself deeper. Hide from the insanity surrounding me.

The two voices continued arguing. Whoever they were, they seemed to know me. They sounded familiar, but as hard as I tried, I couldn't conjure a memory. Bossy came over and nudged my prostrate form, bawling for me to finish the milking job I'd started.

When her long tongue darted out toward my cheek, I tried to move away but found I couldn't even wince. I was trapped in my own body. *A brain aneurysm. That's what must be happening. It's the only thing that could explain the voices and the inability to move my limbs.*

The door creaked open, and I felt someone reach out and touch my arm. "Lily?"

A man leaned over me. His eyes were kind and familiar, but I struggled to identify him. The skin on his face was weathered, like a timeworn leather vest, but most of the wrinkles around his eyes were upturned, as if he spent most of his time smiling.

Hassan! both voices cried at once. *He'll help us.*

"Oh, Lily!" he cried. "I feared something like this."

That didn't sound good. The man disappeared briefly before he returned with my grandmother. She eyed the man like he was a wolf trying to make off with her prize sheep. Still, she worked with him to wrangle me into the house. Once I was settled on the couch, she reached for the old-fashioned phone hanging on the wall.

"Please don't," the man asked in a soft, pleading voice. His eyes cut to my nana and then to me.

I could hear the anger and suspicion in her voice. It was lurking just beneath a layer of forced politeness that was steadily melting away like a snowpack blanketing an active volcano. Nana was fixing to erupt in all her protective grandmotherly glory. "And why wouldn't I call an ambulance?" she asked, daring him to give her an answer. "Seems mighty convenient that you just happened upon my granddaughter in the barn. How do I know you didn't cause whatever's wrong with her?"

"On the contrary. I freely admit, I am partly to blame for her condition, though I would never wish her ill. If I had wanted to make off with her for some nefarious purpose, I wouldn't have retrieved you."

Nana didn't respond with more than a suspicious *hmph*.

The man wrung his hat in his hands guiltily as he spoke. "As to why you should refrain from seeking medical attention, it pains me to inform you that what ails Lilliana is not of this world. I'm afraid a doctor would be of no help whatsoever."

I couldn't see Nana from my fixed position on the couch, but the fact that she wasn't immediately pushing the buttons for 911 meant that she was considering his words. "Explain," she demanded.

"It's rather complicated . . . ," he hedged.

"I would suggest you give me the *Reader's Digest* version, then."

The man nodded, swallowed, then said, "Now, this is a supposition on my part, but I think Lily might be suffering from a form of extreme dissociative identity disorder. She's had a very recent traumatic experience. One terrible enough that her conscious mind has . . . for lack of a better explanation, retreated. It's a way for her mind to protect itself."

"And when, exactly, do you believe this *trauma* has occurred? Lily has been under my care since she arrived."

"That's not precisely true."

"That's enough. I'm calling the police."

"No! Please, dear lady, I beg you. I mean neither you nor her any harm. There is no one more qualified to help her than I. You must believe me."

"Who are you? And how do you know Lily's name?" There was a dangerous edge to her voice.

He sighed. "My name is Osahar Hassan. I'm an Egyptologist by trade. Has she mentioned me at all? Spoken of Egypt?"

Nana came closer to the couch. I could see the uncertainty in her eyes. "Her . . . her parents said she's taken quite an interest in the Egyptian wing at the museum. She's spent all her free time there for the past few months."

Had I? If so, I had no memory of it at all. Why did I get out of bed this morning? I knew something was off. Still, my brain disassociating didn't make sense. Was that where the voices were coming from? And why did my mental state affect my limbs? I tried desperately to move my pinky. Just lift one finger. I concentrated like I was threading one of Nana's embroidery needles. I couldn't produce so much as a twitch.

"Lilliana has been helping me on a . . . a project of great importance. I'm afraid one of the discoveries we've made has put her in some peril." He raised a hand. "She's out of physical danger." He grimaced. "For the moment. It's her mental state that I'm most concerned about. You see, there was a spell. . . ."

"A spell?" Nana lifted her eyebrow along with one corner of her lip.

"Yes, a spell. A very ancient, very powerful one. If you will allow me, I can prove to you that what I'm saying is true." He took a step closer to the couch, but Nana dropped the phone, which was now beeping because it was off the hook. The half smile disappeared from her face as she picked up the rifle she kept tucked in the corner. Nana didn't keep it loaded, but the man wouldn't know that.

"I'll thank you to keep your distance from my granddaughter," she warned.

The man looked at the rifle, then at my grandmother. He gave her a small nod but lifted a finger as if to shush her, completely nonplussed by the gun pointed at him.

"Tia?" he said while looking at my inert body. "Are you there? If you are, I need you to take over for Lily."

In the few seconds it took for me to wonder who Tia was, my focus shifted. I felt smaller. Like I was looking up at the world through a thin layer of water. Instinctively, I bucked against the change. I knew that what was happening to me was connected to something bad, chained-to-an-anchor-and-thrown-in-the-ocean bad, but at the same time, I had the distinct impression that I was safe. Cared for. Loved.

"I am here," I heard one of the voices say, except now it was coming from my mouth. Slowly, my view shifted as my body sat up on the couch. "The fairy is with me as well."

I have a name, ya know, the second voice inside me said.

"The fairy?" The man frowned. "Apparently, Anubis left out some of the pertinent details, as usual."

"Fairy? Anubis? What exactly is going on here?" Nana demanded. "Lilypad, are you all right, honey?"

"The one you refer to as Lilypad is here. It is as Hassan has described. Her mind is fragmented. She is like a river after a rainstorm—clouded with silt. I can only hope that with time she will return to normal."

The man rubbed his jaw. "Yes, perhaps," he said.

"How can you speak of normal when she has a split personality?" Nana demanded. "Tell me exactly what is going on!"

The Egyptologist was about to speak when a new voice, like ethereal musical smoke, echoed around us. "Perhaps you will allow me to explain," it said.

My head moved and fixed itself on a pinpoint of light that grew steadily in the center of the room. I heard a soft gasp from Nana when a beautiful woman with moonbeam-blond hair as smooth and straight as a frozen pond stepped through a glowing doorway. The lighted background diminished around her, but there was still a brightness that never left her form.

"Who . . . who are you?" Nana asked. She looked to Hassan, but he just stared at the woman in awe.

She's a blinkin' fairy like me! the fairy voice said.

"Clearly, she is not," Tia answered. "Do you not recognize a goddess when you see one?"

A goddess? I thought with an inner snort. That's crazy. And I knew crazy. New Yorkers saw crazy every day—guys dancing on the street in Lady Liberty dresses, women jogging in heels, food trucks that looked like cheeseburgers, dogs as fashion accessories. But this was next-level stuff, my-boyfriend's-an-alien kind of crazy.

If I hadn't seen the woman magically appear, I would never have believed it. Even with photographic evidence. Whoever she was, the woman was as out of place on my grandmother's farm as a chocolate cupcake was at the gym.

She is a fairy, the voice continued in a manner I was sure only I, and Tia, could hear. *I'd bet my tree house on it.*

"*She is not,*" Tia said vehemently, using what I decided to call her outside voice. "*She is the sister of Isis.*"

"Nephthys!" the man said as he immediately bowed. "It is an honor."

With a kind expression, the goddess put her hand on his shoulder. "The honor is mine, Hassan." Turning, the beautiful woman approached Nana. "And you must be the esteemed guardian of our Young Lily."

"I . . ." Nana swallowed, the forgotten shotgun hanging limp in her grip. "Yes. I'm Lily's grandmother."

"Good. There is much for the two of you to do." Her smile took in both of them. "It is up to you to train Lily. There isn't much time. Even now, Seth has broken free of the obelisk. He is still shackled, but his minions heed his call. Without Lily coming into her full power, I'm afraid all will be lost."

"What will be lost?" Nana asked.

"The grand vizier Hassan will tell you everything. I cannot remain here. Seth seeks Lily, and though I am shielded by her presence, even an adder stone of her ability cannot hide me from my husband for too long." Nephthys pressed a rolled parchment into Hassan's hands. "Are you familiar with the stories of Hecate? The maiden, the mother, and the crone? The furies? Sirens?"

Hassan nodded hesitantly. "They are not my particular specialty, but I know of the things you mention."

"That is good. You are aware that Lily has taken on the power of the sphinx." She ignored Nana's gasp and continued, "She is to become Was-ret. The concept of who and what Wasret is has been purposefully left vague in Egypt's history. We did this to keep her safe from Seth. How-ever, there are many references to a triple goddess peppered throughout the stories of antiquity. We have placed these things throughout history specifically to hide them from Seth and for you to draw upon. Use this parchment as a guide. Study all of these stories, for they will give you clues as to Lily's potential and power."

Nephthys walked over to me and placed her hand on my cheek. "Wasret is of vital importance. I've been waiting for her to come into being since the dawn of time." She placed a soft kiss upon my forehead and turned around to face the others who stared in our direction with mutual expressions of shock. "Lily has not yet taken on the mantle of what she is to be. You must help her accomplish this. Fix what ails her. Reunite her with those she loves. They will help her overcome the beast.

"Even now, the battle of Heliopolis begins. I wish we could give you more time, but I fear that is the one thing beyond even our power. Good luck to you," she said with a tinge of sadness in her voice. "Good luck to all of us."

With that, the goddess raised her hand in a flourish, and a brightly lit gateway appeared. When she stepped through, it vanished with an explosion of color, and she was gone. In the electric aftermath of the goddess's visitation, the three of us remained silent. The only sound in the room was our breathing.

Then the unmistakable cry of Bossy broke the tension.

"Well, now," Nana said. "It looks to me like there's more to this than I originally thought." Turning to me, she said, "Tia, is it?"

"*Yes,*" I answered.

"You promise me my Lily is safe?"

"*Yes. She is here with me and is listening even now. But she is confused.*"

"As are we all, my dear. Do you perhaps know how to milk a cow?"

My nose wrinkled up. "*I can access Lily's memories of the undertaking.*"

"Good. Then you get out there and finish up with Bossy. And

you"—she pointed to the man—"put that dusty hat on the stand by the door and wash up. I'm making pancakes."

The man nodded. "Yes, ma'am."

Nana put her rifle back in the same spot she'd retrieved it from and started whistling. She then tied on her apron as if it were a normal day on the farm.

When we got back from milking Bossy, the man was sitting at the table with Nana, a bowl of scrambled eggs between them, and a stack of pancakes high enough that I was sure there was no way the three of us could make a dent. I was wrong.

My appetite was voracious. It was like I hadn't eaten in weeks. Also, the persons inhabiting my body kept making strange comments like "The eggs would be better raw" and "The syrup is like the juice of honeybees." I dipped my tongue into the glass of warm fresh milk like a very satiated kitten with a bowl.

Normally, I couldn't force myself to drink it warm; it was a little too close to the musky animal for my comfort. Today, though, I lapped it up and licked the sweet cream from my lips with a shudder of deep-rooted pleasure.

When our breakfast was finished and Tia, who was still in control, stumbled through washing the dishes, the man named Hassan took out the parchment and spread it on the table.

"Now then," he said. "Shall we begin?"

I'm a What, Now?

Nana cleared her throat. "Perhaps we should start over again," she said and then held out her hand. "My name's Melda."

"Call me Oscar," the man replied as he gripped her hand and offered her a warm smile. "Pleased to meet you, Melda."

If I had been in charge of my body, I would have frowned at the slight blush that stained the man's cheeks when he realized he'd been holding her hand just a few seconds longer than was necessary.

"Now then, I think I should begin by giving you the . . . What was it? Oh yes, *Reader's Digest* version of events."

He then proceeded to tell the most fantastic tale of mummies, a necromancer, an evil soul-sucking she-devil, goddesses, and much, much more. As he continued his story, my inner voices listened with rapt attention, making little comments and adding their own two cents when he arrived at the parts where they came into the picture.

Everyone sounded very sure that the incredible things he described had actually happened. I couldn't believe it. It just didn't sound like me. Why would I leave New York to follow a mummy? To traipse through deadly tombs filled with traps and fight zombies? Then I sacrificed my life just so he could save the world? I must be more altruistic than I thought.

Apparently, I was then willing to save the world again by heading into hell, or, I guess, the netherworld, to find this mummy guy and bring him back to the afterlife so he can keep doing his day job. Of course, his day job does sound pretty crummy. Only two weeks to be alive, and then he has to die to keep this evil god in prison, which clearly didn't work, since he was out and was waging war.

It was a good story, and the voices inside my head believed it was absolutely true, but something felt off. What was the motivation? Why would I leave and do all these things? How could I be a goddess? Or a sphinx or whatever? I was no warrior.

When Tia sensed my doubt, she stopped the conversation and said, *"Lily needs to see something."*

Oscar and Nana nodded and proceeded to follow me outside. Tia stopped near the barn, set up a bale of hay, and asked Hassan, *"Do you have our weapons?"*

He nodded and retrieved a pack from a place in the barn. "I hid them here after Anubis left." Opening the pack, he handed me a bow and a quiver of arrows and then set down a harness with two wicked-looking crisscrossed knives protruding from the top.

"I think we'll try the bow first."

With an unexpected smoothness that would come only from years of training, my fingers nocked an arrow, drew back the string, and let the arrow fly with a twang. The arrowhead sunk into the bale of hay with enough power that a puff of straw clouded the air. If I'd had control of my body, I would have clapped for her.

My voice sighed. *"Lily believes the skill comes from me,"* Tia said.

Perhaps the knives? the Irish fairy suggested.

With a shrug, my fingers stretched out and picked up the harness. I whipped it across my shoulders, quickly strapping it into place. Without even thinking, I ran, leapt over a water trough, yanked the knives from behind my back, and did a wicked martial arts maneuver. I tumbled, pressed buttons on the knives that elongated them into spears, and thrust them toward Nana's garden scarecrow. The straw filling in its chest exploded outward, raining down in golden tufts that drifted gently to the ground. The fallen victim collapsed in a heap of cast-off rags.

Wow! I thought. *That was amazing! Good for you!*

We would be even more powerful if you joined us, Lily, Tia growled.

Joined you? Umm . . . I'm already here. Stuck with you guys, so to speak.

This power isn't ours alone. We share it with you. In fact, you already had it before I came on board.

I'm pretty sure I'm not the one doing these things, I said. *Actually, I'm not even sure why I'm talking to you. You're just manifestations of my crazed state. This is probably all an elaborate dream, and I'll wake up in a hospital at some point with a hopefully very handsome young doctor who will tell me I've finally come out of whatever caused this hallucination and he'd like to ask me out. With any luck, it will end up being just a really bad bump on the head.*

Another growl rumbled in the recesses of my mind, and I was frightened. I'd angered Tia. *How dare you!* she said. *You make light of our achievements. Our sacrifices. If you don't believe in our abilities, believe in this!*

My hands were brought up so I could see them clearly, and then I watched in horror as the fingers elongated, forming claws with an extra knuckle. My eyesight sharpened, and I focused on a tiny bug that was crawling over one of Nana's tomato plants. I could even see the little cilia on its back. There was a pop, and I could hear the rustle of leaves though there was no wind blowing through the big tree behind the barn. I then heard the scratching of an animal deep underground as it dug. I sniffed the air to realize that animal was over a mile away.

I panicked and tried to press my palms to my eyes, but I still couldn't move. I looked down at my hands and was horrified by what I saw. *No, no, no!* I screamed over and over again, unable to look away but desperate to do so.

"She is frightened," Tia said forlornly. "She cannot accept what we are. I fear all is lost."

"Nothin's lost until it's dead and buried," Nana called out, her voice resonating with steely conviction. "And even then, I'm not so sure."

She came around in front of me and put her hands on my shoulders. They rested there, warm and heavy and reassuring. "Now, Lilypad, you listen to me." It was comforting having her there, hearing her familiar voice. It was a speck of normalcy in an ocean of confusion. "I understand that this whole thing is a bit disturbing, but I cannot accept a world where you're shut off from me. This is a mighty strange thing, to be sure, but the women of the Young family buck up and do what's necessary. It doesn't surprise me a whit that you've saved the world twice over. The granddaughter I know never walked away from what was important, and this sounds pretty important."

Nana stroked my cheek and then patted it lightly. "What's more, I suspect the young man you loved and lost was the one you went to save, now, wasn't he?"

She peered into my eyes for confirmation, but even if I had known the answer, I couldn't have moved my lips to form the words. For some reason my two inner voices were silent on the matter.

"Hmph." Nana grunted and looked at Oscar, but he just shrugged and raised his hands as if unwilling to comment on the subject either. "All right, Lilypad. I'll give you some time to think on it while I get to know these other two girls visiting with you and we decide what to do next."

She made it sound like I was having a slumber party and she was laying down the ground rules.

"But I fully expect you to make every effort to come to terms with the situation. Denial is a river in Egypt. It has no place on my farm." She sniggered at her own joke and then noticed that nobody else was laughing. She squeezed my shoulder, a hint of apology and worry in her eyes. "The sooner we figure out this mess, the sooner I will get my granddaughter back."

A crack of thunder boomed overhead, and a brisk wind blew back the hair from my face. Dark purple clouds churned across the sky like a speeding herd of desert horses. Stinging raindrops hit the ground, followed quickly by hail. The sound was deafening. I wanted to cover my head with my arm, but the one in charge of my body lifted her face and sniffed. *"What is it?"* she asked.

"The battle of Heliopolis has begun," Oscar whispered.

"Come on," Nana said. "Let's get you inside."

After we finally managed to shut the banging door, we crowded around the little kitchen table, all three of us peering at the window speckled with rain, the fat drops blurring everything outside. Hail pummeled the roof so hard I winced, hoping the storm wouldn't rip off the shingles.

Oscar cleared his throat and turned away from the rattling window with determination. "There's nothing we can do about that right now. Our job is to help prepare Lily."

"And what exactly are we preparing her for?" Nana asked.

"She needs to come fully into her power. Only then can she defeat the evil one."

"Defeat? And how would that happen exactly?"

"There are many things I do not know, but take heart. As you saw, she is perfectly capable of acting the part of a warrior."

"Yes, but . . ."

Oscar placed his hand over Nana's. "She is the world's only hope. We must help her to believe. The rest will work itself out."

Nana put her other hand over his. "That's what my late husband always used to say." She offered him a watery smile, patted his hand, and then swiped her hair back, tucking the flyaway wisps into the bun at the nape of her neck. "Okay, then, where do we begin?"

"I suggest we start by translating the scroll. Would you be so good as to take notes?"

Nana nodded and pulled her to-do list off the refrigerator, tacking the top sheet back onto its white surface and then bringing the pad and pen back to the table. Only Nana would think she still needed to hold on to her shopping list when the apocalypse was coming.

This really was Nana. What was happening to me was no dream. It was real. They were right. I could either fight against it—kick against the pricks, to use a saying Nana often quoted—or I could buckle down and try my best to make sense of it all. As Oscar began to translate and Nana took notes, I paid close attention.

"This passage refers to the Furies. They possess the key that unlocks the storehouse where Zeus's thunderbolts are kept. They travel the night sky singing of justice as the light of the moon marks their path. The wicked hear the voices of the daughters of the earth and know that when their song ends, the windless quiet of death comes for them. They are forever linked to the gods of the sun, the moon, and the stars, and when her life fades, the sun and the moon are eclipsed and the stars fall from the heavens. In sorrow the moon draws her likeness upon his face for all to see." Oscar paused. "I believe this is in reference to Amon, Asten, and Ahmose. They are the gods associated with the sun, the moon, and the stars."

Wait a second. Does that mean we're going to die?

"*Do you speak of our demise?*" Tia asked, echoing my thoughts.

"There's no way to know," Oscar answered.

Tia just nodded as if resigned to the fact. "*Please continue.*"

Why doesn't it bother you? Our death? I asked her.

I've already died once, she replied. *I came to terms with it a long time ago.*

Speak fer yerself. I'm not wantin' to give up the ghost any time soon.

I'll remind you that a ghost is all you are now anyway, Tia said. *Your body has gone the way of the world.*

So's yers, she replied testily.

Obviously.

What's your name? I asked. *I know the one in charge is Tia. But who are you?*

I could sense the pleasure the other one felt at being addressed. *I'm Ashleigh,* the voice replied. *I'm a fairy. At least, I was. Originally from Ireland.*

An Irish fairy. Sure. Why not. *Pleased to meet you,* I said.

I then focused back on Oscar's voice. "The serpent hears her keening and emerges from his den, where she will bind him with a cord. Ah"—the scholar tapped the parchment—"this is a depiction of the Triple Goddess Stone. It's quite famous. The inscription on the stone refers to a goddess known as Qetesh, who goes by many names. The one here specifically indicates that she is the Mistress of all the Gods. Her symbols were the lion and the sphinx. And here, look at the weapons she wields."

He turned the parchment around so Nana could look. She put on her reading glasses and peered at the place he pointed out. "Are those her special spear-knives?"

"I believe so." Oscar tapped his lip, considering the image. "The goddess mentioned sirens. They also sing to trap men. Perhaps Lily's song is what will be used to trap Seth."

"We do not sing," Tia remarked with a snort.

"*Singing* does have to mean something musical. It can be a chant or something like a spell."

"We do have the power of the names." Ashleigh popped up, taking over my body. Even though she used my body to speak, my voice sounded different. There was a pronounced lilting accent.

Nana smiled. "You must be the fairy."

"Ashleigh," she said. *"Pleased to meet you."*

"Can you tell us more about the names, Ashleigh?" Nana asked, pen poised.

"We figure out the true names of things. It gives us power over them."

"Names, names . . . Yes, here is a section that speaks of the power of naming. It says, she who possesses the eyes to see, the heart to feel, and the soul to reach, shall have the power to discern all things. She, and she alone, will possess the power to name and defeat Chaos." Oscar's brows peaked as he sat back. "Can it be that simple?"

Nana thumbed her lip. "Nothing's as simple as it appears on the surface. What about this section?"

"This piece refers to the goddess Hecate."

"Is she Greek?" Nana asked.

"Yes. She is also a triple goddess. In this drawing, she holds a key." He paused. "Interesting. This is the second time a key is mentioned." He continued. "She is guardian of crossroads and is commonly thought of as one who guides ghosts down the right path. It says her destiny is to fight the Titans. She is honored by the deathless gods who will become her adoring kings. Her token animal is the dog, and she is often depicted with them."

"*Dogs.*" Tia snorted. "*We have no use for them.*"

"*Unless it refers to the hellhounds in the netherworld. They became our servants after we named them,*" Ashleigh added.

Oscar lifted his head. "Do you remember any of their names?"

"*Of course.*" Ashleigh laughed. "*Who could forget He Who Voids His Bladder in the Wind? That's a name I'll never forget.*"

"Can you call him?" Oscar asked.

"*Call the hellhound?*" Tia repeated. "*We can try.*" She closed our eyes and shouted, "*Come to us, He Who Voids His Bladder in the Wind!*" Air rushed around us and we heard a whine preceded by a growl.

You must help us, Lily.

I don't know what to do.

Join your mind to ours, Ashleigh encouraged.

I had no idea what they wanted from me, but at their prompting I attempted to do what they asked.

Tia took a centering breath and something inside me shifted. It was almost like folding my arms across my chest and falling backward, trusting Tia and Ashleigh to catch me. They locked me into an embrace so tight, I couldn't tell where I ended and they began. With one voice, we chanted, "Come to us, He Who Voids His Bladder in the Wind!"

The rushing of air whirled through the kitchen. I felt darkness draw near in the same way I could feel the approach of a storm. There was a bite in the air. The smell of sulfur, burned coal, and ozone. It was the scent of an enemy. A dark shadow materialized, jaws snapping as a breathy voice hissed, "What do you wish?"

Nana gasped, and Oscar wrapped an arm around her, pulling her back. He stepped in front of her.

I couldn't remember what this creature did to us, but I remembered the taste of his evil, and the coppery tang of the blood he spilled.

"Do you serve us?" we demanded.

"I have no choice but to do as you ask."

"Have you seen your former mistress?" we asked.

"Not since both of you disappeared." The creature's head turned to smoke and then solidified at a new angle, his eyes turned to the side.

"What is it? Tell me what you know."

"The queen is alive. She fights with the Dark One."

"The Devourer has joined him, then?"

"Yessss." The word was drawn out in a sibilant hiss.

"Do you know their plans?"

"Only the rumors."

"And those are?"

"That the two of them hunt you. They will seek to find you by hurting those you love," he replied.

My mind fragmented. *"Asten!"* Tia cried.

The shadowy creature laughed. "Farewell, goddess."

"I . . . I command you to stay!" Tia called out.

"You've let go of the leash," he said with snap of his jaws. "Run, little goddess, for I assure you that my bite is much worse than my bark."

The creature swiped at me with its sharp claws, but we swatted it back. Mentally, Ashleigh took hold of Tia and wrestled her back into place. We locked together again, and with a united voice, commanded the hellhound to depart. He vanished in a wisp of smoke just as the beast lunged toward Oscar, jaws gaping wide.

"Well, that was certainly interesting," Nana said as the mental hold I had with the other two slowly unlocked.

"If by *interesting* you mean *deadly,* then yes, that was interesting," Oscar said. "It would appear that Ashleigh was correct. There is something to this naming business."

"It would appear so," Nana added. "Is there more?"

"There is the mention of Valkyries," he said and then began to read, "They cross the airy sea. Three girls enter, but one rides ahead, white-skinned under her helmet, sunlight glinting from her spears. The horses tremble, and from their manes, dew falls blood red into the deep valleys." He looked up. "It appears as if they ride winged horses through the clouds and enter battle choosing who will live and who will die."

"Perhaps you speak of the unicorns," Tia said.

"Unicorns?" Nana asked, her jaw falling open. "Can this get any more bizarre?"

"I'm afraid it can," Oscar said. "There is a reference here to Shakespeare's three weyward sisters found in the play *Macbeth.* Specifically, the line 'Fair is foul and foul is fair' is mentioned."

My memory suddenly flashed back to the day I'd had lunch with the girls on my committee. I'd called them the Weird Sisters. Funny. Turns out I was the one who was weird all along. There was a mental block, almost like static that shrouded the memory. For some reason I'd been flustered during the meeting, I'd been in the museum that day trying to pick a college. Something had interrupted the meeting, and I'd had to go outside. That's where the memory stops. No matter how hard I tried, I couldn't access the piece that was missing.

I cannot help you, Tia said. *I can only share the things you've told me and the memories we have together. However, I suspect that the thing you cannot see is Amon.*

You mean the mummy?

Yes. You love him, Tia said matter-of-factly in my mind.

Love?

Was it possible? Had I fallen in love with this guy I kept on saving? I couldn't imagine any guy I'd risk my life for. Especially one who moon-lighted as a mummy. It was a disturbing thought.

"So all will not be as it appears on the surface," Nana said, interrupting my thoughts.

"That much should be self-evident," Oscar said.

"Then what should be our first move?" Nana asked.

Oscar pressed his lips together and squinted at me as if considering the merits of an aspiring apprentice. "There is nothing we can do about Lily's memory except give her time. Until she recovers, I'd suggest we train the girls to use their naming ability and practice their various skills. When she's ready, she can summon the brothers, calling them forth like she did the hellhound. Without the Eye of Horus, there's no way for us to raise them ourselves, and Amon won't have the ability for another millennium."

"Can we not just retrieve them from the afterlife?" Tia asked.

Oscar shook his head. "Until their bodies and souls are united, they cannot leave that realm. But you called the hellhound, and he had physical form beneath all that smoke. I'm certain that you will be able to raise them."

And what if we can't? I thought.

"Lily doubts our ability to do so," Tia explained.

Leaning forward, Oscar spoke with conviction. "I am confident that if we can somehow help the furies within you rise, then we will discover the key to unlock that particular door."

Perhaps the key he spoke of would unlock my memories as well. But, as much as I wanted to remember, a part of me was frightened. What if I couldn't do all that they expected? What if I wasn't ready? What if I caused the destruction of the world? What if the enemy pacing outside the gates, the one I could feel as surely as I felt the presence of Tia and Ashleigh, managed to find us? Now not even my grandmother's farm was safe.

As I considered the help I knew I'd need, I tightened my hands into fists, digging my fingernails into my palms. When I straightened them, I saw little fleshy crescent-moon smiles that mocked me. The idea of raising the brothers made my heart feel tight and my scalp tingle. I wasn't sure if that was a good thing or a bad thing, but there was one thing that was certain: my life was about to change forever. I was so wrought with worry, I didn't even notice that Tia hadn't been the one to clench my fists.

Practice Makes Perfect ...
Sort Of

A week passed and my memory still had not returned. At least, not the memory they all wanted me to have. And everything seemed to hinge on me regaining it.

Hassan was reluctant in guiding me to raise the mummies until I knew what I was doing. Apparently, calling them forth was different from summoning the hellhound. I had to know them—like, really know them—before he would risk it. He worried that if I screwed up the spell, I'd resign them to the afterlife permanently, and that wouldn't do us any good. He didn't seem to believe I was strong enough to defeat Dr. Evil What's-His-Name without their help. Suffice it to say, he didn't want me—or, I guess, *us*—going off half-cocked.

Something was wrong with my—*our*—power. Well, according to them.

The thing was, nothing they seemed to do, no monotonous exercise or regaling of my supposed past deeds, triggered my memory. I remembered my parents, graduating from high school, getting accepted to college, Nana, even the museum. It was just all the weird Egypt stuff I didn't know, and truthfully, if I didn't have crazy lioness girl, who spent hours telling me all about the weirdness of how we came to inhabit the same body, and even crazier fairy girl keeping me constant company, I think I would have hidden in my room with my blanket over my head.

It pretty much stank having a peanut gallery in my brain. Even for mundane, everyday chores, they had to share their opinions. The two of them would argue about practically everything. Eventually, they settled into roles. Ashleigh gathered the eggs, helped Nana in the kitchen, kept notes for Hassan, and took over the showering and dressing of my body. While she'd get us ready, I'd wince, not recognizing who I was in the mirror. It was creepy looking at yourself and not seeing your eyes looking back. Oh, they were *my* eyes, but the light behind them wasn't me. Also the facial expressions were all wrong. It wasn't a horror-movie type of possession, but it was possession all the same.

I retreated further. Sometimes hours passed, and I had no recollection of how I came to be in the barn or on the training field. When it was Tia's turn, I wasn't remotely interested in what was going on. She was in charge during physical training, eating (which she did with gusto), and, oddly, milking Bossy.

Not only was I losing myself, I was losing my own grandmother to my two mental passengers. She seemed to like them a lot more than she did her own granddaughter, which stung more than anything else. Nana gave me lots of sympathetic looks, but I could tell that even she was disappointed in me. The more Nana addressed them first, the more I moved further away.

Then there were the times when we entered the room and caught Nana sitting close to Hassan and whispering. When she noticed us, she'd suddenly sit up and move away, wipe her hands on her apron, and head to the kitchen. Tia thought nothing of it. But Ashleigh was delighted over the idea that Nana and Hassan might be beginning a budding romance. Hassan making goo-goo eyes at my nana was just the icing on the incredibly inedible dump cake that my life had become.

Practicing my abilities seemed to be Hassan's main focus. I just hung out in the background and morosely watched Tia at work. When it came to attacking scarecrows or stalking the chickens, apparently I—*we* (stupid pronouns) were experts. We could sink an arrow into a bull's-eye from great distances and throw the spear-knives with deadly accuracy. But each time Hassan asked us to practice merging our minds or summoning the hellhound again, I balked.

I tried, at least on the surface, but something inside me froze. Tia blamed me. Ashleigh kept plaguing me with a litany of bubbly motivational sayings like "He who is not strong must be clever" and "A raggy colt can turn into a powerful racehorse" and then, my favorite, the one that made me feel guilty: "Forgettin' a debt doesna mean it's paid."

Even at night I couldn't rest. They were always there, the two of them. When it was quiet in the house, and everyone was asleep, there they were, in the back of my mind, their thoughts like white noise. Finally, after a week of restless nights, exhaustion won out, and I fell into a deep sleep.

I wasn't alone in the dreamworld my consciousness escaped to, which wasn't surprising at all, but the minds I sensed nearby were unfamiliar to me, which *was* a surprise. I stood on top of a sand dune, an ocean of desert waves spreading out around me in every direction. The grains of sand shifted, hiding frightening things, like a dusting of snow covering bleached bones.

Then the whisper of a night breeze kissed my face. I looked up at the brilliant stars overhead; I could almost hear them speaking. The bones underfoot were forgotten as voices like the tinkling of bells murmured, overlapping each other as they passed their messages back and forth. It was confusing and chaotic.

One star burned brighter than the others, bathing me in sparkling light. A white bird flew overhead, obscuring all the stars but the bright one before disappearing into the night sky. My senses sharpened. It felt as if I were standing in the eye of an unseen storm and was being watched over, protected.

A man's laughter fell over me like a warm waterfall. I wanted to sink into it and float away. A zephyr wind caressed my cheek, and I spun, touching my fingertips to my face, but no one was there.

The moon rose like a silver phoenix, and the star I'd been so fascinated by gave way to its light and retreated, fading into the background. I lifted my chin to let the glow trace its fingers over my face and closed my eyes. As it marked its path across the sky, I turned my body so I was always looking toward it. I felt caught in its heavy gaze, and the space between us felt full of secrets, longing, and unfulfilled wishes.

The feeling of someone's gentle lips pressed against my forehead, but again no one was there. When I looked up again at the pearly orb of the moon, the silver light reflected two stormy eyes, wild as a hunting wolf. They blinked at me from its surface and then disappeared.

The moon set, kissing my face with its beautiful light one last time before it melted into the horizon. I mourned its passing and expected my star to return then, but it didn't. The loss of the friendly star and the earnest moon sharpened into a knifepoint that twisted in my stomach.

Soon, the darkness surrounding me thickened. It tickled the back of my neck with cold, ghostlike fingers. Almost delicately, it traced a path down my spine. I waited, breathless, for the icy points to tear through the thin fabric of my dress and sink into my flesh like daggers.

Wind whipped around my body, and I lifted my nose to the air. A storm was coming. Or, perhaps, with my protectors gone, the storm could finally unleash its fury upon me. I heard a laugh, cruel and sharp as lightning, the scream of horses, the bellow of a colossal beast, and the cries of tortured men. When I blinked, the desert sand shifted, finally revealing what lay beneath the gritty surface. The land was covered in a vanquished army.

Death littered the ground. The rotted corpses of men mingled with the bodies of fallen beasts. I pressed a hand to my mouth to stifle the scream, and sank to my knees as tears filled my eyes.

Despite the lack of light, the bones took on a sheen of their own, glowing with an inner luminescence that highlighted the empty eye sockets and the hollow rib cages. It was me who had caused this. I knew it. I was to blame. "I'm, I'm so sorry," I whispered. My voice, though soft, carried across the sand. "I didn't mean for this to happen."

Just then, the earth's rim exploded in brilliant flame. Dawn broke over the horizon, tingeing the world gold. The bright sun stretched out its arms, reaching toward me. When the light fell upon the bodies, they disappeared. When it reached me, I was wrapped in an embrace so full of warmth and love that all thoughts of sorrow fled as quickly as the darkness.

Everything stilled and, once more, I existed in a bubble of protection. The dust and the sand, which had been so easily stirred by the breeze, didn't dare show a transient state or reveal their morbid secrets in the face of something so powerful. I closed my eyes.

The rays of the sun traced over my face, instantly drying my tears and leaving behind a pulsing glow. I had thought the light of the gleaming star and the lustrous moon were beautiful, but they were nothing compared to the power of the sun.

I absorbed the warmth. Basked in it. I was like a bee stuck in a comb overflowing with honey. Fulfillment and purpose and destiny and sweetness and summer were all wrapped up in that single embrace. If I could have chosen to remain in that spot forever, even to die in it, I would have.

Slowly, the light withdrew, and I whimpered, "Please don't leave me."

The sun tangled his fingers in my hair. Warm tingles traced over my scalp. The outline of a man briefly appeared in the center of the sun, but the light was too brilliant for me to look upon his face. "I never have," said a male voice that could weave sunlit meadows and warm the white-capped oceans.

A cry escaped my lips. "How will I find you again?"

"In your dreams," the voice said with the fading warmth of dying coals.

The sun slipped below the horizon, and I was enshrouded in blackness again. The absence of the sun suffocated me, pressing down on my chest like an anchor. I ran down the dune, attempting to chase the last rays, but my eagerness caused me to trip and fall, and I jerked awake.

My grandmother's quilt was on the floor and the moon cast a weak glow across the bed—a pathetic copy mimicking the light in my dreams. I wrapped my arms around myself and shivered. Tears trickled down my face. Even though I felt utterly alone, I knew I wasn't. My own two personal ghosts watched me curiously from the recesses of my mind.

Interesting.

It's interestin', all right.

I sniffled loudly and wiped my eyes on my sleeve. "I'm so glad you find my tears interesting," I spat back.

Oh, it's not the tears, darlin', Ashleigh said. *It's the fact that you're back in control.*

"Back in control? You call this *control*? If I were in control, the two of you wouldn't be here."

It's a sign, said Tia. *He called to her, and she heard it.*

I groaned. "Didn't Hassan say haunts like you two slept in the early dawn hours?"

He was talkin' 'bout spooks. We aren't spooks, Ashleigh said with a huff. *Even if ya know nothin' else, ya should know that at least.*

"Well, regardless, go back to sleep and mind your own business."

But you are our business, Lily, said Tia softly. *Without you, what are we?*

"I don't know. An all-expenses-paid trip to Crazytown? Why don't you tell me?"

There was a moment of silence. I welcomed it, thinking I'd finally put them in their place, but I immediately started to regret my words. "Look, I didn't mean it."

You did. We know when you speak the truth, said Tia.

"All right, I did." I yanked the quilt off the floor and bunched it around me, tucking it around my legs. "Still, I didn't mean to hurt your feelings. I'm sorry."

I told ya, Ashleigh said to Tia, *the well fed doesna understand the lean.*

"What's that supposed to mean?"

It means, little miss, that this whole experience was probably a good thing. Now ya know what it's like ta be a passenger.

"What are you talking about?"

You. Now that you're back in control, ya might have just a wee bit better idea of what it's like ta be relegated to the back o' the apple cart.

I heard a tiny growl. *Your hair is slipping from its binding, Lily,* Tia said.

"My hair?" I reached up and pulled out the loose rubber band. I tossed my hair over my shoulder.

"Uh, thanks?" I said with confusion. "I'm not getting your point."

The point is, ya daft girl, we didn' lift yer hand. You did. And yer talkin' on top o' that.

"I did?" I raised my fingers, touching the tips to my face and lips. "I did! I'm moving myself! It's me!"

Yes. You are controlling your body again. I wonder what triggered it.

"Why does it matter?" I asked Tia.

It matters because if you slip into the background again, we need to know how to fix it.

Isn' it obvious what the trigger was? It was Amon, said Ashleigh with a dreamy lilt in her voice.

"Amon?" I echoed, frowning. "You mean the mummy?"

He's only a mummy in the mortal realm, Ashleigh explained.

"Still, I don't see how he has anything to do with it."

Lily, Tia said, *he was the sun.*

"The sun?" Could the man hidden in the light of the sun be real? I swallowed, remembering the feeling of being caught up in his arms. "You mean that really happened?"

Yes. The two of you are connected in your dreams, Tia explained.

"I see."

I didn't see. Not really. At least I didn't want to see. They'd all been telling me that I had a relationship with this guy, but I couldn't remember a thing. It was utterly unlike me to give everything up for a man. I was extremely fastidious when it came to the male species. There was a whole mental checklist I had that eliminated every guy I'd ever met from dating consideration. Most of the guys in my high school couldn't even fulfill the basic five requirements, let alone the full list. So the idea that a *mummy* was the one I'd chosen above all others just didn't make sense to me. I now had a new box to check on my list. *Alive.* Never thought I'd have to add that one.

"Well, this has been a constructive meeting," I said to Tia and Ashleigh. "We've done some good things here. What do you say we reconvene in the morning and assess our progress?"

Why is she talkin' like that? Ashleigh asked Tia.

The lioness growled softly. *She is trying to silence us.*

Oh. Well, g'night, then, girls.

Sleep well, fairy, Tia said. I could almost feel her curling up in my mind, watching me with glittering eyes and a twitching tail. *Good night, Lily.*

"Night." I slid down in the bed, kicking the quilt until my feet were covered. After twitching my toes just to prove to myself that I could, I closed my eyes and fell into a dreamless sleep.

Much to my consternation, Tia and Ashleigh played hooky the next morning. I stretched and enjoyed a leisurely shower, relishing the fact that I was in charge, but later, when I asked Ashleigh if she wanted to do my hair, she simply replied, *No thank you.* Even though I sensed she really did enjoy doing it, she stubbornly refused.

Tia did the same thing with milking Bossy. I tried to get a rise out of her by shooing away the cats. They meowed pitifully and brushed up against my legs. Then they batted Bossy's leg until the cow mooed a warning to them and they scattered into the bales of hay. Tia wasn't happy, but she didn't say anything. Pretty soon, even her dislike was hidden from me.

"I don't know what the two of you think you're doing," I mumbled as I carried the full pail of milk down the path to the farmhouse. "I thought you were all about teaching me what it feels like to take the backseat." They didn't answer. "Oh, well, your loss."

I sank into a chair at the small kitchenette table, watching Nana as she prepared breakfast. A smile lit up my face. She was going to be so excited to find out I was myself again. Well . . . mostly.

Nana placed a giant stack of blueberry pancakes dripping with freshly churned golden butter along with a bottle of maple syrup in front of me before turning back to her griddle.

"I think I'll just have a soft-boiled egg and some tea this morning," I said brightly.

My grandmother froze, spatula in hand, and then turned to me. "Lilypad?" she said hesitantly.

I nodded, my laugh turning to a grunt as she swept me into her arms and squeezed me hard. "How do you feel?" She brushed the hair back from my face and peered into my eyes.

"I'm not sure. I guess the word would be 'hijacked.'"

As I said it, I could tell that both Tia and Ashleigh resented my remark, but I didn't care.

"And, um, the other girls are still with you?" Nana asked.

"Yes. They're still here."

Nana nodded solemnly. Her eyes were glossy, but I couldn't tell if she was sad or happy. She took hold of my chin and studied my face. "You've got circles under your eyes. And despite Tia's eating, you look like you've lost weight. You were already lean to begin with. Now your skin is pulled so tightly across your bones, it looks like you've been cast into a pit to starve for the last month. I won't have it. Hassan?" she called out.

He came hurrying into the room, toweling his hair dry. "What is it, Melda?" he asked.

I glowered at him. "Who gave you permission to use her first name?" I accused.

"I'll thank you to be polite to our guest," Nana said. "If you must know, I gave him permission. And why I did is none of your business."

"Lily?" He took a step forward and peered into my eyes as if he were a medical doctor instead of the Indiana Jones type. "How did this happen?"

I ignored him and turning on Nana, jerked a thumb in his direction. "Do you *like* this guy or something?" I accused. "Don't you think that's betraying Grandpa?"

Hassan's face turned beet red, a remarkable occurrence considering the natural tan of his skin. The red color crept down his neck, disappearing into the open collar of his button-down shirt. He spluttered, "I . . . we . . . I apologize for any infraction on my part."

"Don't you dare apologize," Nana said to him. "You've done absolutely nothing wrong. Lilliana, I'm surprised at you. You of all people know how much I loved—still love—your grandfather. Now, Hassan has been a good friend to me these past few weeks. That doesn't mean we're fit to move in together or walk down the aisle. Even if it did, I would expect you to respect my choice in the matter and at least do me the courtesy of expressing your feelings on the subject in a civilized way. I expect better from you, even if your life is a mess right now. Do you understand me, young lady?"

I looked at her stern expression and nodded, feeling sufficiently chastised and repentant. Even Tia and Ashleigh felt cowed by her lecture. "Yes, ma'am," I said.

The granite of her eyes softened to their normal cornflower-blue color. She smiled. "That's my girl. Now, I'm glad to have you back. Hassan? Best bring out those notes we were working on last night. I know you hate computers, but, personally, I think we should organize it so everything's searchable. Will you bring my laptop, too?" She turned to me. "Eat some breakfast, young lady, and then we'll get busy."

As Hassan left, I folded my arms across my chest. "I don't want to do this, Nana. I don't think I can."

"If anyone is strong enough to do this, you are. Don't ever believe you can't. Belief is half the battle."

Taking hold of her hand, I squeezed her fingers and mumbled softly, "I'm scared."

She shook my hand lightly and stroked my hair with her other. "Of course you are. You'd have to be a fool not to be. And my granddaughter is no fool." Nana sighed. "Let the fear work in you, soften your rough edges. Give yourself over to it so that it runs through your limbs and eats at your stomach and then set it aside. Tell it that it can work its poison of inaction in you no longer. Fear comes upon us like a towering wave, but it will always break upon the rock of your determination. You will get past it, Lilypad, and you will be the better for it."

Nana tucked her finger under my chin and lifted my face so she could look at me. I swallowed and sucked in a deep breath. "Okay," I said finally.

"Okay," Nana replied. "Now then, before we try anything else, we need to get you healthy. Hassan?" She addressed the returning archaeologist. "What can we do? More rest? Feed her?"

He rubbed his chin. "My theory is that Lily's body has atrophied while her mind was hidden. A body cannot exist without a mind."

"But I had three minds in my body all along, so why should that matter?"

"It matters because your body belongs to you. It knows that Tia and Ashleigh are not, for lack of a better concept, good fits. With you back in command of it, memories intact or not, you should begin to see a more positive result."

"But we were still strong and able to do all the things required of a sphinx."

"Yes. But you are not meant to be a sphinx. You are more than that. For you to come into your own power, you must embrace the being you are to become. You must take on the name Wasret as well as all that the name entails."

I stood there immobile for a moment. Nana's freshly cut flowers on the table tickled my nose with their sweet smell. The dusky dawn had given way to a golden sun that winked at me over the ledge of the windowsill, warming my arm where the light's rays touched it. I took in everything. Nana's hopeful look, the mosaic pattern of her kitchen tile, the air moving in and out of my lungs, and the thoughts of the two girls who'd made a home in my brain.

One moment, I was Lily, a girl caught up in an impossible situation as dangerous and as deadly as anything I'd ever read about in stories. And in the next moment, I was something else entirely. As I drew in a breath, I gently guided my two inner consciousnesses toward me. They circled my mind, ideas and thoughts, hopes and dreams mingling until we became one. We became Wasret.

"Shall we begin?" I said, embodying a voice that was as old as the cosmos and as powerful as a newborn star.

4

Lionesses, Hellhounds, and Unicorns ... Oh My!

There was a whine and then the click of claws on Nana's tile floor. The hellhound appeared. With slavering jaw twitching, he answered me with a hiss. "Goddess," he demurred with hatred emanating from his shifting body. "What is it you desire?"

"Where are the Sons of Egypt?"

"They are sequestered in the afterlife. At least, that's where they should be."

"What do you mean, *should be*? Tell us what you know."

"I know many things. You'll have to be more ... specific." He wheezed and then laughed. It was a frightening sound, and when Nana took a step back, the hellhound snapped his jaws in her direction.

Narrowing my eyes, I took a bold step closer. Almost limitless power filled my frame. I was lioness and fairy, human and goddess, and I would not be denied. I grabbed the hellhound's ear and tugged him toward me. He yelped in surprise, and his head turned to smoke, shifting away before taking shape again. His tail drooped down between his legs, and I cocked my head, a small smirk lifting a corner of my mouth.

It was me confronting the hellhound, and yet it wasn't me. Every single part of me was in sync with every part of Tia and Ashleigh. I was able to fully access Tia's predatory nature as well as Ashleigh's unique view of all things otherworldly. But there was something else there—or some*one* else. We weren't three. We were . . . four. We'd opened the door, and someone had stepped in. As one, we moved an arm, asked questions, and processed information, but I sensed the connection was fragile, tenuous.

Pronouns like *I, we,* and *our* lost meaning. I was Wasret. We were Wasret—bound in such a way that carving ourselves away from one another—no, from her—was painful to even think about. Each of us still retained what made us unique, but we were locked in an impossible triangle of power, creating a bridge, unable to tell where one of us ended and another began. There was a definite sense that we were now . . . other. We had become something altogether new. In that moment, we were fearless. We could do anything, be anything, and yet I sensed that there was still a small piece missing. There was a part of *me*, Lily, that was still darkened.

"I'd suggest you tell us what you know we want to hear," I demanded with the voice of a powerful thunderstorm. "Otherwise, your *goddess* might do something . . . unpleasant."

"Nothing you could do to me would be more unpleasant than the netherworld."

Smiling, I sank down, and a chair moved of its own accord, scraping the tile as it positioned itself in just the right place for me to sit. As if the hellhound's presence didn't faze me at all, I crossed one leg over another, kicking my booted foot nonchalantly, and then grabbed a butter knife from the table. I twirled it deftly between my fingers, passing it between my hands before waving it in his direction like it was the sharpest of weapons. "Having spent some time in the netherworld myself, I'm sure I can come up with something."

I rubbed my thumb across the ridges of the knife. "You know, even the dullest weapon can kill," I said. "It just takes a little longer."

The hellhound backed up a step. "You don't frighten me, goddess."

"Don't I?" I planted both feet on the floor and leaned forward, capturing the hellhound's eyes in my gaze. At first he froze as if hypnotized, then the predator in me recognized the signs of submission. The hellhound lowered his head slightly and shifted his weight from one side to the other as if preparing to flee. He bared his teeth, tongue licking his chops, and wrinkled his nose as if he found bowing to me extremely distasteful.

Then, using our combined mental power, we pressed our consciousness forward and sunk behind the beast's silt-brown irises, moving past the bristling fur and scorching skin stretched tight with rage. We pushed into the mind of the creature—a fascinating and disturbing thing. "Are you frightened now?" I demanded.

He didn't need to answer—I could feel his recoil, his horror at being invaded in such a way. Not even his former mistress had been able to rip the very thoughts from his head.

You will tell me, I commanded, mind to mind.

This time, instead of asking, I took. I tore through his memories, seeking the information I needed. The hellhound whimpered and fell to the tile floor, scratching feebly. When I found what I was searching for, I retreated, easing my power back into myself, and warned the pathetic creature prostrating himself before me, "Wrath kills those foolish enough to act in its name. I'd suggest you take up a new hobby, ya manky beast." I thrust my boot into his side halfheartedly. "Now get out of my sight."

The hellhound disappeared, and I turned a triumphant gaze to Nana and Hassan but frowned when I saw the naked fear in their eyes. It droned around and between us like the humming of cicadas.

The human in me was ashamed of our actions, and the fragile hold on our power was broken. Immediately, the power of Wasret left us, and we separated, becoming three individuals, albeit still in one body, once more. I felt drained and shaky; my limbs trembled like I was a junkie needing another fix. It hadn't been a conscious decision to let go of the power. In fact, it was surprising to all of us. It was almost like the snap of a rubber band. Whatever or whoever we'd been was gone. Truthfully, it was a relief to be myself again. I sat back down on the chair, my fingers twitching. "He's gone now," I said to Nana. "You don't need to be afraid of him."

"It's not him I'm afraid of, Lilypad. It's you."

I frowned and rubbed my aching temples. "We did what you wanted us to do."

"No. We didn't want that. Never that." Nana came forward and cupped my chin in her hands. "Now, girls, each one of you listen to me. Never, never forget to stay in the boat. The minute you think you can brave the ocean on your own, you're lost. You all went off the deep end for a bit there."

What does she mean? Tia asked.

"She means we overstepped," I said, my mouth now dry as I translated Nana's metaphor for them. *I wonder if a hangover feels like this,* I thought.

What is a hangover? Tia asked.

It's the pain that comes after imbibing too much o' the devil's drink, Ashleigh explained. *I had to nurse my da back ta health from it every Sunday mornin'.*

We didn't feel pain before, when we used our powers on the Devourer, Tia said. *So why are we feeling the pain of it now?*

I don't know, I answered. *Maybe it has something to do with my memory loss.*

Turning to Hassan, I said, "I apologize for frightening you. I . . . We weren't in control."

Or perhaps we were too much in control, Ashleigh added.

Hassan nodded thoughtfully. "The power you possess is great. Perhaps this is why you need the Sons of Egypt."

"Why do you say that?" I asked.

"I believe they can help you . . . channel your power properly. They have experience with it. Especially Amon, who possesses the Eye." He touched my arm. "You may not remember, Lily, but I was the keeper of the Eye for a time, and its influence is . . . well, it's indescribable. If I'd held it for long, I would have gone mad. Perhaps this power is the same."

"So you think the mummy, I mean Amon, can guide us as Wasret?" I asked as I chewed on a fingernail.

"That is my belief."

"Then it's a good thing I practiced by summoning the hellhound. Even though we got a nasty headache from it, as well as a bad taste in the mouth. I'd hate to lose it like that on the Sons of Egypt."

"You'll have to describe your symptoms for me," Hassan said with interest as he picked up a pad of paper.

"Later, Oscar," Nana said as she dug through her kitchen cupboard for a bottle of aspirin. "Did that beastie tell you where Amon is?"

I shook my head. "All I know is that they haven't been found yet. Somehow, the brothers have managed to avoid Seth even though he's sent his shabti spies into the afterlife looking for them. The hellhound didn't want to tell me, but Seth is planning to liberate the demons from the netherworld and then use them and the Devourer to attack the afterlife as soon as Heliopolis falls."

"Are the gods losing the war, then?" Hassan asked. His pen clattered to the table.

Wincing, I downed my aspirin and nodded. "I'm afraid it looks that way. At least from the beast's perspective."

"Then we must hurry," Hassan said. "We've got to get to the bodies of the Sons of Egypt and summon them before Seth finds them in the afterlife and unmakes them entirely. Anubis assured me that they will be needed in the final battle. Ideally, I'd like more time for you to prepare, but the situation being what it is—"

"It's sink or swim." I slapped the butter knife down on the table and then grimaced, shrugging my shoulders in Nana's direction as an apology. "We'd best get going, then. It will take us a while to get to Egypt."

"Yes, about that . . . I'm afraid I have some rather bad news," Hassan said.

"What is it?" I asked edgily, uneager to hear anything else regarding my celestial mission. Rising, I could feel my limbs still trembling with the recent use of our power. I was like a kettle full of popcorn just put on the stove—untapped energy ready to explode out of my skin.

But what would be left behind after that power was spent? My fear was an inner chink in my armor. It weakened me, and I was unsure how I could repair the breach. What if, after this was all over, I ended up just an empty, useless husk of a girl, wrung out and tossed aside by the gods who used me to fight their battles?

Hassan went on, unaware of my inner turmoil, but it gave me some measure of comfort to know that Tia and Ashleigh shared my fears. Even worse: they expected, after all was said and done, to be relegated to oblivion. They didn't fear being left alone or abandoned by those who had fashioned us into what we were. They had no concept of PTSD and didn't really care much about what happened to my mortal world. No. They were worried that they'd be banished altogether. That they'd simply disappear—ceasing to exist.

I promised them I wouldn't let that happen. At the same time, Hassan just finished explaining, "And that is why we have to get there on our own."

Rubbing my flushed cheek, I said, "Um, what was that again? Sorry. Had an inner conversation going on."

He gave me a small, understanding smile that crinkled his eyes. In that moment, I admitted to myself that Nana could do worse. Hassan was a kind man and handsome for a guy his age, especially when he smiled. If he weren't messed up in all this god-and-goddess/saving-the-world business, I think I'd even like him.

"I was saying that Anubis made it quite clear that the gods would be embroiled in battle. We cannot rely on them for transportation to Egypt."

I placed my hands on my hips. "Well, that's just great. How are we supposed to get to Egypt, then, fly?"

"I . . . I've got some money stashed in the cookie jar—" Nana began.

We don't need her treasures, said Tia.

Hate to share this sad human fact with you, lioness, but we do need treasures to fly. Egypt is an ocean away.

No, we don't, Lily. We'll summon the unicorn.

"Unicorn?" I said out loud.

Ashleigh's excitement exploded in my mind. *A winged one?* she asked. *Oh, how I've missed flyin'.*

I took a backseat and let Tia emerge to explain to all of us how a flying unicorn and his children could be summoned to take us to Egypt. Nana was shocked, to say the least, and Dr. Hassan seemed both thrilled at and terrified of the idea. Apparently, he'd never even ridden a horse before.

At first, Nana didn't want to go. She fussed about the cow and the barnyard cats and the chickens. When I adamantly refused to even consider going anywhere without her, Nana being my only lifeline to what was normal, she acquiesced. She called upon her twin brothers, Melvin and Marvin, to take care of the farm while the two of us went on a "road trip." The twins instantly agreed and said they'd stop by that very evening, which freed us up to leave immediately.

Tia argued that my *elder* would be better left behind and that it was dangerous to bring her. Perhaps it *was* selfish of me to want Nana to come along, but . . . I needed her. There was just no way I was going to . . . to climb on the back of a unicorn and head off to parts unknown. I wasn't particularly brave or heroic despite what Tia and Ashleigh told me. Whatever had inspired me to do what they insisted I'd done before was . . . well, it was missing now.

Tia finally accepted it and explained that we needed a tomb to summon the unicorn. Hassan asked if there was a cemetery nearby. Nana hesitated only a moment and then confirmed that yes, there was one rather close.

No. We can't use that one, Tia, I said. *It's where my grandfather is buried. It will be too painful for Nana.*

"Lily informs me that the place you have mentioned is the burial ground for your mate. Perhaps we can find another place," Tia suggested.

Nana clutched a dish towel in her hands. She gave us a small, apologetic smile and then turned to look out the kitchen window. "No," she said. "If Charles were around, he would have wanted to take part in the action. He would give us his blessing if we could ask him."

"Are you certain, Melda?" Hassan took her hand and squeezed her fingers.

"I'm certain. Let me just . . . Let me just collect a few things."

She retreated to her room while Hassan gathered his things, placing them in a well-used waterproof satchel next to his archaeologist's tools.

Tia shifted back, allowing me to take over again. The problem was, I didn't know what to do next.

"You'd best prepare yourself, too," Hassan said with raised bushy brows. "Your weapons are in the barn. Tia knows where."

"Okay." I headed out to the barn and found the bow and quiver of feather-tipped arrows along with the leather harness hanging on a hook. Fingering a knife, I sank it down into the casing until the magic that locked it in place took hold. I picked up the harness, letting it droop from my fingertips.

I looked down at my rolled-up overalls, mud-slicked boots, and soft cotton button-down shirt. Then reached up to touch my messy ponytail. "This doesn't really look like what one wears to summon a unicorn."

We can make our own clothing, Tia suggested. *It is fairly simple, actually. We just summon the power of the sphinx while you think of what you want to wear, and it appears.*

"Okay," I said.

Do not forget to close your eyes. Oh, and also, you usually like to be cleaned.

My eyes flew open. "Cleaned?"

Yes. We are often in an unwashed state, and you enjoy having a silky mane and fragrant skin. Personally, I think our natural musk is better, but I leave it up to you.

"Uh-huh. Well, I appreciate that." I blew out a breath. "Okay, here goes."

Closing my eyes, I concentrated and felt my power stir. Tiny stinging particles pummeled my skin and I cried out in fear and cracked open an eye.

The sand is normal, Tia said. *It polishes your skin. It shouldn't take this long, Lily. You are not focused. What is the problem?*

"I don't know," I replied and instantly regretted it when grains of sand flew into my mouth. I spat and sent her a mental reply instead. *I guess I don't really know what to wear.*

I'll help, replied Ashleigh's perky voice.

Tia quickly intervened. *No. You do not understand the necessary attire. I will help Lily. You just watch.*

The sand buffeted my body, and the fabric I wore, including my shoes, dissolved in the storm. I wrapped my arms around myself self-consciously, grateful I'd decided to do this in the barn, where only Bossy could see me. My hair was swept up in the wind, and the long strands whipped against my bare back. *It is not working,* Tia said as she attempted to merge her thoughts with mine to summon the power of the sphinx.

What am I doing wrong? I asked.

I covered my face with my hands, my body trembling in the onslaught. Then Ashleigh said, *It can't jus' be the two of you like before. I've got to be a part of this, too.* She joined with us and the sand froze in midair and then settled down on my body as soft as drifting snow, forming clothing as it did so.

Lifting my hand, I stroked the fabric covering my arm. It was patterned to look a bit like fish scales. Each tiny curved plate caught the light, and I turned, reflecting every metallic color under the sun. It was hard like chain mail, but it moved and stretched with my body easily. It felt like a vintage T-shirt. Open-fingered leather gloves were laced up to my elbows and overlaid with beautifully designed metal plates that cuffed each wrist.

My torso was protected by a sort of breastplate that attached to my leather harness, which was now gray to match my leather gauntlets. Soft, textured leggings were tucked into supple boots with shimmering green armored pieces that capped my knees and shins.

A silver cape was the heaviest thing I wore. It hung from my shoulders and was long enough to brush the ground. Concerned that it would block my access to the arrows, I reached up and was surprised to find that the cape fit beneath the harness with a wide opening so that I could easily draw my weapons.

Feeling along the upper edge, I discovered a fur-lined hood that could be rolled up and tucked away when I didn't need it. My hands brushed against my hair, and I looked in the small mirror in the barn. My dark hair was wound up and looped in an elaborate design, fastened at the nape of my neck with little scarab pins.

Around my neck, attached to the cape, was an intricate necklace. At its center hung the most beautiful emerald-green scarab outlined with diamonds and gold. I knew its name. It was on the tip of my tongue, but I could not summon it forth. "It's beautiful," I said, fingering the gem, delighting in the little flutter I felt against my fingertip.

It's Amon's heart scarab, Tia explained.

"Heart scarab?"

Yes. He gave it to you before he departed the mortal realm.

"Did he?"

Hassan found it and kept it for you in your bag.

I pressed my palm over it, and it warmed my hand. Closing my eyes, I could almost feel the caress of the sun on my face. Sucking in a breath, I said, "I guess we should see if Nana and Hassan are ready."

Nana's eyebrows rose when she saw my outfit, but she said nothing. As natural and as magical as it had seemed when I was in the barn, I felt slightly silly walking around in my new clothes on the farm. Tia and Ashleigh assured me that it would be perfect for where we were going, and they were rather proud of their fashion contributions. The cloak would keep us warm, and the armor would protect us. The boots were thick enough to make hellhounds think twice about sinking their teeth in, and I had to admit, they were extremely comfortable.

Nana wore a pair of jeans and her cowboy boots with granddad's felt hat atop her head, the tie cinched tight beneath her chin, and she had a heavy bag slung across her shoulders. She looked like a woman headed out for a day trip on horseback.

I, on the other hand, looked like I was headed to a comic book convention. I gave her a sheepish grin. To her credit, Nana remained tight-lipped about my clothes and distracted me from my thoughts by forcing me to down a bottle of water, pressing a second into my hand, and handing me an apple to eat while she drove us to the cemetery.

With my harness on, I couldn't buckle my seat belt, but I guessed a car accident on a country road with no traffic should have been the least of my worries. Hassan sat in the back of the car, running his hands over the brim of his hat before placing it on his head and mumbling to himself. He checked his bag to make sure he had everything he thought he might need. He barely gave my outfit more than a glance, though he did do a quick sketch of the scarabs adorning my hair. He claimed that they were exact replicas of something or other he'd dug up who knew when.

We arrived at the cemetery all too quickly and trod the worn path, small headstones peeping out from behind tall prairie grasses and weeds. The apple turned sour in my stomach as we approached Grandpa's well-maintained headstone. Nana must have been there not too long before. There was still a little bit of life in the bouquet of flowers placed in the vase at the base of it, which, even if the others had been cleared of weeds, would have made it stand out among the rest.

I turned to look at her and saw that her eyes were sparkling wet, but otherwise her face was set with determination. "It's up to you now, Lilypad."

Tia? I don't know what to do.

I don't know either, Ashleigh said.

Do not worry. I remember how to summon the unicorn, Tia said.

Tia began chanting a spell in my mind, which I then spoke out loud. As I did, the ground shook and a crack opened in a nearby tree, spewing glittering dust into the air. Nana cried out, and Hassan pressed her head into his shoulder, though he looked nearly as frightened as she did.

I closed my eyes and coughed. A thundering gallop echoed in the air around us. It sounded like a stampede, and I stepped back, fearing we were going to be run down at any moment. I spun in a circle, for the noise seemed to be all around us, but still, I didn't see anything. Then light exploded out of the crack in the tree. Shielding my eyes, I reached for the blade at my back and felt a shift in the air around me, like I was in the presence of something ancient, something dangerous.

Hooves stamped. Hot breath washed over my face. There was a deep whinny, and a new voice penetrated my mind. *Ah, young sphinx, we meet again.*

5

Summoning

Unicorn dust and panic mixed together, tasting bitter on my tongue, but when I actually looked at the beast I was in awe. When he shook out his mane, it sparkled with an almost angelic quality, as if it had been touched by the light streaming through a cathedral's stained glass window. In all the world, in all the books I'd read, I could not imagine a more ethereal and beautiful creature.

Hello, lioness, the stomping animal said in my mind.

Greetings to you, too, unicorn, Tia replied.

Ach, he's lovely, Ashleigh said.

Wait, he can hear you two? I asked, stepping away from the unicorn's wet, velvety nose. My movement didn't deter him. He narrowed the gap quickly, pressing his head against me again. It was almost as if he couldn't help himself. I was startled by his ease and sense of familiarity with me.

It would appear so, Tia answered. *Interesting. He wasn't able to hear me before without your aid, though he could sense me. Apparently, our voices are now audible to immortal beings, even ones as simple as unicorns. And don't mind him, Lily. He has a thing for young virgins.*

Watch yourself, lioness, he warned with a sparkling glint in his eye.

You might have proven a worthy companion for Lily, but you have yet to win my trust.

Then I will endeavor to do so, especially as we have great need at the present time. Lily has . . . forgotten herself.

Forgotten herself? The unicorn snorted and shook out his mane. *How is this possible?*

Her mind fragmented when we returned to the mortal world, Tia said.

Umm, hello, I'm right here, and I can speak for myself. Out loud, I said, "So, yeah, I've forgotten all about this Egypt stuff. I'm not, like, incapable of doing anything, I just—"

She doesn't remember Amon, Tia interrupted with a grave tone.

The unicorn turned his head to peer at me with his thick-lashed eye, which narrowed smartly. Up close he smelled of starlight, night breezes, and wintry desert. His stare made me uncomfortable, and I shifted my weight to my other foot. The extra inch or two I gained in space wasn't much, but I still breathed more easily. "Anyway, this is Dr. Hassan, and Melda, my grandmother," I said, pointing to my two companions.

Dr. Hassan was jotting down notes as fast as humanly possible and sketching a crude drawing of the great beast. I could tell he had a thousand questions he was itching to ask. Nana had her hat pushed back and her fingers covering her mouth. I could almost hear the *Well, I never!* even though she was restraining herself from actually saying it. Gesturing to the two of them, I added, "We need a ride to Egypt. We've got to raise the mummies so they can help us battle the bad guy."

Unicorns are not packhorses to saddle up at will.

I quickly backpedaled. The last thing I wanted to do was tick off a unicorn. "No, I didn't mean it like that," I said. Turning to Nana and Dr. Hassan, I added, "Better give us a minute." They moved a ways off and waited, my grandmother whispering questions to Dr. Hassan.

The unicorn turned as if preparing to leave.

You are afraid, Nebu, Tia accused him.

Tia! I mentally hissed, but she effectively ignored me.

I fear nothing, he countered, spinning around. *Even death cannot rip away my integrity.*

But you are unsettled, she insisted. There was a quiet moment as Tia processed what our senses were telling us. *You . . . you fear the Unmaker,* she finally said. *The stench of it has settled on your coat. Do not think to deny it.*

The unicorn lifted his head to the sun as if seeking its blessing. When he lowered it, he said, *This is a battle we cannot win. If Seth discovers I am helping you, he will unmake all of my children. I cannot risk it. I am their only protector.*

Sometimes protection means joinin' the battle, Ashleigh said.

Nebu stomped, then nudged us with his head, causing me to stagger slightly. *The gods have already taken away my soul, the one I love above all others, and then they removed my alicorn. Why should I risk my family to help them? If you have a good reason, tell me.*

I was about ready to give Tia an *I told you so*—leave the unicorn be, when she said, *I cannot justify the actions of the gods. Lions have suffered their punishment as well, but I am able to look outside myself and my pride. Can you not do the same?*

Bah. You have lived as a human for too long. You've begun to think like them, Nebu said. *My children are all I live for, the only hope I have left. How can I endanger them? Avoiding the war and Seth's wrath is the best counsel I can give the herd.*

I did not expect such cowardice from a unicorn.

If I could have waved mental hands to shut her up, I would have. Tia and the unicorn obviously had a prior relationship, even if it was a volatile one. All I could do was sputter, cringe through their bantering, and hope she knew what she was doing. Even without an alicorn, a stallion that size could pound us into powder.

Perhaps, then, you expect too much, the unicorn finally said. *How do I attack without a horn? Without power? I am stunted. Bound in fetters. With what shall I fight?*

You fight with teeth and hoof. With strength of limb and strength of heart, like any other beast! Tia exclaimed.

The unicorn cocked his head. *Strength of heart. How can a heart be strong when it's been broken? You've tasted first love, young lioness. It's puffed you up with courage, possibility, and dreams. I wonder if the one you loved was lost, how eager you'd be to embrace your convictions then.*

That statement stopped me in my tracks. *Whoa there. You're in love, Tia? With who? When did this happen?* I asked.

She ignored me again.

You are a great beast, Tia said, *but great beings are not always wise. Make no mistake. Seth intends to destroy us all. Even should you survive to the last, he will come for you. And when he does, you will meet your death knowing you could have been a hero but that you chose the path of fear instead. You would rather hide in a burrow like a pitiful mouse trying to tunnel deeper while the snake lurks at your door, than risk death in the most glorious of hunts. You are not the creature I thought you were.*

We cannot win, lioness. He is too powerful.

But, don't you see, Nebu? It does not matter if we win or if we lose. We have no control over the manner of our death. We can only choose how we will live. Besides, winning does not make heroes. Heroes are born of those who strive.

The fairy tree always told me, there's safety in shelterin' one another, an' if we do that, we can endure anythin'. Won't ya strive with us? Ashleigh asked hopefully. *Please?*

The unicorn snorted and stomped as he spun and raced back to the tree. Then he kicked up his hind legs, shook his head, and trotted around us in a wide circle. Finally, he came back to me and touched his nose to my shoulder. When I reached up to pet his neck, he closed his eyes and sighed softly. *Very well,* he said finally. *I will go with you and I will ask two of my children who would be willing volunteers to help your elders. The rest of the herd will remain in hiding. I will not endanger them. I hope you are right. For all our sakes.*

I'm glad to see you have regained at least some of your horse sense.

I am as removed from a horse as you are from a housecat, I'll remind you. I'll thank you to show me the respect I deserve.

When you do something to deserve it, I will do so.

"Thank you," I said quickly, patting the beast's shoulder, hoping to interrupt the argument.

The unicorn shook out his mane. *You are welcome, Lily. Come, let's raise Egypt's Sons.* Lifting his head, he whistled, the sound an eerie, chilling pitch that made my heart flutter in my chest. Within the space of two heartbeats, we heard the ghostly gallop of otherworldly creatures.

A golden mare and another stallion leapt from the heart of the tree and approached their leader, nickering and flicking their heads up and down. I retrieved Nana and led her to the mare, linking my fingers together to give her a boost. Nana threaded her fingers in the sparkling mane and patted the sleek neck of the beast.

"Her name is Zahra. She likes you," I told her. "She says she appreciates having an experienced rider."

"Lily," Nana said, bending down. "I thought they were unicorns."

"They are."

"Then where are their horns?"

"Tia tells me it's a long story. She'll fill you in later, but suffice it to say, they were cut off."

"Cut off? Oh, you poor beast. Don't you worry yourself none about that. You're the most gorgeous creature I've ever had the pleasure to ride, not to disparage old Bob. He's a good horse. But you're much more than a horse, aren't you, honey?"

I left Nana to sweet-talk her unicorn and helped Dr. Hassan, who was nowhere near as comfortable climbing on the back of a unicorn as Nana was.

"His name is Kadir," I told him. "He says if you hold to him tightly and keep your legs clasped to his side, he won't let you fall."

"Yes, well, I'll endeavor to do my best," Dr. Hassan said.

I was about to leave when Tia suggested I give him a warning. "Tia says you might want to put your hat in your bag. If you lose it on this journey, there will be no going back to retrieve it."

"I'll keep that in mind." Even as he said it, he took off his precious hat, ran his hand through his thick white hair, and gave it some serious consideration.

I took hold of the unicorn's mane and kicked up onto his back with relative ease. *You don't remember me at all, Lily?* the beast asked as I settled.

No, I'm sorry.

So am I. I'd like to think our time together was notable.

I have no doubt it was, I said.

Still, there's something to be said for getting a second chance at a first impression.

With that, the unicorn reared up, beating the air with his shiny hooves, and raced headlong toward the opening in the tree. It looked entirely too narrow to fit the width of his body, but in the time it took for me to raise my hand up to protect myself from the impact, we were through.

Everything turned inside out, like the whole world was now a negative-exposure photo. The bright countryside, which had had an almost Sunday-morning sweetness, had become cold and dim. It was as if everything wholesome and good in the world had been siphoned away, leaving only the moldering, unwanted bits lying beneath. We were galloping through a grove of trees, but instead of leafy tops bursting with growth, the trunks were barren and skeletal, their long limbs stretching upward as if they begged the cold blue moon above for death.

Where there would normally be a farm with crops, I spied fields of blood that provided the only color in the otherwise bleak landscape. As we grew closer, they were actually covered with tiny crimson flowers, but that fact didn't make me feel any better. Ashleigh and Tia shared my concern. Then, tiny snowflakes began to fall, but instead of melting when they touched the warmth of my skin, they burned like hot ash.

Unicorn, what is this place? I asked, chilled by the fact that I couldn't hear a single bird or leaf stirring on the wind. The woods were hushed, and it was as if the countryside languished in an eternal midnight, when only the dead ventured out.

Call me Nebu, the stallion replied. *This path is not one I would normally choose, but it is what you would call a shortcut. I thought it best to take the Road Less Traveled so that we might avoid unwanted attention.*

The Road Less Traveled. A terrible sense of foreboding took hold of me, the feeling a razor-sharp spearhead twisting in my gut. I shivered, frightened of what lay ahead. Cold seeped into my skin, and I lifted the fur-lined hood over my head, expressing gratitude to Ashleigh for coming up with the idea.

Hassan and Nana were quiet as they galloped along on either side of me. Even my inner companions were silent. We continued without rest for several hours. Finally, when I thought Nebu might stop, giving us a break, he informed us that we were close to our destination. The path narrowed, and the trees around us, thick with wintry mosses, laced their fingers together overhead, becoming more and more intertwined until we could no longer see the dreary sky peeking through.

We raced through the ever-darkening tunnel. The jagged limbs of the trees jutted out like a mass of sharp, protruding teeth, causing the dim path to look like an openmouthed hungry monster. Then we plunged through the very center of its mouth and hit an almost viscous barrier.

As we fell through the other side, I felt the warmth of the sun touch my body before I could see anything. It hurt my cold skin, but it was painful in almost a good way, like sinking into a too-hot bath. Gravity shifted, and just as we burst into a morning sky I realized that we were high above what I presumed was Egypt below, and we were falling.

Wind rushed around me, and I heard Nana and Hassan call out just as Nebu snapped open his heavy wings. We leveled off, and Ashleigh whooped with such delight that I was able to let go of my fear and appreciate the flight along with her, even though my thighs burned from gripping Nebu's sides. I wasn't sure if I'd ever be able to untangle my fingers from his mane.

Hassan must have given his unicorn instructions, because we banked and turned toward the east, where the sun had just crossed over the horizon, tingeing the land pink and orange. We touched down on the desert sand, far away from any of the modern cities of Egypt. Giant carved stones littered the ground where there must have once been a temple. They were piled up like lost puzzle pieces, their secrets long ago forgotten and yet to be discovered.

"Where are we?" I asked as I tried to walk off the wobbly feeling in my legs. Even Nana, as experienced as she was, seemed a bit worse for wear after our ride.

Hassan was so eager to get us where we needed to go that he actually stumbled from his mount. We helped him up, and he gave a sheepish look at Nana before he answered, "We're at an old abandoned temple about forty-five minutes outside of Luxor. I brought the boys here and was going to move two of them to other hidden locations, but I haven't had the time yet. As you know," he said, giving me a meaningful glance, "we've been rather occupied as of late."

He dropped his bag near one of the still-upright structures. It fell in the sand like bread dough on a floured board. Sepia dust puffed up around it in a cloud, falling softly around us, coating our shoes. The first thing he did when he opened his leather satchel was remove his hat and place it on his head.

Good call, I said to Tia.

Hassan next took a tool from his bag and carefully touched it to a series of hieroglyphs, cleaning the rock's surface with a soft brush before pressing the last one. The rock shook, dust falling like a cascading waterfall around it, and it shifted away, revealing an opening.

"Follow me," Hassan said as he replaced his tools and gathered up his bag. We descended into the dark space underground, and the temperature dropped at least fifteen degrees in the course of a few steps. Tall, carved columns held up what was left of the temple ceiling above, casting deep shadows over what little light came in from the opening. I traced my hands along the stony surface and blinked quickly as my eyes adjusted. An eerie greenish tint lit the room, and I could easily make out my surroundings.

The stone opening above us closed, and yet even without light I could see. *Night vision?* I asked Tia.

Lions naturally see better than humans in the dark, she replied.

Nana stumbled against me, and I held out a hand to help her. I guided Hassan with my voice, telling him how many more steps he had left, and then a shaft of light pierced the darkness as he turned on a flashlight.

When we got to the bottom, he guided us to a room and proceeded to light torches. Even before he did, I could easily make out the shapes in front of me. Three coffins, ornately carved and painted, rested on raised daises. When Hassan lit the first torch, my vision shifted from night vision, which was sort of a play on shades of greenish gray, to the full color spectrum.

They were magnificent.

I wanted to reach out and touch the polished wooden sarcophagus nearest me and trace the brightly painted scarab adorning its surface. Walking around it, I frowned as I studied the depiction of a battle by the pyramids embellished on the side. My eyes narrowed when I saw a girl standing with a boy on top of a pyramid. On the lid of the coffin, where a mummy would have crossed arms with a face in repose, I saw not one but two figures wrapped in one another's embrace.

The female had long, dark hair with streaks of blond running through. Her face was in profile and covered half of the male's image, but unlike her, he had been painted looking straight ahead. One dark eyebrow, as elegant as the sweep of a painted bird in flight, drew low over a brilliant green eye that seemed to look right through me. Behind him, haloing his head, was a sun. His full lips were pressed together like there was something he needed to say but couldn't. *What a beautiful tabernacle to house a dead man's bones.*

"This is Amon," Dr. Hassan said. "You must use your power to summon him. We can't call him forth like we did before because neither of us possesses the Eye of Horus."

"Even if I knew what that was, I wouldn't remember how to use it."

"You can do this, Lily," he said. "It's just like calling the hellhound. You just need to figure out his true name."

"How am I supposed to do that? I have to look into someone's soul first. Tia already knew the hellhound's name, and this guy's not exactly here to give me any clues."

Dr. Hassan thought about this for a minute. "Perhaps it would help to see him."

He began to shift the lid of the sarcophagus, and a kind of horror seized me.

"Oscar," Nana said, gently taking hold of his wrist, "I'm not sure this is the best idea."

Pausing, he glanced at her and then peered at me. "You've seen them in their decomposed forms before."

"Maybe I did, but I don't remember."

Nana pressed, "Even so, she didn't love him then."

I shuffled my feet. "Technically, I don't love him now either, so . . . I guess if you think it will help."

Nana gave me a pitying glance but nodded and came over, wrapping an arm around my shoulders. Goose bumps shot down my limbs when the lid fell to the floor with a heavy thunk. Gently, Dr. Hassan peeled away the wrappings that covered the face of the dead man and gestured me closer. "It's really not bad," he said. "Anubis has a lot of experience in preserving the flesh."

Swallowing thickly, I replied, "Good to know," and took a few halting steps forward. Beneath the white wrappings was a face. Even in death, the chiseled features were handsome. He looked like a grayish carved statue of an Egyptian god, and I understood why I might have been attracted to him. I tried as hard as I could, but I couldn't remember a single thing about the man lying there.

What did his voice sound like? Was he a serious person? Melancholy? Did we have anything in common? Did he have a sense of humor? I couldn't imagine the two of us fitting together in any kind of situation. Surprisingly, Tia said nothing. Apparently, she wanted me to try to figure all this out on my own.

"Can you do it?" Hassan asked, interrupting my thoughts.

"I'll try," I whispered.

He indicated that when the breath of sife—whatever that was—stirred, then Nana should help him release the mummy's powers by opening the canopic jars he'd stored inside a neat little opening at the base of the sarcophagus. When they were ready, Hassan gave me a nod.

Tia and Ashleigh merged their minds with mine, and I closed my eyes. Stretching out my arms, I felt our power fill my frame. In the voice of Wasret, I cried out, "Amon." I sucked in a breath. "I summon you from the afterlife. Return to your mortal form. Use my energy to guide you. Come to us!"

We waited, but nothing happened. I lifted my head and called him by another name, one that Tia supplied. "Revealer, we call you. Come forth!"

Again there was no change. Tia and Ashleigh broke off. "It's not working," I said.

Perhaps it is because you cannot remember him, so you cannot discern his true name, Tia suggested.

But isn't that our power?

Yes, but we struggled ta find the true name of the Devourer, too, Ashleigh added.

Maybe it would be easier if we start with Asten, Tia offered.

It didn't matter to me, so I told Hassan we wanted to move on to Asten. He nodded and stowed the first mummy's jars. He then removed the top of the second sarcophagus and pulled away the linen covering the face. Tia rushed to the forefront. *"Asten!"* she cried, using my voice before she quickly retreated back again, allowing me to take front stage. Her sorrow buffeted us in waves.

Ah. So this is the one you love, I said. *When did this happen?*

He . . . I . . . It is complicated, she said finally. *Asten . . . thought it was you.*

You mean he thought I was falling for him?

Yes.

Apparently, you and I need to have a girl-to-kitty-cat talk, my friend.

Do not mock my feelings, Lily. I did not set out to complicate things. It just happened. I have tried to ignore my impulses for your sake, but I . . . I've missed him.

As Tia looked at the man's face with my eyes, I could feel the waves of longing sweeping through her. This fellow was handsome, too. *Perhaps a little too handsome,* I thought. Definitely not my type. I didn't trust guys who were that gorgeous. I did like the little cleft in his chin, though. It added character.

Just as we were locking our minds together again to attempt to raise Asten, a shimmering light filled the room. A goddess stepped out of the light and collapsed to the ground before us, dropping a box she had tucked under an arm. Desperately, she scooped it up.

"My lady!" Hassan leapt forward and helped her stand.

The woman's hair was disheveled. Her smooth, dark skin was mottled with bruises, and her dress was ripped. Yet she stood as proudly and as stiffly as her body allowed.

"You cannot raise him," the goddess said.

I took a step forward. Before I could ask the question, Tia provided the answer. "Ma'at," I said. "It's nice to meet you."

"Nephthys told me you'd blocked your memories. I certainly hope you recover them in time."

I wanted to ask *What do you mean, I had blocked my memories?* and *In time for what?* but I was afraid to hear the answer. Instead, I asked, "Why can't I raise him? I thought that's what you all wanted me to do."

"You can't raise him because the afterlife has been compromised. I've hidden the Sons of Egypt in an oubliette to keep them safe so you'd have time to bring them forth."

"Oh, well, can't you just magic them out of there?"

The goddess put her hands on her hips. "The point of an oubliette is to forget. Not even the gods can find it. I, myself, couldn't tell you where it is."

"Well, that makes this a little complicated, then, doesn't it?"

"Not necessarily. There's still a way."

She dusted off the box, murmured a spell, and then opened it. From inside, she pulled out a feather.

It's the Feather of Justice, Tia said.

"Take it," Ma'at said. "You will be able to protect it better than I."

"Okay," I said, taking the feather between two fingers. "So you just want me to hold on to your feather for you?"

Ma'at sighed with exasperation. "No. Yes." She took a deep breath and explained, "You will use it to summon the heart of the only Son of Egypt who has not yet been judged. He is the pathfinder. With his help, you'll find the oubliette and free the other two. But do it quickly. We can only hold off Seth for so long."

She lifted her head as if listening to something we couldn't hear. "I must go now. Anubis has need of my help." Ma'at took hold of my shoulder. "Good luck, Lily. Make haste." She turned but then paused. "Oh, and after you have raised him, leave the Feather of Justice in the safekeeping of your elder. It is best not to risk its being lost in the battle of the cosmos."

With that, the goddess disappeared, shimmering dust falling to the spot where she'd last stood.

I sucked in a breath. "It doesn't sound like the battle is going very well."

"No," Hassan replied. "It doesn't."

"So I guess we should raise this other one. Pathfinder?"

His name is Ahmose, Ashleigh said.

"Ahmose. Right." Without waiting for Dr. Hassan to remove the lid, I shifted over to the third sarcophagus. Gripping the Feather of Justice in my hand, I locked my mind with Ashleigh and Tia and, with the voice of a cyclone, cried, "Pathfinder, with the Feather of Justice I summon your heart and command you. Return to your mortal form!"

The feather gleamed as if lit from within, and the light moved down my arm. It filled my body until the glow became so bright that Nana and Hassan had to shield their eyes. A gust of wind whipped my hair straight up, and Hassan dove for the hidden cupboard, pulling out the canopic jars and opening them in quick succession.

Silver particles burst from the top of each jar like four moonbeams. They coalesced into balls of light except for one that became a long-necked bird. One by one, they sunk into the still-closed sarcophagus and disappeared.

When my power dimmed, Tia, Ashleigh, and I broke apart. Hassan, Nana, and I all stood there looking at each other, wondering what to do next.

Then we heard a boom and I leapt back, drawing my knives from the harness. Another boom sounded, and Hassan ran to Nana, holding her against him as she gasped in fear. Dust rained down from overhead, and I narrowed my eyes and cocked my ears, listening for the source of the threat.

When the third boom came, the lid of the sarcophagus exploded upward like a bomb had gone off beneath it. I twirled my knives, shifting my weight to attack, when a wrapped figure suddenly sat up.

I swallowed as the mummy tore the wrappings from its face and arms. Then it turned to look at me. Taking a moment to clear its throat. Its voice was dry and raspy. "Do you think I could get a little help, Lily?" the mummy asked.

A World Apart

I stood immobile, gaping at the creature peeking out at me through torn wrappings.

Lily! Ashleigh said. *Snap out of it. It's just Ahmose.*

I don't . . . I'm not . . . I . . . can't, I said with a pathetic whimper to my two companions.

Then let me.

All too willingly, I stepped aside and let Ashleigh take over. She quickly walked right up to Ahmose, clucking at him like he was a naughty boy who'd been busy playing in the mud.

"Now look what ya've gotten yerself into, laddie," she said. "This'll never do."

Efficiently, she unwrapped the bandages around his head. When it was finally free, he cracked his neck as he twisted side to side.

"Yeah, no doubt you'll 'ave an ache in the neck for most o' the day. But ya should count yerself lucky. Better'n bein' dead, I'd wager."

"That it is," the man said and smiled warmly at me . . . her . . . *us* while Ashleigh moved down his arm, unwinding the yellowing linen as she went.

Good heavens, I thought. *This one's as good-looking as the others. His smile could melt the moon.* Wait a minute. That didn't sound like me. It was hard enough to remain sane when two other girls shared your head. It would never do to have our thoughts bleeding together. *Tia,* I accused, *stop thinking so loudly.*

It's not me, she groused. *Perhaps it's you. Though even I admit this one does have nice teeth. If he were a lion, it would mean he'd be an exceptional hunter and protector. Also, his build is very muscular. I quite enjoyed being held in his arms.*

What? No. You know what? I don't want to know. Don't tell me anything else about his build. Okay? Just . . . just stop.

I do not understand why you are upset. If I recall, you enjoyed being close to him as well.

I . . . gah! I really hated the idea that Tia knew things like this about me, about us, or my past. It felt wrong. Almost like my body had been stolen without me remembering it. Wait. That was exactly what had happened.

Ashleigh had moved down to his hand. Each finger was wrapped individually, and the man flexed each one as it was freed from the cloth. Nana moved to his other side, quickly getting over the fact that she was unwrapping a mummy. She always handled things like delivering calves or caring for wounds on her animals like an experienced medic. I suppose this wasn't too different. I'd be jealous of the ability if I actually cared about doing such things myself. In this case, I was happy to let Ashleigh handle it. It was bad enough I could still feel everything.

Nana introduced herself as my grandmother, and the man gave a respectful bow, at least the best he could when he was bound like he was. He said that he was honored to meet one of Lily's elders. The fact that she was even there in Egypt didn't seem to faze him at all.

When both arms were done, Ashleigh began unwrapping his chest, asking him to lift his arms when she passed his shoulders. He did so, pushing the dark hair that fell in his face away from his eyes. Tia had been right. This guy's arms and shoulders were thick with muscle.

Nana moved down to the foot of the sarcophagus to help Hassan unbind the man's feet. Soon, his chest was exposed. His very naked chest. His very naked chest, which was as hard as granite. If I were in charge of my body, I would have gaped at the guy.

When Ashleigh neared his waist, she leaned across him to pass the bundle of wrappings from one hand to the other, but he stopped her, taking her hand, *my hand,* and pressing it against his chest. "Thank you," he said. "I think I can get the rest."

Even with the cloth between his chest and my hand, I could feel the warmth of his body. I'd expected him and/or the sarcophagus to smell of rot and decay, but he didn't. The smell of cedar was more prominent that anything else. Without meaning to, my nostrils flared and the power of my enhanced senses kicked in.

Luckily for me, the mummy's personal scent was pleasant. Almost like a moonlit forest in the fall. Even the wrappings smelled more like recently tilled earth and old leaves. His face was inches away, and his gray eyes were assessing me curiously. My pulse quickened.

I don't think I'd ever been that up close and personal to a man before. At least, not that I could remember. I found I didn't mind it so much. In fact, the newly freed mummy was about as handsome a man as I'd ever seen. The idea that I found him attractive made me uncomfortable in all kinds of ways.

Ashleigh said cheekily, "Are ya certain, then? I don' mind unwrappin' all o' ya."

Ashleigh! I scolded, suddenly embarrassed and realizing we'd been touching the guy way too long. Granted, he hadn't let go of my hand yet either, but, regardless, it had been too long to pass off as casual contact.

I told her to move away, but she stubbornly ignored me. Then the man laughed, a bubbly, happy sound, like a wave capped with foam breaking on the shore. I found I was more attracted to the man's laugh than his looks, and that was saying something. "Perhaps next time I awaken."

"Right, then." Hassan stepped forward. "I think it would be best if I help Ahmose with the rest. You ladies can take my flashlight and wait in the adjoining chamber."

The reasons I had for fearing the mummy-turned-man were crumbling as easily as the pillars of the temple above us. *I think I'm okay now, Ashleigh.*

Are ya sure? I'm vera comfortable with Ahmose. I don' mind takin' the lead for a time.

I'll be fine, I replied. *Besides, I need to get used to all this. It won't help me to remember if I hide behind the two of you every time something scares me.*

I could sense Ashleigh's reluctance, but she switched places with me willingly. While we waited, I promised both her and Tia they'd get a turn at being in charge very soon.

When Hassan called us back, I was surprised to see the new member of our team dressed as a warrior, complete with leather tunic, thick leggings, soft boots, and wrist braces decorated with silver. After giving him the once-over and swallowing back the girlish giggle that rose up from just standing next to a guy who could have clearly stepped off the pages of *GQ: Medieval Knights Edition*, I asked the only intelligent question I could come up with. "Where are your weapons?"

He tilted his head curiously. "I summon my weapons from the sand. Do you not remember, Lily?"

"I'm afraid Lily doesn't remember anything," Dr. Hassan said.

"What do you mean, she doesn't remember?"

"She forgot everything about Egypt when she entered the mortal realm."

"Has she been injured?"

"Hello there. I'm right here," I said, waving a hand in the air. "You can ask me, you know."

"I apologize, Lily," Ahmose said. "Were you injured in our last battle?"

"I don't think so. Tia?" I asked.

We were not injured in any way that would disrupt your mental process.

"She says no."

He took a step closer and held up his hands. "May I?"

I frowned, feeling slightly nervous next to the big stranger. "May you what?"

"One of my abilities is to heal with magic. If I can touch you, I will be able to sense what's causing the damage and fix it."

"O . . . kay. I guess so."

Hassan and Nana looked on curiously as the man narrowed the gap between us and lifted his large hands, placing them on my neck. His touch was gentle and light, which was surprising for a guy that could probably lift a truck by himself. He closed his eyes, and I felt his energy humming in my body. It tingled, and a gentle buzz sped through my limbs. It didn't hurt, though. It actually felt nice. Like getting a shiatsu massage from the inside out.

"Well?" I asked when he removed his hands and stepped back. His hooded gaze told me the news wasn't good.

"There is nothing to be healed. She is well and whole, as are the two hearts linked to hers."

"Ah," I said. "And you're upset because . . ."

"Lily," he said hesitantly. "If there is nothing wrong with you physically . . ."

"Then there's something wrong with . . . what? My soul? My . . . my brain?" If I had to choose, I think I'd rather something was wrong with my soul than my brain, but really my preference would be neither of those things.

He placed a hand on my shoulder. "There's no way for me to tell. Perhaps I can sense more once we leave the mortal realm."

"So Hassan told you I can't raise the others?"

Nodding, he turned to look at the bodies of the other two mummies. "I'm going to have to take you to them. You will need to enter the oubliette before you can reunite them with their bodies."

"And you're sure this oubliette isn't, like, in Arizona or Taiwan or something?"

He shook his head. "It is not. The place Ma'at hid us was tucked away at the far corner of the cosmos."

"The far corner of the . . ." I trailed off, unable to finish. I turned, eyes wide, to Nana, who reached for my hand and squeezed.

"It'll be all right, Lilypad."

"I'm afraid you and Hassan will need to stay here," the man said, directing his comment to Nana. "Mortals cannot traverse the paths we will go."

Turning to Hassan, he added, "You will need to stay and guard the bodies of my brothers. Watch over them, lest Seth's minions discover their hiding place. I will cast a spell to hide this temple from all but the most discerning. There is a certain power the grand vizier has in caring for his charges. As long as you are alive, their bodies cannot be destroyed."

Dr. Hassan straightened proudly. "I will, of course, fulfill my duty."

"Good," the man replied. "Can you fetch me the items necessary to raise them when we access the oubliette?"

Hassan nodded and disappeared back into the chamber with the sarcophagi.

The mummy touched my shoulder briefly. "Now I will leave you to say your goodbyes while I seek out the best path. We need to make haste, Lily."

With that, he marched up the narrow, sand-dusted stairs heedless of the waning torchlight. I was left to gape at his departure. "Nana, I can't," I sputtered, gesturing wildly. "You guys really expect me to just head off to who-knows-where on the other side of the freaking cosmos with this, this . . . stranger?"

He's not a stranger to us, Ashleigh said.

Pipe down, I replied. I could feel their frustration with me. *Keep in mind that he's pretty darn strange to me.*

Nana put her arm around me as Dr. Hassan entered with his bulging pack. "Oscar, are you certain we can't go?"

"If Ahmose says we can't, then it is impossible. The fact that Lily had to become a sphinx to traverse these paths before is proof enough to me that we wouldn't survive the journey."

Neither of them offered anything else. I could tell Nana didn't want to try to sway me one way or another. She wrapped me in a hug and squeezed hard. "What do you want to do, Lilypad?" she murmured in my ear.

My grandmother always knew exactly what I needed to hear. She would let me rant, get out my frustration, and then turn the problem back to me. Nana expected me to act responsibly, consider my options, and make the right choice.

I sighed against her soft shoulder and acted the part of the grown-up I was supposed to be. "What I want to do is go shoe shopping. What I'm *going* to do is head off to the middle of the cosmos and raise some more mummies."

When I stepped back, she cupped my chin. "You've always been a brave girl."

"I don't feel particularly brave. I think this is one of those cases where greatness has been thrust upon me whether I wanted it or not."

"You've always been great to me."

"Yeah. Well. Put that on my tombstone."

"Don't be morose, Lilliana," she said and then tempered the comment by taking hold of my shoulders and kissing my forehead.

She almost never called me Lilliana, and it hit a nerve. Probably too close to the truth. She didn't want to think about having to bury me next to my granddad. That is . . . if there was anything left of me *to* bury.

The more likely scenario is that we'd end up lost in space, floating through the stars, Tia said.

Great. Thanks for the clarification.

We probably wouldn't die, though. At least not for a few millennia, she added.

Even better. Well, girls, let's get this show on the road, I said.

"Will the two of you be okay here?" I asked as we headed toward the stairs.

"I have some contacts in the area that can drop off some supplies for us," Hassan said.

I nodded feeling a little depressed over the idea of leaving him and Nana behind.

Climbing the stairs, I noted that I didn't even need to rely on my night vision. The passageway above us had been left wide-open. I put my hand on my blade as I exited, scanning the desert in both ways, but relaxed when I saw Ahmose crouched down in the sand tracing furrows with his fingertip while the three unicorns looked on curiously.

When he saw us, he stood and strode over to me. "Nebu and Zahra will take us. Kadir will stay near and help if Hassan and your grand-mother need him."

"Gotcha," I said, narrowing my shoulders and striding toward the unicorn that trotted up to me. Apparently, I'd be riding Zahra this time. Kicking up onto her back, I turned and gave Nana a weak smile and handed her the Feather of Justice. "Wish me luck," I said.

"You girls take care of my Lily," she replied.

Tia was going to respond, but the mummy guy beat her to it. "I vow to protect her with my eternal soul," he said as Nebu trotted up beside me. Nana gave him a tight nod, while I just lifted an eyebrow.

The mummy lifted his arms and began chanting a spell:

Great ancestors who rest in your tombs

You who built this place,

You who have found rest,

The walls you raised have crumbled to dust

But the power you imbued in it remains.

Lend your strength to this stronghold.

Secret it from our enemies.

Protect it from the Unmaker,

From the one who never sleeps.

As you obeyed your pharaohs

Obey me now.

Serve the gods,

Serve the Sons of Egypt,

And your hearts will be weighed with favor

On the day of judgment.

A rumbling shook the ground, and little pockets of sand hissed all around the area in a wide circle. Something tunneled beneath the sand, and I gasped when dozens of snakes emerged, their black bodies writhing. They positioned themselves end to end, creating a vast circle of reptile flesh around the temple. Then they opened their jaws wide and clamped on to the tail of the snake preceding them. Once they were all attached, they froze in place and turned to stone.

"Can . . . can they cross that circle?"

"Do you mean your grandmother?" he asked.

I nodded.

"Crossing the boundary isn't recommended, but the spirits of the dead will not cause them harm."

I looked over at Nana, who was breathing quickly, but she gave me a bright if not entirely genuine smile and wave.

After returning the gesture, the man leapt upon Nebu's back. "We must go now, Lily. Do not worry over them. They are safe for now."

With that, Nebu spun and raced toward a sand dune that opened up like the mouth of a cave. Zahra followed, and I turned to look back at Nana until we plunged into darkness right behind him.

Even with our combined senses, I couldn't see. Not even my hand in front of my face or the gleaming mane of the unicorn. Finally, I could discern a light far in the distance and a dark shape moving in front of it, which I assumed was Nebu. Zahra assured me the darkness was natural in this passageway, but every part of me strained toward the light.

When we burst out of the darkness and into the sunshine, I expected the terrain to be similar to the Road Less Traveled, but this landscape was totally different. It was almost . . . alien. No. It *was* alien. We emerged at the opening of a mountain cave overlooking a wide valley. A glistening river wound across the plain before us, twisting and turning, but the water wasn't blue. It was violet.

Tall trees stretched out wide arms, but the shape of them was umbrella-like. Beside us was a thorny sort of cactus with arms that branched out and made it look a bit like an upside-down, living Chihuly chandelier. Spiky, almost black, plants were topped with golden flowers that gave off the scent of caramel.

The birds nesting on the mountain side looked more like lizards. Their wings were speckled blue membrane instead of feathers, and their long tails and the skin of their bodies were scaled. Though I noticed when one squawked in alarm that they did sport feathers, after all. They had crests of them on the tops of their heads.

Two moons graced the sky: A reddish one, currently a crescent, was thin and wide like a Cheshire Cat smile. And a smoky blue–colored second moon peeped just over the horizon like a winking eye. Both of them were visible despite the fact that a burning orange sun sat at high noon.

Where have you brought us, Nebu? Tia asked as the unicorn unfurled his wings, preparing to leap off the side of the cliff. *This is not the same path you took us on before.*

No, he replied. *It is not. This is the only remaining passage open to us, and it is the most dangerous. The others are compromised. Seth's guards have destroyed the one we took before. His sentinels watch for us everywhere.*

Nebu leapt off the side, the mummy clinging to his back, and Zahra quickly followed. This time I couldn't enjoy the flight like Ashleigh did. It was all I could do not to throw up at the quick descent. I clung desperately to Zahra's back. When we neared the bottom, both unicorns touched the ground, skidding slightly as they tucked their wings. They slowed to a walk and proceeded ahead, picking their way gingerly alongside the river, their hooves clicking against the bed of smooth, multicolored river rocks that sparkled in the alien sun.

Why aren't we still flying? I asked Zahra.

There are creatures here that would devour us. They consider unicorn flesh a delicacy.

Then wouldn't it make more sense to get out of here as quickly as possible?

The distance is too far for even a unicorn to navigate quickly. Besides, the vegetation becomes . . . agitated when animals move too fast through it, and it would alert the hunters that fly through the air. Our bright coats make us easy targets when we take to the sky in this place. They can see us from far off.

So . . . that means we move at a snail's pace?

Not quite that slow, but yes. We go carefully here. It will take us the better part of one of your weeks to cross this path, more if our going is slowed by the fauna.

I'm not sure what I expected, but it wasn't that I'd be gone that long. Clothing I had covered thanks to my abilities, but we had no other supplies. My two inner companions appeared not to be overly worried. I glanced at the purple river and swallowed, already feeling thirsty.

We didn't bring any food, I said to the unicorn.

We can graze, Zahra said.

Yes, I answered impatiently, *but what about us?*

We will hunt, Tia said.

Yes. You will hunt, Zahra echoed. *We will tell you which animals are edible and won't hunt you in return. There aren't many, but edible grasses are plentiful and there are many fish in the river. Some of them don't even bite.*

Perfect. I was suddenly replaying all the monster fish shows I'd seen on the National Geographic Channel. Drinking from the river became even less appealing, especially when I realized that all the basketball-sized, potbellied, green melons spread out in the sunshine were alien frogs. They cried out and collapsed at our approach, tumbling over one another to escape into the river, where they peeked at us suspiciously, blinking Ping-Pong-ball-sized yellow eyes.

We continued on for several hours traipsing through an episode of *Land of the Lost* meets *My Little Pony*. I spent the time asking the unicorn questions in an effort to avoid listening to Tia. It hurt her feelings that I was ignoring her, but everything she talked about seemed to involve our past history together or devouring bloody meals, and it made me uncomfortable.

When I wasn't talking to the unicorn, I studied the man scouting the path ahead of us. He often got off Nebu, walked off a ways, and crouched down to study the ground. His shoulders were stiff, his body taut, like he was as uncomfortable in our environment as I was. I was hyperaware of him, though. It was like he was a silent pillar of fire that moved around me. Sometimes he was in front, sometimes behind, but I could always feel him there watching over me.

Nana loved studying the Bible, and so I knew the story of the Israelites following Moses through the wilderness. I didn't know if this mummy could part the purple sea or pull water from a rock, but there

was no denying that I felt a kind of comfort being in his presence. I was
content to follow my own personal pillar of fire, even if my nerves prickled when he drew near. Both Tia and Ashleigh trusted him implicitly.
They were irritated every time I thought of him as a mummy instead of
a man, but they didn't push me to talk to him.

Once, he froze holding a hand in the air. Nebu nickered softly and
angled his head at a copse of thickly shaded trees. There was a shuffling
sound, and a family of yellow-fleshed, prickly-backed animals broke
cover, heading to the river. My senses heightened, and I pulled my bow
and let an arrow fly without even thinking about it. I let out a breath I
didn't know I was holding and felt as if I was collapsing in on myself. My
hands shook as I moved the bow back across my shoulder. To say I was
surprised at my own action was an understatement.

Tia? Did you? I asked.

It wasn't me.

Ashleigh?

Me either.

Well, it wasn't me, I insisted.

Nebu trotted over to us with Ahmose on his back.

"What just happened?" he asked.

"I . . . *we* aren't sure."

He cocked his head, studying me with steady gray eyes. "Will you
give me your hand?"

When I did, he cupped it in his own and murmured a spell. Then
he turned it over and studied my palm as if he was checking out my
lifeline. "It was the power of Wasret," he finally said.

"But none of us can remember wanting to shoot that animal. Even
Tia hadn't thought of hunting it yet."

"Wasret ensures your survival."

"You're talking as if Wasret is a person."

"She is, in a way." He must have seen that I was clearly distressed
by this revelation. "Come," he added. "We will talk more of this. There

is much you need to understand. This is as good a place as any to make camp for the night. The unicorns say it is best if we do not travel in the dark."

I was grateful to stretch my legs anyway. I collected wood for a fire while he inspected our kill. He noted with interest that I had not used one of the precious arrows given to us by Isis. Since those were all that rested in the quiver, the plain wooden arrow tipped with blue feathers, which looked suspiciously like those that adorned the lizard birds, was of great interest. Where had it come from? How had I known to draw that one instead of one of the others?

Thankfully, he prepared the meat, so I didn't have to gut anything. He started the flame by snapping his fingers together. It served to create a sort of lightning from his fingertips that soon sparked on the kindling I'd gathered.

By the time the meat was propped up on spits, juices dribbling, the sun had gone down and another moon had risen. This one had an apricot hue. The scent of the meat was making my mouth water despite my reservations. "Look at that," I said, pointing at the purpling horizon. "Another moon." I turned to my companion, only to find he'd wandered off into the woods somewhere. Nebu and Zahra had gone off to find a good patch of ground to graze on. For the moment, I was alone.

Of course, I was never truly alone. I always had Tia and Ashleigh with me. The idea of it didn't bother me so much anymore. At least not like it did at first. I suppose I was getting used to having them around.

"I guess it's just us girls," I said. Apparently, I spoke too soon, though, because right after, Ahmose emerged from the trees carrying a dripping leather bag.

"Whatcha got there?" I asked him.

"Water," he answered, handing the bag to me.

I took it, peering at it dubiously. "Is it, uh, purple?" I asked.

"It is. That is the natural color of the water in this world, but it is clean. I summoned it from the sky and have ingested it myself. The unicorns assured me that it is safe for drinking."

"Huh," I said after taking a tentative sip. "It's sweet." I tipped back the skein of water, drinking deeply.

"I find it delicious also." The man took a seat beside me and leaned forward to turn the meat.

"So you can summon water from a rock, eh?" I said, wiping my mouth. "I guess I got that Moses analogy spot-on."

"I forget that you do not remember my powers. One of my names is Bringer of Storms. I can call upon wind, rain, and lightning."

"That's handy."

His smile was slight, as thin as the crescent moon above. "It is, on occasion."

The flickering flames of the small fire danced in his eyes like a blushing gemstone beckoning from their storm-gray depths. I got the impression that there were many secrets hidden behind those eyes. Perhaps even a treasure trove for a hunter bold enough to seek them out. I also sensed, not danger, but movement, as if a surging tide stirred through him, daring anyone to swim without being drawn beneath. Though he appeared as still and as calm as a frozen lake on the surface, there was more to this man. Much more.

"So," I said. "Since we're getting to know each other all over again"—I stuck out my hand for him to shake—"I'm Lily. It's nice to meet you."

He took hold of my hand but not to shake it. He held it gently and then let go almost reluctantly, our fingers lingering for just an extra moment. Then he smiled, and it was full and genuine and, I noted, as beautiful as a poet's love sonnet. His expression of solemnity had been chased away by his smile, as if the two things couldn't exist simultaneously. "It is nice to meet you again, Lily. My name is Ahmose."

"Ahmose. I like it." I drew up my knees and wrapped my arms around them. "It's not your only name, though. You said Bringer of Storms is one of your names. You have others?"

"Yes. I have many. Pathfinder is another."

"Names are my superpower, you know."

"Wasret has many abilities."

"Right. Speaking of that, what's your theory on the whole killing-the-alien-critter thing?" I asked, gesturing at the meat on a stick.

"I think . . ." He paused, looked at me, and then leaned over to pull the skewer of meat from the fire. He blew on it before handing it over. "Careful, it's hot."

"Go on," I said, nibbling at the meat. It tasted a bit like gamey pork. "You said you thought Wasret was a being separate from us."

"Perhaps 'separate' is not the proper term, for I do not believe she can exist without you, at least not fully. Wasret is you, but she is all three of you. She comes into being only when you are locked together."

"Well, right, we already know that." I pulled off a chunk of meat with my fingers and popped it into my mouth, chewing heartily and licking the juice from my thumb.

"No, you don't. Not really. Lily, I've traced your path, and at the end of your journey, the one where you defeat Seth, there is only Wasret. Tia, Lily, Ashleigh . . . The three of you cease to exist. Wasret is born of you. Your thoughts, your feelings, your desires, are something she can access, but she is not you. Not any of you, not entirely."

I swallowed, the meat sticking in my throat. Tia and Ashleigh were gripped by the cold fear I felt. "We will disappear completely? Are you . . . are you sure?"

"I am as certain in my abilities as I am in wielding my cudgel."

"You sound pretty certain, then," I said staring at the fire, my skewer of meat all but forgotten.

"For what it's worth, I am sorry to be the bringer of this news," he said. "I know this must be traumatic for you. And you are already in a fragile state. . . ."

"Yeah." I set the skewer on the rock so he could finish my portion, and pasted a pathetic form of bravery on my face. "If you'll excuse us. I . . . we . . . need to head to the little girls' room."

When his brow furrowed in confusion, I explained further, "We won't be gone long."

He appeared to figure it out and nodded.

After I passed the tree line, I started running. My breaths came heavy. My senses heightened, and I heard the far away hoot of an alien bird, the scratching of rodents underground, and the rustling of something moving through the grass. Angry at these enhanced abilities, and wanting nothing more at that moment than just being human, I tried to stifle them and turn them off. I panted at my efforts, and panic blossomed in my chest. Ahmose's words had effectively strangled the little seed of hope I'd nurtured that I'd come out on the other end of this thing okay.

It took a few moments for me to notice the golden streams of light that turned on behind me like spotlights trailing an actor on a stage. I staggered and slowed, turning to see the wreckage I'd rent upon the land. The light of the three moons made the landscape glow like the inside of an oyster shell. Plants of all kinds that had been green or greenish purple had exploded with color. They were lit up from the inside as if someone had painted them with glow-in-the-dark paint, and the moons acted like a black light.

Not only was there a long, lit path tracing back the way I'd come, but the plants had angled themselves in my direction. I heard a thwap as something hit my cloak. I pulled the fabric toward me, and I saw a thick fruit had been thrust at me. It was about the size of a kumquat, but it was soft and fleshy and, apparently, easily destroyed. It had burst upon impact and plopped to the ground, trailing a gleaming path of sticky juice and seeds behind it.

Hesitating, I backed up a few steps, and another plant spat at me, but this time with thorns. One pierced the thick cloth covering my thighs. "Ouch!" I cried, pulling a thorn as big as a knitting needle from my leg and dropping it.

We've got to move slowly, Tia reminded me. *We've agitated the plant life. The unicorn warned us of this.*

Right. Slow.

Taking measured steps, I moved out of the path of the glowing fauna and through the darkness, letting my night vision take over. I kept the luminous plants in my sight but moved far enough away that they couldn't lob their fruits or needles at me. But then, one by one, the lights winked out, and I was left in the dark again with only my senses to guide me back along the path I'd come. That wouldn't be a problem, since a lioness can follow scents like nobody's business.

I walked along, careful with my footing, moving quietly, when I sensed something. A presence in the forest that was animal. It was a hunter. And it was big.

We've got to run, Tia said.

No, hide! Up in a tree, Ashleigh cried.

If we run, the plants attack, I said.

Better the plants than the beast, Tia argued.

I agreed with her and began running.

We were close. Only another minute or two until we'd be back at the campsite. We entered an area of ground covered with large, bulbous pods, and as we ran through, the animal hunting us fell back and left off pursuit. I was just about to breathe a sigh of relief when one of the large spheres suddenly rose up in front of us. It glowed yellow, its light pulsing. It gave off a rich scent. Like that of recently turned earth and flowers.

Slowly, I took a step back and another, but then the bulb opened, peeling back brilliant orange petals. It was the largest flower I'd ever seen in my life. The smell was heavenly. Like chocolate-covered strawberries. It dripped with thick nectar. As pretty as it was, I knew I needed to get out of there.

I backed up some more, but then a long orange stamen shot out and wrapped around my arm. It was strong. Stronger than me. I pulled, but it held fast. Reaching behind me, I yanked out my knife, raising it above my head. Then the tiny needles shot out from the flower's leaves.

Most of them hit my cloak, but a good number struck my hand and my neck. I staggered and managed to use my knife to free my arm, but as quickly as I did, another two swollen appendages shot out to replace the one I'd cut. Whatever was in the needles worked fast. Soon, only the plant was holding my body upright.

Before my eyes closed, I tried to cry out to Ahmose or Nebu, but my lips were numb, and I could no longer even feel my face. Tia was already asleep, which I found interesting. I would have thought all of us would go unconscious at the same time. Ashleigh's voice was the last thing I heard before I became senseless, too. In her mind, over and over again, Ashleigh cried out one word. *Ahmose.*

In the Shadow of the Moon

The sound of wood crackling and popping woke me. I groaned and tried to move, but my limbs were heavy.

"Just relax, Lily," a voice said. "I'm right beside you, and you're safe. I have healed your physical injuries, and your body is fighting off the toxins, but it's slow going. You were hit by multiple needles, and my power seems to have no effect on your immobility."

"Ahmose?" I tried to say, but my tongue was like an alien object in my mouth. I shifted slightly and felt the heavy weight of my cloak draped over me like a blanket of snow. It was warm and comforting until my senses sharpened. I came to the full realization that my body felt as numb beneath it as if I had indeed been buried in a snowbank. The soft fur tickled my nose. The memory of being lifted up and into the mouth of a giant flower made me shudder.

It was going to *eat* me. This planet that housed a plant with an elongated hacksaw-like protuberance that sparkled like a ruby was apparently my own personal Little Shop of Horrors. All those beautiful glow-in-the-dark flowers out there wanted meat, and I could provide plenty of it. If I could have moved, I would have kicked Zahra in her hindquarters for her vagueness. She had said the fauna had become agitated. *Agitated? Really? Hungry* was more like it.

Opening my eyes, I looked past the fire and toward the foliage. Now every green, growing thing seemed to wink at me with malice as the leaves shifted in the breeze. They waited to hedge up my way at best, devour me at worst. The nearby trees smelled deceptively normal—like cypress, moss, and pine. They didn't give any indication they were predators. If I'd been a lioness, my fur would have bristled just thinking about it. Speaking of fur, the resident cat in my head was still out of commission.

Tia? I inquired.

She's sleepin' it off, Ashleigh replied.

I don't understand why it wouldn't affect all of us the same. I mean, you're sharing my body, so you should be unconscious when my body is asleep, too.

Don't think it works in that manner. I was awake the whole time the plant was tryin' ta mince us inta stew. I heard Ahmose fightin' off the plant. Could feel 'im carryin' us, too, at least until yer skin lost sensation.

So you weren't affected by the toxin?

I guess I wasn'. It was a bit like bein' trapped in the fairy tree. I couldn' open yer eyes or move. Yer body wasn' respondin' ta me at all.

Is that normal? I asked. *Do fairies heal quickly or something?*

Ashleigh took a moment to consider. *Not sure it applies when the body I'm inhabitin' isn't my own. Still, I've ne'er been hurt by a plant before. The fire scorpions killed my fairy form, so obviously animals can harm me. One time I got a splinter. It was right sore, but soon as I pulled it out, the wound closed of its own. Maybe the tree gave me a gift o' healin'.*

Could we do that before? Before you, I mean?

I don' know. Wasn't with you before, and we never talked 'bout it. We'll have to ask Tia when she wakes.

You don't think she's in . . . danger, do you?

I don' believe so. No more so than ya were. When ya were asleep I still sensed ya there, there wasn't any trauma to yer consciousness. Ya were just . . . unresponsive. Tia feels the same.

Good.

I shifted again, and this time my tongue cooperated. "Ahmose?" I said with a croak. A shuffling sound came from a place outside my vision. Then he was there, kneeling in front of me with a skein of water. Gently, he helped me sit up and bade me drink. He wasn't satisfied until I'd drained all the sweet purple liquid from the bag.

When it was gone, he dragged a log over so I could prop myself up with my back against it. Feeling had come back to some parts of me while other parts tingled painfully as if they'd fallen asleep. One of my arms regained enough strength, and I was able to position my legs so they weren't tucked awkwardly beneath me. Ahmose moved over beside me and sat back against the same log.

"The unicorns are on guard duty," he said, "so we can sleep."

"How long was I out?"

"A few hours."

"You can go on and sleep if you need to," I said, seeing his shoulders slumped with fatigue.

He shook his head. "Not until you do."

"I don't think I'll be able to for a while. At least not until I know what happened. We were chased by a large animal. Tia wasn't able to figure out what it was, but she was scared, and if Tia was scared, I don't really want to know what it was."

"There's nothing out there now. The unicorns would warn us if a large predator was circling. I don't think it was willing to cross the tuber plants, and they seem to stretch a good distance around us. When we continue on tomorrow, we'll have to pass through some more of them, but it should only take us a short while."

"Well, at least that's good news."

"Nebu said that the plant that seized you is called a fisher bulb. They lure in prey with their pretty lights and then latch on. Apparently, there are three varieties here—the fisher, the pitfall, and the trigger. One entices you in, one waits for you step into its trap, and the third produces a sticky sap on the leaves when you step on its trailing vines and then it grabs on to you. It seems not even unicorns can escape the third one. Luckily, you were caught in the easiest one to escape."

"The easiest one? Seriously? I didn't escape it. You helped me."

"Yes. But now we know why we must go slow through this area."

"And watch our step. Seems to me flying would be safer."

"The unicorns say that the pitfalls do not grow around the fishers. Too much competition. They also said that the predators hunting the sky are much more dangerous than the foliage and the beasts on the ground."

I folded my arms. "You're kidding, right?"

"I don't know what that means."

"It means you are teasing me. You can't be serious."

"I am always serious."

Glancing at his expression out of the corner of my eye told me that he was indeed telling the truth. The thought of trekking across the surface of this inhospitable place for another six days at best was a frightening prospect. To distract myself from worrying about it, I decided to change the subject.

"So you're always serious, huh?" I remembered when he laughed at Ashleigh's comment while she was unwrapping him, and the open joy behind it had been . . . well . . . amazing. Contagious, even. I felt curious about him and wondered what secrets he was hiding. "Why?" I asked.

"What do you mean, why?"

"Why are you always serious? I sense you don't like to be."

He shrugged uncomfortably. "My life is . . . complicated, and happiness is fleeting."

"Why do you think so?"

"You might not remember, but once, I loved a girl. She was the exact opposite of everything my life was made of. She was spring and hope, life and laughter. When I was with her, I forgot myself. I was spellbound by her quick smile and the sparkle in her eye. Her happiness and joy in living filled up the empty places in my soul.

"It was during a time of our awakening. The two weeks passed quickly, and never had I been so content. Then, two days before the ceremony, I found Asten locked in a passionate embrace with the one I loved."

"Oh man, that . . . that's not right."

"No, it wasn't. I vowed that I would kill him for seducing her. Never in my entire existence had I struck another person with anger. I never lose control of myself. It's not in my nature. It's not that I'm unwilling to fight. It's just that I know . . . I know I won't lose."

"How can you know that you won't lose?"

"It's because I know the path each of my opponents will take. But after a few moments of pounding Asten until his face resembled a bruised tomato, I came to myself enough to finally hear the laughter. The girl I loved was mocking the two of us. She thought it was delightful that she'd been able to twist two gods around her finger. It took me more than two hundred years for me to forgive Asten.

"Asten ruined everything, but he was right in his reasoning. I would have sacrificed all for her. I was too blind, too sick with love for Tiombe to see what she truly was. Eventually, my sacrifices and affections for her would have been mocked and rejected."

"I'm sorry, Ahmose. She was a fool to discard a man like you. But don't stop seeking happiness. You deserve it."

"Seeing your familiar face makes me very happy. You are my . . . Well, you might not remember, but you are my friend."

"I'd like to have a friend. I don't have many guy friends. Or any, now that I think about it. It's kind of weird to have a friend who's a mummy in his off-season, but I could do worse." I bumped my shoulder against his and was rewarded with one of his stellar smiles. "Friends, then?" I asked.

He took my hand and threaded his fingers through mine. It was a little more intimate than I'd be with a guy I considered a friend. I figured there was probably a cultural difference or an immortal difference, and it might not mean what it did where I came from.

"So since you're a pathfinder, have you looked at my immediate path? I mean, not the Wasret one, but mine? Am I going to get eaten by a plant or anything like that? I'd like to think you'd give me some warning next time."

Ahmose froze, his fingers stiffening in mine. "Paths shift. I see possible futures. Ways you can go. Choices you can make. Some are stronger than others, and those are the ones you are most likely to follow. I did not know you would run away because I was not studying your current path—I tend to focus on the big picture for the most part—but to answer your question, yes, I have looked at the path that lies ahead of you."

"And?" I asked with fascination. "Are we successful? Will we raise your brothers and defeat Seth?"

"The path that leads to my brothers glows the brightest at the moment. I can say with a good amount of certainty that we will raise them. After that, the path shoots in different directions."

"What does that mean?"

"It means you will have choices to make. Sacrifices. What you will do is unclear."

"Sacrifices?" I swallowed. "Are you referring to the Wasret thing and losing myself? You said at the end of my path you saw only Wasret. If that's what you're talking about, I have to say I really don't want to know."

I was hoping he would tell me that my choices ahead had nothing to do with Wasret. That he could be wrong. That Tia, Ashleigh, and I would come out okay on the other side. Of course, I didn't know how okay I'd be back in the real world with a mental pet lioness and personal feisty fairy, but I'd rather have the two of them in my head for the rest of my life than disappear forever so Wasret could be born.

Ahmose turned to me, still clutching my hand. Concerned gray eyes gazed into mine. The light of the moon touched his face, and he almost glowed. "I see many things in your future, Lilliana Young, many of them dangerous, many of them heartbreaking." He briefly touched his fingertip to my jaw. "More than anything, I wish I could take away the hurt and hide you from the danger. Though my life path is entwined with yours, I know I cannot influence where you walk. It would be wrong of me to be a stumbling block to what you will become."

Tears came to my eyes. "I don't want to lose myself, Ahmose. I don't want to become Wasret."

He pulled me into his arms and hugged me tightly. Then he took hold of my shoulders and moved back. "Do not think of Wasret now. You must first focus on the task at hand. Climb the hill today and the mountain tomorrow. As you move forward, there will be loss, but there are also many things you will gain. Such is the burden of mortality. Always remember that the power of choice remains yours."

Sniffling, I wiped my eyes. "Thanks. Thanks for being my friend. I didn't realize how much I needed one."

"I, too, am in need of someone such as you." Under his breath, he added, "You have no idea how much." If I didn't have the super hearing of a sphinx, I might not have caught those last words. I decided not to comment on it, though, at least not until I'd had more time to think about what it meant.

After repositioning myself against the log, I started spilling out all the worries and fears of my heart. I shared how strange this whole experience was and caught him up on everything that had happened since I'd been at my grandmother's farm and met Hassan.

He asked about my feelings regarding raising Amon, and I said I wasn't ready to talk about Amon yet. Sensitive to my tension regarding my supposed boyfriend, he graciously changed the subject and instead shared stories about Asten and Amon and him from when they were younger, keeping it light. Finally, he said, "You need to rest now, Lily. We have a long day of travel tomorrow. Please sleep."

"Will you rest, too?"

"Yes. Soon. Make yourself comfortable."

As I lay down, I watched him as he sat back against a log, his head angled up as if he studied the stars, and realized that for the first time since I had woken up with voices in my head, I felt safe. It was like finally here was a person who understood what it was like to know too much, to be responsible for too much. Ahmose could identify with me in a way that Nana and Hassan couldn't.

Ahmose was someone I could trust. I knew instinctively that he wouldn't make me do or become anything I didn't want to. "Good night, Ahmose," I said.

Looking down at me, he gave me a soft smile. "Good night, Lily. Sleep well." My heart skipped a little beat as we looked at each other. Then he tilted back his head again to stare at the moons overhead. I wondered what paths he saw in the sky and looked up at the constellations myself. My eyes fluttered closed, and then I drifted in a state of partial consciousness—half-awake and half-asleep.

I soon heard the murmur of voices. They tumbled over each other like the sound of the river moving across the rocks, soothing and steady. It was almost as if I watched the scene play out in my dream.

"You need to let Lily's body rest, Ashleigh," Ahmose's said.

"How'd ya know it was me?"

"A man who pays attention to a woman can tell."

"It's nice ta hear ya been payin' attention."

"Go back to sleep, Ash," Ahmose said with a chuckle.

"It's just for a little while, darlin'," Ashleigh responded. *"I wanted to ask a question."*

"What is it?"

"Ya said ya healed us. Were ya able ta see what's wrong in Lily's mind? Ya said ya might have a better chance when we were no longer in the mortal realm."

"I tried. It's strange, but there's a space there. It's hidden, and I cannot access it. I think it has to do with her power. Ma'at says she is an adder stone. Somehow, this is separate from you and Tia. But it is this ability that keeps you hidden from Seth, so I dare not tamper with it. I'm not sure I could heal it even if I were to make the attempt."

"Perhaps Amon will be able ta fix it once we waken 'im."

"Perhaps."

"Do ya want ta tell me what yer hidin', then?"

"Hiding?"

"I can read ya, handsome. I know when a man evades the truth. The fact that ya lied ta Lily put the heart crossway in me. Why would ya do such a thing?"

He smiled then and, with a teasing glint of moonlight in his eyes, said, "And what do fairies know of men?"

"I know enough. Once, I was a mortal lass, and though I've been beaten, bent, and born inta somethin' new, I still remember what a boy looks like when he's holdin' somethin' back."

Ahmose cocked his head. "You remind me of the moon," he said. "Most of the time you are hidden in the shadows of others, but when you shine down in your full splendor, there's no escaping your light. Did you know that I can see you, even when you wear Lily's face? It's just a vague outline of your features, but there's no mistaking who you are."

"As pretty as those words may be, I'll kindly remind ya that yer evadin' the question, lad."

Ahmose sighed. "Lily doesn't need to know about the things I've seen. It will only confuse her."

"Bah, you're as full of secrets as a tick that's found himself at the butcher shop. I can help, if you let me. My magic is o' the earth, but it's powerful, too."

"I know it is. Did you know I can follow paths both ways?"

"What do ya mean?"

"I mean I can trace the past as well as the future." Ahmose glanced at the ground. "For what it's worth, I'm sorry about what happened to you."

"I've found it's best not ta look back with regret. Only with lessons learned. Misfortune can follow ya all o' yer life. Ya end up with only two choices. Bemoan yer fate, slow down ta let it catch ya and then hold out yer arms to embrace the sadness, or keep runnin' so's it can' ever catch up. I choose ta do the latter."

"Then you are a wiser person than I've been. I let misfortune catch me."

"Then escape its grasp. My ma always said, 'Love is sweet, as sweet as honey, but the best honey is found in the quiet, forgotten places. Don't go lookin' for it in a busy hive, lest ya get stung.' Sounds ta me like ya got stung, Ahmose."

He smiled all sweet, the otherworldly moonlight melting in his dark hair, making it shine like his eyes. "That I did."

"Good night, Ahmose."

"Good night, Ash."

The next morning, Tia was back, and we filled her in on all she missed, though it seemed she remembered bits and pieces of it as if in a dream. We speculated as to why she had been most affected by the flower's drugging effects, and the best we and the unicorns could come up with was that Tia was closer to their natural prey than Ashleigh or I were.

It was disturbing to think that the toxins could affect Tia and Ashleigh's consciousnesses. I'm sure Hassan would have come up with a more solid theory than we could. Tia didn't want to dwell on it. She was more interested in the animal that had hunted us than the plant. She considered death by vegetation to be about as ignoble a thing a lioness could ever suffer.

During the next few days we fell into a routine. Tia taught me how to stalk and hunt prey. Each time we drew an arrow, the shaft ended in a blue-tipped feather. Though, when we checked, the quiver was still full of the feathers Isis had given us.

Ahmose had all kinds of idea about why this phenomenon might occur, the foremost being that we were unconsciously saving up our most powerful arrows for the upcoming battle. I didn't like thinking about that. My theory was that the quiver was somehow spellbound to just produce whatever arrows we had need of. Tia didn't believe any of this and preferred avoiding the arrows, encouraging us to hunt with our claws or knives.

Sometimes, as we dined on strange alien fish, wild lettuce, edible flowers, and the sweet water he summoned from the sky, I felt Ahmose's gaze linger on my face longer than was necessary, and he rode alongside me more often than not, engaging me in conversation.

He was interested in quite a variety of things. We spoke at length about the modern world, and he asked me numerous questions. Ahmose wanted to know everything, from how water was brought into the city and made hot for showers, which was something he loved about my time, to what I studied in school, to how cars worked.

But he also, very politely, asked Tia about her life as a lioness, about her lost sister—something I didn't know, or at least didn't remember—and engaged Ashleigh in long discussions about her home life in Ireland. I let each girl speak for herself when he asked questions and was happy to give them time to be in control.

Ashleigh told him an interesting story about how when she was a young girl of ten, she used to gather apples for an old woman who was so bent over she could no longer reach her tree. One day, her curly red hair got caught in a limb of the tree, and she cried and hollered until the old woman came out. "What do ya expect me ta do, lass?" she'd asked. "I can't reach ya ta help ya get unstuck."

"Take up an ax," Ashleigh had cried. "Chop the tree down. A girl is much more important than an apple tree."

"Ah," the old woman had said, "but apple trees take years o' nurturing ta bear fruit. I've cared for this tree since I was a young girl. 'Tis vera important ta me. Its apples feed me all year long. Birds sit in its branches and sing ta me when I'm lonely. I'm afraid without the tree, I'd perish."

"But what 'bout me?" Ashleigh wailed. "I canna stay up here forever!"

"This was when I learnt the most important lesson o' my young life," Ashleigh told Ahmose, who listened with interest. *"The old woman didn't*

say anything else. She didn' argue or offer other reasons. She didn' hesitate. She jus' picked up the ax an' got ready ta swing. But right before she did, I called out ta her.

" 'Wait! Don' do it.' Instead I asked her ta 'and me 'er kitchen knife. Even though I sobbed somethin' fierce, I hacked off all my pretty red hair till I was finally freed. I'd thought o' doin' it first thing after I got stuck, but I didn' want ta give it up. I was a rather vain little girl, an' I'd rather someone else make a sacrifice instead o' me, even though mine would cause the lesser pain. I learnt that day that I had ta stop bein' a selfish child. Ta this day I canna see an apple an' not think o' the woman."

"It was nice of you to help her."

"Oh, I didn' wan' ta. Everyone thought she was a witch, and my da was scared o' her. When she asked for me, he was too frightened ta say no."

"People often think those who are different possess magic."

"That's the thing, isn't it? She *was* a witch. She was the one introduced me ta the fairy tree. She was its guardian an' knew she wasn't long for the world. The day she died, I became its caretaker."

The unicorns moved ahead, and Ahmose and Ashleigh were silent for a time. Then he said, "You miss your red hair."

"Aye, I do. It was lovely. As curly as a pumpkin vine an' as red as the wild corn poppies. I miss it." Quickly, Ashleigh fidgeted with my own hair, tucking it into the arrangement she had done that morning. *"Not that Lily's hair isn' pretty. I jus' miss feelin' the curls, that's all."*

Ahmose reached over and patted my leg, giving Ashleigh a sympathetic look but saying nothing. She retreated after that, wanting me to take over.

Soon, I began to notice other little kindnesses Ahmose did. Things like helping me down after a long day of riding, or leaving a bright red flower on top of my cloak when I headed into the trees by myself. He'd always notice when it was me or Ashleigh or Tia, congratulating Tia on a skillful catch at the river, or just saying hello to Ashleigh and asking what she thought about one thing or another that the two of us had talked about.

By the sixth day, my mind swam with little half-remembered stories and dreams from Ahmose and Ashleigh's nighttime conversations. One dream was of a fairy with green eyes and a small, slender body. She was made crazy by the moon, and she danced and feasted beneath its light, singing softly to him. The lovesick fairy cried each night the moon set, thinking him dead, but rejoiced when he was reborn the next night. She believed that when a fairy died, the moon would send a shaft of light to catch her and bring her up to live with him. But a fairy cannot choose when she dies, so she waited, looking up at him with longing, night after eternal night.

There was another story or dream about a man trapped in the moon. He looked down upon the mortal realm and spotted a beautiful girl. Instantly, he fell in love with her. But, alas, he knew they could never be together, so instead he watched over her and learned to love her in new ways every day. But this one could choose when she would die.

The pretty girl discovered that she was to be given in marriage to a man she didn't love, and she threw herself from a tower rather than marry him. The moon, desperate to save her, reached out with his brilliant arms and caught her, but his light was too powerful, and he was weakened by his efforts. The girl became blind—moonstruck, they called it.

He begged the gods for help, and they put her in a deep sleep. She would not age, and her beauty would not wane, so he could look upon her face forever. The woman he treasured would never die. He could hold her with his moonlight arms, but their hearts still could not be together. His love brought him no comfort, for he was a man tormented by the feast set before him and yet he could not taste it. The light around him dimmed, and the moon was haloed by darkness.

Time passed as the man in the moon mourned. Finally, he told the gods he was ready to let her go. To let her find peace. The gods smiled and touched their fingers to the girl's eyes. She woke and looked up into the moon, finding there the face of the man who loved her. "Now she is truly yours," they said. "For you have proven that her welfare means more to you than your own."

His new bride ran into his arms and laughed as he spun her around. The two of them were freed from the confines of the moon, and the fabric of space was drawn together so that they might begin life anew in another world. As their feet touched down on a sea of undulating blue grass, they looked up at the haloed moon and knew it as a reminder to always think of the other before one's self.

If they forgot and became selfish, they would be separated once again. The moon would warn them when they were in danger. This is why a haloed moon is a portent. At the least, it was a sign of inclement weather. At its worst, it was an omen of imminent loss and heartbreaking sorrow.

I pondered these stories as I followed Ahmose along the river's edge. Something was changing between us. When he climbed a ridge seeking a path, I found myself captured by the sight of his muscled back and stared at his rigid forearms as he stretched them over the ground. Despite his dislike of battle, his was the build of a warrior. And, after spending days by his side, I realized not only that he was as beautiful on the inside as he was on the outside, but that I couldn't imagine not having him there.

It amazed me how quickly I'd come to rely on his steady presence. On his companionship. Maybe it was my fear of what lay ahead that spurred me to act, but what I felt didn't seem wrong. Everything inside me, the very beat of my heart, told me it was right. Perhaps it was premature. Maybe I should have waited to talk with Tia and Ashleigh about it first, but I didn't sense any trepidation on their part. In fact, they were quietly hopeful. At least, that's the innate sense I got.

Ahmose had said I had choices to make. Since I'd woken on my grandmother's farm, it didn't feel that way. The weight of the world rested on my shoulders, and I'd been told stories of what I'd done and who I loved, but I couldn't remember any of that. All I knew was now. My feelings were real. Right or wrong, they were there. So I made a choice.

Ahmose returned to my side, and I found myself breathing quickly. My heart pounded at his approach. When he placed his wide hands around my waist to help me down, I wrapped mine around his neck. I didn't step away after I found my footing. His dark hair looked flecked with gold in the setting sun. Boldly, I brushed a lock of it away from his cheek, relishing the rough scrape of his unshaven stubble against my fingertips.

Gently, he took my hands from around his neck and pressed a kiss against my wrist. "Are you certain this is the path you wish to take?" he asked softly. His gaze was shuttered, as if he didn't really want to know the answer, but I could still make out a piercing gleam in his silver eyes, and that brightness beckoned me closer. My heart beat so fast, I felt like I was a new star, gleaming and fresh as a new diamond, outshining the setting sun. I could have lit up the world all by myself.

"This path makes me happy," I said simply.

Slowly, deliberately, he lifted his hand and cupped my cheek. The expression on his face changed from one of careful soberness to a joyful, boyish kind of delight. "It makes me happy, too."

And he kissed me. A sweet, drowning kind of kiss. The kind that could drive you to your knees. In fact, it did take us to our knees, but he still refused to let me go. His hands splayed on my hips and remained fixed there as he tugged me against his warm body. The hard planes of his chest reminded me of a shield—one that protected his heart. Enemies should fear the strength and power found there, and yet, for me, he bent.

He tangled his hands in my hair, and Ashleigh's careful arrangement came undone. Golden scarab pins dropped haphazardly to the ground. It didn't matter, though, not when he trapped the loose tresses and curled them around his warm fingers. I wrapped my arms around him, drawing him ever closer. It seemed we couldn't get enough of touching and kissing. When he broke away, we were both panting, but there was a satisfied grin on his face a mile wide.

As he traced his thumbs across my cheekbones, my breath hitched as I anticipated the velvety soft touch of his lips on mine again. Ahmose was such a beautiful man. It was every girl's dream to have a guy like him looking at her the way he now looked at me, as if I were his whole world. Even though I didn't want to do anything to ruin the moment, my curiosity got the better of me. "Did you see this path? Us, I mean?"

Ahmose's smile softened, sobered, and he spoke in a voice low and heavy, "I've known it was a possibility from the moment we first met." His eyes fluttered closed then, and the happiness in his face dimmed slightly. "You must know I did not cause this to be," he said, as if I might wish to blame him for my feelings. "There were hundreds of choices you could have made that would have led you in a different direction."

"But this was the path with the strongest possibility," I said.

"It was," Ahmose admitted. "And I do not regret this course." Capturing my hands, he slowly kissed each palm. "I hope that you do not either."

"I don't," I murmured softly and was rewarded by the renewed gleam in his silver-gray eyes. The short, stubbly hairs on his cheek moved across the sensitive skin on the inside of my wrist, sending shivers down my spine.

When he lifted his head, I swayed, but he steadied me. "Of all the wonders I've experienced. Of all the paths I've seen. You are the only true magic I've ever beheld. Ever *held* in my arms."

Then the Master of Beast and Storm, the man known as pathfinder, healer, and most of all, Ahmose, stood, drawing me up. He wrapped his big body around mine, tucking me into his chest. There I felt safe, protected, warm, and above all else, loved. But even in that safe haven,

I felt a drop of rain hit my forehead. Another drop plinked against the knife handle sticking out of the harness that I'd let drop carelessly to the ground.

Ahmose looked up at the sky. The sun had set and the blue moon had risen. There was a dark, foreboding halo circling it. Frowning, Ahmose said, "Come, love. A storm approaches. We must find shelter."

Storm of Evil

The heavens opened above us, and dense rain hit the river rocks in heavy sheets. It pummeled our backs with stinging, angry drops. The storm smelled bitter—like creosote and ash. Ahmose moved off a few steps, attempting to find a path, and when he returned, his hair was slicked back and dripping wet. Even the unicorns lowered their heads and trudged forward. Their long lashes stuck together while beads of lavender rain trickled from their pointed tips, trailing down their white cheeks like tears.

Dark purple-black clouds obscured the moons and the stars. Lightning struck nearby, and the smell of ozone and burned wood filled my nostrils. The plants seemed to fold in on themselves, rolling their leaves in little curlicues and pulling the stems in tightly against their trunks. My heart beat quick and frantic when thunder boomed, shaking the ground.

I took hold of Ahmose's thick arm. "Can't you stop it?" I cried, needing to raise my voice above the noise of the storm so I could be heard.

Ahmose shook his head. "Something is wrong," he shouted back. "My powers aren't working. But I found a cave not too far from here. It's big enough for us and the unicorns." He tried to give me a reassuring smile, but it was too tight, more of a grimace than a smile. Something was more than wrong.

Finally, after being beaten back and battered by the storm for more than an hour, we came upon the cave. Ahmose ducked inside first, but he quickly returned after scanning it and took my hand, guiding me in. The unicorns followed, their back muscles twitching and their heads shaking to shed the rain from their coats and heavy manes.

I gathered my spilled, sodden hair over my shoulder and wrung it out. I wasn't able to see more than five feet in front of me, even with Tia's night vision, so I wasn't sure how Ahmose was able to make his way around without stumbling. He returned shortly after he left my side, saying he wasn't able to find dry-enough wood for a fire. Instead, he murmured a spell and his skin lit from within. His eyes burned like shiny headlights in a fog, which explained how he could see in the dark so well.

"What is that?" I asked in wonder, taking his hand and turning it over in mine to examine the light emanating from it. A kind of heat, warm and pleasurable, seeped from his bare skin into mine. His body glowed silver in the dark cave, but I was more interested in how his power lit me up on the inside.

"All my brothers have this ability. You might not remember it, though."

"It's . . . it's amazing," I said, taking his hand and pressing to the space over my collarbone. I gasped as my heart fluttered wildly at the touch. "Does it hurt you?"

Ahmose laughed softly. "No." After stretching his fingers and grazing them lightly over my jaw, shooting tingles up to the roots of my hair and down my spine, he said huskily, "There will be more of that another time, love."

He stepped back and picked up some large rocks, then he rubbed his hand across their surfaces, one by one, murmuring some words in Egyptian. The rocks began to glow with the same silver light coming from his skin. He set them in nooks and crannies throughout the cave and then told me he was going to fashion some new clothing and change. I somewhat reluctantly turned my back to him and walked to the edge of the cave to give him some privacy.

Thin strands of yellow thread that might have once been the web of some alien spider fluttered across the rocks as the wind whipping into the cave tore at them. I touched the edge of one, and it stuck to my finger. Then I raised the gleaming rock in my palm and upon closer inspection found the half-destroyed remains of a web glistening with rain.

Shuddering and expecting to see a glow-in-the-dark plant spider or something even worse ready to leap at me, I wiped my finger against the rock to get the web off. I then stepped across the mouth of the opening to the other side. Far below the cave, the purple river was almost black. It rushed its banks like a jilted suitor, determined to destroy and spoil everything that had once shaped and tamed him.

Ahmose stepped up beside me wearing dry clothing and holding another gleaming rock. He'd let his own inner light dissipate, and I found I was slightly disappointed. I wanted to touch him while he was lit up again. When drops of rain struck the rock he held, they hissed and disappeared as if the stone burned like fire. Curious, I reached out to touch it and found it warm, but it didn't burn my skin.

"I'll wait here," Ahmose said softly. "You go ahead and change."

Nodding, I left him standing there in the opening of the cave and moved to the shadowed spaces in the back. Inside the depths of the dark mountain cavity, I felt vulnerable, unfocused, like I had wandered into some kind of dreamworld. Tia and Ashleigh were strangely quiet considering the events of the past few hours, but they joined their energy to mine to create new clothing.

Sand spun around us, whipping my hair dry in its wind. When the storm abated, I wore a supple linen tunic in green, a color I suspected had been selected by Ashleigh. This was accompanied by comfortable leggings and soft-soled shoes. A belt with golden discs of diminishing sizes cinched my waist and swung in perfect synchronicity as I moved.

The green scarab sat at its center. I pondered what it symbolized, and for a moment felt that it was a very beautiful but, at the same time, very solemn, shackle. It was a reminder to me that I belonged to a man I didn't remember, and I resented the idea that I had no choice in who I loved.

Carefully, I removed the gemstone and placed it in the quiver to keep it safe. I knew I should feel guilty about my newfound relationship with Ahmose, but I didn't. The girl who loved Amon was gone. Maybe forever. I ran my hands down my body and over my hair, surprised to find it hung long and loose down my back instead of in one of Ashleigh's complicated updos.

Happy to finally be warm and dry, I headed back to Ahmose, feeling inescapably drawn to him. All the pieces that made up my new being coalesced and moved, shifting toward one thing. Ahmose. I was a mass of iron filings, and he was my magnet.

When I reached him, I wrapped my arms around his waist and pressed my cheek against his back, clinging to him. "The barriers are down," he said quietly, cupping my locked hands and pressing against them.

I turned my face, my chin jutting into his spine. "What does that mean?"

"The fact that I no longer have power over the storm means that Seth, or at least his minions, have seized control of this land. We can no longer expect that our journey will be easy. Fortunately, we are nearly ready to leave this world."

With a snort, I said, "You call what we've been through easy?"

"Relatively, considering everything."

As if to prove his statement, the wind whipped frenziedly. It howled through the cave as if it were a fettered beast that had finally been let off its chain, and caused a small avalanche of rocks to tumble over the lip of the cave. I remembered the haloed moon and dread filled my frame. I hoped a storm was all the moon warned us of. The idea that Ahmose could be ripped away from me was unthinkable. My fists clenched against his stomach. I wasn't going to let that happen.

"It's a bad wind that doesn't blow good to somebody," I murmured softly and then realized that the thought hadn't been my thought. It had come from Ashleigh. We were bleeding together again.

"Agreed," Ahmose said distractedly as he stared into the stormy night. He took my hand and drew me in front of him. He tucked my head beneath his chin. My arms remained locked around his waist. Absentmindedly, he stroked my hair, his fingers wriggling through it to knead the soft flesh at the nape of my neck.

Lighting struck again and again, brightening the landscape with cruel lashes. I looked out at the land and then back at him. When the light fell on his face, it shadowed Ahmose's features and for a moment, he looked like his brothers in death. Still handsome but with dark hollows that made him seem more like a seductive demon of the night who only rose from the coffin to seek out the one he wanted to carry away with him to the grave.

He looked down at me, and the remoteness in his eyes, the fatigue and worry I saw in them, melted away until all that remained was the bright, cool luster of contentment.

"Come, love," he said. "There is nothing we can do until the storm abates."

"And what if it doesn't?"

"I can still sense its power. This storm will last until the morning. We'll take our rest and head out once again tomorrow. Nebu assures me we are close to the jumping-off point."

I nodded and followed him deeper into the cave. The unicorns were sleeping standing next to each other, angled so one of them faced one way and the other faced the opposite direction. "Why do they sleep like that?" I asked.

"They each guard different directions. That way no one can sneak up on them and catch them unawares."

Ahmose positioned his big body up against the wall of the cave, drawing his cloak over the two of us. I sat beside him, cradling my head against his shoulder. Even relaxed, I could feel the corded muscle of his arms through his shirt. The gleaming stones that shone like pewter, combined with the subtle light coming from the coats and manes of the unicorns, painted the cave in dreamy, romantic softness.

My head nodded sleepily, and my thoughts became unfocused, and still I couldn't help but stare up at the finely wrought features of the man holding me as if I was the most treasured thing in the world. Finally, I slipped into the quiet space between wake and sleep and heard low voices speaking. They soothed and comforted me. It was like falling asleep when someone you loved was reading a story.

"You both need rest, Ash," Ahmose said.

I could see him and hear him and feel his touch, but somehow I knew it wasn't me he was looking at. *"I know,"* my mouth said. *"There's just . . . there's just somethin' I need ta know."*

"What is it?"

"Who do ya love?"

My dream self looked at Ahmose and saw his shining moonlight eyes. That they appeared stark, and distant, like he was keeping secrets, might have been my imagination.

"What are you asking me, Ashleigh?"

"It's quite a simple question, handsome. I'm askin' which o' us do ya love. Is it Tia, Lily, or me?"

"Does my affection need to be limited to only one of you?"

"Does ours? I thought you didn' so much like sharin' with yer brothers."

His body tightened for a moment, and his expression became as dark as a sea that had suddenly been chilled by a distant storm. It made me shiver. But then, as quickly as the storm within him had risen, it abated, and all was calm on the surface once more.

"My brothers are a hurdle we'll cross when the time is right."

"Lily might believe she loves ya now, with yerself all dashin' and strappin' an' smiles an' sweet, sweet kisses, but how do ya expect to hurdle Amon if she ever remembers herself?"

"I suppose in that case she'll have to weigh her options and make a choice."

"She's not the only one decidin', ya know."

"I'm aware of that. How could I not be?"

"It might help ya, lad, to have someone in yer corner, so ta speak."

Ahmose smiled. "Are you in my corner, Ash?"

"I don' think I can rightly say. Amon is a handsome sort."

He paused, touched his finger to the tip of my nose, and then asked, "And who would you choose, Ashleigh?"

"It's not fair to ask me that question when ya haven' answered my own."

Exhaling, he picked up my hand and entwined my fingers with his. "I'm not sure it's possible to separate out how I feel about each of you," he said. "I respect all three of you. I care for all three of you."

"But do ya love all three?"

Ahmose smiled softly, but it was a haunted thing, a slipshod and sad imitation of the happy expression he wore before.

"Ah, we have our answer, then, don' we?" My heart hurt in my chest like a hot stone had been set in the space where a heart should go.

I continued, my mouth wrapping around the words carefully though they numbed my lips as I spoke. "Vera well. If it's a drownin' ya intend, don' torment me with shallow water, love. Jus' get the breakin' o' my heart over with quickly." I taunted him with words to add more fuel to the fire. Gave him leave to let his tongue slip recklessly and beat me with the truth. I was nothing to him except the sad, pathetic remains of a girl long ago uprooted from history.

That I was intoxicated by his nearness; that I longed to touch and be touched by him; that I considered him finer than precious gemstones in all their faceted, sparkling splendor, and his arms more comforting than the softest nest in a fairy glen, made no difference. His next words would vanquish me as certainly as he did his enemies. They would be a knife driven through me that would undo me utterly. Tears leaked from my traitorous eyes and trickled slowly down my cheeks.

Ahmose cupped my face and wiped away a tear with a thumb. "You wore a crown of apple blossoms in your hair the day you hid in the tree."

"I . . . yes, I did," I replied, startled.

"Did you know the man would have killed you as easily as he did the tree?"

"Better the trouble that follows death than the trouble that follows shame."

"He would have shamed himself, not you. If I had been there, I would have killed him."

"But ya don' like killin'."

"No. I don't. But any man that would have spoiled the sweet innocent you were—the sweet girl you *are*—isn't worthy of walking the face of the earth, or any other place, for that matter."

Gently, he trailed his fingertips over my forehead, dislodging the strands of hair that stuck to my tearstained cheeks, and tucked them behind my ear. My wrung-out heart thumped once, but the sound was shallow, ruptured, like a stick hitting the torn skin of a drum.

Fairies could die of a broken heart. And once they found someone to love, they could never love another. I'd never thought that would happen to me. How could I find someone to love in the netherworld? Had the fairy tree gone to all the trouble to save me just so I could perish on this lonely planet? Unloved and unwanted?

I wished Ahmose would just get it over with. Get all the hurt done at once instead of trying to rub honey all over the knife he was going to skewer me with. Each stroke of his fingers was a torment. A reminder that I was simply wearing the face of the real girl he loved. The one who could touch him back and hold him in her arms. What could I offer a man like him? What did I expect?

Finally, he spoke, "Ashleigh," he said. "Believe it or not, there are things I don't know. Paths I cannot see. Most of the time when you speak, I know it's you. I know Lily's voice. And Tia's. But sometimes there's a mixing. A blending of souls. The different parts of you, the things that define Lily or you or Tia, are all things that interest me. They are pieces that I've come to love. I know this isn't what you want to hear. Not exactly.

"But there's something else I want you to understand. I've traced the life paths of all three of you. I've watched you grow up. I've seen the choices you've made. And I've spent the most time watching yours. Hours, no, days, in fact. During the weeks we were apart, while I was supposed to be guarding the afterlife with Asten, I followed your path.

"I know you. I know the person you were as a mortal. I know the impish fairy version. And I know what you are now.

"So if you are asking me if I could love only the slight-framed Irish girl with the curly red hair, the one who stomps her foot when she's irritated and narrows her green eyes with temper—if you want to know if I could spend hours tracing the patterns of the freckles on her shoulders and kissing her apple cheeks and the sweet mouth that draws up like a bow hiding the most beautiful present when she smiles, then the answer is yes."

A little gasp escaped my lips. *"Are ya certain, then? 'Cause once ya say it, I'll take ya at yer word."*

"Why do you think I've been sacrificing much-needed sleep night after night just to sit next to you and listen to your stories? Even when I do sleep, I chase you in my dreams like an eager puppy. I long to lie in a meadow of clover, my head in your lap, with you threading your fingers through my hair, and fall asleep with the lilt of your voice caressing my ears. The truth is, you've been in my thoughts since you first spoke to me."

I placed my hand on his cheek. *"And ya've been in mine."*

His smile was quick and tender. With eyes half-closed, he kissed me, and it felt like it was at once different and new. This kiss was distinctive. It was mine and no one else's.

"You taste like strawberries, heather, and fairy dust," he murmured, his stubble rough against my cheek. Ahmose whispered sugared assurances, tickling the soft skin behind my ears, and mending the little hurts in my heart with all its tiny leaks. Soon, they were stopped up, and the love I felt for him was trapped inside, full to bursting and pulsing through my veins once more.

I wrapped my arms around his neck, squeezing him tight, feeling like the happiness would erupt out of my body and rain down sparkling joy on everything around us. Ahmose closed his eyes and held me loosely, content as I explored his cheeks and jaw with my lips, leaving a trail of soft fairy-wing kisses behind as I went.

Cupping his hand around my head, he pressed me to his chest and hummed a light-hearted tune, one I remembered from when I was a child. It reminded me of summertime naps in patches of wildflowers, eating ripe berries straight from the bush, and dipping my bare toes in ice-cold streams. Smiling, I closed my eyes and drifted to sleep feeling like somehow everything would work out and I'd get to be with Ahmose like that forever.

It was the sweetest of dreams. But, it turned out, that forever didn't last as long as I hoped.

I woke with a jolt. Ahmose was gone, and the predawn air crept into the cave, silent, and with a cold bite that seemed somehow threatening. The glowing rocks had gone dim, and the only light came from the thin, orange moon winking through beat-back clouds. It stretched through the opening of the cave, tingeing everything red like it was the rising floodwater of hell.

The unicorns were awake. They shuffled quietly, as nervous and jittery as if they sensed a far-off stampede. "What is it?" I asked Nebu. "Where has Ahmose gone?"

Before Nebu or Zahra could answer, a dark figure entered the mouth of the cave. "Lily?" Ahmose said. "We need to go, quickly. We are being hunted."

"Hunted?" Immediately, I rose and picked up Ahmose's cloak. After shaking it out, I made my way over to him, handed him the garment, and began strapping on my harness. He turned me around to help, and then I felt the solid weight of his cloak as he placed it around my shoulders.

"Is it the same beast that made a try for us before?" Tia asked, asserting herself.

"I'm not sure," he said. "But whatever it is, it seeks our destruction."

Ahmose kissed my forehead quickly and gave me a boost onto Nebu's back. "Nebu's the fastest," he explained. "If something happens, I will tell him the path to take, and we will separate so I can draw off the beast."

I placed my hand on his arm. "No, Ahmose. We do not separate." I said, back in control of my body.

He tried to give me a reassuring smile. "We will avoid it if we can."

We can take to the sky, if we must, Nebu said. *The distance to the edge is not too far.*

Ahmose nodded, agreeing with Nebu's assessment.

We set out from the cave, following the path only Ahmose could see. The half-moon peeked over the top of a layer of clouds that were moving quickly across its face. Ahmose stopped often, constantly changing course, but whatever he saw left his expression grim. A strange bird cried out from the dark trees, hooting like an owl but with a screeching sound at the end. I wasn't sure if that was the natural sound or if the animal had caught something else and silenced it with a deadly talon.

Even when the sun rose, thick mist licked the tops of the trees, making the sunlight that did touch the ground seem sinister and strange. Ahmose had summoned his weapon from the sand and his fingers twitched toward the handle every time he heard a sound. There were hollows beneath his eyes, and his handsome face looked haggard and worried.

Though the storm had passed, the trees were still drawn into themselves. With flexible limbs raised and leaves rolled up, they reminded me of tall ostriches tucking their heads in the sand, hoping no one would notice that the bulk of their forms was obvious to everyone. The spiny green plants that resembled aloe had wrapped themselves so tightly that they looked like tall sticks just planted into the ground. It was eerie seeing them. They stood in their beds like rows of unmarked graves.

As the sun rose higher, we came to the crest of a hill and looked down into the valley just as the first animal burst into a clearing. It stood up on its hind legs and sniffed the air, shifting its head back and forth. It was huge. If a velociraptor and a saber-toothed cat had a baby, it would look like this animal. Its skin was armored, which was likely why the stinging needles from the plants couldn't slow it down. When it turned its head toward us, it bellowed again, spotting its prey.

I saw the flash of not one set of glow-in-the-dark eyes but two or perhaps more, set in its face. It looked like something out of a Godzilla movie. Where was the giant lizard when you needed him? "Ahmose?" I called out. "I think we're in trouble."

Almost as one, the pack of creatures leapt from the trees and made their way up the rocky mountainside as agile as goats, scrabbling with claws and tearing up the distance in great bounds, the sun flashing off their bodies as they triumphantly bellowed. They'd be upon us in minutes.

"Nebu, go!" Ahmose shouted. With that, the unicorn began running. The awakened plants responded, stretching out branches to catch my hair and cloak. Holding on to Nebu's mane with one hand, I pulled out one of my spear-knives and hacked at the offending branches. Then, almost instinctively, I nocked an arrow and fired it into the trunk of a nearby tree. To my dismay, I saw I was pulling the arrows of Isis from the quiver. The branches immediately stilled upon being struck and withdrew. I used two more arrows on the other species of tree attacking us, and both species stilled. In my mind I thought, *Eight, seven, six. Six arrows left.*

Terror swept through my veins like water through a desert arroyo, crashing and aggressive as the creatures behind us swept upward, still coming for us. At least the surrounding trees were no longer barring our path.

Ahmose turned around and barreled past me, meeting the first beast head-on and bashing in its skull with his cudgel. *What was he thinking? That he could take on a whole pack?*

He's drawing them away, Tia said. *It's a noble thing.*

It's a stupid thing, I countered. "Turn around, Nebu."

I will not, Lady Sphinx.

"You will."

He will not risk himself overmuch. Trust in this man. He knows what he is about.

I did trust Ahmose, but how could I let him endanger himself? He was powerful, but so was I. Nebu turned, heading up a new switchback, which gave me a good view of what was going on below. I nocked another arrow and fired it. It barreled into the chest of one of the beasts. *Five,* I thought. The animal struggled and stumbled but the others kept coming. I shot again. *Four. Three.* Ahmose was safe for the moment. Three of the creatures were tumbling down the mountainside, either dead or severely injured, but they did not respond to the arrows as a species like the trees had. Ahmose was barreling upward again, taking a new path that I knew would soon intersect my own.

We came to another switchback, and Ahmose caught up to us quickly and shouted, "Are you all right?"

"We're fine," I shouted back.

"We've got to fly!" he called. "I'm sorry, Nebu, but we don't have a choice."

Very well, Nebu said. *Let's hope fortune favors us.* The unicorn's muscles bunched beneath me and, all at once, his wings snapped out and he leapt into the sky with a whoosh of air. Zahra followed, and we soon left the mountaintop with its cap of carnivorous trees far below us. The scrambling pack crested the peak and howled at the loss of their prey.

A moment later, as the unicorns angled west, away from the rising sun, a sound like a thousand cicadas rose around us. The chittering rose and fell as if an invisible swarm circled around me and then Ahmose. It was more frightening when the sound disappeared. We angled up, flying so high I dared not look down, but I did anyway, and when I did, I couldn't help the scream that erupted from my lips.

Below us, a giant creature rose upward. Its wide mouth full of teeth gaped open like a shark. We flew into a cloud bank, and I couldn't see it clearly for a moment. But then, the tips of the wide featherless wings, which looked much like an ocean ray's, pierced the clouds. Its nose and sleek, torpedo-like body followed.

Hurry, Zahra, Nebu warned.

Tiny birdlike creatures swarmed around the large predator, trailing alongside it like remora fish. The chittering noise returned, and I realized that they were serving as a sort of echolocation for the creature, because when they made the noise, it angled itself anew and pressed on. Coming closer, it snapped at Zahra's heels.

Ahmose chanted a spell, and the creature paused momentarily, flapping its wide wings, and then continued toward us.

I tried to help by channeling my power to find the creature's name, but the swarm surrounding it made singling out the main threat difficult. It was as if they encircled the beast with static or a sort of white noise that diffused my abilities. I tried a precious arrow, which found its mark, but it didn't slow the creature. *Two,* I thought.

Save the rest, Tia said. *This one won't respond to it.*

We're almost there, Nebu cried.

I could just make out a dark hole in the sky. The unicorns stretched out their necks and hurried toward it. We were going to make it. Then the swarm fell upon us. I realized they were more like giant bees than birds. They buzzed and hummed and the sky-shark drew closer.

He cannot follow us in! Nebu exclaimed. *Hold on!*

Nebu and I passed through the opening first. Nebu's head and forelegs disappeared into the black. The swarm hit the barrier and, stunned, buzzed off in different directions. This confused the predator chasing us. A few of them hit me in my back and bounced off my cloak. My hands and arms entered the void. Just before the rest of me went through, I felt a sting on my neck. Reaching beneath my hair, I pulled out a thick stinger and dropped it over Nebu's side.

Ahmose came through quickly after us. When I turned to look behind, I could still make out what was left of the swarm and see the confused sky-shark turning in circles wondering where we'd gone. The purple-pink of the sky shifted into the dark of space, and we were soon encompassed by stars.

"Where are we?" I whispered to Nebu.

This is the transition place, the Place Where Dreams Are Born. You crossed it once before, though you don't remember it.

"I did?"

You did.

I rubbed my arms. *It's getting cold.*

Tia did something and my body soon warmed. *Thank you,* I said to her.

The adrenaline rush that had fueled me before subsided, and my limbs grew heavy. We flew at a relaxed pace. The tired unicorns beat the air with slow but steady wing strokes. Now that we weren't being chased by things that wanted to eat us for breakfast, Tia said, *We need to talk.*

"What is it?" I asked.

Privately, she said.

Oh. Are you okay? Is something bothering you?

I think we need to talk about him.

Him? You mean Ahmose?

Yes.

Do we really need ta do this now? Ashleigh asked.

I think we . . . I think we . . . should.

Tia? I said. There was no response. "Tia?" I said out loud.

I think she fell asleep, Ashleigh said, then hesitated a moment. *Oh no.*

Ash . . . leigh? My mind felt fuzzy, like it had when the plant stung me. Reaching behind my neck, I touched the place where I'd been stung.

There was a lump there, and a sticky liquid oozed from the puncture wound. "The bug . . . the bug . . . must've . . . drugged . . . ussss."

No! Nebu shouted in my mind. *Ashleigh, you must take over. Lily cannot fall asleep here! She cannot!*

I . . . I can't, I started to say, but then my head rolled back and I felt suddenly weightless. I heard Ashleigh's scream in my mind, and then all went dark.

That Sleep of Death

"Lily!"

Someone was screaming my name, screaming it over and over like it was the end of the world. All I wanted to do was sleep. Was that too much to ask? It was summer. College hadn't started yet. So why were my parents yelling so loudly?

My head hurt. Especially at the base of my neck. Then, suddenly, the voice shouting my name was cut off and the pain ceased. The silence was blissful. Peaceful. I was detached from all my worries, from every niggling thing weighing down my conscious mind.

I don't know how long I slept, but when I came to myself, I woke slowly, stretching out my arms and legs and rolling my shoulders like a drowsy cat. For the first time in a long time, I felt unhurried, unneeded, and unanswerable.

When I finally blinked open my eyes, I didn't understand what I was seeing. Heavy mist covered my body, and when I sat up, it flowed around my waist, covering my legs. I was clothed in a simple white dress that swirled around my body. Above me, the sky was full of nebulas and churning galaxies in every color of the rainbow. But in each direction, as far as I could see, there was nothing but a white mist. When I waved my hand by my bare feet, I saw that the floor was also white. It wasn't granite or marble, but it was slick and hard.

Where am I? I thought. *This is the weirdest dream I've ever had.*

A sad voice answered, *We fell.*

Like a boulder rolling down a hill, everything suddenly came back to me. Well, not *everything,* everything, but enough. I wasn't at home in my warm bed in New York City. I wasn't on a well-deserved summer break. I'd been riding the back of a unicorn on another planet. And, oh yeah, I had two passengers hitching a ride in my cranium, was half in love with a mummy come to life, *and* I had to save the universe.

"Ashleigh," I said simply, "where's Tia?"

She's still sleepin'. The toxins in that world affect her the most.

"Right. How long was I out this time? And where's the bow and quiver or the harness with the spear-knives?"

I don' know. There's no way for me ta keep track of time here either. I'm not sure if we lost our weapons or not.

"Do you think this is heaven?" I asked. "Did we die in the fall?" It wasn't the worst outcome I could think of.

Not ta be insultin', but I'd like ta think that if I die, I'd be a ghost all on my own instead o' hauntin' yer mind.

"Right."

I began to walk, even though there was nowhere for me to go. Both of us were relieved when Tia awoke. She suggested we try using our power. It didn't work. We couldn't even use the abilities of the sphinx. After an indeterminable length of time, something changed.

At first, we thought it was rain tumbling from the sky, but the droplets were too large, and they never actually touched the ground. When they got closer, we saw they were more like bubbles or twirling glass disks. The shining panels soon surrounded us, and as they floated there I could see pictures reflected in them. Moving pictures.

"What are they?" I asked, stretching out a fingertip to nudge one.

"I wouldn't touch that. At least not yet," a male voice behind me said.

I spun around and Tia rushed to the surface, pushing me out of the way in her eagerness to speak. *"Asten!"* she cried.

The handsome man smiled a bit cockily, with one side of his mouth lifting higher than the other. If Tia hadn't blurted out his name, I'm not sure I would have recognized him from his sarcophagus. There was so much life in his expression, I couldn't reconcile it with the body I'd seen before. "Hello, lady lioness," he said with a slight bow. The man's easy grin was too charming for his own good, in my opinion. I didn't trust men with easy grins. Then again, I hadn't fully trusted Ahmose either when I first met him.

This is the one you love? I asked Tia.

He is the brother of Ahmose, Tia explained, without adding anything else.

Yeah. I figured out that much. How is he here? Ask him where we are and what exactly happened to us. Ask him about my memory, too. And where are Nebu and Ahmose? Can he lead us back to them?

Tia sighed. *You'd better ask him yourself,* she said, and switched places with me.

Before I could ask him any of my questions, he asked one of his own.

"What have you girls done?"

"Done? What do you mean? We haven't *done* anything." I put my hands on my hips and frowned at him. "I'm Lily, by the way. Nice to meet you. Tia's told me a lot about you."

She hadn't. Not really. Other than his role with all the Egypt stuff. Clearly, she had skipped over some of the more interesting tidbits.

He folded his arms across his chest and scrutinized my face with way more than casual awareness. "Hello, Lily," he answered, eyebrows raised. "It's, uh, nice to *meet* you, too." He gestured in my general direction. "We'll figure out what's going on with you later. First we have to get you ladies out of here."

"Right. And where exactly is 'here'?"

"It would seem the three of you have gone and gotten yourselves trapped in the Place Where Dreams Are Born."

"Okay," I said. "So how do we get untrapped? Is there, like, a doorway or something?" I asked, looking around hopefully.

"I'm afraid you don't understand the severity of what's happened. You see, all three of you have become a dream, a figment of the imagination. The only way to escape from here is if someone dreams you back into reality."

"I don't understand. Then how can *you* be here?"

"I'm not here. Not really. My dreaming self is here. It's a part of my power as a Son of Egypt."

"Uh-huh. So then why don't *you* dream about us? Unless this already counts?" I added optimistically.

Asten shook his head. "I am not currently in possession of my mortal body. I'm stuck in Ma'at's oubliette."

"Well then, Ahmose or Dr. Hassan?"

He rubbed his jaw with a palm. "It's possible, but they'd have to bring you back one by one. You see, each of you has a different dreamworld, and you can only access the mortal realm through a dreamworld of your own making. I wouldn't hold out much hope for Hassan. His dreams as of late have been about someone much closer in proximity. Ahmose is our best bet."

"Nana," I mumbled.

"Your grandmother?" he asked.

I nodded. "I think she and Dr. Hassan have a bit of a crush on each other."

"Interesting." Asten blinked; then he smiled and held out a hand. "Shall we go find Ashleigh's dreamworld? Ahmose is most likely to dream her into existence first. Providing, of course, that Nebu explains what has happened."

"Why is he most likely to dream up Ashleigh first?" I asked.

Asten glanced at me sharply but chose not to answer. The fairy in my mind didn't add any insights either. We walked along quietly for a time, Asten giving me strange looks as we did. "Ah," he said, stopping and pointing at a floating, mirrored disk. "Here we are."

The picture rotated toward us, and the inner scene was a picturesque Irish meadow with a large tree shading it and blue flowers popping up among the green. I could hear the gurgle of a nearby stream and feel a robust, summer-kissed breeze blow lightly across my skin.

"Now, when you touch it, you will be in Ashleigh's dream. Ahmose will join her there and pull her out. When he does, you and Tia will move on to her dream, but Ashleigh will be gone."

"What do ya mean, I'll be gone?" Ashleigh said, rising up and taking over my body.

"I mean you will be in the place where Ahmose is dreaming in his physical form. You will be like a ghost. He won't be able to touch you or see you, but Nebu will. Tell Nebu that Ahmose will have to dream of Tia and Lily in succession as well. Once Lily is back in her physical form, assuming, of course, that Ahmose and Nebu have retrieved it, you and Tia will naturally enter her mind again."

There were a whole lot of *ifs* in his what-is-going-to-happen-next speech that made me all kinds of uncomfortable. I would have addressed them, but Ashleigh was currently running the show.

"Can ya really tell someone ta dream about somethin' and make it happen?" Ashleigh asked, her mind full of doubt. I agreed with her there. I had never heard of inducing yourself to dream of someone before.

"You'd be surprised what influence your will can have on your dreams," Asten said softly. "Trust me. I'm kind of an expert." He raised his head and closed his eyes. "Yes. He's ready. Go ahead and touch the dream. Good luck. I'll see you two soon," he added. I assumed he was indicating me and Tia.

One of my hands stretched out toward the dream while the other reached out seemingly of its own volition and took hold of Asten's arm. He had turned to look at another disk that circled behind us, but at the touch on his arm, he paused and met my eyes. "Don't worry," he said tenderly, while taking hold of my hand and squeezing it. "I'll come find you. I promise."

Just then, my other hand touched the bubble, and it sucked me inside. Asten and the white fog were swept away, and we spun in a vortex, the sky swirling above us. Finally, the blue and white streaks slowed and stopped. I was lying on my back, arms behind my head, looking up at the fresh blue of a spring sky.

The ground felt soft and giving beneath me. I plucked a handful of greenery and began to count the leaves of clover, looking for the elusive four-leafed variety. Turning my head toward a noise, I saw I was lying in a bed of red, springy stuff.

Quickly, I sat up and discovered the red stuff moved with me. It was my hair. Tugging a piece, I found that it was long. So long that I could stretch out my entire arm while holding the end of it. When I let it go, it sprang back into the mass spilling over my shoulder.

The sound nearby was that of a chittering squirrel as it hastily climbed up the thick trunk of a nearby tree. Large roots stuck out of the ground, and as I marveled at the sheer size of it, I realized the trunk would have to be that big to support the considerable weight of the heavy canopy above. Fluttering spring-addled birds tweeted as they chased each other in happy delight, darting in and out of the branches.

I held out my arms and saw that I was as delicate-limbed as a deer and as pale as Bossy's milk. My skin was spun sugar and cream. Against the green clover, my bare legs looked like soft butter spread over fresh green peas. Touching my face, I felt the outline of my lips and cheeks and jaw and knew that the shape was very different from my own. I had a small, pert nose, and I wished I had a mirror so that I could see what I looked like. A bubbly giggle escaped my lips. I finally looked the way I was supposed to.

My feet were still bare and now slightly dirty. I wiggled my toes in the morning sunshine and then tucked my feet and legs beneath the voluminous skirt of my green homespun dress. Untying a ribbon tickling my neck, I swept away my straw bonnet, fluffed out my curly hair, and dug in the wide, deep pockets of the apron tied around my waist, finding, to my delight, a handful of wild strawberries.

Plucking off the stem, I placed a fat berry in my mouth, enjoying the burst of sweetness.

"I hope you saved one for me," a familiar voice said.

I was about to answer when I found I couldn't. Someone else spoke for me. *"I always do, handsome."*

Ahmose sat down next to me, snuck his arm around my waist, and opened his mouth, waiting to be given a berry. Pulling another from my pocket, I tore off the green top and pretended like I was going to give it to him, but stuffed it into my mouth instead, laughing.

"Oh, you're going to pay for that," Ahmose said.

"Is that right?" I teased. *"And who 'round here is man enough ta do such a thing?"*

"Are you, a mere wisp of a girl, questioning *my* manliness?" Ahmose said with mock outrage as he pushed me back into the grass, my hair spilling on either side. He put one arm on each side of my head and lowered down until his lips were just inches from mine.

Ahmose's strong features seemed smooth and relaxed. The tension that lent sharpness to his jaw and cheekbones had melted away. Leaning down, he kissed my lips gently, softly, moving across them as if he wanted to memorize the shape of them by the touch of his. When he lifted his head, he murmured, *"Have I told how beautiful you are?"*

"Yer a silver-tongued devil, ya are. Are ya perhaps thinkin' flattery will get ya the lion's share o' the strawberries?"

His carefree laugh warmed my heart. He sat up, pulling me up with him. Taking hold of my waist, he shifted me onto his lap and held me close, pressing his nose to my neck. Ahmose proceeded to drive me crazy with kisses, trailing them from one ear, down my jaw to the other side and back. I shivered when he touched his lips to the tender spot just beneath the corner of my jaw at the hairline.

When he finally raised his head, I was trembling, but he wore a wide grin and opened his hand to show me he was now in possession of all the strawberries from my pocket.

I gasped. *"Yer more than a silver-tongued devil, ya are. Yer a red-handed thief!"*

"Better a thief than a beggar in the game of love. Are you going to make me plead for more of your strawberry kisses, Ash, or shall I steal them?"

"Ya think ta make me all moony-eyed with honeyed words, but I'm made o' stronger stuff. Besides, a truly wicked thief wouldn' waste time on words, he would just take. Yer not foolin' me, Ahmose. Yer more beggar than thief."

His smile was as crisp and tart as the green apples that grew in the orchard a bit farther down the creek. Just looking at him made my lips pucker like I'd already helped myself to a not-quite-ripe piece of fruit. With Ahmose, I'd brave all the sour things in life just for a little taste of the sweet in being with him.

His wintry seashore eyes beckoned me closer, and I pressed my lips against his again. This time his kiss was deeper, darker, like a moon-pulled tide drawing me out of my element and taking me to a place I wasn't entirely sure I wanted to go, but the mystery of it enticed me all the same.

When we parted, he stroked my hair. His smile was sweet and sad all at once. "We need to go, love."

"I don' want ta." Fiercely, I seized his hand. *"Can't we jus' stay here? Where it's peaceful and I can have ya all to meself?"*

"And what about Lily? You can feel the hurt in her heart right now as much as I can. She's suffering, seeing us like this."

"Lily can find her own happily-ever-after. This one's mine."

"Ashleigh." His reprimand was mild, like soft desert rain, but she could still feel its effects even after all signs of it disappeared. "I'm surprised that a girl who only exists because another gave up their life is so willing to abandon others. Lily needs you. In this place it's easy to forget the real world. To hide away, ignoring the sun rising and setting day after day. To focus only on love and laughter. But this meadow isn't real. The animals, rocks, and stream take no notice of us. This isn't living.

"I want to make a life with you," he continued. "To make the most of living, or at least try as best we can." Ahmose nudged my chin up so I'd look at him. Tears had filled my eyes, and I felt like my heart was breaking. He went on, "Ash, you once told me that it's easy to halve the potato where there's love. As much as I enjoy sharing your dreams with you, following your steps along this path, the girl I know wouldn't let her two friends, the ones she loves like sisters, suffer alone."

I sniffled loudly. *"What's ta become of me? Of us?"*

"I don't know," Ahmose replied frankly, hugging me close. "I wish I did. I wish I could see the path clearly, but it stops at Wasret. What happens after that is unknown."

"I don' wanna lose you."

"And I don't want to lose *you*. We can't change the direction of the wind, love, but we can align ourselves in such a way that it doesn't break us."

"Will . . . will you promise me somethin'?"

"Anything."

"If . . . if something happens to me, you won't forget me. Like I am now, I mean?"

Ahmose cupped my cheeks with his big hands and smiled sweetly. "Seeing you like this is something I'll never forget. Even if I go on to live for millennia, every time I close my eyes, I'll see your lovely face in my dreams."

I placed my hands on top of his. *"Okay, then. I'm ready, darlin'."*

The green meadow around me shifted, and my body rose in the air like I'd been whisked into a vortex.

When the spinning stopped, the world shifted. Instead of a blue sky dotted with puffy clouds, there was a wide expanse of black, lit with stars.

Around me a vast plain of seemingly unending grasslands. Ashleigh was gone, and her dream had gone with her. The space in my mind where she lived now felt empty and wrong. But as quickly as the thought came, my mind seemed to forget it.

Tall grasses swayed in a balmy breeze that carried with it the scents of a nearby river and the heady musk of night-blooming flowers and sun-warmed acacia trees. Winged creatures fluttered overhead, their cries ringing across the savannah as they hunted insects that emerged after sundown. I was the only large predator around as far as I could see. Though I liked the idea, it made me feel somewhat lonely.

The part of me that was Lily knew that something was missing, that my heart hurt, but that part wasn't in charge right then. This was Tia's dream, and she felt . . . peaceful. At home. I sank into her dream as if it were my own and experienced every taste, scent, and sound as she did. I walked through the grasses, the tops of them prickling my bare calves, and climbed up a series of rocks until I came to the level peak. My arms and legs were supple and strong, and my skin was soft and a darker hue than the sepia rocks I climbed.

After finding a good spot, I sat on a flat stone, still warmed from the heat of the summer sun, and leaned back on my palms. Shuttering my eyes, I half dozed and half reflected on what I now was. It surprised me that I took human form in my dreamworld. I found I missed my tail, and my sharp teeth, but I liked the curves of my bare shoulders and my hips. I longed to run and test out my long, long legs, which stretched out beneath the short dress that was the same color my fur had once been.

Now I had a mane, too. I'd often complained about caring for a mane, but this one was perfect. My thick hair was swept back from my forehead and ended just where it brushed the tops of my shoulders. I could run my hands through it quickly to work out any tangles, and it wouldn't require too much maintenance. I had no idea what color it was, and found I really didn't care overmuch.

The wind rustled the tall grasses and I sat up. The light of the stars blanketed my skin, giving it a glossy sheen. I found I couldn't get enough of looking at my hands and arms. They were mine. My face; my skin; my tall, curvy body; my scent. Mine. Not Lily's. I don't know why that was so important—or why the concept hurt the silent watcher inside me—but it was. So very, very important.

The shadows of the rocks stretched like inky pools across the land, and the leaves sighed softly in the trees. The breeze passed through them, kissing each one and whispering its secrets before moving on. It caressed my new body, sending tingles across my skin and making the little hairs at the nape of my neck stand on end. It hinted of things to come.

"There you are," a voice said from the ground below. It bothered me that I hadn't sensed his approach. Such must be the burden of humanity.

I looked down. *"Hello, Asten."*

The handsome man cocked his head, a half smile on his face as he perused my altered form. His white linen pants and loose, flowy shirt stood out starkly in the dark night, but they still couldn't compete with his stellar smile. I let out a soft sigh, pleased at seeing him but dreading it at the same time.

"Is there room enough for two up there?" he asked politely.

"There is," I replied. *"You may join me, if that pleases you."*

"It does."

I listened to the sounds of his progress, though I didn't turn to watch him. I felt like my heart was fighting a battle I didn't understand, and no one was aware of it except me. As he closed the distance between us, his nearness became a palpable thing. I wanted to growl, to warn him that he was approaching a formidable foe, one that would not be easily bested. But I remained silent knowing he would effortlessly breach every invisible defense I could possibly muster.

When Asten settled himself by my side, I glanced at him out of the corner of my eye. He wasn't looking at me like I expected a conquering victor would. He didn't even adopt the demeanor of a lion staking his claim. Instead, he was quiet, his thoughts turned inward as he gazed out at the landscape surrounding us. "I like your dreams," he said finally. "They're peaceful."

Since I didn't know what to say to that, I said, *"I thought Ahmose would be joining my dream, not you."*

"He will. It might take him a bit of time, though. Ahmose doesn't know you as well as he does Ashleigh. It's going to be difficult for him to track down your dream."

I sniffed and shifted slightly, plucking at the hem of my dress. I suddenly felt awkward wearing it, like I was an impostor playing human. *"Yes, well. It's certainly true that he knows Ashleigh best."*

A quick grin appeared on his face, and it looked like he was itching to say something more, but then he bit his lip, a gesture I found fascinating for some reason. He chose to keep whatever he'd thought of private for the moment. In its place, he said, "I thought you wouldn't mind having company while you waited."

Asten turned to me then, his handsome face so very close to my own. When he closed one eye in a wink, I noticed his long lashes were like tiny feathers. It was one more thing I could add to my list that I found beautiful about him.

I should have felt embarrassed when he caught me openly admiring his features, but I didn't care that he knew. Not anymore. A door had closed between us, and I now sat dejectedly on the other side of it, wishing I could open it again and step into the same light that touched his face.

"You don't seem like yourself, lady lioness," he said. "Apart from the obvious, of course." He indicated my new body.

Pulling up a long leg and tucking it under me, I angled myself toward him and stiffened my back and shoulders, my face a taciturn mask. *"I feel I am more myself now than I have ever been. But if you believe that I am overstepping by assuming human form, then say it outright. Do not feel as if you must coddle me in any way, Asten. I am a lioness, and I prefer candid speaking."*

"Yes," he agreed softly, seriously. "I know. Your straightforward manner is something I appreciate about you. I don't begrudge your taking human form. In fact, I think it suits you."

I nodded. *"Thank you. Then I wish to speak plainly to you on the matter of our relationship, Asten. I know that you must be disappointed by what passed between us in our dream before. You thought it was Lily you held in your arms. You believed it was Lily you kissed. It was not.*

"I cannot go back into the past and correct this mistake in judgment, but I do not regret having had the experience. The fire that blazed between us once has now turned to ash, and the wind has carried it away, but I can still feel the heat from it branded onto my memory."

"Were all the things you said in that dream true?" he asked.

"I did not attempt to mislead you, if that is what you mean. The words I said to you were in earnest and are a true representation of how I feel."

Asten did not speak for a long moment. My heart beat heavy and thick in my chest, pounding like the sound of an elephant moving through the jungle.

"Thank you," Asten finally said.

"What is it you are thankful for?" I asked, surprised. His response wasn't what I had expected.

"Thank you for finding something in me to love."

I wanted to tell him that I'd found a great deal in him to love. That though there were perhaps other men who would make worthy mates for Lily, and, in fact, might make her happier, I knew in my heart that Asten would be my choice if I were given one. The sad fact was that no such option existed for me. I had no more right to choose Lily's mate than I had to this body.

All those thoughts seemed too complicated for a lioness to express, so I said simply, *"Love is not something I ever thought myself capable of."*

He picked up my hand and played with my fingers, not looking me in the eye. I liked seeing our fingers intertwined, the different colors folded together. It reminded me of the evening sky—stars and silky night. It also reminded me that in my dreamworld at least, I was my own person.

"But you are, aren't you," he said, not meaning it like a question. "You're a lioness capable of love."

I let out a soft breath. *"Lily tried to help me comprehend it. To know the difference between passion and love. It was confusing at first. Now I think I understand what it is. Perhaps that means I have changed into something more than a lioness,"* I confessed. *"Though, in truth, I don't know what I am."*

"You certainly don't look like a lioness any longer."

"No," I answered softly. *"I don't."*

"So, you wanted to know the experience of love, the kind that exists between a man and a woman. That's why you came to me in a dream, isn't it?"

"Yes."

"I see. And were you satisfied with your explorations?"

"What do you mean?"

"I mean you've tasted it. Tested it out. Did you find it to your liking, or are you ready to move on to something else? Some other new human experience?"

I frowned. *"The human experiences I've had have been varied and unique. Some I've enjoyed. Some I've not liked. And some were confusing. If you're asking me if I enjoyed our encounter, then you should know that I've reflected on it many times since."* I bit the inside of my cheek. *"It is my most treasured memory in all the time I've been with Lily."*

"But now you've experienced that with Ahmose."

"Yes, but . . ." I smoothed my palms on my thighs, unsure about how to explain myself.

"But?"

"It is not the same. Not for me. There is heat and tenderness and kindness, but when he looks in my eyes, he sees someone else."

Asten reached out for my other hand. "So," he said, "you believe what has passed between us is now over and gone forever."

"Even if I held out hope that you could feel about me the way you felt about Lily, how can it be otherwise when Lily chooses another?" I placed my palm on his cheek. *"Your form is pleasing to me, Asten. Your heartbeat is like the hot sun warming my back. When you speak, your words ring true to every part of me. Your smile is as a sky full of stars. I yearn to be near you in spirit and body. But knowing that when you look at me you see Lily, that you kiss her lips and hold her tight, burns within me like a raging fire. It is cruel. Like a predator playing with its prey.*

"I would, instead, beg you to find a way to ease my torment. Help me escape. Send me on to whatever fate awaits me rather than trap me in a pretty box in this half-life. You said that you dreamed of Lily. That you saw a future where you loved one another. If this is to be, then please, at least wait until we have defeated the Unmaker. After I am gone, you can do as you will."

"And what about my torment?"

I looked up at him sharply.

He continued, "You speak of the Dreams That Could Have Been. You were right about me seeing a life where Lily and I were together. But there were other dreams, too. Dreams I never told Ma'at. I thought it was because I was broken, but now I'm not so certain. Events have happened that helped me see things a little more clearly. And one of those things is you."

"Me?"

"Yes. I am certain of it." He reached up to trace one of my eyebrows. Slowly, gently, he trailed his fingertip across it and then down my cheekbone to my lips. "I like you like this," he said. "It's easier to see you, the real you, without having to look through Lily's face."

"I only feel real when I'm with you." Had I said those words out loud? If I did, he didn't respond to them. I had closed my eyes, relishing the feel of his caress, and when I opened them, he still touched my lips and his eyes had drifted in the same direction.

I sucked in a breath as he dipped his head. His kiss was different than I remembered. This one was hungry and possessive, and I responded to it with a little growl. Asten moaned, wrenched me closer, and tilted my head, his mouth almost devouring mine. "Tia," he murmured huskily, his lips still hovering near my own.

"*Say my name again,*" I said while lifting my chin so he could kiss my throat.

He smiled. "Tia," he said again. "Don't give up on this. Promise me you won't. Give me time."

Tears stung the back of my eyes. "*There is no time. This is all I have, Asten. Right now. Right here.*"

He took hold of my shoulders and pushed me gently away. "No, it's not. Didn't anyone ever tell you that cats have nine lives?" he asked with a teasing glint in his eyes.

"*That's a myth.*"

"Is it?" he provoked, stroking my bare arm. "The souls who are the most resilient are the ones who suffer the most hardships. The things you have endured would break lesser people. This is why Lily needs you. Why you three need each other. When this is done, we'll see about starting that second life of yours. Well, technically, a third life, since I suppose being in Lily's head counts as one."

"*And this is what you seek? A life with me and not Lily?*"

He grinned. "Usually, it's the man that does the pursuing."

"*Ah.*" I put an arm on the stone by his leg and moved closer, pushing against his chest until his back was pressed up against a rock behind us. When both of my hands had trapped him, making his escape impossible, I angled my head until it was even with his. "But I am the huntress."

Asten lifted his head, slightly baring his neck, a sign of submission. I stared hungrily at his throbbing pulse, but the hunger I felt was not for the kill. It was for something else. With the stars reflecting in his eyes, he lifted his hand to cup my neck and pull me closer. "In this instance," he said, "I don't mind being chased."

He drew me down and kissed me with the kind of passion I craved. His arms cradled me tenderly, in such a way that I knew he wanted me as I did him. My worries that he might not feel about me the same way he felt about Lily flowed away like flotsam in a fast-moving river.

When I lifted my head, he brushed my hair fondly away from my face. "I like this body," he said. "I hope you can keep it." I raised an eyebrow and pushed away from him.

"You tease me, Asten, by speaking of something that isn't possible for us. Why do you waste the few moments we have together by dreaming of something unattainable?"

He sat up. "Tia, you can believe in things that are proven or you can believe in dreams. One of them is the key to power. It's how miracles are made. The other one is the easy road. I didn't take you for the kind of girl who sticks to the easy path."

"You . . . you called me a girl."

"And so you are . . . a lady lioness." He ran his thumb up my jaw. "And the prettiest girl I've ever kissed."

A tear did slip from my eye then. Asten wrapped his arms around me and stroked my back, only to pause a moment later. "Ahmose," he said softly.

Ahmose stood quietly below us looking up. The scrub grass shifted slowly around his ankles. I frowned, thinking I'd missed the signs of an intruder again. The insects that had serenaded the night with their sweet, familiar song had suddenly gone quiet. I'd been so enraptured by Asten that I hadn't noticed.

Ahmose's arms were crossed over his chest, and he stared at Asten with an I-want-to-kill-you-very-slowly kind of look. When I unwrapped myself from Asten's arms and leapt from the tall rock, falling through the air easily and landing in a crouch as nimbly and as quietly as a cat, Ahmose turned his gaze on me. My appearance obviously shocked him.

"Tia?" he asked.

"Yes. Are you ready, Ahmose? Is Ashleigh well?"

"Ashleigh's fine."

He took hold of my hand in what I thought was a slightly possessive manner, and I looked from Ahmose up to Asten, who now stood upon the rock. The starlight dusted his hair and made every part of him shine as if he were lit from within. I'd never seen anything so beautiful before. I hoped he was right. That a place for us existed somewhere in the stars. But if it didn't, at least I'd gotten a last tender moment with him.

I lifted a hand in farewell and caught the soft murmur of his voice on the wind. It could have been a trick of my imagination or wishful thinking, but I thought I heard him say, *I love you.* I would have responded, but before I could, I was pulled into a vortex.

Around and around I spun, and when my feet finally met the ground, I knew exactly where I was. Manhattan.

Here Comes the Sun

The street I stood on was as familiar to me as my bedroom. I knew each business, each building, even the names of the horses who pulled the carriages across the street in Central Park. But the vibrant city I called my home stood empty. The towering edifices that stretched high into the sky swayed slightly and stared down on me with dark-eyed windows.

For the first time in this new second life I'd experienced since I'd woken on Nana's farm, I was alone. Ashleigh was gone. Tia was gone. I shivered and rubbed my hands over my arms as a wintry wind swept through the gloomy city. I wondered why my dreamscape in particular would be so horrible, so dim, so lifeless.

Tia's and Ashleigh's dreams had made sense. They were void of people, too, but they were peaceful. This landscape was anything but peaceful. In fact, it was downright creepy, apocalyptic even. As I walked down the block, looking for someone, anyone, I noticed the gray snow that lay pushed up against the sides of the buildings. It clung to the shadows as if fearing the sunlight that would be its demise.

With snow on the ground, I would expect the city to feel happy and hopeful like it did around Thanksgiving, Christmas, and New Year's.

But if Christmas was coming, there was no sign of it. No lights graced shop windows. There were none of the usual gift displays, glitter, or garlands. In fact, the shops that did showcase their wares looked like no one had been inside them in more than a decade. Dust covered everything.

When I tried the door to the opulent hotel where I lived, I found it locked. I rang the buzzer repeatedly but no one answered. I blew out a breath, fogging the window, and stared at my reflection in the murky glass. The visage of the girl reflected there was familiar. It was the girl my mother had molded, a young woman who was precise and perfect in every way she could be. My long brown hair hung smooth and glossy, so tamed it barely shifted in the wind. My posture was straight and sure, much like my father's.

My clothes were designer—fitted slacks, a thin leather belt, a silk button-down shirt—right down to my high-heeled sandals, where perfectly painted toes peeped out. Though I was dressed like me, I wasn't dressed for the weather. My poor toes were turning blue in the cold. Shifting uncomfortably, I stamped my feet partly in frustration, and partly to bring some feeling back into them. I blew a puff of air at my reflection.

The confident, unshakeable New York City socialite on the verge of making a name for herself was in this dream. The person everyone expected me to be. The kind of girl who would belong in this city. A perky, privileged young woman ready to head off to college and begin her life.

But nothing I felt fit this mold. The thin veneer cloaking my outside hid something much different on the inside; I frowned at the girl who stared back at me and decided it was time to move on and leave her behind.

Figuring I'd try the next block, I walked briskly through the uninhabited landscape and came across an abandoned newspaper stand tilted precariously, one wheel over the curb. It swayed in the breeze like a drunken man had heaved up its contents all over the road. Rubbish littered the street and sidewalk.

Newspapers and a torn canopy clung to its sides as if blanketing the display to protect it from more damage, while ads and bits and pieces of refuse caught between it. The road fluttered wildly, trying desperately to escape. I picked up a wind-torn sheet of newspaper and looked at the date. Where the date should have been, the paper was curiously blank. The words on the articles were just jumbles of letters and symbols that didn't make sense.

Was I going crazy? Could I have fabricated everything in my mind? Egypt? Mummies? My powers?

The idea that I was not in a dreamscape after all, but was sitting in a mental institution somewhere going slowly out of my mind, didn't sit well with me. I tossed the newspaper aside and continued on, passing hot dog carts, the sausages spilled onto the sidewalk, the meat as cold and gray as intestines, and an outdoor market full of rotten fruits and vegetables. One vacant store after another.

Each block looked eerily similar to the last one. No people. Not even vacant cars. The big, unoccupied buildings felt haunted. As the wind whistled through them, I imagined each fluttering curtain or shifting blind harbored something evil.

Garbage was piled up in great mounds, the bags ripped open with their contents flung everywhere, as if a wild pack of dogs had gotten into them. And more unnatural than anything else was the absence of the sounds of New York. The only thing moving in my nightmare city was strewn litter. It tumbled and shifted from place to place as if it, too, sought to escape.

Thinking the park might provide me a safe haven, or at least a change of scenery, I headed across the street and entered the trees. At first, I felt safer. The park felt clean. It was supposed to be peaceful, so the fact that there was no one around didn't make my nerves tingle as much as it had in the city.

Snow covered the ground and foliage, but the paths were clear. I took one and headed deeper into the park until the sidewalk abruptly stopped. A large crack ran across it, and snow covered the ground in front of it. Steam came from the depths of the crack. It only took a moment for me to decide I didn't want to investigate further. I spied another path and trudged through the snow, my feet stinging with cold, until I set foot upon it and immediately felt better once again.

When that one ended after a few dozen steps in a crumbled block of cement, too, I stopped and looked around me. Stretched out as far as I could see were paths. They were jagged and broken, and some were . . . shifting. When they were connected, they held their shape for a brief time, and then, if I listened carefully, I'd hear a groaning and a popping noise as they moved and settled into a new place.

I suddenly realized I was back at the street again. Somehow the path had returned me to the place where I'd begun. It was like being stuck in an M. C. Escher painting. If I hadn't been freaked out before, I definitely was now.

Turning around, I started running, leaping one crack after another, navigating the labyrinth walkway and knowing that I needed to keep going no matter what. Someone was playing with me. I felt eyes on me no matter which way I turned. Shadows lurked behind the trees, but when I looked directly at them, I couldn't see anything.

My breath heaved in my lungs. I was frozen and exhausted. Tears filled my eyes, and I sank down, wrapping my arms around my knees, when I came upon the end of another path. How could I be expected to move forward when I didn't even know where I was going? I was like a bridge built without supports. One tiny quake and I'd topple, carrying everything down into the river with me.

Then I heard the laugh of a woman. It wasn't a pleasant sound. There was nothing warm or sweet, cinnamon or sugar, about that voice. It was cold and full of spite, saucy hand-on-a-hip and glaring hatred, wrapped in a smooth dark-chocolate coating. What's worse? I recognized it, and the sound of her voice triggered a tremor in my body that couldn't be stilled.

I didn't know her name and wasn't sure where I'd met her before, but I did know that she represented everything I hated. She was the one who belonged in a place like this. It suited her perfectly. I felt the press of an arctic hand on my shoulder, heard the click of slick-painted nails tapping on a glass and the crunch of a high-heeled shoe as it stabbed the ice-covered sidewalk. When I stood abruptly and turned, I saw nothing. I might have screamed if I thought there was anyone around to hear it.

I attempted to summon my power, but nothing happened.

Then I heard the voice. *Run, Young Lily,* it said. *Run to the center of the park. You can find me there.* The voice was warm and familiar, different from the woman's. I trusted it.

I ran.

When the path broke and shifted beneath me, I stumbled and fell, scraping my palms and knees. The injuries stung, but I got up and kept going. The barren trees around me shifted, blocking my way, and hundreds of dark birds lifted into the sky. I hadn't seen them in the trees before. They circled and then headed toward me, chasing me as if I were an enemy scarecrow and they wanted revenge.

I tore my way through the trees though the branches clutched at my hair and clothing. My shirt came untucked and fluttered behind me as I ran. The broken paths soon disappeared altogether, and the trees were wrenched from the ground. They ripped in half before vanishing from the landscape in dark holes in the sky that opened up to swallow them. I cringed waiting for the tree-devouring monster to seek out a taste of my flesh.

Soon the gray skyscrapers faded away, too, as if they'd been covered by a dense fog. The trees were all gone now. With the snow-covered field broken up only by fallen pinecones and ripped branches that littered the ground like bones, the wind shrieking around them, I knew my dreamscape had turned into my worst nightmare. On and on I ran, the light from a thin moon chasing me from behind a veil of clouds until it finally set.

After the moon disappeared, the skyline grew dark and ominous. Freezing rain mixed with snow fell, stabbing me like sharp needles. I coughed and wiped the icy droplets from my face. I swept back my sodden hair. My legs burned and my breath clouded the air in front of me as I ran and slipped over the terrain. I couldn't feel my feet, nose, ears, or fingers anymore, but I did feel the pounding of my heart in my chest.

I'd never been so terrified. My heart was in a grip so tight that I gasped and clutched at my chest. The woman's laugh returned. A green glow filled my vision, eclipsing the predawn light of the snow packed ground, and the breath was stolen from my body. I struggled, but I could not escape the grip of whatever invisible beast held me in place.

Then a light pierced the storm, and the hold on my heart disappeared. A single ray of dawn sunshine settled on both me and a golden temple that had suddenly appeared in the white landscape. The sunlight lit a path directly to its door. To my knowledge there was no such temple in the middle of Central Park, but nonetheless I was grateful to see something, anything, that would provide shelter from the storm and protection from the demon who sought to consume me. With all the remaining energy I had, I pushed toward it.

At my approach, golden doors burst open, and when I entered, they shut with a resounding boom. The storm outside was immediately silenced. Leaning over, I panted and wiped a shaking hand over my face clearing the rain from my eyes. When I recovered my breath, I moved forward through the wide hall, leaving slushy footprints in my wake. I marveled at the beautiful carved reliefs on the marble walls. They showed pyramids and gods, battles and monsters and warriors.

I came upon another set of doors, this one with a golden carving of the sun. After tracing my fingers over its face, I pushed on the door and stepped into a room with a domed ceiling and columned arches. A dais with a marble statue of three women was the focal point in the room. They stretched their arms upward, fingertips touching, and they were bathed in a pure white light that shone down on them from the ceiling.

Walking around the statue, I studied it from different angles. The faces of the women were lifted, like they looked up at the sky and reached toward something. They seemed familiar to me.

"It is the birth of Wasret," said a voice from behind me.

Spinning around, I saw an alcove hidden by a curtain of opulent fabric. A light stirred behind it.

"Who are you?" I asked, moving closer. I could tell the voice was the same as the one that guided me when I was lost. "Why are you hiding?"

"I'm not hiding from you, Young Lily," the voice said. A gleaming hand pushed aside the curtain and a man that glowed so brightly I could barely look at him stepped through and approached me. "And you already know who I am."

"No, I don't," I said, taking a step back, my leg hitting the statue.

"You do."

The man came closer. Looking at him was like staring into the heart of the sun. My body warmed as he approached, and I leaned toward him without thinking. Steam rose from my dripping-wet clothing. I wondered if I would burn my hand if I touched his vibrant skin. Despite my inner reservations, I knew it was safe. That touching him would be a sort of healing. That his light would dispel all the darkness.

Reaching out, I placed my cold palm on his chest. I was surprised to find not only that feeling quickly returned to my fingers, but that a sense of warmth shot through my entire body. No, it wasn't just warmth. It was peace, happiness, *belonging*.

"You're cold and hurt," the man said, stretching his glowing fingertips to my hair. "Let me help you, Nehabet." He whispered some words, a spell of some kind, and light bathed my body. When it receded back into him, I was wrapped in a sumptuous robe of silk and soft slippers.

The stinging cuts on my palms and knees had vanished. My body and hair were dry, but strands of my hair, now gold, were still wrapped around his fingers.

Slowly, he dropped his hand and stepped away. Though I couldn't see his face, there was something sad in his stature, the slump of his shoulders. I tightened the belt at my waist and relished the feeling of being warm and safe, though I would have preferred to be wearing a bit more clothing.

"You . . . you're Amon. Aren't you?" I asked the man.

"Yes," he replied softly.

"Why can't I see you? Why don't I remember you?" I turned in a circle, looking around me. "Where are we? How can you be here? Why aren't I in a dream, and where's Ahmose?"

He laughed. "You still ask too many questions. At least that hasn't changed." The glowing man held out an arm, indicating his alcove. "Would you like to sit and make yourself comfortable while we wait? Ahmose will come, perhaps too soon for me and not soon enough for you."

"Th-thank you," I said stiffly, not knowing how to feel. I followed him to a plush couch layered with plump pillows in rich jewel tones.

Delicately, I perched on the far edge of the couch. He seemed to consider me for a moment before choosing a seat in the middle. Though I tried to be discreet as I shifted my body away from him, I got the sense that he not only noticed, but was wounded by it. The robe slid up around my smooth thighs, and I hurried to adjust it, embarrassment coloring my cheeks. Since I couldn't make out his features, I couldn't tell if he'd seen it or not. If he had, he didn't say anything.

"I suppose most of your questions can be answered by telling you a secret," he began.

"A secret?"

"Yes. One only the two of us know."

"And what would that be?" I asked, shifting uncomfortably and dragging a pillow into my arms for some added space.

"Do you remember what a heart scarab is?" he asked.

I nodded, wincing slightly as I thought of the brilliant gemstone that had been his. The one I'd removed and tucked into the quiver of arrows. "I do," I answered.

"We are currently inside yours."

"What?" I exclaimed, mouth gaping. "How is that possible? I thought I was supposed to be inside my dreamworld."

"Your dreamworld was seized by the Devourer. She cannot actually do you harm while in it, but she can trap you there, confuse you. Asten had to spin some new dreams to distract her while I helped you to escape here. Now that you are safe, he will find Ahmose in the dream realm and guide him to where we are."

"How was she able to find me?"

"That's my fault, I'm afraid. The Devourer has tasted my heart, and because of that she was able to enter the world of my dreams and access yours."

"I see. So, I know Asten has the power to enter dreams and Ahmose is supposed to find me in mine. That doesn't explain why *you* are here now or how she was able to find me through you."

"I'm here because we are still bound. And . . . and because I am in possession of your heart scarab."

"What does that mean, exactly? Are we, like . . . engaged or something?" I was half afraid to hear the answer, but I needed to know. To understand what was going on.

"You gave me your heart scarab just before you returned to the mortal realm. You wanted me to be able to find you as you were able to find me." He cocked his head. "What is engaged?"

"It means planning to marry."

"Ah." He paused as if considering his next words carefully. "What do you remember of us?"

"Um . . . nothing. Not really. I just know what the others have told me."

He set a gleaming hand down on the couch between us, and there

was a part of me that wanted to cover it with my own. Instead, I clutched
the pillow tighter to my chest.

"Lily," he said, "it means only what you want it to mean."

"But what does it mean to you?"

"I'm not sure we should be talking about that right now," he said
dolefully.

"Then what do you think we should be talking about?"

"We should speak of weightier matters. Such as the reason you cannot remember."

"Do you know why?"

"The heart scarab was only one part of the secret. There's more.
You caught a glimpse of your future when you fought the Devourer. You
channeled the power of Wasret for a time, though you do not remember it. The transformation frightened you." He leaned back and placed
his arm along the rim of the couch. If I leaned an inch toward him, his
glowing fingers would be touching me. I shifted farther away, and this
time I knew he recognized I was avoiding him.

He sighed. "You have a tendency to hide your feelings, Young Lily.
You put on an air of confidence at times when you'd rather run. Instead
of making peace with your path, and the two who reside in your mind,
you broke it and tore yourself away from them." He hesitated and then
added, "And from me."

I sat immobile listening to his words. I knew they were true, but I
wanted to press my hands over my ears and deny them. *How could I be
such a coward? So weak that I'd rather give up and run away than fight? Maybe
there was more to it than what he knew,* I thought hopefully. *Maybe I had
other reasons for running that he wasn't aware of.*

Amon waited a beat and then continued, "Just before you returned
to the mortal realm, you channeled the power of the adder stone to
take your memories from your mind, then you hid them here, in your
heart scarab, and gave it to me for safekeeping. Not even Tia or Ashleigh
knew what you'd done."

"Wait. You're saying my memories are locked in here? Then why can't I access them?"

"This is only a dream version. Though there are bits and pieces stored in the murals and carvings. Your lost thoughts will return when I give you back your scarab in person."

"So," I said sadly, "I'm a deserter. I'd rather run and hide from my problems."

"I'd hardly call Seth and his minions mere problems, Lily."

"Still. I gave up. I ran away to the other side of the cosmos when the gods needed me. When Tia and Ashleigh needed me. When"—I swallowed and looked up at him—"when *you* needed me."

"I will always need you. There is nothing shameful about fearing an enemy. Any hero would be a fool not to take his enemy seriously. Especially one as powerful as Seth. Besides, you underestimate yourself. I'd like to think I know your heart better than anyone. It is not a man you fear, even one as powerful as he is." Amon lowered his head. "It is also not love you fear. This you have given and still give freely."

I bit my lip then, thinking of Ahmose. Was it possible Amon knew what had happened between me and his brother?

"What you fear is losing yourself," he said.

"Losing myself how?" I swallowed, marveling at how his words rang true to the deepest parts within me, those I have tried to ignore.

He looked pointedly at the statue. He'd called it the Birth of Wasret. "Oh," I said. "That."

Before I realized he'd moved, he stretched out his gleaming hand and touched mine. Warmth stole into my skin, filling my frame with sunshine. The contact was brief, but for some reason it brought tears to my eyes.

"I do not . . . ," he began and then started over. "*We* do not blame you for this. There was a time I, too, ran from my destiny. Perhaps if I hadn't, you wouldn't be in the position you're in now. But it's too late to change our past. All we can do is prepare for the future. And, like my brothers, there are pieces of your future that I cannot see, even with the Eye of Horus."

Quietly, he admitted, "A part of me was, in fact, happy when I learned that you couldn't remember. I would rather lose you to a mortal life than lose you so something else, *someone* else can be born. My lo—my *feelings* for you are not contingent upon your saving the cosmos. Whatever you choose, whichever path you decide to walk upon, I will support you and be at your side for as long as you allow it. Do you understand, Young Lily?"

There was no denying that this man knew me and cared about me. He somehow discerned what I feared in the deepest parts of my soul, and he didn't think I was a weakling for it. It was what I needed to hear. I wasn't sure Asten or even Ahmose would have said the same thing. That it was okay for me *not* to be the hero. Even Nana hadn't said that. I was pretty good at recognizing disapproval, even in its most subtle forms. This guy wasn't going to judge me. He saw who I was, who I could be, and who I wanted to be. But, most important, he gave me the freedom to just . . . be.

"I . . . I think I do. But there's still something you haven't told me," I said.

"What is that?"

I took his hand and wrapped it inside both of mine. He looked down at our clasped hands, and I heard his small intake of breath. The cold, hard ruby that was my heart seemed to dissolve into sand. I felt weak inside. Vulnerable. "Why can't I see you? I mean, I can see Asten and Ahmose, even Tia and Ashleigh in their dreams. Why can't I see *you*? It doesn't make sense."

Slowly, he lifted his other hand and touched my jaw. I turned to look at his glowing face, relishing the warmth of his touch. "When two people are bound to one another, the way we are," he began softly, "there is nothing on earth or in heaven that can keep them apart. There is only one reason you can't see me, and though the reason breaks my heart, I understand it and accept it."

"What is it?" I whispered.

"The reason you can't see me, my love, is because you don't want to."

"No." I shook my head, my eyes filling with tears. "You're wrong. That can't be it."

"Shh, Nehabet, be still." He gathered me in his bright arms and held me close. I could feel his heartbeat against my cheek. Amon stroked my back and hair, fingers slipping through the loose strands like water, as soft tears trickled down my face.

"Why? Why would I do this to you?" I asked, an unexpected and intense emotion bubbling up inside me like a hot spring. I was angry. Not with him but with myself. My heart pounded, hot and tight, like a wolf chasing prey. I wanted to rip into whatever was causing the pain, but I knew I'd destroy something precious in the process.

"It doesn't matter," he murmured in my ear.

"It does matter, Amon," I said as wrapped my arms around his neck and closed my eyes. "Don't," I began and kissed his glowing cheek.

"Don't what?" he asked tenderly, pulling slightly away.

It was almost painful to look at him and know it was my fault his features were hidden. But I forced my eyes open and said sincerely, "Don't let me forget."

He paused only a moment before he lowered his head and his lips touched mine. At first his kiss was light and soft, like a feather brushing against my skin. I wanted more.

Amon seemed to sense my mood, and I was quickly enveloped in sunshine. I could feel it wrapping around me—protecting and soothing but, at the same time, teasing and tantalizing.

I could have happily drifted in the dreamy state that was Amon forever, but he pulled away. When he did, I was dismayed to see he was still just a golden being of light seated next to me on a couch. He stroked my face. "You'll see me when the time is right."

Wrapping my hand around his wrist, I looked straight into the place where I knew his eyes should be. "I will figure this out. I promise you."

"I know you will. And I will wait for you. Until the death of the cosmos, I will wait for you. Do not doubt it."

"I won't."

A chanting voice echoed in the room and light pierced the center of the golden doors. With a resounding boom, they crashed open and Amon rose as if preparing to protect me.

"Lily!" a voice cried. It was one I knew well.

I scrambled to my feet. "Ahmose!"

The big man glanced between the two of us. If he thought it was strange that Amon appeared in the form of a gleaming figure, he said nothing. Or, perhaps, Amon looked like he should to everyone else, and it was only me who saw him as I did.

Amon turned to me and stretched out a hand. I took it and he drew me close. His warmth enveloped me one last time, and I wanted to stay and bask in it. "Go with Ahmose now, my love. Be safe." He pressed a kiss on my forehead.

"I'll come find you," I said.

I couldn't tell from his face that he smiled, but I heard it in his tone. "I await your arrival with breathless anticipation," he said, then looked behind me. "*Hakenew,* Ahmose. Take care of her."

"I will, of course, brother," Ahmose answered.

Giving Amon a crooked smile, I then looked past him to Ahmose, who was anything but smiling. "Are you ready, Lily?" he asked, as grave and polite as a starved dog looking for a meal.

"Yes. Let's go."

I walked over to Ahmose, and with a backward glance at Amon, I stretched out my hand. Ahmose took it, and a vortex opened up above us. It lifted us into the air. The golden temple disappeared, along with the golden boy I'd left behind.

11

O Captain! My Captain!

We spun at a dizzying speed through golden light, but we quickly left that light behind, and I was sad to lose it. Ahmose clutched me tightly, and I pressed my face into his chest, closing my eyes. When we finally slowed, he nudged my chin up. We hovered over a dark beach. A small campfire was crackling quietly, and I spied the unicorns keeping watch over two bodies sleeping beside it.

Ahmose murmured a spell, and one of the bodies lifted into the air. It was mine. A chill crept over me as I saw myself in this out-of-body-experience way. My head drooped, and my hair hung around my face in limp wet ropes. Almost without intending to, my dream self drifted closer and closer to my body until my hand touched a shoulder, and then there was just . . . me.

I opened my eyes and dropped lightly to the ground, my bare feet sinking into the black, wet sand. I was surprised to see I still wore the thin robe Amon had created for me and not the clothes my real body had been dressed in when I fell from Nebu's back. Ahmose quickly returned to his own body as well and walked up behind me.

Shivering, I rubbed my arms and stepped away from him to take in our location. The nighttime view was beautiful. A thin crescent moon brushed the surface of the ocean with silver sparkles. The waves were soft and quiet and broke upon the rocks and driftwood trees with a shushing sound that made me feel sleepy. I was so tired. Exhausted in body and mind.

Ahmose moved in front of me, filling my view. He took hold of my shoulders, and asked, "Are you all right?" His face was tight with an emotion that sharpened his features. The closeness we'd shared together before, the emotion that had made me feel as happy and free as a forest sprite dancing beneath a harvest moon, was gone. I knew it and Ahmose did, too.

The sun had been eclipsed by the moon for a while. Now that I knew the sun was there, I could no longer ignore it or the warmth it provided. Without Ashleigh and Tia in my mind, my emotions were my own. I had a new and different perspective. And from what I could see, it seemed like Ahmose did as well.

Even though he held me gently, he was distant. Hard. Ahmose had become an imposing cliff too sheer to even think about scaling. The warmth of his gaze had leached away.

"I'll be fine," I managed to say.

His gray eyes spoke volumes, but I couldn't read the text. The air was thick with tension, and I brought my hands together at my waist and wrung them. I stopped myself and began to play with the ties of my robe instead, unable to maintain eye contact. The space between us was full of blades, and each second we went without talking cut me deeply. When he finally did talk, it was to call out to Ashleigh and Tia. "It's time, ladies," he said, turning away from me and looking out at the space around us. "Your host has returned."

My breath caught. Host? Was that all I was to him? Just a body that housed the girl he really loved? How could he be so cruel? It wasn't like him. At least, I didn't think it was. But how well did I know him, really?

He was likely angry. Especially because he'd seen Tia with Asten and me with Amon. Any guy would be upset about that. But didn't I have a right to be upset, too? He knew it had hurt me to see him with

Ashleigh. He'd even admitted as much when he was with her in her dream. I thought there had been something special between *us*. The us that was Ahmose and Lily. Something new and precious. I'd relied on him. Needed him. I'd thought I was beginning to . . . beginning to love him.

For one moment I was, if not blissfully, then at least peacefully, alone. The next, my two inner voices were back. My mind suddenly felt too crowded, my thoughts confused. Somehow, I managed to stretch myself to accommodate the two girls, and I felt better afterward for having done so. I was surprised to find I'd missed them.

Ach, Lily, Ashleigh said, a tinge of sorrow in her tone. *I'm sorry.*

Me too, I replied.

I'm sure the daft boy didn' mean it the way it sounded, she said.

Tia didn't add anything, but a soothing purr soon resonated in the space where she curled up comfortably.

It was like having two best friends come over to console you after a heartbreaking experience. While I grieved in my mind and in my heart, the two of them mourned along with me. Tears slipped down my eyes as I thought of what I'd lost. What *we'd* lost—for all of us had lost something.

We stepped away from Ahmose, leaving him and his searching gray eyes behind, and walked along the beach. Nebu trailed along after us but didn't speak. Everyone seemed to sense we needed time to readjust. To relearn which pieces of our experiences belonged to us as individuals and which we shared.

Wet sand stuck to my feet. Each step left a footprint at least an inch deep. The water that licked my toes was warm and welcoming. I felt like I was a porous rock and each sweep of the water filled me. When it receded, I was again empty, bleached, and desiccated. Holes of truth had ripped me open from the inside out, and I wasn't sure I could fix them.

When we were far enough away, we fused together and used our power to make new clothing. Sand rose and then swirled around me, buffeting my skin almost as painfully as Ahmose's words had pummeled my heart. I was surprised when I looked down afterward and found I wore a comfortable, warm flannel shirt over a soft tee with a pair of jeans tucked into sturdy yet fashionable boots.

"Thanks, girls," I murmured and turned around to head back to Ahmose's small campfire. I patted Nebu's back and walked alongside him as we returned. By the time I got there I was wearied enough in spirit that it didn't seem any amount of talking would fix what was wrong. I sank down onto a cloak and cradled my head on my arm. "I'd like to sleep for a while, Ahmose. You should, too."

He sat down across the fire from me and replied, "You go ahead. I've been sleeping a lot lately."

When I closed my eyes, I was out quickly, though I dreamed I heard Ashleigh's voice. She was lecturing someone sharply. Her wrath was something I realized I didn't want to encounter personally, and I felt sorry for whoever it was that had upset her. Eventually, even her raised shouts weren't enough to drive off my sleep, and the world went dark.

When I woke, it was to the sound of waves and seabirds. My body was stiff, my joints sore. I sat up with a groan and found a stick to stir the cold embers of the fire, but there was no reviving it. Ahmose was gone, as was Nebu, but Zahra was close by.

"Where are the others?" I asked.

They are obtaining breakfast, the unicorn replied.

Ahmose soon returned and set several fish on a rock, then knelt and rekindled the fire. He glanced up at me briefly but quickly looked away, his mouth pursed as if he wanted to talk but couldn't muster the words. I watched him openly as he gutted the fish and went about cooking them. A nearby seabird was more than happy to scoop up the innards and cawed with excitement as it watched Ahmose with beady black eyes.

When the meal was ready, he gave me a share and then sat down and picked at his but didn't eat. I chewed a few bites, but the food stuck in the back of my throat as if my tongue had swollen too much to gulp it down. Finally, I set it aside and nudged his foot with my boot. "Just say it, Ahmose. I can tell you want to."

Prickly nerves shot over my skin when he looked at me. My eyes felt hot and bruised. He turned back to his fish. "I'm not sure what you want me to say, Lily."

"Tell me that you're disappointed with me. That it was all a lie. That you never loved me at all. That our paths don't merge together like you thought. Any of those. All of those. Just . . . tell me." I pulled up my knees and wrapped my arms around my legs. Even though he hadn't said anything yet, I already felt like he'd punched me in the gut.

I thought of the way Ahmose had kissed Ashleigh. The two of them surrounded by clover, the buzzing of lazy bees, and the heavily scented apple-blossom breeze. The way his eyes crinkled and his cheeks rounded into plump little moons when he looked at her. The way Ashleigh loved his lips on her skin and his warm breath tickling her bare throat.

Ahmose frowned. "I can't tell you any of those things, Lily."

"Why not?" I asked, anger tingeing my words around the edges.

"Because none of those things are true. My feelings aren't a lie. I do love you. Our paths do cross. I've seen it." When I gave him a doubt-filled look, he added, "Why don't you ask me what you really want to know?"

What was he talking about? Did he want me to come right out and accuse him of loving Ashleigh more than me? Did it matter? It did to Ashleigh. She was quiet, but I could sense her sorrow, her acceptance, and her concern for my feelings. At the same time, the love she felt for Ahmose was a palpable thing that colored my perception whether I wanted it to or not. Those sentiments swelled around me, and I responded to them. I wanted to be held in his arms, have him comfort me and stroke my hair. But I was also my own person. His affection for Ashleigh was not the thing that plagued my mind the most.

"Why didn't you tell me about him?" I asked finally with a soft voice.

Ahmose nodded stiffly, indicating it was the question he'd been waiting for, but his lips were drawn tight at the edges as if he didn't want to answer.

I continued, pressing, "You knew I'd lost my memory of him. You took advantage."

"I did," he said simply. "That doesn't mean what I've seen and what I feel are wrong."

"Then why does it feel wrong to me?" I murmured. "In fact, everything about this situation feels wrong."

"Don't say that."

"Why not? Does it hurt you? Well, good. I'm glad it hurts you, because you hurt me. I was a witness to Ashleigh's dream, and your attachment to her is obvious."

"That doesn't mean I feel nothing for you."

I rose and walked up to the edge of the shore. "It's not the same. Not even close," I said, my voice carrying over the sound of the ocean.

Ahmose came up behind me and wrapped his hands around my arms. His mouth tickled my ear, and I found I still wanted him to love me, to kiss me and hold me like he had before.

"I respect you," he murmured. "I admire you. Your face, your form is beautiful to me. I want to keep you close and protect you from harm and care for you the rest of my days. We could be happy together, Lily. Comfortable and content. Isn't that enough?"

I turned around, and as I did, he wrapped his hands around my waist, attempting to pull me into his arms, but I pressed my palms against his chest, keeping us apart. "A part of me wishes it were," I said sadly. "Perhaps it doesn't matter." I gave him a wan smile. The urge to step closer, to lose myself in his kiss, was strong. Ashleigh wasn't the only one who wanted it, but something had changed for me, for all of us, in the dreamworld.

We didn't know what the future would bring, but even if there was a happy ending ahead for one of us, it would mean a disappointing ending for the other two. None of us wanted to dwell on that. "I think it would be better if we set aside our feelings for the time being and focus on the task at hand," I said.

"If that is what you wish," Ahmose said formally. He slowly moved away from us, his back rigid.

Ya've hurt 'im, Ashleigh said. *Did ya hav' ta be so fierce about it? He's a sensitive type.*

He hurt me first, I responded. *Besides, what difference can it make now? We have a job to do, and we've had enough moony drama over men for the time being. We should be concentrating on Seth.*

I agree, Tia said. *There's no sense in wishing for things. They will either happen or they won't. Odds are, Wasret will choose our mate anyway and we will have no say in the matter.*

Wasret. Wonderful. I'd almost forgotten. I quickly shared with them the things I'd seen in my dream with Amon, and they were both shocked by the infiltration of the Devourer. When I mentioned it to Ahmose, he nodded and said Asten had told him about it. The fact that Wasret had regained enough power to take over in such a way didn't bode well for us.

"There's more bad news, I'm afraid," Ahmose said. "I've scouted our path, and the quickest road to my brothers lies along the Cosmic River. The unicorns don't do well there. The flight is too long. They tire, and there's no safe place for them to rest along the way."

"Then what can we do? How will we get to your brothers?" I asked.

Tia suggested, *Why not summon Cherty?*

"Cherty? Who's Cherty?" I asked aloud.

Ahmose looked up, a spark of interest in his eyes.

"Do you think he would take us?" he asked, and rubbed his chin. "He did seem to like you."

Of course he liked us, Tia said. *We can summon him with the coin he gave us.*

"What coin?"

The one Hassan hid in the quiver. It lies beside Amon's heart scarab.

My heart skipped a beat at her words. Without explaining my actions to Ahmose, I headed over to the campfire and found my leather harness, spear-knives still sheathed, and the quiver of arrows with the bow. Reaching into the depths of the bag, I wrapped my hand around the heart scarab and pulled it out.

I stared down at the object for a long moment. My fingers tightened around it, and I looked up to find Ahmose studying me. Keeping it clenched securely in my palm, I dug around until I found a coin with a bird stamped on it. I handed it to Ahmose. When he wasn't looking, I slipped Amon's heart scarab into the pocket of my jeans.

"The benu bird," he said reverently as he turned the coin over in his palm and traced his fingers over the other side. He showed me the image of a boat and a man hunched over a pole. "I have never seen one of these coins in my lifetime, though I've heard stories of them. It's dual-sided. It means you have the protection of the benu bird as well as the ferryman. Do you know how rare this is?"

I shrugged. Tia volunteered, *We've seen the bird in Heliopolis. This coin looks similar to the coin the bird paid for our first passage. It might, in fact, be the very same one.*

When I related her message to Ahmose, he gaped at us openly. "You actually *saw* the bird? He paid your way?"

"Yes. At least Tia says we did."

Ahmose stared at us, his eyes neatly cutting through me as if searching for answers I couldn't give him. It seemed he was about to say more, but I interrupted. "Will it work? Can we call this Cherty with it?"

"Oh yes," he replied. "I should think it will work very well." He placed the coin in my hand and beckoned. "Come with me."

I followed him to the edge of the water, and he told me what to do. Reaching back my arm, I cried out in a loud voice, "Ferryman! With this coin I claim passage!" I thrust my arm forward, tossing the coin as far out into the water as I could. In the morning sun, I saw the flash of gold as it spun in the air, and when it dropped into the water a beam of light shot into the sky and disappeared overhead.

"What happens now?" I asked.

"He'll come for us if he's able."

"Why wouldn't he be able?"

"Cherty will be busy ferrying the dead, especially in a time of war such as we are in currently."

"But didn't Ma'at say the afterlife had been compromised? Where is he taking the dead, then?"

"I'm not sure. It's possible he's still taking them there. Dropping them off and leaving them to fend for themselves until order has returned. This happens occasionally when we are in the mortal realm. The dead wait upon our arrival. There are usually large groups to lead to judgment after our two weeks on Earth. Some of them wander off on their own but end up getting devoured by various beasts that prevent the dead from leaving. There isn't a safe way to escape the afterlife, not really. Unless you're a god. They can come and go as they wish."

"Oh . . . and, uh, are you given leave to come and go like the gods?"

Ahmose glanced down at me. "No," he answered. "We must remain in the afterlife until we are called forth to our bodies to fulfill our purpose. Though now that Seth is freed, there is no longer a reason to grant us a mortal sojourn."

"So you're saying, when all this is said and done, assuming we survive, that you, Asten, and Amon will . . . what? You'll end up in the afterlife, just staying . . . dead?" I tried to swallow the lump that suddenly formed in the back of my throat, but it didn't help.

"That is the likely outcome."

Did you two know this? I accused Ashleigh and Tia.

We did, Tia replied.

Then . . . then what's the point of Ashleigh loving Ahmose or of you loving Asten? What difference does it make when there's no way to be together? Not even for one of us? I asked them.

Ashleigh responded, *Ah, darlin', that's why these rare stolen moments are so precious.*

I folded my arms. "Well, I don't accept it," I said out loud.

"Don't accept what?" Ahmose asked.

"There has to be some kind of boon." I waved my arms, gesturing wildly. "Some kind of reward for saving the cosmos. Right? Isn't that how things are supposed to work? You said you've seen us together. When? Where? In New York? In the afterlife? Where did you see us get our happy ending? Were we alive or dead?"

"I told you the ending was hidden from me. I am not given the where or the when. All I know are the emotions I felt. All I've seen are moments of happiness. Of contentment. Of love. These are the glimpses I've been given."

"And do your glimpses include me or Ashleigh or Wasret? Which one of us do you get to be with?"

"I've seen all three of you."

"Right. Well, that's convenient, isn't it?"

"You are angry."

"Of course I am. It's bad enough that I've got to sacrifice my identity to become this Wasret person so I can save the cosmos. I was just discovering who Lilliana Young was going to be. Narrowing down a major seems pretty silly now, doesn't it? And here I was worrying about which guy I might be in love with when actually it doesn't matter one little bit. You're all dead. There's no having a life with any of you. So you know what?" I jabbed him in the chest with my finger. "Why don't you just keep these visions of yours to yourself? And while you're at it, why don't you leave Ashleigh alone, too? None of us need to put our hopes on a guy, on a future that doesn't exist."

My chin quavered as I stared up at him with icy eyes. I wanted him to tell me I was wrong. That everything would work out and that I'd get a happy ending. That at least one of us would survive and have a good life. Instead, my trembling body heated with an inner anguish. He touched my face lightly and answered, "If that is what you want, Lily, then I will do as you ask."

Before the tears that built in my eyes had a chance to spill over, I whipped around and stomped back to the campfire, doggedly tugging on my leather harness and the bow and quiver. *I don't want to hear it*, I warned Ashleigh and Tia before they even said anything.

Zahra nudged me with her head, and I ran my fingers through her mane, working through the tangles and smoothing the strands over her shiny coat. My thoughts felt just as knotted as her hair. I heard Ahmose cry out, "He approaches!" and turned to look over my shoulder, one hand still on the unicorn.

Shading my eyes, I looked out over the water. "I don't see anything!" I shouted back.

"He's not out there," Ahmose said, indicating the ocean as I strode toward him. "He's up there!" he finished, pointing at the sky.

A large, dark object appeared within a layer of clouds. I could only make out bits and pieces until it sank lower. I'm not sure what I expected, but it wasn't a flying boat. It dropped down, circling overhead until it finally fell with a splash into the ocean. It was too far out to wade to. We'd have to swim out.

Ahmose turned to the unicorns. "Thank you. You've risked much in helping us."

Zahra nudged his arm, and I hugged her around her silky neck. "Take care of yourself," I whispered in her twitching ear. She whinnied in response and then spun and quickly galloped down the beach. When her body hit a wave, she dissolved into sand and disappeared.

When I turned to Nebu, he said, *Climb on my back, young sphinx. I'll take you to the ship.*

"What about Ahmose?"

He can get there on his own.

Ahmose gave me a boost, and when I was settled, Nebu unfolded his great wings and ran on the sand, wings pounding until they caught the wind. I looked down at Ahmose and gasped as he turned into a beautiful silver bird, the largest winged creature I'd ever seen, apart from Nebu. *Did we know he could do that?* I asked as I watched him fly.

You once told me they had this power, Tia said, *but they had no access to it in the netherworld.*

He . . . he's beautiful, I said. And he was. Ahmose in his bird form was a sight to behold. The sun glistened off his shining silver wings. He drew close to us and flew alongside us, his long legs extended out behind and his neck stretched out ahead. Ahmose tilted his head, peering up at me with an expression I didn't understand. When he approached the boat, he flapped several times to slow down and then switched back to human form, dropping lightly onto the deck.

Nebu circled the ship, not slowing as I'd expected. *I wish to say good-bye,* he said.

Thank you, I replied. *Thank you for everything.*

I have not done much.

Still, we wouldn't have gotten this far without you. You are very brave.

No, I am not. Not when it comes to risking my own.

I felt Ahmose's eyes on me, but Nebu still circled the boat. *What is it?* I asked the unicorn.

If I could, I wish to share a piece of advice and a warning before I go.

You may, I said.

Then my warning is for Ashleigh. Be careful, young fairy. Do not let new love divert you from what's best for all of you. Lily might have fought off the sting of the sky-fish if you had not wearied her body each evening. She fell and trapped all of you in the dreamworld because you were selfishly using her to further your own desires.

Ashleigh, stung at his reprimand, retreated to a corner of my mind and clouded her thoughts from our view. *We'll talk about this later,* I told her gently. *And your advice?* I asked Nebu.

Do not take away their hope. You are hurt and are frightened for the future. I understand this, but remember that without you they all have nothing. Keep that in mind.

How can I have hope when I cannot convince even a unicorn as powerful as yourself to join our cause? I asked.

Perhaps, when you ask me again, I will be ready to stand at your side and remain there for the duration.

I'll test you on that, I warned.

I expect you will. Good luck, young sphinx. And farewell. For now.

"Farewell," I said as he dropped down toward the boat. I lifted my leg and gauged the distance. When I was ready, I slipped from the unicorn's back and landed light as a cat on the deck. Nebu neighed loudly, tucked his wings, and plummeted into the ocean. I darted to the side of the ship, but the only sign of the unicorn was a sparkling layer of sand that slowly sank beneath the waves.

Turning, I found Ahmose arguing vehemently with the captain, the one I assumed was the ferryman. Angry red splotches had crept up the man's neck. His face was at once sea-worn and ageless, his eyes as unfathomable as the depths below. "I'm tellin' ya!" the man yelled. "Ya can't travel that way, Pathfinder. It's no' safe. Apep'll gobble 'er up before ya can blink!"

"And I'm telling you, we *will* go that way. If Apep finds us, so be it. We'll fight him off together."

"Ya only say that because ya haven't seen the beastie. If ya had, ya'd know there's no fightin' such as 'im. There's only avoidin'. Anythin' else jus' shows ya don't belong on the river in the firs' place."

Ahmose just folded his arms and stared the man down. The captain threw his hands up in the air with a frustrated grunt and turned away as if hoping Ahmose would disappear when he was no longer in sight.

The man fixed his gaze upon me, bushy brows lifted, and a big smile gracing his face.

"Hello there, girlie. Glad ta see yer still in one piece. So ta speak."

Through the Wormhole

"Hello," I replied hesitantly. "It's nice to meet you."

The man's bushy eyebrows met at the little crease that formed between his eyes. "Meet me? What're ya talkin' 'bout, girlie? I can' believe ya forgot 'bout me already."

"Yes. Well, apparently, I've purposely removed all my memories from before. I locked them away for reasons I can't recall."

The man grunted and squinted at me, one eye nearly shut and the other one wide-open as he cocked his head. "Didja, now?" He rubbed the scruff along his jaw making a sandpapery scraping noise. "Well, can't say's I blame ya. Looks ta me like ya ignored my advice and kept on with the soulless," he said, jabbing his thumb over his shoulder to indicate Ahmose. "Please tell me ya didn' do somethin' reckless an' give over the last boyfriend only ta lash yerself ta another o' the same ilk. One o' them is bad enough."

I grimaced. His assumption was a little too close to the truth. "The soulless?" I asked, wishing he'd change the subject.

"Yah. The guardians." He snorted and spat over the side of the ship. While Tia clarified that he meant Asten, Ahmose, and Amon, the man continued, "Seems ta me they ain't been doin' too good a job o' guardin' lately. They've been missin' for a while, an' the dead are so thick now, they got no recourse but ta hold on ta the sides o' the ship."

I nodded. "The afterlife has been compromised. Ma'at hid the . . . the guardians to protect them from Seth."

"I suppose that would explain it. Each time I drop off a new boatful, the dock's so crowded with souls beggin' ta be let back on, my ship's almost capsized a few times. It's gotten so bad that now I just throw the dead overboard when we get close enough."

A little flare of alarm rose in me, and I glanced nervously from side to side. "I don't see anyone."

"Ya will once we get airborne an' pass through the portal. The souls o' the dead can't be seen in the light o' day, 'less they've got a special attachment ta some mortal."

"Oh." I rubbed my arms and glanced at Ahmose, who was doing some kind of spell to double-check our path.

"Are ya certain ya want ta follow that one?" he asked. "This path o' his takes us inta dangerous waters. We ain't too likely ta come out o' the other end with our skins intact."

I blew out a breath in a half laugh. "That's nothing new."

The man leaned closer, a serious expression on his face. He smelled of spice, wax candles, and the sea. "If ya want me ta throw 'im overboard, jes' give me a sign," he said, thumbing his nose. "Won't kill 'im. Least, I don' think so. Jes' give the word."

He lowered a thick eyelid in a secretive wink, and I almost giggled in response, but Ashleigh surged to the surface, bristling with indignation. *"Ya barnacled ol' bear! Ya'll do no such thing ta my Ahmose!"*

The man blinked, his eyes round with surprise. Mottled red shot up his neck, and he pointed a broad finger in my face. "And who gave ya leave ta mouth off in Lily's stead?" he argued back. "I see ya in there. Come out right now and go back ta where ya belong, on the side o' the ship, ya wicked fairy. Ya got no call hauntin' this lovely young woman."

"I'm not wicked," Ashleigh declared with my voice. *"And I'm not hauntin' her either. I'm just as much a part of Lily as Tia is."*

The man folded his thick arms across his chest. "Are ya, now?"

"Yes, and what's more—"

"Cease this!" Ahmose said. We hadn't even noticed his approach. He stepped between me and the burly captain. "I'll thank you to treat Ashleigh with respect, Ferryman. I think you've wasted enough time getting reacquainted, so, kindly do your job and please get us under way." Ahmose's expression was as hot and dangerous as a hellhound's. "Immediately," he added.

Ashleigh retreated, a bit smug after Ahmose's gesture. I slowly rose to the surface, taking control over my own body again. I glared at Ahmose, not happy with his show of force. The captain hadn't meant anything. At least I didn't think so. Ahmose caught my look and turned away, heading back toward the bow of the ship, saying nothing.

To see the big captain step back from Ahmose and lower his head bothered me for a few reasons. The first was that, to my surprise, I liked the boatman. Second, Ahmose seemed too overprotective of Ashleigh, which irritated me, and his rude approach was uncalled-for. Also, I wanted to hear more about the haunting idea the captain mentioned.

I bit my thumbnail. Could it be possible that I *was* being haunted by two spirits? Was I possessed? I knew what everyone else believed, that we were destined to become Wasret or whatever, but I didn't want to rule out any possibilities. Especially since the captain seemed to indicate that there was a way Ashleigh's soul could be removed from my living person.

It felt like a betrayal just to think about evicting my tagalongs. I really did care about them. At the same time, it was my body, wasn't it? Didn't I deserve to have a life? If there was a possibility that I could be myself again, whole and complete and normal, was it wrong to harbor that desire? To try to find a way to make it happen?

The boatman mumbled his disgruntlement under his breath as he yanked on various ropes and pulled up the anchor, which he'd apparently attached to the top of a mountain. Ahmose stayed at the front of the boat, watching our progress for a while, and then turned to stare out at the ocean. I could tell he wanted me to head forward and stand beside him, but I decided to stay by the captain's side instead. When he asked me to help, I was happy to. It felt normal to be asked to work alongside him. He reminded me of my nana in that way.

"Offer still stands," the man said in a stage whisper as he helped me coil a rope. "It would be ma pleasure ta help one o' the wanderin' ta wander o'er the side."

I did laugh this time, and though Ashleigh wanted to get up in his face again, I forcibly held her back. She didn't like that and sulked in the back of my mind. "I think we'll let him stay. For now," I replied to him in a breathy whisper of my own, raising my eyebrows meaningfully and grinning to show I was teasing. "Will you tell me your name again?" I asked a bit louder. "Tia said it a few times, but I can't remember it. I know you're Charon the ferryman in mythology, but you don't look much like the myth."

"Yeah. Lots o' people say that. Name's Cherty. 'Ferryman' is all the wanderin' three ever called me. Don't show me much respect, those three don't."

"That's a shame. They're really not as bad as they seem, Cherty. Maybe they just don't know you well enough."

"Our paths cross enough, they should at leas' treat me cordial. Jes' 'cause they hate their job don' mean they need ta take it out on me. Not my fault they got stuck with it. Not like I got ta choose my job either."

I was going to ask him more about their jobs, but Cherty nodded toward a crate, indicating I should make myself comfortable and hold on. Tia told me to wrap my arms through the rope on the side and that she'd answer my questions as best she could later. I did as she asked, and a stiff wind filled the sails until they billowed out like great balloons.

The previously calm ocean heaved below. Giant waves rushed toward the beach, the tops of them brushing against the hull of the ship though we were far above the land. When a large one sprayed foam over the side, Cherty yelled, "Hold on!" The boat tilted at a deep angle, riding down the backside of a wave at roller-coaster speed, and then climbed the next and the next, each one increasing quickly in size until I feared we'd tip over.

I called out a warning to Ahmose, thinking he would fall, but he stared straight ahead, ignoring me, feet rooted in place as if they were locked into steel bands. The only sign he struggled to keep his balance was when he wrapped a hand over the railing. Then, just as we crested a wave big enough to sink a cargo ship, we were airborne again, rushing upward at breakneck speed. When the sea was far, far below us, the ship balanced out and steadied to a comfortable rocking rhythm.

Soon thin wisps of clouds passed around us. Before I could unwrap my arm from the rope, we were deep inside a cloud bank. I held out my hand in front of me and was unable to see it. Dew settled on my arms and face, and the air I breathed was wet and cold.

We went higher and broke through the tops of the clouds. An ocean of them stretched out beneath us. The sun burnished their puffy tops, making them resemble a landscape of fluffy pink cotton candy. They were so thick and solid-looking that I wanted to pull one close and take a nap. We kept going and the air grew colder. My cheeks and ears became numb, and I shivered.

"Almost there," Cherty said. "Hang on, now."

The blue shifted subtly at first, and then darkness overtook the sky. The air was too thin. I sucked in deep breaths, a hollow ache stabbing my lungs, but Cherty put his hand on my shoulder, and my breathing eased.

"Ya'll be fine once we enter the portal," he promised.

He pointed ahead to something dark and jagged that yawned like an open mouth eager to swallow us.

"What is that?" I asked.

"A tear in the fabric o' the universe. Well, more o' a rift than a tear." Cherty grunted, rubbing his jaw. "'Tis like a canal tha' leads from this partic'lar realm ta the Cosmic River." Cherty moved the rudder, and the sails shifted. The boat groaned and creaked as we altered course. "Steady, now," he said, speaking to the ship and patting the rail. "Steady."

The bow hit the opening, and the whole ship shuddered. I lost my footing and stumbled against the side. Immediately, my lungs seized. I coughed and grabbed at my throat, trying vainly to open my airway. Ahead of us, Ahmose and the entire front of the ship disappeared. *Ahmose!* I mouthed, terrified that he'd fallen over. Cherty grabbed on to my arm, and blessed air surged into my body again.

"He's fine, girlie. Ya'll see 'im in a moment."

I only had time to blink once before the blackness enveloped us as well, and not only could I not see Ahmose or even Cherty, but I couldn't hear them either. The only thing my senses told me was that I was still on the boat. Even when I tried to activate my lioness night vision, I was completely blind. I gripped the railing and screamed when the boat suddenly dove. We dropped down quickly, angling forward like we were rolling down a mountain, then we listed to one side and the other. If I hadn't been holding on, I would have fallen overboard.

Finally, the boat steadied, and Cherty let go of my arm as I took in my surroundings. My night vision finally kicked in, and it was powerful. Black starlit eddies swirled around the sides of the ship like an inky river, and above us the stars twinkled like they had in my long-ago dream. I could hear the rustle of their voices whispering like shushing reeds along a river. It was comforting and peaceful.

"It's beautiful!" I said.

"This is the best part o' the river," Cherty said. "'Tis why Apep makes 'is home in this part o' the cosmos."

"And Apep is . . . ?"

Cherty opened his mouth to answer, but before he could speak I let out a bloodcurdling scream. All around us, wispy ghosts began to appear. Some of them stood quietly looking over the railing. Others curled up on the deck in little balls, sobbing bitterly. A little girl sucked her fingers as she stared at me with big eyes. A man that was part horse and part human shifted uncomfortably as other ghosts pressed close to his sides. He swished his ghostly tail in irritation.

At my scream, they all looked at me. More and more ghosts

materialized. So many that I felt trapped. Surrounded by the dead. Their dark mouths split in a silent scream that echoed mine as those nearby pressed hands to their cheeks and copied my movements. I spun in circles, my claws emerging as I slashed at the air to keep them away. My daggered fingertips just tore right through their forms as if they were composed of nothing but air.

When I figured out that my sphinx claws didn't work, I scrambled backward until I hit the railing of the ship and clutched the side desperately, hoping to escape. They drew closer and closer, peering at me curiously. Perhaps it was my mortal body that threw them for a loop, but they reached out and pawed at me. I whimpered and closed my eyes, trying to ignore the chill that crept through my veins every time a ghostly hand passed through my body.

I didn't open my eyes until I heard Cherty shouting, "Back away. Back off, ya wretched ghosties!" The shining beings on the deck moved off a bit, their bodies blending into one another.

The ferryman had not been kidding when he'd said the ghosts were so thick there was no room for them on the ship. They were packed together in all shapes and sizes so tightly that there wasn't enough space to slip a sheet of paper between them. Most of them stood with arms and torsos overlapping, and I could tell they didn't like it. It looked painful. Like the fusing, though possible, wasn't comfortable. I wouldn't like it either. I glanced over the side again and saw that not just dozens of ghosts hung over the rails, but hundreds.

Those that couldn't grip the wooden beam had attached themselves somehow onto the other ghosts, forming a ghoulish chain that disappeared down into the black water. Bobbing heads floated in our wake like downed skiers, but instead of dripping rope, they clung to the sallow limbs of their fellows. It was ghastly and horrific. I couldn't imagine a worse means of transportation. Cherty's boat was a hellish bride traipsing down a dark aisle trailing a long veil of the dead behind her.

When Cherty approached, casting aside ghost after ghost, even tossing some overboard, I took hold of his arm, needing something solid to focus on. "Won't they . . ." I gulped. "Drown out there?"

He shook his head. "They're already dead. Most likely they'll get eaten. Then they'll be *dead,* dead."

"Eaten?" This was getting worse. "What kind of a monster eats ghosts?"

"The Devourer, for one." Ahmose came close, and I was grateful for his presence. He placed his hand possessively on my arm and lectured Cherty. "You should have warned us you carried so many."

"An' whose fault is that? Ya summoned me in a busy time. Besides, if you an' yer brethren were doin' their jobs, I wouldn' have so many clingers-on right now!" the boatman shouted, his face turning purple.

I summoned my courage, which took everything I had, and stepped away from Ahmose, who frowned. "It's . . . it's all right," I said, patting Cherty's arm with a grimace of a smile. "I'll get used to them." There was no indication as far as I could tell that I would, but I didn't want to be thought of as a coward. Tia said we'd seen something similar in the netherworld, and we'd made it through somehow before. I stiffened my spine despite the itchy, bugs-crawling-on-my-back feeling and tried to make the best of it.

Cherty ducked his head down. "'Tis better this way, girlie. Apep'll be distracted, with this many to fill 'is belly. We might even have a chance."

"Are you sure this is the right path?" I asked Ahmose, hoping he'd say no and we could go somewhere else. Preferably somewhere we could disembark our passengers.

"It is. As far as I can tell, the oubliette where Ma'at hid the three of us is located on the Isle of the Lost. It is found far beyond the outermost edge of the Waters of Chaos, past the boundaries of the gods. Even they do not dare venture out so far."

"If it's so dangerous, then why did Ma'at trap them there?" I asked, my curiosity piqued despite our audience.

"She's not the spell caster Isis is. It's likely Ma'at used a particular spell that sent them to a place where Seth could not go," he answered. "Spells are tricky in their wording. The fact that she sent us somewhere so remote and inaccessible is a sign of how desperate she was."

"If it's dangerous for the gods, then how are we expected to survive?" I asked.

"It'll be fine, love. I'll keep an eye on the path."

I furrowed my brow. "Don't call me love. You don't get to do that anymore."

Cherty snickered as he manned the rudder but didn't look our way.

Ahmose stepped closer. "Not *all* of you feel that way," he murmured quietly.

"No? Well, the others aren't in charge right now. I'm afraid you'll have to deal with me."

"I don't mind dealing with you, Lily," Ahmose said softly. He lifted his hand to brush his knuckles down my jaw. Little tingles shot down my arms despite my resolve to be angry with him. He seemed to sense my weakening and ducked down to kiss me lightly on the temple. "I've got to keep my eye on the path ahead so Cherty can steer us in the right direction. Will you join me at the bow? I'll try to keep the ghosts away."

I wanted to. I mean, I really wanted to. The yearning Ashleigh felt to be close to him came at me in waves of desire so poignant that it nearly brought tears to my eyes to resist it, but somehow I did. I shook my head. "I'd prefer to stay with Cherty, if you don't mind," I said, wondering if that meant I was resigning myself to cozying up with creepy dead guys.

Ahmose looked up at the boatman and sighed deeply in resignation. "Be careful," he warned. "Cherty will keep the dead away from you, but there is trouble ahead, and I want you close to me when it comes. Will you promise to come to me then?"

I peered up into his moonbeam eyes and nodded. "I will."

Satisfied, Ahmose moved back to the front of the ship, walking through the numerous host of the dead as if he didn't even see them. I shuddered and found a crate to sit on right beside Cherty. It appeared that Ahmose had been right. There was a circle around the ferryman that the ghosts wouldn't cross, so I slid my crate as close as I could and tried to ignore the prickly sensations of invisible fingers trailing along my back, tickling my spine, and making my hair stand on end.

"Ya've gotten yerself into a mess o' trouble with that one," Cherty said, clucking his tongue. "The fairy pines for that fella, ya know. I fear ya won't be free o' his sway till she's gone. I can cast out yer lingerin' ghosts, girlie, if that helps."

"It's all right, Cherty," I said. "The girls are a part of me now. We're going to see this through, the three of us, until the end."

"An' what happens after the end?" Cherty asked.

"We . . . we don't know," I answered quietly, then smiled weakly. "We'll probably end up as ghosts on your ship." I looked around at my fellow travelers and couldn't imagine losing my mortal body. "Will you tell me about Apep now?" I asked, hoping the distraction would help me ignore the creepy feeling of being surrounded by the dead.

The wizened old boatman glanced down at me with sharp, discerning eyes, and then looked back up, slightly adjusting his course to follow Ahmose's signal. "The isle," he began, "it's called the Isle of the Lost fer a reason. When ya venture close, it comes inta view, beckoning. An' what a view. 'Tis a beautiful place. Looks like a utopia land. Real peaceful-like. But the trick is, it slips away. When ya get close, it vanishes. Drives boatmen mad. Those who see it pursue it the rest o' their days."

"So you've seen it, then?"

"I've been in its vicinity. Didn' plan on it. Apep drove me there. 'Tis his home, ya see."

"Did you go mad when you saw it?"

"Naw. Was smart enough to blindfold meself when I got close. Drove my passengers mad, though. Ghosts can't cover their eyes."

"What happened?"

"They jumped. Every last one of 'em jumped ship and swam for it. Easy pickin's for Apep. I kept my blindfold on until the boat reached gentler waters."

I swallowed. "So we'll need to blindfold ourselves, then?"

"I reckon we will."

"And all these ghosts will . . ."

"They'll be food for the monster." I looked at the ghosts surrounding us, focusing on the little girl who sat just at the edge of Cherty's circle and watched me with wide eyes. Suddenly, I felt sorry for them. They didn't seem as frightening to me anymore. Not after knowing they were headed to a second sort of doom.

They were just shadowed versions of the people they once were. Somewhere, somebody mourned them. They were fathers, grandparents, doctors, kids, teachers. Some of them were not entirely human, but I imagined they had families, too. It was a terrible thought that their afterlife would end in such a gruesome way.

Tia spoke up then and told me all about the second death. I knew the basics of what the Devourer could do, but when they told me back on the farm, I was trying to ignore them. Pretend it all wasn't real. The thought that Asten, Ahmose, and Amon could experience this second death didn't sit well with me. If we died, Tia and Ashleigh would experience a second death. They'd blink out of existence. Maybe I would, too. I wasn't sure it would work like that, since technically I was still alive. At least, I thought I was.

A bevy of ghosts clung to the masts, their bodies shifting in the breeze like torn flags. Their faces wore a variety of expressions, but the one most common was resignation. A prickle of foreboding crept over me, the sensation as unsettling as bugs crawling on my skin. Ahmose had mentioned something dangerous was coming. He knew.

"So Apep eats the dead?" I asked.

"Oh, Apep'll eat pretty much anythin'. He's gotten a bit fat an' lazy the las' few centuries. Hasn't had ta work as hard as when 'e was young."

"I see. And what, exactly, is he?" I continued, not really wanting to hear the answer.

"Didn' I tell ya? Thought I did."

I shook my head. "No."

"Oh, well, Apep, he's a giant snake. The original one. Some call 'im the devil. Some say he's a dragon. But I've seen him up close an' personal-like. An' he's a snake, sure as anythin'. A special one, o' course. Bigger than anythin' ya've ever seen. He slithers among the stars. Makes the river his huntin' ground. But his home, his nest, is on that island. Drawn ta it, he is. He only ventures out when he's hungry. Which is pretty frequently."

"And Asten and Amon are trapped there?"

"Seems so."

"Are they safe?"

"If they're in an oubliette, they should be safe enough. Apep'll leave em alone so long as he can't see or smell 'em."

"No wonder nothing can get to them," I said. "They're protected by a giant cosmic snake."

"I wouldn' say 'protected.' Like as not, he don' know they're there."

Later, after rejecting Cherty's dinner offer of a black eel he described as one of Apep's offspring, I drifted off to sleep. Then, what must have been hours later, the ship lurched, and I jolted upright. The soft murmurs from the ghosts had turned into a frenzied trill, like the ominous buzz of cicada wings times a thousand. "What's wrong?" I shouted, darting to my feet. Cherty strained as he pulled ropes and tied them down.

"Apep's found us!" he cried. "He's pickin' off the ghosts in our wake!"

I spun around and peered out at the water behind the ship. The ghosts thrashed around, desperately trying to grab on to their fellows. Cherty pointed to a surging beneath the waves, and I saw a huge coil rise and sink below the water. It sparkled. The scales as beautiful as rainbows. When I looked closer, I could see that the body was actually black, but it was so shiny that the stars glinted off its form turning the scales green, blue, and gold.

If I hadn't been deathly afraid of it, I'd have loved to see the animal up close. I spied one loop and then another but didn't catch a glimpse of its head. Pulling the bow across my back, I nocked an arrow, aiming for a hump when it emerged from the water. "No point, girlie," Cherty said, placing a hand on my arm. "Yer arrows won't work on such as him."

"Even the arrows of Isis?"

"Even hers."

"Then how do we fight him?"

"We don'. Bes' we can do is hope he fills 'is belly fast and then heads home ta sleep it off."

"So there's nothing we can do to protect them?"

"Nah. Try ta ignore it."

"Ignore it?" I echoed incredulously. "They're screaming out there."

"Yeah. Ya would, too, if ya were getting devoured by such as 'im."

The pitiful cries of the ghosts rose over the water. I caught a glimpse of the tail, and it was thicker than a semitruck. If that was the caboose, I'd hate to see the engine. I tried to follow Cherty's instructions. I had no interest in the ghosts. There was no obligation to save them, but something tore through me, and I knew I had to act.

Tia joined me first, and then Ashleigh added her power to ours. We summoned Wasret. A great wind rose around us, and power filled my veins. My voice was thunder as I reached for the creature's true name and sent howling gales to pummel the beast. "Hollow Serpent," I cried, but all three of us knew it wasn't quite right. "Come to me."

The thrashing in the water stilled, and the six visible humps sunk beneath the waves. I wasn't sure if I'd committed enough to the power of Wasret to actually use it effectively. It was something I was still frightened of. I thought if I truly gave myself over to it, to her, one hundred percent, I'd lose myself. So I held back. Each of us did. None of us wanted to lose our identity. We all hoped it was enough.

Nothing happened for the space of several minutes, but then next to the ship, the waters parted, and an enormous head lifted from the Cosmic River and swayed in the air above us. Black droplets showered down on our heads. Angling its body, Apep peered at me with opal eyes the size of a witch's cauldron.

Foolish mortal, it said in my mind. *Those who disturb my dinner, become my dinner.*

13

The Isle of the Lost

I stood horrified, frozen in place, my mouth gaping. A long, forked tongue darted out from the monster's mouth and tasted the air. My body shivered uncontrollably at the sight. The two of us peered at one another, unmoving, even when Ahmose and Cherty both stepped between us.

The former summoned a gleaming weapon that materialized from unseen sand particles caught between the boards on the deck of the ship. He brandished it threateningly, his corded arm ready to swing. The latter clutched two long sticks with sharpened points, holding them in his chapped, knuckly hands loosely enough that I could tell he had much experience in their use.

"Don' look 'im in the eye, girlie," Cherty said. "Apep's stare's hypnotic. Can convince ya to walk right inta 'is belly and make ya think yer strollin' through a flower garden."

The snake opened its jaws in a wicked imitation of a smile, showing off thick fangs that sharpened into deadly points and gleamed in the starlight. *You spoil all my fun,* Apep said petulantly, his voice penetrating our minds. *You know I like to give my prey a fighting chance. Most of the time. Not that they have a lot of fight left in them by the time they end up on your ship.*

Apep swung his head back and forth as if trying to shove Cherty and Ahmose aside, but neither man was intimidated enough to move, which I found remarkable. All things taken into account, I didn't think we stood a chance against the creature. Not with the puny weapons at our disposal. The snake was too large. He could crush our ship with just the tiniest effort and then pick us off, swallowing us down at his leisure.

"The girl didn' mean anythin' by it," Cherty said interrupting my thoughts. "Take yer fill o' these an' leave the livin' alone. There's plenty here ta keep yer belly from achin' without actin' greedy."

I thought Cherty's words were pretty bold, considering. Apparently, his conscience didn't suffer much at the idea of losing his passengers. The snake hissed and lifted a heavy coil out of the water, then slapped it down. Part of his body must've hit the ship heavily enough, because we listed to one side and had trouble keeping our footing.

Ah, the snake said. *What you say is true enough. The scent of the dead you carry is strong, which indicates your boat is full to capacity. Well, it was, until I finished my first course. But now that my appetite is whetted, I'm ready for dinner.*

At his words, the dead moaned and shook. They pushed and shoved one another to the far corners of the ship. Each was desperately trying to get away from the creature, who flicked his great horned head to see them better. I caught a glimpse of the snake's underbelly, which gleamed as if it had been covered in smooth garnet stone. Again I was struck with how lovely my impending death looked.

Even if they did fill me, Apep said, *I cannot allow a young girl who wields such power to enter my realm. You should know better, Cherty, than to bring one such as her to this place. It's been a long time since you've dared enter my waters.*

Ahmose spoke next. "Great Apep, we are about the business of the gods. Seth has been freed, and we must stop him at all costs. Even you must be aware of the chaos he engenders. We promise that we will not remain in your territory long. If you allow us peaceful passage, we won't cause you any harm."

The snake reared up, his great sides spasming at the gills, pushing out brackish water that effervesced and trickled down the beast's scaly body. It splashed on the wooden deck, where it steamed and festered. It took me a moment to figure out that Apep was laughing and not churning out poisonous muck in an attempt to smother us. He whipped his head around and then, quick as a flash, sank right down to stare at Ahmose. The snake's black eyes twinkled with malice. All it would take was a snap, and Ahmose would be no more.

You pathetic weaklings cannot harm me, the snake declared with a hiss. *The very idea of it is nonsensical. As for Seth and the other gods, I pay them no heed. They can destroy one another and their realms for all I care. It just means more food for me. Now, why don't the two of you step aside and let me talk to the little girl who thinks she knows me?*

Apep hesitated only for a second to wait and see if he'd be obeyed. Then he reared his head back and slammed it down on the deck, splintering it. Both Cherty and Ahmose fell through the gaping hole. Instinct had made my claws come out. I dug them into the side of the ship, which prevented me from falling in after them.

Before I could consider a wiser course, I scrambled to the broken edge of the deck and cried, "Ahmose? Cherty?"

There was no answer, and I couldn't see either one of them in the black innards of the ship. They might be impaled on a shaft of wood or lying with broken bones, unable to get up. The boat trembled and groaned and then, slowly, before my eyes, began repairing itself. The splinters and shards lifted into the air and positioned themselves back into their proper places. In the space of just a moment, the deck was repaired, sealing the two fallen men inside the dark hollow of the ship.

I gasped in shock and pounded a flat hand against the deck. "No!" I cried. "Ahmose? Can you hear me?" Again there was no answer, at least not until I heard a hiss. I froze in place, my back to the predator that hunted me. I felt a funnel of hot, moist air lift the hair on the back of my neck. Another whoosh of it blew over me again, and I knew it was the fetid breath of the beast—reeking and repellant. Slowly, I turned and stood to face the monster alone. I drew my weapons from over my shoulders and pressed the buttons to turn my knives into spears.

An odious ecstasy lit the snake's face. As I considered him, a disgustful curiosity overwhelmed me. There was something broken in the creature. Wasret's abilities still buzzed through my body, and the need to name him became crushing. Though he was powerful, I saw in him a gauntness, a haunting sickness, an unending hunger that could never be satisfied. He was . . . malformed. Unnatural. He didn't fulfill a purpose in the cosmos. Apep was an aberration.

Though the snake was close enough to wrap his jaws around me, he seemed as curious about me as I felt about him.

"What made you?" I asked.

What? What did you say? the snake demanded incredulously.

"I asked what made you? I know it wasn't a who. It wasn't Amun-Ra. You're older than Amun-Ra, aren't you? That would make you older than the cosmos. Right?"

I had an awful feeling rolling through my body, a premonition that I had asked something I shouldn't have. That whatever happened next would taint the world and cause evil to sprout up like mushrooms on rotten ground. The snake gave a great shudder, as if my words had cut him deeply enough that he could feel them in his blood.

Beads of water trickled down my temple and through my hair. I wasn't sure if it was from the ocean spray or sweat. Either way, it chilled me down to my bones. The water droplets felt like tiny worms slithering across my scalp. The ghosts had stilled, watching our exchange with mouths pressed so tight, not even air could escape. They huddled in the dark corners of the ship like cockroaches hiding from the light, their pale limbs knotted together like macabre pretzels.

I took a step toward the creature. "The place you come from, it's deep. Unfathomably deep. You swallow up these poor beings so you yourself aren't swallowed up and sucked back into the place you came from."

Who are you? The snake asked in a whisper of a voice. *How did you come to know these things?*

Retracting one of my spears and putting it back in its sheath, I pushed my sea-tangled hair away from my face and stretched out one hand. The snake, shocked at my action, shifted away, causing the boat to rock wildly, but it didn't retreat to the water. I crossed the deck and touched my hand to its black side. Despite my expectations, the snake's body was warm.

"Yes," I said softly, channeling my power with greater ease than I ever had before. "Your path has been broken. Grief and the weight of what you've lost have sharpened your fangs."

When I touched him, my mind swam with visions of a darkness so complete that not even light could escape from it. He'd existed in a void. Like a black hole. The pressure, though terrible, was at least familiar. Then there was a rending, a thrashing, and an expelling. Apep had been torn in two. Split down the middle. Part of him had been cut away, and then there was the part that made his home here. That was the piece that we saw.

The snake's mind was utterly foreign to me. The place in which he existed now was eerie and frightening—the worst kind of prison. But the blackness wasn't the place that scared him; he was afraid for that part he'd left behind.

"Now I understand," I said to the creature, stroking his smooth black scales. "You are the hunger, the desolation. You're a slave to your disposition. The part that was left behind made you whole. More than anything, you long to be reunited. Do you know how it happened?"

I do not, the snake hissed. *I have ranged to the edge of the cosmos and back. I have found no trace of my other half. Perhaps the splitting was an accident. Perhaps it was a surgical cut devised by a villain in the grand theater of the cosmos. I was the unwanted portion, tossed aside. There's no way for me to know.*

"Maybe you can be healed," I said. "I can try to help."

There's no help for one such as me. My nature makes me what I am. And what I am is hungry. His eyes changed. The very countenance of his face blackened to even darker than his shiny skin.

Come to me, young one, he said silkily, his voice making all the noise of the ship and the churning water around me disappear. *You are the tincture that will soothe my parched throat. Come into my mouth, and I will cover you like a storm covers the sea. You will drown in me, but it will be a peaceful death, like lying on a carpet of moss as the pale moonbeams slowly drain the life from your body.*

I obeyed. I climbed up onto the mossy hill and lay down, cushioning my head on the spongy bed. It *was* peaceful. The voice was right. This was my path, my purpose. My body would feed the hunger of the cosmos. There was a horrible sting, a pressure on my leg. But I soon forgot about it and rested again. My mouth tasted funny, like I'd bitten into a rotten peach. The bitter, swollen taste turned into a burning that licked my veins with fire. I whimpered.

Then a great explosion rocked me violently from my bed. It was dark, with just a strip of light at the base of the door. My leg was pinned to the bed, and it hurt badly. Suddenly, the door flew open, but it opened the wrong way. The thing poking my leg wrenched away, and I realized exactly where I was. In the mouth of the snake.

I'd walked right into Apep's mouth. His fang had pierced my calf, and the poison was already working. Moving through my system and numbing my limbs. The snake's body wrenched back and forth, and I slid out of his mouth, hanging on to his slippery fang as he flung himself side to side.

My stomach fell as the snake dove toward the boat, and I caught sight of a wrathful Ahmose, dripping with wet from the Cosmic River. Beautiful in his fury. As we passed him, his eyes opened wide and he made as if to catch me, but the snake moved too fast. Ahmose lifted his arms above his head and chanted a spell. It was loud enough that when the head of the snake climbed high over the boat, I could still hear it. Ahmose's spell caused great flaming boulders to drop from the sky. Heavy meteors fell all around us, some splashing into the Cosmic River with a sizzling hiss, others hitting the snake's coils, each one causing an explosion.

The poison did its work, and my arms could no longer support my weight. I plummeted toward the river, dropping as hard as one of the heavy, bitter-smelling meteors. I was alert enough to hope that I wouldn't die upon impact. When I hit the water, bones audibly shattered, but the pain died quickly as I sank beneath the waves. The last thought I had before I blacked out was that the snake had been right. Death was like a peaceful drowning.

Sadly, pain returned. At first it was irritating, like something tickling my ribs, and I groaned, hoping it would stop. But it quickly worsened. I slapped at whatever it was like I'd inadvertently walked into a spiderweb. I grabbed on to my pain stubbornly, tucking it deep inside me and holding it there like a cat would hold on to a mouse, unwilling to let it get the best of me. "No," I slurred. "Leave me alone."

"I've got to heal you, love."

My nerves tingled, stinging like a thousand hornets. There was a pop, and water leaked from my ears, trickling down my neck. That's when I heard the sound of crickets. They chirruped together, sawing their little legs back and forth, wondering if I was dead like them or still among the living. Their song was wild and annoying.

"Stop it," I called out to them.

"Stop what, love?" the glowing man leaning over me said.

"Stop the bugs. They're so noisy."

"I think she's talkin' bout the ghosties," a familiar voice suggested. "Shut it!" the man demanded.

The buzzing suddenly ceased, and I rolled my swollen tongue over my numb lips. "Thank you," I mumbled and promptly fell asleep.

When I woke again, I lay still for a moment assessing my body for injuries.

Ahmose healed us, Ashleigh said.

Tia? I asked.

I am here, Lily.

Are you guys okay?

We are fine, Tia said. *Though we need to have a frank discussion about turning your back to a hunter.*

I know. I'll add it to the list. I'm sorry I endangered the two of you.

Slowly, I cracked open my eyes and saw Cherty at the rudder. "'Bout time," he said. "Was thinkin' you'd sleep the whole way ta the island."

"Ahmose?" I called out softly.

"He's sleepin' it off," Cherty said, nodding his head to something behind me.

I turned around and saw Ahmose, back propped up against the deck of the ship, his head hanging low to his chest as he slept.

"Took a lot out o' him ta bring ya back from the brink," Cherty said. "Didn' think he was gonna make it."

"I was that bad off?" I asked.

Cherty leaned forward, bushy eyebrows raised. "Ya was dead, girlie. Don't rightly know how he did it, but he did. Fished ya outta the river himself."

I nodded and scooted a bit closer to Ahmose. His golden skin had a dusky pallor, and his fingertips were as blue as if they'd been nibbled on by hoarfrost. A gray bruise colored his jaw, and his cheek was slightly swollen. I knew I didn't look much better. My clothes were still damp in places, and the parts that were dry were scratchy and rough. I didn't even want to look down at my bone-white limbs or the scar on my leg that was still sticky with blood though it had healed over.

"Are we safe?" I asked. "What happened with Apep?"

"The burnin' rocks were too much fer 'im. He ran off ta lick his wounds. Don' worry, though. He'll be back. Did plenty o' damage before he left. *Mesektet* had ta heal herself. Apep broke 'er apart in frustration before he hightailed it outta here. Lost more'n half my ghosties."

The ship did look considerably less crowded. "How much time do you think we've got until he returns?" The idea that the giant snake would be coming back for round two filled me with horror. I hadn't done well before. Sure, I'd distracted him for a short time, but ultimately we'd lost. I wasn't sure we'd survive a second bout.

"Hard ta tell. Could come back soon or could leave us alone for the duration. Depends on 'is mood. If we're lucky, we can grab the two boys and skedaddle from his island before he even knows we're there."

"Let's hope so."

After a brief moment of hesitation, I reached over and smoothed Ahmose's thick hair away from his forehead. His lips were slightly parted, and the worries he carried with him like a cloak upon his shoulders had lifted away as he slept, revealing a slight trace of the happy, carefree man who'd spent an afternoon in Ashleigh's sunshiny, strawberry dream.

Despite everything, I loved him. It wasn't all Ashleigh. It was time I admitted it to myself. I wanted Ahmose to be happy. It would be a travesty to never see that moonbeam smile again. To never feel the comfort and warmth of his arms around me. Maybe the others were right, and we should grab every moment of happiness we could. It wasn't going to last. An end was coming. We all knew it.

I draped the healing stela around his neck, hoping it would work its magic as he slept, and scooted back against the boat, positioning myself alongside Ahmose and dropping my head on his shoulder. He stirred only slightly when I took his hand and twined my fingers through his.

"Best rest while ya can," Cherty said. "Won't be long till we reach the island, and ya'll need ta have yer wits about ya."

I gave him a grateful smile and closed my eyes, my body rocking with the motion of the boat.

Lily. Sunshine filled my mind. I startled awake. "Amon?" I murmured groggily, reluctant to rouse myself. Ahmose shifted beside me and rubbed his eyes.

"Good thing. Was gonna fetch ya in a moment anyway," Cherty said.

"What is it?" I asked, clambering nervously to my feet. "Has Apep returned?"

"Naw. It's the island. We're here. Found 'er an hour ago, but she disappeared. This is the second time I've been able to spot 'er. Don't look at 'er directly, else she fades away in the mist again."

"I can find it without looking now that we're close enough," Ahmose said as he turned me toward him. After he inspected my former injuries, his eyes found my face. His fingertips followed his gaze and he touched my cheek, the contact as fleeting as a butterfly's wings, but still my skin burned. I wondered what he saw when he looked at me. Was it Tia? Ashleigh? All three of us? Maybe it didn't matter anymore.

"How do you feel?" he asked. "Are you still in pain?"

"I was going to ask you the same thing. Cherty said you brought me back, expending your own energy to do so."

"It was nothing."

I took his hand, cupping it in mine. It was a bold move on my part, but it somehow felt right. "No, it wasn't."

He looked down at our hands, and then his eyes flickered up. For a moment he studied me and a corner of his mouth lifted in a small, hopeful smile. Ahmose squeezed my hand, not painfully but possessively, and I took a step closer. "I'd do it again, love," he said as he bent down to my ear, his breath warming my cheek.

When I nodded, he pressed a soft kiss on my jaw next to my earlobe and goose bumps shot down my body. Wrapping my arms around his waist, I tucked my head against his chest and said, "Thank you."

His big hand cupped my head and stroked my hair softly. I was so lost in the moment that I was surprised when Ahmose said to Cherty, "Bear right." The ship listed, and I would have had to grab on to the railing if Ahmose hadn't kept me solidly planted against his body. "Now straight on," he added. "That's it. I can feel them nearby. Keep your eyes tightly closed, Lily," he said.

"You best do it, too, lad," Cherty said. "Don't look straight upon it."

"You can sense your brothers?" I mumbled against his chest, both of us swaying with the ship.

"Yes."

After another moment, Cherty said, "You two can open yer eyes now. Lost a few more ghosties what looked on the island, but now we're anchored ta her, so we're safe enough. Nice havin' ya aboard, lad. Came in real handy."

Ahmose reluctantly left me to help Cherty with the sails, and I rubbed my arms, feeling cold after having been enveloped in his warmth. I felt a combination of giddiness and guilt over my feelings for Ahmose. Indulging my desire to be close to him, even knowing everything I knew, made me feel like I was an addict passing by a bar. I was walking slowly enough that temptation seeped from the windows, beckoning. My limbs trembled with wanting something I shouldn't have. I approached Cherty and asked, "Will the island move now that we're here?"

"Naw. She can't drift away once we're anchored to 'er."

I nodded, shifting my gaze from the coarse beard on Cherty's face to the view off the bow of the ship. A heavy mist obscured the island at first, but then spears of sunshine pierced the clouds. I saw the top of a green mountain part the gray billows like a shark fin on the ocean. When it disappeared again, a sense of foreboding and danger swept over me just as surely as if we were indeed being encircled by a school of the dangerous predators.

Channeling the powers of Wasret, we created new clothes and I reached up to find my windblown, salt-ridden hair was now clean and hung in a loose braid down my back. I wore a white T-shirt tucked into khaki cargo pants with a long-sleeved white button-down shirt tied around my waist, and a pair of supple hiking boots adorned my feet.

Ahmose appeared a moment later, also freshly changed. His hair, as dark as the churning water of the Cosmic River, was swept back from his face. He offered me a tired smile and gave me back the stela. "Thank you for loaning your token from Horus," he said. "It's done all it can for me," Ahmose added cryptically. I draped the necklace around my neck and wondered exactly what healing me had taken out of him. I made a mental note to find out.

Cherty took my hand and helped me into a dinghy that had magically formed on the side of the ship. "That's convenient," I said as I stepped into the boat and took a seat. "Bet the captain of the *Titanic* would've appreciated having that ability."

He clambered aboard and started pulling on the ropes to lower us down. "I was watchin' that, ya know. Terrible thing ta see a fine ship such as that one find its home at the bottom o' the sea. Carried many o' those souls on their last boat ride. Didn't have the heart ta tell the captain everythin' he did wrong. Least he went down with the ship. Gotta give 'im credit for bravery."

When we were bobbing on the Cosmic River, I looked up to see Ahmose drawing in the ropes, then he raised his hands, and his body lifted into the air and floated down toward us. He settled into the craft on the bench next to me, but I could see how using his power drained him. I took hold of his hand and pressed it between mine. He squeezed my fingers weakly.

Cherty sat by the rudder and twirled a finger in the air. We shot forward, heading toward the island as quickly as if there were a motor speeding us along, but as far as I could see we flew across the waves on whatever power Cherty had at his disposal. Starry flying fish raced alongside our craft, and a larger animal that looked like a cross between a black dolphin and a sea horse leapt from the water and reentered with a splash.

I caught glimpses of the island that teased me with flashes of green, but most of it was covered in swollen clouds so thick it was really difficult to make out the size and shape of it. Then, when the boat ran aground, the mist dissipated before us and the Isle of the Lost showed itself in all its splendor. A magnificent green paradise rose out of the depths of the black Cosmic River. Mountains loomed high overhead, their tips hidden by the clouds. Trees of all kind with heavy canopies that shifted in a warm breeze butted right up next to the thin black beach.

"It's lovely," I murmured in a hushed voice.

"It's lovely, all right," Cherty agreed. "Lovely until ya get all twisted and turned around in the forest wonderin' if ya'll ever see the light o' day again."

"What do you mean?" I asked.

Cherty rubbed the stubble on his cheek as he considered the jungle ahead. "The whole island is . . . well, it doesn't like ta let ya go once ya set foot upon it. Now, me, it doesn't much care for. Nothin' it can get outta me. But two kickers like you? Well, let's just say, it's not too likely ta let ya go easy-like."

"But Ahmose can find a path."

"He might. He might. Then again, islands are confusin' things. An' keep in mind ol' Apep lives here. Could be he's waiting for us ta walk into his mouth again. If he's not bad enough, ya should know that the island can hypnotize you as well as the snake. It's got ways o' trappin' ya."

The thought of walking into the mouth of the snake again froze me in place. Fear crept through my veins, forming icy rivulets, and my breath hitched.

"You might have told us that before we set foot upon it," Ahmose said, placing a comforting hand on my shoulder. I inhaled shakily.

"Oh, I mighta. Wouldn'a changed yer minds anyhow," Cherty replied.

"He's right," I said, putting my hand on top of Ahmose's. I turned to face him. "We have to save your brothers. We don't have another choice." I added hopefully, "So if the island isn't interested in him, then we can have Cherty lead the way instead of you."

"I'd like ta be able ta help, but I'm tied ta my ship. Can' leave *Mesek-*

tet. Bad enough the ghosties still aboard have ta wait. I can only give ya a day or so ta find the other two guardians. After that, the pull o' the dead will force the ship ta continue on an' I'll have ta go with 'er."

When he saw my fallen expression, Cherty stiffened. "I'll not have ya givin' me a coward's name," he said, his chin tilting up.

I shook my head and stepped toward him. His rough, chapped hands twitched at his sides. "I'm not thinking you're a coward, Cherty. I'm just a little scared of the unknown."

Cherty peered at me with one eye shut, then nodded gruffly and pulled me aside. "As am I. But the lad is a good one," he said, indicating Ahmose, who had crouched in the sand and was waving his hands over it, seeking a path.

Ahmose's thick hair, as black as the sand, hung over his forehead, obscuring his moonbeam-gray eyes. "I judged 'im unfairly before," Cherty continued. "He clearly loves ya and is willin' ta risk himself ta save ya. I thought the guardians were cold men with hearts as unfeelin' as a crocodile's hide, but seein' 'im with you changed my thinkin'."

"He's not coldhearted at all," I found myself saying. "Ahmose jes' keeps his feelin's all bottled up inside, so he does. Ya might think he's intimidatin' an' stern if ya jes' look on the outside, but once ya break through ta his heart, he's as soft an' sweet as a newborn kitten at Christmas, the poor darlin'."

I stood there, staring dumbly at Ahmose with a goofy expression on my face. I wasn't even aware that Cherty was still there until he cleared his throat and spat into the sand. Blinking, I jerked and turned to face him.

"That was disconcertin'," Cherty said. "Ya should be ashamed of yerself, fairy."

"What?" I said, confused.

"Yer fairy. She plum took over and ya didn' even notice. The three o' ya are blurrin' together more an' more."

Ashleigh began sobbing in my mind. "Stop it," I said to Cherty. "You've hurt her feelings. She can't help the way she feels."

"Maybe not. Jes' . . . jes' be careful, Lily. Bad enough ta be confused here, where it don' mean much. It's 'nother thing entirely ta be turned about out there." He pointed toward the jungle, where dark branches and trunks gave way to soaring greenery that beckoned us closer. "The three o' ya got ta keep tight control o' yerselves. If ya show the island yer weaknesses, it'll exploit 'em, sure as a sharkie zooms in on a flailin' fish."

"We'll be careful," I promised him. "Will you wait on the beach?"

"Yes. I'll stay here as long as I can, but if fer some reason, me and my boat are gone, don' look back on the island when you leave. It'll trap ya sure as a kingfisher. If Apep returns, I . . . well . . . let's jes' hope he don'. Be safe, Lily," he said. "An' hurry."

"We will," I answered with more confidence than I actually felt. I adjusted my leather harness containing my spear-knives and the quiver of arrows over my shoulder.

"Are you ready?" Ahmose asked, coming up behind me and shifting my bow to a more comfortable position. His face looked grave and serious, the dark hollows beneath his cheekbones made him look severe, almost like a starved and desperate animal.

"Yes," I answered, longing to see the happiness and sparkle return to his eyes. To see him as he was in Ashleigh's long-ago dream. I gave him what I hoped was a reassuring smile and cupped his cheek with my hand. He pulled it down to kiss my palm, his lips as light and soft as flower petals. I squeezed my eyes shut for just a moment. Then he wrapped his hand around mine, leading the way forward.

Together we walked to the edge of the jungle and, with a last look at Cherty behind us, plunged into the dimness beneath the trees of the Island of the Lost.

14

Trouble with the Natives

The jungle closed around us. Within a matter of moments, I could no longer hear the sound of the waves hitting the beach. Ahmose had seemed confident before we entered, but once we were beneath the trees, his smile slipped and his steps became less sure. Not ten minutes later, he stopped and turned in a slow circle.

He crouched down and spread out his fingertips searching for a direction. After several tries, he blew out a breath in frustration. "The path to my brothers is unclear. When I channel my power, not one but many paths appear, and as soon as I follow one, I find it broken. They cannot all be the right way. I fear leading you down the wrong one."

"Are there any that seem to be stronger than the others? Can you still feel your brothers?"

"Yes and no. I know they are close, but I can't pinpoint their exact location."

"Cherty said he could only wait for us for a few days at best. What do we do?"

A group of large birds squawked loudly overhead. I glanced up and a shiver ran through me as I realized they were watching us. Their long beaks snapped shut in a series of clicks that sounded like they were communicating. They reminded me of miniature pterodactyls looking for an easy meal.

Ahmose studied the paths for a moment, grunted in frustration, and then said, "Whatever we do, we shouldn't stay here."

"Agreed."

We trudged ahead through the jungle. Sweat trickled from my temples down to my neck. I swiped at it distractedly. When the trail ahead dead-ended, Ahmose murmured a spell and a wicked pair of golden machetes materialized in his hands. He cut away the undergrowth so we could pass, but soon as we did, the jungle knit itself back together behind us. Apparently, getting out was going to be just as hard as getting in.

Despite the heat, the power of the sphinx gave me energy to burn and the ability to regulate my temperature. I could have hiked through the jungle for hours without tiring. Ahmose was a different story. To distract both of us, I asked Ahmose, "What does it mean when a path is broken?"

"A broken path is an aberration. It's unnatural. Every object in the cosmos has a path that begins at the Waters of Chaos and spreads out from there. A broken path means something has physically damaged or moved that object before it reached a natural end."

"You mean like Seth unmaking something?"

"Yes."

"Is that why this island was hidden? It's been unmade?"

"No. Seth hasn't touched this island. If he had, it wouldn't exist at all." Ahmose rubbed his jaw, the machete barely missing his jugular. "From what I can gather, I'd say that this island predates Seth."

"Interesting. So it's like Apep."

"Apep?"

"Yes. He's broken, too. Part of him was split away. He doesn't know what did it, but he longs to be reunited with his other half," I said as I shoved aside a thick green leaf and stepped through the hole Ahmose had just made. "The part we see is the hungry part. The sad thing is, it doesn't matter how many ghosts he eats, he'll never be full. Not until he's put back together."

Ahmose lifted his weapon and struck. A thick, leafy vine fell at his feet. "Apep by himself is bad enough. I'd hate to encounter his other half, too," he said, clearing the way for me to follow.

"Yeah."

I asked if I could help, but Ahmose shook his head stubbornly. He made sure I stood back far enough that his blades couldn't reach me by accident. Following behind gave me the opportunity to admire his sculpted back and arms. His muscles weren't the result of protein bars and a gym like most of the brawny boys I knew. Hard labor and actual battle had fashioned Ahmose.

I could see it in every swing of his arm, the angle of his weapon, and the stance he took as he faced his foe—in this case, a thick copse of undergrowth. The hard body that glistened with sweat wasn't meant to impress women or the guy on the weight bench next to him or to get him a minor role in an even more minor film. Ahmose had earned every inch of sinew. Watching him in action was like watching Hercules in his labors. I didn't just admire the view; I admired him. And, what's more, I respected him. Ahmose was simply breathtaking. My two inner voices agreed with me.

We moved ahead for an hour and then another and another. The jungle was hot, and my skin grew feverish and sticky. I was thinking about my jetted tub back in New York when Ahmose stopped and leaned over panting. He was clearly exhausted but still doggedly refused to let me assist. I was pondering the stupidity of not having brought a canteen along when he stood up and froze. His eyes were glued to something over my shoulder.

I spun around, but at first I couldn't see what had captured his attention. All I noticed was a tree. At least, I thought it was the trunk of a tree. Upon closer inspection, I found it was a thick post with an intricately carved face. Torn fabric floated around it like ghostly apparel, and strings of seashell necklaces hung around the indentation where a neck should be.

"What is it?" I asked, my breath hot against my sweaty arm as I swiped my face. I stepped up to examine it.

"A totem. It's a warning. If we cross, we acknowledge that our lives are in peril."

"That sounds just about perfect," I said matter-of-factly. "Bad enough a snake lives here who wants to munch on us for breakfast."

Ahmose moved up behind me and studied the carving. Without even consulting me, he stepped boldly past it and said, "I don't think we should worry about it too much."

Something shifted. I reached out and yanked his arm to stop him in his tracks. *"Are ye spinnin' blatherskite, my 'andsome boy?"* I put my hands on my hips. *"Don'tcha think we oughta be jes' a wee bit careful?"*

Ahmose came back to my side of the totem, which made me sigh in relief, and took hold of my shoulders, peering into my eyes. "Ashleigh?"

"Aye?" I answered with a saucy grin.

"Where's Lily?"

"She's right here. But Lily's a more trustin' sort than I am. I thought it best ta make sure ya know what yer about before ya go off prancin' around in a haunted jungle."

"Are you saying you don't trust me?" A wicked gleam twinkled in his eyes.

Heat rose in the space dividing our bodies, and though he didn't move, I could have sworn that the distance closed between us. I lifted my hands to shrug him off but ended up pressing my hands against him instead. As I became aware of the contours of his chest, all thoughts of my aches and pains melted away like snow in the desert. Good heavens, his body could have been carved from stone. *"Ach, now,"* I said, trying to engage my brain cells. *"Trust goes two ways. I'd think ya might be showin' me a little bit o' gratitude for pullin' ya back from the brink."*

He lifted a hand from my shoulder and captured a strand of hair between his glowing fingers, changing the color to a gleaming silver. "And just how should I be showing my gratitude, Ash?"

"I'm sure I could come up with somethin' if I gave my mind over to it," I said with a grin. I tilted my face up for a kiss. His breath hitched, and I closed my eyes and waited for it, but the kiss never came. I cracked open my eyes, my brows knit together in confusion, and his expression was one of regret coupled with his familiar obstinacy.

"In our case, Ash, trust is a *four*-way street. Six if you count my brothers. And to save my pride, I'd rather leave them out of the equation. I won't take advantage of Lily and Tia in that way."

I punched his chest, fiery temper flowing through my veins, heating up my already overheated body. *"Yer a wicked lad, ya are!"* I shouted. *"I will . . ."*

My words were cut off as Ahmose pressed his lips against mine. He pulled me so tightly against his body that his warmth enveloped me and a seeming volcano erupted between us. His heartbeat merged with mine until they sounded like wild, pounding jungle drums. When he angled his head, a little moan escaped me, and I was no longer Tia or Ashleigh or Lily. I was just a girl being kissed by a boy she loved. His hands were at my waist, then at my neck, then knotting in my hair, loosening my braid.

By the time we broke apart, all I could do was look into his gray eyes full of stormy passion and try to breathe. He kissed my damp forehead sweetly. "Now stop teasing me, woman, else I'll have to kiss you until you're senseless enough not to argue with me anymore. And not one more word from any of you about how you'd rather kiss Asten or Amon. I may be on the quiet side, but I'm a jealous type." He took my hand and led me past the totem.

An hour later, we were crouched down in the undergrowth, peering at a small village. When a very short person emerged from a hut wearing nothing but a skirt of leaves to cover himself, Ashleigh whispered excitedly, using my voice, *"It's one o' the wee folk!"*

No, I said to her mentally. *I don't think it's a leprechaun. Do you see any pots of gold?*

Ahmose held a finger to his lips. He studied the few villagers we saw for a long enough time that my legs began to cramp. Ashleigh retreated reluctantly, and I took over. Leaning close to him, I asked, "What are you watching for?"

Ahmose turned to look at me, his eyes narrowed. "Lily?"

I nodded.

"I'm looking for weapons, soldiers, a hint that they have magic," he answered.

"Have you seen any of those things?" I asked.

"No. But something feels off."

"Yeah. It does," I agreed.

"Tia?" he asked. "What do you sense?"

Tia was surprised at being directly addressed. She appreciated it. I stepped aside mentally and let her take control. My head tilted to the side, and my nostrils flared. "There are more villagers than we see," Tia said. "Many more."

"That's what I was worried about. But where are they?"

Tia inhaled deeply, and when the air cycled through our lungs, she froze. Tingles shot up my spine, and all my nerves stood on end. "Above us!" she hissed.

At that moment, ululating cries echoed all around us as small bodies dropped from the treetops and slid down on vines. Before we could even stand up, they surrounded us, spears jabbing into our sides and dozens of arrows pointed our way. The tallest warrior came up to my belly button, but that didn't make them any less fierce or formidable. Their faces and dark bodies were painted and coated with ash, making them appear ghostly.

They spoke in a language I didn't understand but Ahmose and Tia did. By accessing her thoughts, I was able to discern their meaning.

"You trespass on our hunting grounds!" the largest warrior said as he stepped forward.

Though Tia caught the meaning of his words, she couldn't speak back. Ahmose, who had raised his hands in the air to show he meant no harm, spoke for us. Tia translated mentally. "We did not mean to offend. I am seeking my lost brothers. Have you seen them? They are hidden in a dark place."

The warriors looked at one another and talked briefly until one of them hissed and they all went quiet. "We do not go to the dark place. It is forbidden. Those who seek it out do not return."

"We have no choice. We must find my brothers. Can you guide us?"

The men shook their spears angrily as arguments broke out among them. "We do not help those who trespass!" he shouted at Ahmose, despite the fact that it would take two or three of them standing on each other's shoulders to even reach his height.

Ahmose folded his arms across his chest. "Then perhaps we can petition your king. We have much to offer in trade."

I looked up in alarm. We had nothing to trade. We didn't even have water. I licked my chapped lips and swallowed drily. Ahmose's expression was cool and confident. Even Tia was worried, and if she was worried, I was nearly petrified.

The tallest man fidgeted as he considered our proposal. Then, finally, he gave a stiff nod and shouted out instructions to his men, who jabbed at us with spears. Ahmose pulled me close to shield me, and we allowed them to march us unceremoniously into the village. The few women who were milling about shouted and drew the children into their arms. They disappeared into small homes patched together with leaves, bits of cloth, and tree branches.

We were made to sit by a large fire pit with several cauldrons, their thick contents bubbling. "You stay here," the big warrior warned. "I bring back king. Maybe he help you"—he peered at me with a wicked grin, his stained teeth sharp—"maybe he cook you for dinner." The man laughed uproariously at his own joke. At least, I hoped it was a joke.

He leaned closer and closed his eyes, sniffing my neck and hair. "You good and tender meat," he said with another gleeful belly laugh before disappearing into the largest hut. *Maybe it wasn't a joke.* We didn't have to wait long, but I felt every minute. Nausea overwhelmed me as I pondered why there were so few women and children in the village. Were these people really cannibals? I wondered. Did they eat the weak ones of their tribe? I grimaced, listening to the sounds of their dinner pop and sputter as it cooked over the fire.

Tia thought the whole idea was fascinating. She regaled me with a story about a lioness who ate her cub when it died. I'm sure my face was a mask of horror, but Tia talked about it with a tone of reverence, explaining that it was natural and instinctive. The mother was re-absorbing the energy of the lost cub so she could continue to feed her other, healthier ones. Still, we all agreed that none of us wanted to be added to the menu.

Soon the entrance flap of cloth covering the hut fluttered, and the warrior emerged. Just behind him another man exited. He was clothed in a skirt of colorful fabric, though his chest was bare. Instead of a painted face, he wore an intricate mask, similar to the carved totem we'd seen before. The king was slightly taller than the other men, maybe all of four feet and a few inches, and I wondered if that fact alone was what had qualified him for leadership. He came boldly toward us but instead of looking at us or engaging in conversation, he addressed his people.

"These interlopers come to us begging favors. Shall we grant them?"

"No!" the people shouted over one another.

The barefooted man stepped around us shaking a stick, the shells at his ankles and on his stick rattling noisily. "They seek the forbidden place," he said. "They ignore our warnings. Do they come to steal our food or to become our food?"

All Tia heard was "food" over and over again from the crowd. We couldn't tell which way the wind was blowing.

"Perhaps they are sent by the gods. It is my job as your king, to find out why."

Shouts of agreement spread around the camp. I reached for Ahmose's hand, and he wrapped his fingers around mine, squeezing them reassuringly while giving me an indiscernible nod.

"Bring me the diviners!" the king shouted, and a man hurried into the main hut. He fetched a bag and what looked like the head from one of the long beaked birds. I stared into its empty eye sockets as the man dumped the contents of the bag into the skull, plugged the openings, and shook it back and forth. Finally, he raised it over his head, his hands cupping the bottom of it. As the beak opened, out fell six rocks with painted symbols. They rolled across the ground, one stopping near my shoe. Upon closer examination, I noticed they weren't actually rocks at all.

Palm nuts, Tia said in my mind. *Tribes in Africa use them for a similar purpose.*

Despite her knowledge, she couldn't discern what the nuts might be predicting for us. The man hunched over the nuts, turning them with long bony fingers as he made various grunting noises. When he was satisfied, he stood. A wide, eerie grin appeared below the mask. *Please don't kill us,* I thought.

Tia gave me the mental approximation of a lioness snort. She considered our captors easily overcome. I wanted to feel assured by her confidence, but my practical side wouldn't allow it. Instead, I replayed all the adventure movies I'd ever seen where the heroes of the story had been bushwhacked and tied up. It never turned out well. Of course, we weren't tied up. At least not yet.

Raising his hands in the air with a triumphant expression, the man silenced the crowd. The jungle also seemed to go spookily still as the man proclaimed his findings. With dramatics worthy of any Emmy Award–winning actor, he said with a flourish, "Our two interlopers are to face . . . the Calabash Trials!"

The warriors surrounding us stomped their feet and shouted their excitement. "What's a calabash?" I asked Ahmose, leaning close to his ear.

"It's a gourd."

"Oh. That doesn't sound so bad. How can a trial by gourd be dangerous?"

As if in answer to my question, three small warriors approached. They each carried a decorated brown gourd with a short neck and a dark hole at the top. They shook them ominously, dancing around us, then set them down in front of the king, who now knelt on a braided mat. "First we celebrate, then the trial begins!"

Some stringed instruments were brought out, along with a variety of drums. The warriors lined up and began stomping and singing, their voices merging seamlessly in a series of clicks and whistles as they moved around the fire pit. One of the women began pounding on a trough of water, producing a drumming rhythm that reverberated in my bones. The boiling food hanging over the fire was scooped out and passed around, along with gourds of water that were shared among several tribesmen.

A fragrant bowl of the simmering stew was passed almost beneath my nose, but none was offered to either me or Ahmose. The smell was bitter and earthy, like burned meat mixed with decaying plant material coated with exotic spice. Ashleigh groused, *Wish it was stirabout. Got a real cravin' for it. Coulda offered us somethin'. At least water.*

What's stirabout? I asked to take my mind off how thirsty I was.

Kind of like a porridge.

I'd take that over whatever they're eating any day.

We can hunt for ourselves once we show these people our claws, Tia said. *I don't understand why we aren't making a move.*

Ahmose knows we can't find the others on our own, I said. *He's probably waiting to see if they're going to help us. We'll just play along until we get a feel for things.*

Lionesses don't play along. They go for the kill or they slink away, Tia replied.

Well, humans have learned to get the biggest bang for their buck, I said.

A buck sounds tasty right about now, my inner lioness growled.

I sighed. *Well, what does your instinct tell you?*

To trust Ahmose, Tia admitted.

Me too, Ashleigh added.

Then we'll wait.

I tried to be patient, to sit still like Ahmose was doing. His arms lay on his knees, and he sat quietly, resting and watching as if he were a celebrated guest at the feast and not dying of hunger and thirst like we were. To pass the time, I tried to fix my unruly hair. The tie had slipped away. I didn't want to reveal all our cards yet by summoning my power just to pull it back again. Instead, I fluffed it out, knowing it probably looked like a mess of wild straw poking out in every direction.

Almost an hour passed before the villagers settled down and the music and dancing ceased. The empty bowl was taken away from the king, and he dusted off his hands and stood up, beckoning us to do the same thing. Then he summoned the three men who held the gourds, and they approached, bowing low and holding out their offerings before them.

"Before you are given the privilege of choosing a gourd," the king said, "you must pass three trials."

"Three?" I echoed with a grimace.

The man frowned at my interruption.

"But know that even should you pass all three trials, only one gourd hides the treasure you seek. In one gourd, you will find a map to the forbidden place. In another, you will find disease. In the third, you will find death."

I held up a hand. "Wait a minute. You're saying we have to pass three trials, and then our prize for accomplishing that might still be death?"

The man just looked at me dumbly. Ahmose "interpreted" my

words but changed them to suit his purposes. Instead, he said, "We accept the challenge of the calabash and understand that the outcome might be different than we hope."

I elbowed him in the ribs, but he ignored me. Instead, he took my hand and locked my fingers in his.

"Very well," the king said. "Then we shall begin."

He lifted his fingers and whistled. A small boy with leaf skirt barely hanging on to his hips ran forward and placed an empty, hollowed-out gourd in the shape of a bowl into his king's hands. The king gave it to Ahmose.

"Your first task," he said, "is to fill the bowl to the brim with water." He raised a staff and shook it in our faces. "But you cannot fill it using our well, a lake, the river, or a pond. If you are successful, you may drink from it."

I stood there dumbfounded, thinking this must be a riddle of some sort, like the puzzle of the sphinx. Tia, Ashleigh, and I mentally whispered back and forth, trying to come up with something. We didn't even notice what Ahmose was doing until his voice rang out around us in a spell. The warriors crouched down, their hands over their ears, quaking in fear. Their king stood upright, a gleam of interest in his eyes.

Ahmose wove his spell, and clouds gathered overhead. When he raised his arms, I could see them trembling with exertion. Lightning cracked and thunder boomed overhead. The clouds darkened, and then heavy rain began to fall. In a matter of a few moments, I was completely drenched. The warm rain felt refreshing as it washed away the sweat and grime of our trek through the jungle. I opened my mouth to let the water trickle down my throat, soothing my thirst.

As the minutes passed, the bowl slowly filled while the villagers watched curiously. When the bowl brimmed with water, the rain stopped and the clouds parted. The sun shone down and steam rose from the ground, curling upward. The packed dirt was now as black as the bark from the trees. The face paint and ash adorning the bodies of the warriors had washed away in patches, leaving the remaining paint clumpy and awkward.

"Good!" The king laughed with delight. "Now you may drink!"

Ahmose offered me the bowl, and I took it gratefully. I gulped from the edge, drinking deeply. The contents sloshed over the side and wetted my shirt even more, but I didn't care. When I'd had my fill, I handed it back to Ahmose, who drank down the rest. Water trickled in little rivulets from his mouth down his throat and disappeared in the valley of his chest. When the water was gone, he handed the empty bowl to the king.

"Very good," the king said. "Now, on to the second trial."

He bade us to follow him. Before long, we'd hiked out of the village and through the jungle until we came upon a certain tree. "Your next task is to cut this tree down for our firewood without using any tools. But beware the ants," he said, indicating a pulsating mound of brown and red that I now recognized as a mass of living creatures. "They won't take kindly to your disturbing the area."

With that, the villagers left, giving the nearby ants a wide berth. Ahmose and I walked around the tree, pushing on it and testing it for weaknesses. It was wide and strong and deep-rooted. It would take a long time to chop down even if we did have an ax. Ahmose immediately summoned a weapon from the sand but then stopped as he remembered that wasn't allowed.

"Would my claws count as a weapon?" I asked him.

"I wouldn't risk it," he answered, allowing his own weapon to dissipate. "Ow!" he said as he slapped his neck. Then he danced a bit and brushed several ants from his arms. "Step back," he warned. "They're dangerous. These are the type that can kill living organisms, strip the flesh from their bones."

Tia took over. *I've had much experience with these before. I've seen them overwhelm aging lions and cubs who couldn't outrun them. The next morning, nothing remains, and even the skeletons are hardly recognizable.*

Really? I asked her. *What are they called?*

Wait a minute, Ashleigh said. *We can figure out what they're called. We'll use the ants!* She said excitedly.

"*Ashleigh has an idea,*" Tia said. Without even explaining to Ahmose what we were going to do, the three of us merged and summoned our power. The voice of Wasret echoed, "*Heed me, small ones.*" The mass of ants exploded outward and surged toward us. As individuals we began to panic, but we held on to each other tightly even though ants crawled up my legs and torso.

Ashleigh tried to break away when they began biting. *There's too many!* she cried. *We can't name them all!*

But Tia doggedly corralled her, bringing her back. *We must find the commonality,* she encouraged. *We must name the colony!*

No, I mentally shouted. *Name the queen! She controls the others.*

We pushed and stretched ourselves, finally breaking free of the pain inflicted by the ants as they bit and crawled beneath our clothing. In a voice carried by the wind, we cried as one, "Abyssinia the Fierce! She Who Brings Death and Life! The Queen of Honey and Fire! Heed our commands!" We felt the bending of the queen as she listened to us and within a moment, her ants moved, obeying her instructions.

The colony surrounded the tree and went to work. I was surprised at how quickly they were able to weaken the trunk. After an hour passed, we heard the crack and boom of the tree trunk splitting. Ahmose drew me to the side as it fell in the jungle, taking several other branches from nearby trees down with it. The power of Wasret went out of us with a whoosh.

A lone warrior soon appeared and guided us back to the village. The king emerged from his hut, his mask lifted on top of his head, stroking his jaw. He sat down on his mat, indicating we should do the same. He gave a nod to one of the women, who sat down next to us. She brought with her a bowl of white pasty goop that smelled slightly medicinal but otherwise highly pungent.

She rubbed the stuff on our ant bites, and though I wrinkled my nose at the smell, I was immediately appreciative of the ointment as it cooled the bites and soothed away the sting. As she worked, the king demanded, "Tell me how you accomplished this! A medicine man can bring the rain, but no one has survived the ants, let alone brought down the tree."

Ahmose shrugged. "If we complete the trials and gain your help in finding my brothers, perhaps we will give you a demonstration of our power."

The king, who had been kneeling, sat back abruptly as he considered Ahmose's words. "Bah. It matters not," he said with a wave of his hand. "No one can survive the third trial."

"What's the third trial?" I asked.

Ahmose translated faithfully. The king answered, "You must eat first. Consider it a last meal."

This time an entirely different meal was brought to us. The sun was setting, drawing out the long shadows of the trees. Villagers exited the huts piling dishes before us filled with smoked fish, some kind of roasted meat with mushrooms, boiled eggs, stewed vegetables resembling carrots with a fragrant spice, honeyed yams, a fruit I didn't recognize, and a bowl of what were unmistakably termites. The king scooped up a handful of the wriggling bugs and popped them into his mouth, munching happily. A few escaped his lips, but he tucked them back in, licking his fingers as he did so.

Avoiding the termites and the mysterious roast, I picked at the yams and carrots and nibbled on the fruit while Ahmose lifted up the entire plate of fish and went to town. The musicians came back, this time dancing wildly with a frenzy that made me nervous. It reminded me of the crazy, drugged dancing of the natives before they sacrificed the blond girl to King Kong.

After wiping my hands on my khakis, I asked again, "What's the third trial?"

The gleeful king, without taking his eyes off the dancers, answered the question, translated by Ahmose. "Not too bad," he said. "Just need to defeat Ananse."

"And Ananse is . . . ?" prompted Ahmose.

"Ananse is very hungry. Not as bad as snake, but nearly. She doesn't like ghosts, though. No. What she craves is flesh."

The king finally looked our way and grinned, his sharp teeth gleaming in the light of the fire. "Ananse lives on far side of jungle. When she stirs, we sacrifice a woman. She likes woman flesh the best."

I gulped. "Woman flesh?"

Ahmose pressed again. "What exactly is Ananse?" he asked intently.

The king blinked. "Ananse is giant spider."

Caught in a Web

Folding my arms across my chest, I said, "Sounds like your Calabash Trials equal death, death, and, oh, surprise, more death. I don't think we're going to keep playing your game."

Ahmose didn't translate. He stared at me with a mixture of you-probably-shouldn't-have-said-that and unabashed pride, his gray eyes crinkling as a corner of his mouth lifted. When I raised my eyebrows and gestured for him to do something, he let out a breath. Ahmose expressed my sentiment correctly, even if he didn't have the same huffiness in his tone that I'd had in mine. The king tilted his head, considering my words. There was no doubt the man was sharp-witted and enjoyed taunting us.

I'd come across men like the king before at my father's parties. Granted, those men had had million-dollar smiles and imposing statures, but the diminutive islander royal that sat next to us nibbling bug du jour was no less shrewd than the guys in expensive suits in New York City. In fact, he was probably smarter than most of them and certainly more confident.

The king sipped from a bowl filled with a hot and fragrant liquid. Curls of steam lifted from it, smelling of fresh and not-unpleasant spices.

I caught the scent of something resembling cinnamon or perhaps anise. If we were offered any, I might be tempted to try it. His craggy face appeared younger, smoothed out by either the steam from the tea he drank or the glee of pondering our demise.

"Once begun," he said between sips of tea, "the Calabash Trials must be concluded. Your man agreed to the challenge, if I recall. You are both bound to finish what you start, dangerous as it may be. My people don't take kindly to those who go back on their word."

"Go back on our word?" I countered. "It's not like we had a choi—"

Ahmose placed a hand on my knee and interrupted, "Then, if you have no objection, we'd like to meet this Ananse as soon as possible."

"Of course. Of course," said the king.

"Ahmose," I hissed, grabbing his arm, "I don't think this is a good idea. We're wasting time here entertaining this guy when we should be looking for your brothers."

"I know it seems that way, Lily," he answered quietly. "But this king and his village are the only things I've found so far on this island that don't have a broken path."

"What does that mean?" I asked.

"I don't know exactly. It's just that when I studied the possible paths after I saw the calabash gourds, one path shone brightly. I think I know which one to pick if we could just get to the choosing part of this game."

"Okay, but to get there we have to defeat a giant spider. Not something I wanted to cross off my bucket list, if you get my drift."

"I'm not sure what a bucket list is, but facing a spider should be no different for us than facing the ants. In fact, I would imagine it might be easier, since we're only dealing with one creature."

"Okay, I can see how you might think that, but in every movie I've seen with a giant spider—"

What's a movie? Ashleigh asked as I tried in vain to halt the replay of *Arachnophobia* in my brain.

I sighed. "Never mind. The good news for you guys is that you haven't got fixed mental images thanks to Hollywood versions of long-legged things that go bump in the night. Maybe this giant spider won't be all that bad," I said, attempting to convince not only them but myself. Tia wasn't creeped out by spiders at all, and Ashleigh actually liked them. She'd even had a pet spider at one point in the netherworld and, in fact, had woven its web fragments to make herself a sleeping hammock.

Apparently, I was the only one in our group freaked out by the idea of a giant spider wanting to consume my flesh. I threw up my hands. "Fine. But if we get eaten, expect to hear I-told-you-sos until our untimely demise on this island of death." The big man by my side gave me what should have been a reassuring smile, but I refused to be comforted in such a situation.

I wasn't some dumb blond actress who screamed about bugs, but giant spiders? I wasn't an idiot. When Godzilla comes to Manhattan, New Yorkers are smart enough to head out of town. This felt like a get-out-of-town situation. Seemingly, I was the only voice of reason in the group, and no one was listening to me.

The little king stood up and clapped his hands. "You will leave your weapons here."

"I don't think so," I said, tugging my bow as a warrior yanked it off my shoulder.

"We will keep your weapons safe," the king assured us.

Since Ahmose wasn't really giving me a choice, I reluctantly assented and watched my weapons disappear into the king's hut. Two soldiers came forward and wrapped our wrists together with a homemade rope that chafed. I raised my bound wrists to Ahmose and gave him a deadly look, then reluctantly followed him and our captors into the jungle again.

When we arrived at the designated spot, a tall wooden pole in a small clearing, the short man led me right up to it. He made a big show about binding me to the pole, girl-being-sacrificed-to-King-Kong-style. At any point I probably could have knocked him over with a slight push, but I gamely went ahead with everyone else's wishes. I grunted and tried to kick him in the shin as he pulled my ropes tightly enough to hurt. When he believed I couldn't escape, he went to help his cohort.

Meanwhile, Ahmose was actually aiding his captor in locating a tree he could be bound to. "Come on. Really?" I mumbled under my breath. As far as I was concerned, this little game had gone on long enough. After Ahmose was tied up sufficiently, my guy hit some sort of hanging bell. "Nice," I said as he soon skedaddled out of the clearing. "Ringing the dinner bell. Could we be any more obvious?" I shouted after his retreating form.

The canopy of trees shook, and I glared at Ahmose from across the clearing. "Just so you know, I totally blame *you* for this," I hollered.

"All will be well, love," he called back to me across the space between us.

"Uh, no. You don't get to shout endearments at a time like this!"

"Just concentrate. Use your power," he said, lifting his voice in such a way that it was soothing but understandable. I wrenched my body to try to break my bonds, but the ropes were too tight.

Can't wait ta see the beastie, Ashleigh said.

I, too, am curious, Tia added.

"Just shut it," I said, angry at everyone about our predicament, and finally settled myself against the pole. "Concentrate."

Closing my eyes, the three of us channeled our power. But before the link was complete, a tree branch snapped. I looked up and gasped when I saw a giant, hairy, brown leg emerge from the trees and lower delicately into the clearing. Once down, the thick limb resembled a thin tree trunk, and I blinked, wondering if my imagination had conjured it. Then another leg followed, and another.

Cold fear shot through my veins, and my mouth went dry. Why were the people I loved such idiots? Tia and Ashleigh were clamoring in my mind, but their voices felt distant, as if they were muffled or trapped behind glass. I couldn't get past my fear to hear them. The long legs lifted and set down again. All I could do was watch their progress. I didn't dare look up higher. I didn't want to see the mouth, the fangs, or a bunch of eyeballs reflecting my image.

Ahmose shouted from across the clearing, but his words also had no effect. Finally, the legs stopped moving. Two of them had passed over me. Two were on the edges of my peripheral vision. Now that they were closer, I saw the tips of the legs ended in a hard, pointed casing like a claw that sunk into the ground. I felt the creature's presence. It was ancient and old, and as it watched me my skin prickled. Once again I was in over my head, and there was nothing I could do about it. The air stirred. It was cold against my sweaty skin. All the hair on the back of my neck stood on end.

The legs quivered, and I wasn't able to stop myself from looking up. The body of the spider was hairy, too, and a bit darker than the legs. The abdomen was huge, with protruding nubs on the back that I thought must be the spinnerets. It lowered itself until its head and body almost rested on the ground. On either side of me long feelers twitched. Finally, I looked straight at the creature.

A half dozen or more black jewels winked from a hairy bed on top of the head. It took me a moment to realize they were eyes. Greenish lumps adorned the back of the spider. They looked like a cross between mushrooms and moss. I wondered if that was natural or if it was just a growth, a result of Ananse making the jungle its home.

Two thick, jointed jaws as big as a pair of doors twitched open and closed like kitchen shears, and a long, black fang hung from each one. A drop of white liquid oozed out of one. I trembled and pressed my back into the pole. King Kong was looking pretty good right about then. The giant gorilla had nothing on this spider.

The creature shifted the feelers, reaching out to probe me. It took everything in me to swallow back the scream. The feelers didn't hurt, but they were bristly and got caught up in my hair. The tips felt a bit like the pads on a dog's paws as they ran across my arms and swept over my neck. The feelers moved back, and the head came closer. I noticed the fangs were not only sharp at the point, but they were razor-edged on both sides. I swallowed thickly as the thought occurred to me that the edge might help the creature dismember the girls it ate.

Tia? I stammered in my mind. *Ashleigh?* But my inner companions didn't answer. Instead, a new voice penetrated my brain.

Well, hello, I heard in my thoughts. *It's very rare to encounter a girl who can speak with her mind. You're not the typical offering. It seems you wandered into the wrong place at the wrong time, my dear.*

Now desperate, I tried to shut out everything and reach for Tia and Ashleigh. But try as I might, I couldn't find them at all. A feeler slammed me back against the pole. It felt wrong not having access to my inner companions, like a part of me was missing or drugged. The feeler pinched me. "Ow!" I cried. When I looked down, my fuzzy brain realized that it wasn't a feeler but one of the fangs now embedded in my thigh.

Now, now, don't worry about your inability to communicate. My venom makes a lot of things difficult.

The trees of the forest had started disappearing. One by one they slowly faded from existence. The edges of my vision were becoming white. My body jerked once. Twice. It wasn't painful, not really, though it should have been. The venom must have paralyzed me, because all I felt was a tugging sensation and the slight tickle of the hairs on the spider as the legs brushed over me.

Oh, bother, the voice said. *I don't like it when they tie you up so tightly. They know I don't like my prey damaged.*

I felt tears dripping down my face, but I couldn't lift a hand to wipe them away. With a last jerk, my body fell forward, but I was picked up around my waist before I hit the ground. Prickly hairs rubbed against my back and legs, and then I was moving quickly through the clearing. The last thing I remembered before the world went dark was hearing Ahmose scream.

When I came to my senses, I was staring up at the soft light of a full moon. My leg throbbed slightly, but the pain felt dull and distant, more like an echo than anything that needed attention. I rocked gently back and forth in a comfortable sleeping bag, and the night air felt cool and soothing on my skin. The stars twinkled high above me. What a strange dream I'd had. I wanted to call Ahmose's name, but my tongue was swollen and my mouth tasted funny.

A woman was humming nearby. *Ah, good, you're awake,* she said. Her voice was comforting. Like a beloved aunt. *I'm almost done with your tapestry.*

That sounds nice, I thought and settled back, letting my mind drift as I thought about handsome knights, castles, and beautiful tapestries.

A few minutes passed, but something prevented me from falling back to sleep. An irritation stirred, telling me that my pleasant dream was wrong. I blinked and realized my eyes were very dry. In fact, there was dirt in them and leaves on my face. Shifting in my sleeping bag, I tried to lift a hand, but my arms were stuck. I looked down and stared uncomprehendingly at the white fibers around my body. All at once, everything came back to me. *The spider!*

"Whhaa . . ." I licked my lips and tried again. "What have you done to . . . to me?"

There was movement to my left and then the rustle of leaves overhead. I searched the shadows through the spinning leaves that drifted down. *I've been busy working on your tapestry. I do one for all my girls.*

"What?" I asked, twisting my head, feeling grateful to get the leaves off of my face.

I'll show you, the spider said. *Just be patient.*

As I hung there swinging back and forth, the spider danced around, invisible in the dark, and my limbs started tingling. I flexed my fingers and summoned my claws. It took several moments, but finally they appeared. I knew now that even if I couldn't hear Tia or Ashleigh they must still be with me if I could harness the power of the sphinx. As quietly as I could, I sawed back and forth on the sticky fibers that held me captive.

"Where's Ahmose?" I asked to distract the spider as I worked.

Do you mean your man? He's here. I don't usually eat males. They're too . . . gamey for my taste. My preference is women. They're much softer, you see. They dissolve more easily. Makes for a smooth and satisfying meal. But in this case, I'll give your man a try. He looks clean and might be tasty if I soften him up enough. Of course, he'd have to wait a while. Two of you this size is entirely too much to eat at once. It would just ruin my figure to be that greedy.

I paused when I heard the word *dissolve* and then continued sawing even faster. Finally, I got one arm free and then a leg.

Stop wriggling so much, the spider said. *You'll ruin your tapestry.*

Ignoring her, I freed my other arm and my leg. I then grabbed on to the web, swinging wildly as the cocoon holding me dropped to the forest floor. The line of web was sticky and dense. Looking down, I saw dozens and dozens of translucent ropes crossing and looping between thick branches. I reached above me and grabbed another thread, and then as carefully as I could, started making my way across, hand over hand and foot over foot, toward the nearest tree.

My foot almost slipped off, but I righted myself easily enough and kept going. When two threads crossed, I felt along the new thread until I felt comfortable. Then I whipped around the line bridging them to go down the new path. I finally spotted another cocoon several levels below in what I would guess to be roughly an Ahmose shape. I changed direction.

It took me several minutes to reach him, and though I pushed on his cocoon, slapped his exposed face, and called his name, I got no reaction. I wasn't sure what to do. With the power of the sphinx, I was strong. Maybe even strong enough to carry him. But I couldn't make my way across the web and lug him along, too. I decided I could at least try to free him and hope he'd wake up before I was finished.

I was only halfway through freeing him when the spider discovered me. *There you are,* she said. *There's no point in doing that. He won't wake up for at least another hour. He's a big one. Had to give him a double dose. Come along now. It's time to see your tapestry.* The spider, who had somehow crept up on me without me sensing her, which was an amazing feat considering my enhanced senses, shot out a web that wrapped around my ankle.

Before I could even mutter a word, the spider took off, and my leg was yanked above me. She dragged me behind her. Each web vibrated at my passage, and once she thumped my head against a tree branch. *Oh, sorry about that,* she called down to me as she continued to climb. *Hope I didn't bash in your brain. That's my favorite part.*

I didn't bother to answer her and tried again to reach Tia and Ashleigh. Neither of them responded. How was I supposed to access the power of Wasret when Tia and Ashleigh were missing? I thought.

I've blocked out the other two minds, if that's what you want to know, the spider said, as if reading my thoughts.

The beast paused, reeling in the long web that attached to my ankle and pulling me up toward her. When I was in the position she wanted me in, which happened to be at the end of a web attached to the uppermost limb of a tree, she moved her giant body. She circled the web like a gymnast before locking my leg in place. I shifted so I could sit up in the crook of the tree, which was so thin it barely supported my weight. Luckily, the web was strong enough to support the weight of an elephant.

"What do you mean, you blocked out the other two minds?" I asked as the pounding blood in my head spread back to my limbs.

Ananse, the spider, moved out on the web, her legs walking along the thread as delicately as a ballerina. Her gemstone eyes reflected the light of the twinkling stars above. *They were distracting,* she said. *The tapestry would be too complicated if I included them. Besides, they would only muddy the overall theme.*

"My tapestry has a theme?" I asked.

Oh yes! the spider said, an edge of excitement in her tone. *I used to weave the cosmos, darling. I'm the one who connected each planet to a star and each orbiting moon to a planet. The remnants of those great pieces can still be seen in the night sky, though most can no longer derive meaning from the fragments.*

No web was greater than mine. No territory vaster. The tales that men and gods spun when they looked at the stars came from my great celestial tapestries. Nowadays it's mostly guesswork on their parts. Only I know the true stories. Only I have followed the origins of the cosmos before it was born. Now I just remain here in almost total obscurity, weaving the boring and pitiful tapestries of an inconsequential tribe of islanders. Still, I like to practice my skills. Even if the subject material is dreary, my work is still as beautiful as I can make it.

"I see," I said. "But wouldn't you rather keep a person as interesting as I am around for a bit? You know, just in case I inspire you to create more works of art?"

Oh, I don't think that will be necessary. You see, now that the tribe has sacrificed the two of you, they are likely to ignore my needs for a few years. Besides, each person only gets one tapestry. Now that I've seen yours, I won't need to keep you around. Of course, there's also the fact that my web is, in itself, venomous. The poison has been seeping into your veins for many hours already.

I looked down at my leg, and my skin suddenly felt hot. "P . . . poison?" I said sickly.

Yes. Oh, it would take days to actually kill you. Weeks, even. You'll be long gone before then, I promise you.

"Ah, good," I said. "I'd hate to have to waste away."

I wouldn't want that either. I prefer my meals as nutritious as possible, and the web saps your energy, leaving less for me.

"Right. So, let's see this tapestry you made for me, then."

Patience, dear. Patience. It's not something you just toss at somebody. It's a work of art. It needs to be appreciated as such.

"Oh, I know art. Have I told you about the museum I frequent in New York? Lots of artwork there."

Really? They keep their art on display?

"Absolutely. Sometimes they rotate exhibits between different museums around the world. That way everyone has a chance to appreciate it."

I would like that. To have people see what I do and get the chance to talk about it.

Drawing up the leg that wasn't bound to the tree, I wrapped my arms around it and said, "Then tell me. Not just about my tapestry, but about the other things you've created. I'm happy to listen. I'm a captive audience, if you will," I said with a small laugh, betting the spider wouldn't catch the joke.

She didn't. My purpose in distracting the spider was twofold. I wanted to postpone my impending death, and I wanted to buy Ahmose time to wake up. My hope was that I'd sawn through enough of his cocoon that he could break out without my help. With any luck, he'd get away.

Well, to understand what and how I create, I'd have to start at the beginning.

"Fine with me," I said.

I cringed, knowing that if there was any way for us to get out of this intact, then we had very little time to find Amon and Asten before Cherty left. But one thing at a time. First I had to survive the spider.

I wasn't always the best weaver, you know, she began. *Others of my kind were much more talented. But I was a clever youngling, hovering in the shadows of my elders. I was an expert mimic. That came in very handy.*

My thigh wasn't bleeding, which bothered me. Perhaps something in the spider venom had made the blood clot. It didn't hurt either, even though I could clearly see the puncture wound. It didn't go through my thigh, but I was sure the muscle was severely damaged.

Meanwhile, the spider continued, *When I was assigned to weave the stories of kings and empires, I watched carefully how they rose above their peers and seized power. I took their wisdom and their craftiness into myself, and though I wove their triumphs, I purposely hid their methods for rising to* greatness. I became a flatterer and a cheat. You must understand that only one of my kind can be a Weaver of Destiny, and that was what I aspired to be more than anything.

One by one I manipulated the threads, seeming to give my enemies that which they wanted the most. Then I pulled the weave out from under them, trapping them in my web. I then devoured them and in doing so, absorbed all that they were into myself. I grew ever more powerful. Soon it became clear that no obstacle could stop my progress.

Finally, there were only two of us left: me and my master, Sibriku the wise. I spent centuries learning at his side, growing ever stronger and more powerful.

When I was ready, I challenged him to a game. I told him that fate would determine who would triumph. If it was to be him, then I would roll on my back and let him absorb me, but if I won, then I would become the most powerful creature that had ever existed and learn all the secrets of the cosmos. I then did something that Sibriku did not expect.

"What was that?"

I cheated. He did not expect it. This was how I beat him. How I beat all of them. But you remember he was called Sibriku the wise. He came to recognize my duplicity, but it was too late. Sibriku rolled over on his back, and I dissolved his body, absorbing his knowledge into myself.

"But now you are alone," I said. "There's no one left of your kind in the entire cosmos except yourself. No one to record your accomplishments. No one to help you spin your celestial tapestries."

That is right. Soon after Sibriku's death, I realized my folly. In gaining all the wisdom of the cosmos, I destroyed the one thing that drove me, for there was no one left to best. I tried to devise a new path for myself and tore into the fabric of creation. But even I, with all my wisdom, couldn't put it back together.

Then the gods were born. It was a result of the cosmos trying to restore equilibrium after what I had done. I retreated and watched as a powerful seer arose. We peered into each other's eyes, and I could not bear to see my reflection, so I hid in the deepest, darkest place in the cosmos. When the Unmaker came into power, I trembled, knowing he rose so that I might fall. I created this *place where all the lost and broken things could hide. I let go of my celestial web and fell.*

Now, here I am. Alone. Forgotten. Purposeless. I've tried to content myself with what I have and the fact that I still exist. But so many eons have passed, and I have given up hope that I will ever weave a celestial web again. Now I only feel pleasure when I eat. Speaking of which. Come, Lily. It is time.

The Fateful Tapestry

I wasn't ready to die. My great destiny was apparently to be supper for a cosmic spider. Not the way I thought I would go. Then again, a thousand strange ways to die had crossed my mind since I'd learned what I was. What had happened to me. I suppose death by spider wasn't the worst of them.

Ananse came closer and drew a sharp fang along the web binding my leg, freeing me.

If you like, you may come of your own accord, she said. *I will show you the way to your tapestry. It isn't far. If you aren't too squeamish, you may ride on my back. Oh, and don't think to use your tiny claws on me. They would break against my skin. My hide is older than your own sun and made of much tougher stuff.*

"Well, I guess I'd be safer riding on your back."

That is wise. You may climb my leg. There's a place behind my head where you should be comfortable.

Awkwardly, I rose to my feet. My injured leg felt stiff and swollen, but there was still enough strength in my arms for me to pull myself up the jointed spider leg. I grabbed on to the stiff bristles, and when I was seated comfortably on Ananse's back, she set off.

The giant spider moved quickly through the trees, her body twisting and turning lithely on the strong webbing. When she came to the end of a web, she leapt into the air, her big body almost floating like a kite as she spun out new webbing behind her. She landed on a branch and then leapt to another. The spider pulled herself up, me holding tightly to her back.

She headed toward a large tree. The largest I'd seen in the jungle, in fact. Ducking under branches, she wound her way around the trunk. I began to notice tiny bulges in the webbing. I guess people weren't all she ate, though most of the animals in the jungle were probably too small to feed a creature as large as Ananse. Finally, at the tip-top of the tree, which swayed slightly under her weight, she turned and showed me her handiwork.

There it is, she said, almost reverently. *Tell me, do you think it's accurate?*

I gasped softly. There, twinkling in the moonlight, was the most intricate web I'd ever seen. Dew glistened along the translucent threads, making them sparkle, and there was a slight green sheen to the material. It took time for my eyes to adjust so that I could see the depth of it and make out the shapes. When it finally came into focus, I realized it was a three-dimensional piece of art and what I was seeing was only the surface.

"It glows?" I asked, puzzled by the pulsating light in the web.

The spider answered, *A little. I used to be able to control all the colors in the cosmos, but this one is all I can manage now.*

"It's beautiful," I said, in utter awe of what she'd created.

Yes, yes, but is it accurate?

"I'm . . . I'm not sure what you mean."

Look closer, Lily. What do you see?

The spider moved down the trunk of the tree, her long legs clinging to the branches, and when she did, the web shifted into a series of pictures, like scenes in a great mosaic masterpiece. Shapes exploded before my eyes. I saw the entire skyline of New York. A brilliant sunset that cast tall shadows. Central Park had been re-created in great detail. Even the horse carriages twinkled in the moonlight. In the crook of a tree I could make out pyramids and starbursts of light that looked like tiny fireworks.

Ananse started walking down a long branch, and I marveled at how large her web design actually was. I thought the entirety of it was contained between two large trees, but when she turned, there was another section, this one a re-creation of my grandmother's farm. It was slightly different than I remembered. In the graveyard there was not one tombstone, but three. I wanted to go closer to see if the spider knew what names might be engraved there, but the angle we were at prevented me from seeing it in focus.

We went down another tree trunk, and on each level as we descended to the jungle floor, there was another scene. One was of a little countryside church and a bride and groom standing at the door, him carrying her down the steps while a few onlookers cheered. Another showed a vast desert with flat plateaus and a valley full of a living crop that quivered with pulsating light.

There was a monstrous crocodile surrounded by demonic creatures and a woman with horrible birds resting on her shoulders. I saw an old man sitting in a rocking chair with a group of children surrounding him, three in his lap, his head thrown back laughing. Then there was a man and a woman studying hieroglyphs inside a tomb.

In another section, I saw a dead man lying on a slab, a knife buried in his chest. A woman fell over him, weeping, while an Egyptian god stood guard. A young girl stood next to a unicorn, her hand wrapped around the beast's horn as it lowered its head. Light shone from the horn. The same girl, but now with wings, flew into a dying sun and brought it back to life. There was an old man placing an old woman into a sarcophagus while an Egyptian god looked on, his dog lifting his head in a howl. Other, younger people stood by watching. The woman was still alive.

I shivered.

The spider leapt to another tree, bringing an entire new web into focus.

In this one a dragon hovered over a slain knight, fire and smoke pouring out of his mouth as the girl knelt at the knight's side. The spider turned, and I saw a vast city being rebuilt. It was unlike any city I'd ever seen before. The buildings were connected by walkways and bridges. The next scene showed a girl soaring through space on the back of a unicorn leading an army of such riders. She brandished familiar weapons, and her face was lit with determination.

I pointed to her as the spider paused. "That's not me," I said. "If this is supposed to be my life or my fate or whatever, I think you've gotten a few things wrong. I can't exactly recall everything I've experienced, but some of these images aren't mine."

Keep in mind, the spider said, *the tapestry includes images not only of your past, but also of your future. These scenes depict all of the things that you will do in your life.*

"I get that, but how can I do these things in the future if you're just going to eat me?"

Ah, many misunderstand this. I suppose I shouldn't expect more of you than the native girls despite how special you are. You must remember that even though I have the ability to weave your fate, it is the fate you would have known had you not set foot upon the Isle of the Lost. Once here, your path is broken. I just give you a little glimpse of what could have been. It's a kindness. I think. To be able to see your life in such a way before it abruptly ends.

"Well, that's debatable. But regardless, you still have it wrong."

Oh? How so?

"Well, take this, for example," I said pointing at the winged girl speeding toward a dying star. "That's not possible. I can't do that. I don't have wings. I'm not a goddess or anything."

Are you certain? the spider asked. *Can you not sprout them?*

"Nope. Maybe it's Ashleigh. She was a fairy in another life."

No. No. I specifically blocked out the others.

"Right, but they're a part of me. I don't see a lioness here or the

African pride she came from. You've left out a big piece of my life by ignoring them."

Surely they aren't important pieces.

"I'd say they are. I can't remember how they came to be with me, but they've made a huge impact. There's no leaving them out. You'll have to add them if you want the tapestry to be right. Unless accuracy doesn't matter so much to you. I would have assumed a powerful being such as yourself would be capable of discerning those details. Perhaps you're not really as good of a weaver or as full of wisdom as you think you are."

Yes. Well, you see, the thing is, I can't just add the ways they influence your life. I'd have to weave an entire tapestry for each of them. It would be very complicated. Their webs would have to intersect yours at many different points. It's the only way to be precisely accurate.

"I see. Well, I guess if it's too difficult, I'll just have to accept an incomplete tapestry. It's a shame, really. Don't get me wrong. It's a beautiful accomplishment. And I can live with the discrepancy—well, live for the short time I have left—if you can. Of course, as an immortal creature, you'd have to live with the inaccuracy for quite a while. Perhaps it's not something you can accomplish at this point in your life anyway."

What do you mean by that?

"I just mean that you're not as young as you once were. Being out of practice is nothing to be ashamed of. I mean, look at what you were able to do after being stuck here on the island for so long," I said, extending an arm in a sweeping gesture. I wasn't sure if her gemstone eyes could see me or not, so I didn't take any chances with my expression.

The spider rubbed her two front legs together while she contemplated what she was going to do. I strained my ears, listening for Ahmose, but the only sound I heard was the rustling of the leaves in the night breeze.

I may be out of practice, Ananse said, *but I certainly still possess the skills necessary to create multiple tapestries. I once wove the tapestries of entire world populations. Three little girls shouldn't be a problem, no matter how intricately they are connected.* The spider clicked its fangs together. *Very well,* she said. *I will need to access the thoughts of the other two who reside in your mind to see how they have shaped and influenced your fate.*

"I think that would be best," I said. "Tia alone will be a very interesting addition. She's had quite a complicated life path. I think you'll find her tapestry very compelling."

Then it's decided.

A pressure I didn't realize was in my mind lifted, and I heard the familiar, now very confused voices of Tia and Ashleigh. Audibly, I said, "Tia, Ashleigh, I'd like to introduce you to Ananse. She is going to weave your tapestries. You should be very *quiet* so she can do her work."

Both girls fell immediately silent.

Ananse scurried across a thread and leapt quickly from tree to tree. When she'd gone a sufficient distance from my tapestry, she stopped. I climbed down and sat in the crook of a tall tree. "Do you want to bind my leg again?" I asked genially. "I don't mind. How long do you think it will take to finish? I'm so excited for the girls to see what glorious work you do."

Yes, Ananse said distractedly. *I mean, no. You're high enough now and the poison has likely weakened you sufficiently that you won't be able to climb down on your own. It will probably take me the better part of two more days. Of course, I'll have to weave night and day to get it done in that time frame.*

"Perfect," I said. "We'll just be waiting right here."

The spider turned, grasping a higher web, and hoisted her body upward. She quickly scampered down the thread and added as if speaking to herself, *I'll have to consume the boy first so I'll have enough energy for the task ahead. I've never done a tapestry so complicated.*

"*No!*" Ashleigh cried out using my voice. I clapped my hands over my mouth as the spider scurried back to me, as quick as lightning. Ananse lowered herself back down to my level, her back legs steadying the new web she hung from. Twisting her head so her fangs were within stabbing distance, she prodded me with her feelers.

What was that? the spider said, an edge of malice in her tone.

"Um, it's just that, before you eat him, you should know that Ahmose has a very big place in my tapestry, too."

Ananse cocked her head. *Be that as it may,* she said, *I cannot construct something so vast without energy. Do you think my body can generate threads out of the air?*

"Umm, no?"

"No" is correct. I have looked into the minds of your companions, and their potential fates are vast. In fact, the resulting tapestries might end up covering the entire island.

"But—"

She interrupted. *I assure you I'm up to the task, but it will require a great deal of energy, and I am depleted. I'm sorry if your man is important in your weave, but I'll have to leave him out.*

"It's okay." I assured her. "We understand. Don't we, girls?"

Of course, Tia chimed mentally.

Ashleigh didn't answer at first. I could almost taste her bitterness at having to play nice. *Do what ya hafta do, beastie,* she finally said.

Apparently, it was enough, for the spider moved off again, heading back to the part of the jungle where she'd cocooned Ahmose. When I thought the spider was a sufficient distance away, I mentally said, *Now!*

We concentrated, joining our minds together as Wasret. I knew that fear was a barrier for me. I had to let go and absolutely trust in my two inner companions. "Hurry!" I shouted aloud. I heard the crash and rustle of the trees as the spider rushed back to us at top speed. A bubble of pressure built up in my mind again as Ananse tried to block us, but she was too late. We connected fully for the first time, being spurred on in our desperation to save Ahmose, and were filled with power.

Completely calm, I opened my eyes and raised my arms. The light of the stars fractured and trickled into my frame. I looked down at my swollen leg and pulled energy from the trees and the animals and the cosmos itself, smiling as the wound closed and the poison was cleansed from my body. The spider landed on my branch with a resounding thump, jaws clacking and fangs dripping with venom.

What have you done? she demanded.

I ignored her and twisted my hands. My body became as weightless as moonlight. Slowly, it lifted of its own accord. When my legs felt straight and strong, I placed my feet on the branch. The part of me that was fairy knew how to balance instinctively. The part of me that was lioness knew I needed water, so I called water to me. It came from the air and rose from the river. When I cupped my hands, it pooled in the center. I drank until the lioness settled.

Lily, you have overstepped— the spider began.

"No, Ananse," I said, my voice quiet as distant thunder. "It is you who have overstepped."

The spider backed up, feelers twitching in the air. I knew she was desperate to touch me. Knew her feelers were how she read the minds of her prey. When I lowered my hands, her feelers mimicked my action and became useless.

"But you are not really Ananse, are you?" I said. "This is the name the mortals have given you."

How do you know this? the spider asked. *Why do you speak to me in such a way?*

"I know many things, fallen one. I know that you were once brilliant and beautiful. You were born a *megaraneae*, a cosmic weaver, entrusted with the most important task, creating balance and documenting history. But you sought power, and you broke the fundamental laws that governed your kind. When the cosmos could no longer ignore your crime, justice came for you, but you hid from it. Just like you hide from your true name."

You do not know of what you speak.

"Why, of course I do. Oh, it's not the name you started out with. No, this name is one you've crafted for yourself. It's your true name. It's branded on your heart. Isn't it, Abject Anthropophagus?"

In my mind, the spider screamed. Her long legs trembled, and she fell off the branch, landing in a web several feet below that held her quivering body. The human in me thought the spider looked like she'd been hit with a giant can of bug spray.

I leaned over the branch, looking down upon her. "Do you hear that name echo on the ocean of emptiness in which you live? Despite your ravenousness," I continued, "you will refrain from eating." The human in me cautioned that I must get my wording exactly right. "And when justice comes for you"—I leaned forward, staring into her jeweled eyes—"and I assure you it will, you will embrace your own fate with open arms—or legs, in your case."

When I stepped closer, the spider scrambled back, limp feelers trailing, hanging loosely on either side of her head. "I'd suggest you use the time between now and then to ponder the selfish choices you've made in your too long life. Then take the opportunity to weave your own introspective tapestry. Make sure you include your own ending. If it's any comfort, it will be the grandest work you've ever done."

The spider only trembled as it answered, *Yes, mistress.*

"Very good. Now I suggest you lead the way to my traveling companion and free him from your web. We have much work to do."

As you wish. Ananse righted herself weakly and, on shaking legs, made her way down, pausing only to make sure I followed.

She took me on a winding path through the trees of the jungle and down strands of webbing, creating new webs where they had become weak. I trailed behind, stepping lightly and confidently, my balance perfect, my mind and spirit harmonious and focused. In fact, it wasn't until we approached Ahmose, and the spider drew her fang down the side of the cocoon holding him, that I felt my control as Wasret slipping.

The fairy part of me struggled to break free, but I maintained enough power to place my hand on his cheek and direct the moonlight into his body. There was something wrong with him. Something inside that I couldn't fix quickly, and time was of the essence. I was, however, able to eradicate the poison. He took a deep breath and blinked open his eyes.

"Lily?" he said.

I shook my head. "You speak to Wasret now, Son of Egypt."

If I'd wished to use my power upon him, I could have, but I balked at the idea. I did not wish to control him and, besides, Ahmose had not yet reached the time when a final name should be assigned. His true name would be revealed later. I closed my eyes. There was something to come regarding this man and his brothers, and it was related to my own future. I considered turning my power upon myself to discover my own true name. Wasret was the name given to me by the cosmos, but I was more than that. I sensed it at my core.

The spider had woven the fate of Lilliana Young, at least partially. I wondered what she'd see if she'd had the ability to weave my fate. Then again, I knew no one in the cosmos, not even the last remaining megaraneae, could discern what I would become. I'd have to wait and find out for myself.

The fairy continued to pull, breaking pieces of her conscious-ness away as Ahmose shifted and freed himself from the web cocoon. Alarmed at the fairy's strength and determination, and too weak to stop her, I commanded the spider to leave us and told Ahmose to follow. I stepped off the web and fell lightly to the ground. Despite the distance, my body absorbed the impact easily.

Ahmose followed as I made my way back toward the clearing. Once there, I turned to look on the spider's domain. Closing my eyes, I sensed her watching us but as long as I was Wasret, she could not act against me. Not while I used her true name.

"Come," I said to Ahmose. "We must return quickly to the village. Your brothers await."

The fairy bucked against me as Ahmose took my hand. "Are you all right?" he asked, concern etching his voice. He pulled a leaf from my hair and cupped my neck. "I saw the spider bite you."

"Yes," I replied. "She did. But I have healed myself."

"You can heal?" he asked.

"It's a simple thing," I replied, cocking my head. "You yourself have this ability."

"True. I didn't know Wasret did, though."

I nodded, ready to move on but then paused and cupped the back of Ahmose's head, bringing his lips down to mine. He pulled me against his body and ran his hands down my back until they circled my waist.

After a lengthy kiss, he raised his head. "What was that for?" he asked, a smile lifting the corners of his mouth.

"I was merely trying to appease the fairy. She wishes to dissolve our connection, but we must maintain it for at least a while longer. My ties to your realm are still too fragile. Come, Ahmose."

I took hold of his hand and pulled him along behind me. He squeezed it and changed our hand positions so he could walk alongside. The fairy settled, and I knew that a companion such as him was an important piece of the puzzle in determining what I was, what I would become. When we entered the village, the guards wore shocked expressions. They clearly had not expected us to return.

Lifting a hand when the crowd gathered around us, I said, "You do not need to sacrifice to the spider any longer. Her time on this island is short. Still, it would be wise for you to avoid her domain. If you get caught in her web, the venom will still affect you."

If they were surprised that I could suddenly and fluently speak their language, they didn't show it. "What have you done?" the tiny king demanded as the crowd parted to let him through. "If you've angered Ananse . . . ," he threatened, shaking a finger at me.

"Insidious imperator, you will bring forth the calabash gourds immediately. If I so choose, I could have you groveling at my feet, but we are short on time. We have completed your tasks. We have survived the spider. Do as I say before you suffer the consequences."

The men scrambled even as the king stared sullenly. I knew he was trying to find a loophole. Some way he could punish me to instill fear in his followers. To show he was the man in charge. My fingers twitched to humble him, but it was not necessary. The king took a step back and bowed, if not sincerely then at least obviously. His soldiers followed his example, and three of them stepped forward, producing the gourds.

I smiled, narrowing my eyes at the king. I'd guessed his game. He'd never intended to give us what we sought. In one gourd, there was a snake. A poisonous and deadly one. In the next was a rotten fruit teeming with tiny insects. One bite from any of them would cause a terrible sickness. The third gourd was supposed to contain a map. It did, but what Ahmose had not been able to discern was that the map was drawn on Ananse's web. It would leach poison into anyone who touched it, also bringing death.

"What a clever king you are," I said. "I'd like to offer you a bargain."

"A bargain?" he asked, fingers twitching greedily.

"Yes. If we choose the map, you will carry it for us and lead us to our destination personally."

His eyes became thin slits. "And should you choose something else?"

"If we choose a different gourd, then Ahmose will give you his power to summon the rain. And," I added, "you may keep my weapons."

The king frowned at this. I knew he'd intended to keep my weapons all along, but he rubbed his jaw as he considered the possibility of gaining Ahmose's power.

The crowd erupted in excitement. It was something the king wouldn't be able to deny. The fact that the people showed no fear of losing their king meant they didn't know what he had done. I wondered how he'd accomplished it. Had he made a deal with Ananse while we were figuring out how to chop down a tree using ants? I knew the villagers coveted Ahmose's ability and would pressure him into doing as we asked.

Reluctantly, he agreed, probably thinking we were going to choose the wrong gourd anyway. Wanting to waste no time, I made a show of choosing the gourd, more to appease the people than the king. I saw his eyes alight as I placed my hand over the gourd containing the snake. I whispered its true name, and the poor creature settled down and slept. Hovering over the gourd containing disease, I paused. Then I went to the one with the map, stopped, and looked between the two of them, finally resting my hand on the one with the deadly map.

Reaching inside, I took out the map and raised it triumphantly in the air. The people cheered. With a smile on my face, I bowed my head and handed it to the king. He wrinkled his nose in distaste and immediately tried to summon his best tracker to guide me instead. "No, great king," I admonished. "You promised to lead us yourself."

I shoved it into his bare chest, and he leapt away as if I'd thrown him a burning torch. It had already touched his skin, but he carefully picked up the map using the edges of his colorful skirt and shouted to his people to make way. When I reminded him about my weapons, a warrior quickly produced them, and I deftly strapped them onto my back.

The king dropped all pretenses of civility once we were surrounded by the trees.

"I can heal you, you know," I said as I followed him. "If you lead us faithfully and quickly, I'll remove the venom from your body."

"How did you know?" he asked.

I shrugged. "I just do."

Desperate for the gift I'd offered, the king discarded the map and led us straightaway to the place we wanted to go. When we came upon the stone well hidden in the copse of trees, he said, "There. I've brought you. Now do as you promised."

"You haven't deceived us, now, have you? I'd expect nothing less from you."

"No. This is the Well of Souls. Once you go in, there's no way to get out, at least as far as I know. So I'll thank you to heal me before you go down."

I stepped up to the edge of the well and peered down. There wasn't a pail or a rope to indicate it was used to collect water. It was just an empty opening that felt . . . hollow. Like the depths of the well existed beyond the edge of the cosmos. Even with my abilities, I couldn't hear or see anything. Ahmose picked up a pebble and tossed it in. There was no sound. Still, it felt like the right place. The king was sweating and rubbing his hands together.

"Very well," I said, and closed my eyes. I considered letting the poison remain. With the little contact he'd had, it would take years for him to die, but those years would be long and painful. Decision made, it only took a moment to wipe away the effects of the spider venom from his system. "It's done," I said. "Try to lead your people with wisdom rather than fear."

"I'm glad to be rid of the two of you," he said as he scrambled away from the well and disappeared into the trees.

I leapt up onto the edge, the fairy in me delighting in the way my body moved. The lioness balked at leaping into the unknown, as did the human, but I ignored them. My intent was to jump into the well, but Ahmose took hold of my arm. "Shouldn't we fashion a rope?" he asked. "How will we get back out?"

"Fly, I should think," I said, and gave him a cheeky smile before stepping off the edge.

17

The Well of Souls

"Lily! I mean, Wasret. Wait!" Ahmose cried out. He even reached out to try to snatch me from the air, but I'd already fallen too far. The man standing beside the well gave a frustrated cry and then soon followed after me. His large body blocked out the little light that filtered down from the diminishing opening above.

The shaft of the well was wet with damp, and the air grew cooler the farther we descended. The stones smelled of life and death, growth and decay. It seemed fitting for such a place. Ahmose was able to control the speed at which his body dropped as well as I, so he didn't hit me on our way down but stayed just above. A silvery, pale gleam lit up the stones on either side of me, and when I glanced up, I smiled, seeing Ahmose glowing brightly in the dark.

When the yawning pit I sensed beneath us opened, the two of us dropped lightly to the floor of a vast underground cavern, our feet hitting stone. Ahmose's light filled the space as if he were a lightning bug trapped in a clay water jug. When I asked if he was injured at all, his negative reply echoed, bouncing off rock and scurrying down dark passageways. Each *no* seemed to warn us not to proceed any farther.

He asked if he should draw down the power of the moon to illuminate the cavern to ease my passing. I glanced around. The small opening we had passed through cast a weak beam of light, but with my catlike eyes, it was as clear as moonlight on an open plain. I told him to preserve his energy. Saving Lily's body had weakened him severely.

Scanning the surface of the dome, I saw other pinpricks of illumination. Each one shone down on us, brightening the Well of Souls. Without my power, I might have mistaken them for holes in the dome that let in light from above. But with my senses I knew each beam was the remnant of a soul, a dying light too forgone, with no hope of moving on.

The spider had been right about this island being a place for the lost and the broken. The Well of Souls was full of beings that flickered in and out of my vision. Ahmose sensed something otherworldly, but he didn't have my power to name them. When I did, they flared into view. I knew what they were and, more important, what they'd been. I saw no reason to cause Ahmose unrest by describing the scene in full detail, so I let him enjoy the pretty lights and kept my knowledge to myself. If he asked, I'd tell him. Otherwise, it might be a more pleasant journey for him if he didn't know the sorrow of the place.

I could smell the cool dankness of the Cosmic River as it worked, beating against the well. Over time it had caused small breaches. Little pools of the black water had collected here and there in hollowed-out, stony places. I crouched down, peering into one, and saw the lights of the hundreds of tiny creatures that made the river their home. They were no longer living.

It was easy to understand how the human part of me had mistaken them for stars. They weren't, of course, but the human mind was very limited. Admittedly, the lioness, the fairy, and the human had been exposed to much more than the average sentient being. Still, their perception of the cosmos was fractured. Hampered by their narrow views.

The Sons of Egypt weren't much more advanced, though they did have vast potential. That was appealing to me. I'd need a companion who could learn and grow.

I stretched out my hand to Ahmose, and though he eyed me

curiously, he took it and asked, "Do you know where to find them? I cannot sense their path." His gleaming eyes peered at me in the darkness and then searched ahead, taking in things mortal eyes couldn't.

"No. You wouldn't. Not down here. Even I cannot discern which chamber holds them. At least, not yet. I can tell you that this tomb, for this is indeed a tomb of the lost and broken, contains dozens of chambers, caves, and cisterns all attached by tunnels. To search them all, we'll have to pass through them, and I guarantee that not all of them will be empty. Some of the things in here have been locked away for a long time. And some of them may be unhappy at being unearthed." I paused and looked up at my companion. "Will you be able to retrace our path once we begin?"

"Yes," he answered.

"Then shall we proceed?"

He gave a slight nod, and I turned toward an opening on the right. There was no particular reason to head in that direction except that the brush of air against my skin on the right was slightly warmer than on the left. I considered why I'd chosen it. The lioness was drawn to warmth. The human knew of fantastic stories that told of ghosts being drawn to cold spots. She was right about that, though ghosts resided everywhere in the Well of Souls, not just in the cold. The fairy in me believed first impressions to be lucky, but I knew there was no such thing as luck. Taking these various concepts into consideration, I thought it might bode well for us to continue through the right passageway.

We initially proceeded through a series of caverns without any harm. They weren't exactly empty, but the beings residing there did not represent any danger for us. They were fading ghosts of creatures clinging to long dead bones, most likely the lost villagers from above who'd wandered down seeking either adventure or death.

I studied Ahmose as we walked, letting him lead the way. Truthfully, it didn't matter which path he chose; we'd have to continue our search until we found his brothers, no matter what we came across. Once he placed his hands on my waist and lifted me over a section of broken stone. I could have easily levitated over it, but I liked the feeling of his hands on my waist.

He took my hand possessively in his, and we proceeded. I glanced up and noticed that his hair curled just beneath his glowing ear. It was still raven black and glossy against his sparkling skin. The contrast was quite becoming.

The different girls whose minds I had access to all admired Ahmose for various reasons. One liked the rugged edge of his jaw. Another, his eyes. Ahmose had broad shoulders and a strong back. He was soft-spoken and kind. His lips invoked pleasant memories that tickled the edges of my mind.

When I looked at him, all these feelings and thoughts were a part of me. They influenced the way I saw Ahmose and created a foundation, a connection to him that I wouldn't otherwise have. The first glimpses I'd had of the world around me had come through the eyes of Tia, Lily, and Ashleigh. I understood who I could be and what it was to live as one of them by seeing into their hearts and minds.

The human, still connected to me, had labeled me as some sort of monster. She thought I was like a Frankenstein. A creature made from different parts. One who terrorized and destroyed. But that wasn't how I defined myself at all. The reason I'd come into being was not to ravage, but to unify. To see what was missing and add it. To discover what was unnecessary and remove it.

But despite my dislike for her viewpoint, in a way, she was right. I was an amalgamation of sorts. I wasn't wholly Lily or Tia or Ashleigh. I'd taken the most interesting pieces of each of them—the best parts of a human, a fairy, and a lioness—and grafted them onto myself. Granted, my body belonged to Lily, but there were subtle shifts inside the body that the human girl couldn't have made happen on her own. I had some of the traits of the fairy and the lioness, but, unlike when they were a part of Lily, those traits were fully integrated into my body.

For example, I could now infuse my human cells with the energy of living things. This ability was partially due to the fairy, who absorbed energy from forest trees, but the other part, channeling the power of the starlight, was something even she couldn't do. As Wasret, I could regenerate indefinitely, the one noted exception being the removal of my head from my torso.

Where Tia lent Lily her claws, I made them unbreakable. The arrows of Isis no longer limited me, for I could forge arrows of my own making if necessary. All I had to do to defeat an enemy was to whisper his name to the feathered shaft, and it would seek out the heart I'd named, no matter where it hid in the cosmos. But my purpose, despite what they believed, was not that of an avenging angel. I at least knew that much about myself.

Then there was my ability to communicate mentally. It was no longer limited to my own internal workings like it had been with Lily, Tia, and Ashleigh. If I wanted to, I could mentally converse with Ahmose. But for the moment, I wanted to practice sharing my thoughts verbally. I delighted in the idea that I finally had my own voice, and yet now that I did, I didn't know what to talk to him about first. I was so new and raw, I couldn't yet be certain that anything that came to mind would be from my own thoughts and not from those of my predecessors, regardless.

Despite the fact that I was powerful and knew things instinctively that others didn't, my inner voices made me cautious and doubtful where Ahmose and his brothers were concerned. The emotions I felt when I considered them were raw and volatile. I didn't experience these sentiments when confronting others.

The idea that one or more of the Sons of Egypt might reject the opportunity to become my companion stung a part of my being that I didn't yet understand. Perhaps this was due to the pieces of each girl I carried inside me. Though I knew I was unique, I couldn't deny my own innermost workings. My way of viewing the cosmos and the beings who resided in it was tainted by their views, and yet I knew I could form my own opinions, which might or might not be widely varied from theirs.

Where that thing that made me Wasret came from, I didn't know.

In fact, this joining was the first time I had become truly aware of myself as a distinct and separate entity. It was almost as if I'd been asleep, adrift in a womb-like space. The three girls had called to me, pulled me closer each time they came together. With each connection, I gained more sentience. At first I was simply a source of power. A merging of the three of them and their abilities. But now I was also something more.

We came upon a cavern that housed what Ashleigh would believe to be a banshee. The creature wailed, singing of Ahmose's death. Both his demise as a human from long ago, as well as each death he'd experienced since, and would yet encounter in the future. I could see the moment when Ahmose heard her beautiful song.

"She sings of death," I explained.

"Strange that singing of death would be so beautiful."

"Your afterlife is not death, you know. True death is an instantaneous transition. It's beautiful beyond anything you've ever experienced. It's glacier blue and sun-drenched gold. It's harmony, contentment, and perfection. You see, death is an awakening, not an ending, like most beings believe. Her song is just a tiny glimpse of what awaits you."

"The idea of peace holds appeal for me. Do you . . . do you believe that a true death is still possible for me? For my brothers?"

"Yes. It is still within your reach. A true death is even possible for me."

"Wasret?" he asked.

"Yes, Ahmose?"

"Is Ashleigh or Tia or Lily dead?"

I wrinkled my nose as I considered his question. It didn't hurt me that he asked. Not really. The fairy surged up at his inquiry, blooming like a dying flower, and Ahmose's words were the sustenance she needed. She wanted to break away, free herself from the bond. But I was stronger now. I was able to hold her back and stay in control.

"No. They are not dead. They reside in me. They are a part of me." I did not deceive him. The three girls *were* still with me and would be until my steps in this realm were certain and I did not need to lean on them for aid. Even after that their voices would remain as echoes in my mind that would forever influence me.

"I see."

"Does this bother you?"

"No. I am glad that they aren't dead."

"But you wish they were here instead of me." I didn't know why I said it. There was something inside that desperately wanted to know the answer to the question, even though logically, I knew the answer didn't make a difference. Not with the future looming before us, hovering like a great stone over our heads. It would drop long before we were ready.

Ahmose considered his reply for a stretched-out minute. "I am happy to be here with you. But I am also happy to know that they are not gone forever. You must be aware that I have seen glimpses of you and I together like this when I studied my path."

"Yes. I know of it. It frightened the three that were here before me."

"It particularly bothered them because they thought it might mean losing themselves." He winced slightly. "And my two brothers."

I frowned. "Your brothers might not accept me and what I am as easily as you do. As for the three girls, they are not lost. They are still here," I explained to Ahmose patiently. I sensed it would take time for him to understand this concept.

"They are," he said. "But they have no control. They cannot decide where they will go or what they will do. Their existence is limited now."

"Limited? How are they limited when they will be witnesses to wonders beyond their imagining? When their lent strength will brighten the dark corners of the cosmos?"

Ahmose appeared ready to continue the conversation, but then he held back and offered me a small smile and his arm instead. "Speaking of my brothers, we should find them, don't you think?"

"Yes," I answered, taking his arm.

The man at my side slid his eyes away from me, and a prickly inner turmoil erupted as a result. He was quiet as we passed through a series of empty caves. I bit my lip, concerned that something I'd said had upset him. I didn't want him to misunderstand me. The human part of me had read his body language and knew something was wrong.

Strangely, the fairy was racked with emotions of grief. The lioness wasn't terribly concerned with his reaction to what I'd said or done. A lioness didn't bother with emotions. She relied on instinct and focused on the task at hand without letting her mind wander to other things.

Weighing my options, I decided to adopt the response of the lioness in this case and, as soon as I made the decision, the weeping of the fairy and the concern of the human melted away quickly, like starlight through spread fingers. It was a relief not to have a cacophony of opinions attempting to sway my own, each possessing the illusion of control.

We trod a path through a long corridor and came upon a fork. "Which way?" Ahmose asked, more to himself than me, as he pondered the choices.

As I stared down the one on the left, my eyes glazed, something whispered softly to me from its depths. My mind churned, laboring like a grindstone over wheat, and yet the thing that transfixed me remained elusive. It beckoned as it moved through holes in the rock and sank itself farther into the dark, panting its hot breath into the air.

"Can you hear it?" I asked Ahmose as I stared into the blackness ahead.

"No," he answered. "Do you hear my brothers?"

"It's not them that call to me. It's something ancient. It doesn't belong here."

"What is it?" Ahmose asked, sliding in front of me and adopting a battle-ready stance.

In a singsong voice, I chanted, "Winding paths and rivers, hiding the sun and stars, the bite that causes shivers, we've lost what once was ours."

I don't know how long I stood there singing softly to myself, but I came to alertness only when Ahmose shook me soundly. "What lies down that path, Wasret?" he demanded. His gray eyes flashed like desert thunderclouds.

"Are you angry with me?" I asked, pressing my hand against his solid chest.

He let out a shaky breath. "No. It's just . . . I don't want to lose you, too."

"Lose me?" I questioned, cocking my head. "That isn't possible. I cannot *be* lost." His expression didn't show relief like I assumed it would. "Ah," I said, supposing his continued concern was for more than just myself. "You should know that down that path lie your brothers," I told him. "Your brothers and . . . and something else. Let's hope that we find them before *it* finds us."

Ahmose clapped a hand against his neck and rubbed it, then nodded. "Agreed."

We passed a hollow containing a ghost wearing a coat of leaves, each one as worn and threadbare as the autumn forest just before the snows come. When he spied us, he shuffled hurriedly in our direction, losing several leaves in the process.

Desperately, he gathered them up, clutching them to his bosom, and begged us to help him sew them back on. I knew when they disintegrated he'd have to face what lay beneath them—a skeleton. It wasn't his own but represented a person he'd murdered and buried beneath a pile of leaves in a long-ago place and time.

Disgusted, I pulled Ahmose past him.

The next cave held a creature clothed as a woman wearing an old lace wedding gown. She'd never been a mortal, but she'd tricked a mortal man into marrying her. She'd wanted to love him, but she'd craved human flesh more. During their honeymoon she lost control of herself and consumed him, starting with his toes. Now she rocked back and forth in her dingy gown as she sang softly to the groom who would always be with her, just not in the way he'd expected, and picked at her toes until they bled.

We passed a cavern with something that looked like a horse but was really a mortal who'd beaten his horse to death. He ran and ran over rocky terrain that gouged into his soft feet, though he actually went nowhere. Then he gorged himself on shoots and thick clumps of grass that grew from the stony ground, eating until his belly distended and split open.

Ahmose, thankfully, saw only tiny glimpses of these things because these were the oldest beings in the tomb. The ones almost wrung out of energy. It took a monumental effort on my part to pass by those that still deserved their punishments, but I somehow managed to do so, clinging to Ahmose and shutting my eyes when the view was the most dreadful.

There were others. Those who sat quietly, their vitality long spent. For those ready, simply giving them permission to let go was enough, and they were able to move on to their true deaths. There was a kind of satisfaction I found in helping them break away from the thing pinning them to the place.

Then we came upon a large chamber that was blocked with stone. Energy pulsated from the other side. I placed my hand upon the barrier and closed my eyes.

"Are they in there?" Ahmose asked in a whispered voice.

"They are," I answered. "But something else is in there with them." Letting out a hissing breath, I said, "I cannot move the stone. Unfortunately, I've spent much energy in grappling with the spider and dealing with those beings we've passed by. My physical body is weak, and my soul is as a wide-eyed newborn's. There isn't much living here I can draw upon other than you, and I won't deplete you more than you've already been. You've already sacrificed more than you should have to keep us alive."

If he was surprised at my words, he didn't show it. "I can try to find a path through the stone," he said quietly.

I nodded and stepped aside. Ahmose found a tiny chip in the rock and followed it with his fingertip, murmuring a spell as he did so. The stone shifted and split. A beam of silver light shot through the crack, and as I watched, it widened. Ahmose pulled me back several steps and moved me behind him. Finally, with a resounding boom, the stone broke into several large chunks, while one section shattered, shooting rock fragments and debris through the passageway. Dust rained down softly upon our heads.

There was a loud groan, and a whoosh of hot air blew my hair back. Ahmose stepped forward and summoned his favorite weapon, a cudgel, from the dust. It gleamed in the darkness, glowing with an unearthly light matched only by the illumination shining from his skin. "We'll proceed cautiously," he whispered, drawing me close to one side as he raised his weapon with the other.

I had weapons of my own, but I did not draw my bow. If I needed my spear-knives, I could access them quickly enough. But something told me my mind was the weapon I'd need more than anything else. The cavern we entered was larger than any of the other formations we'd crossed through. There was no doubt that his brothers were here somewhere. Ahmose would have called out to them if I'd let him, but I cautioned against it. We didn't want to attract the attention of the other being that resided there.

We wound around rock outcroppings and beneath stone arches until we finally came upon two knights that stood frozen in place. It was as if they were guarding the entrance to a yawning pit that fell away behind them. The ground rumbled at our approach, and we paused. When the quaking stopped, we gingerly stepped ahead.

Ahmose lifted the visor of the first knight. "It's Asten," he whispered excitedly.

While he made his way to the second, I wrestled with the lioness. She was disturbed at seeing the Son of Egypt in that manner. I, too, was unsettled by his appearance. He looked dead. When Ahmose verified that the second knight was indeed Amon, he stepped back and asked the question I didn't have an answer to.

"Why are they like that?" he asked. "They don't respond to anything, and I can't sense them, even standing right beside them."

"They are here—there's no mistaking that—and yet I cannot access their minds either," I admitted. "Whatever happened to them must have occurred after Lily summoned you to your body. Even if I tried to raise them now, I couldn't. They wouldn't hear me."

The cavern shook angrily, and we staggered and almost fell. The two knights remained rigidly in place. I tilted my head, considering, and stepped carefully to the edge of the pit they guarded. Staring into the darkness, I sought out the creature, the ancient one I knew shared this resting place with the Sons of Egypt. It was powerful, and it resented our intrusion. Its name evaded me, and it reminded me of something. Something I'd faced before. The thing stared up at me from its shadowy abyss with resentful and deadly yellow eyes.

"Come to me, Winding One," I called. "Come and tell me why you keep these men prisoner."

I fell to one knee as the large creature slid up from the shadows, causing the ground to shift beneath me. The tongue shot up out of the chasm first, tasting the air. Then a giant head appeared. I knew in an instant that it wasn't Apep. No. This was Apep's other half, his polar twin. Desperately, I reached for his name, but like Apep's, it eluded me. The name almost crossed my lips, but then it slithered back into shadowy realms.

Why do you disturb me? The great snake opened its jaws, fangs glinting in the light cast by Ahmose's body as it lifted its head and set it down on the lip of the pit. *You have no business in my domain, goddess,* it hissed as it glided ever closer.

"I did not mean to disturb you," I said. "We've come for the Sons of Egypt—the two guardians you've trapped in your tomb with you."

You cannot have them, the snake said. *They are mine.*

"You didn't consume them. So why do you wish to keep them here?"

The snake paused. I knew what the crafty creature was up to. He wanted me and Ahmose to be trapped here just like the other two. But I wouldn't allow that to happen.

Mine is a lonely existence, he answered. *They are my companions.*

"But in this state, they cannot talk with you."

True. But they cannot leave me either. The snake resumed his progress, creeping closer to me and Ahmose, who raised his cudgel in warning but lowered it when I shook my head.

"I know why you are alone," I said. "I know where to find your other half. The one who hungers."

Foolish goddess, he hissed. *I know where my other half is. I just can't escape my prison. Even if I could, we would only rend the cosmos in two in an attempt to consume one another.*

"Yes. And now I understand why." I took a step closer and lifted a hand, palm up. "I can give you what you seek if you will sacrifice your two companions."

How, little goddess? How can I trust you when the last one I trusted did this to me?

"Surely, you can find the strength. I promise you that I will not only reunite you with your twin and restore that which has broken within you, but I will also punish the one who put you here."

What can you offer me to prove you tell the truth?

"I will whisper the name of the one who ripped you from your home. You will feel the truth of it in your bones. Come closer, great one," I said.

The snake wrenched his body farther out of the pit and moved his head alongside me. I shivered despite myself when the great fangs passed me by. A vivid memory of the snake's twin impaling my leg and filling me with his poison clouded my vision for a brief moment. Leaning over, I bent my head close and whispered, "She who harmed you has been named. She is Abject Anthropophagus."

The snake lifted his head and an enraged scream echoed in the chamber, causing great rocks to fall and break on the ground next to us. When he finally settled, he said, *Very well, goddess. You may take my companions. But if you fail to fulfill every part of your promise, I will haunt you in your dreams and consume each soul that resides in your form.*

The snake lifted his head and bit down on a rock, pumping two pools of white liquid from its fangs on either side. *Take some of my venom and rub it into their wounds. They will wake soon enough. But be warned that they are trapped here in spirit as much as I am. Without their bodies, I'm afraid they won't be able to leave either.*

"Thank you," I said to the snake as he descended into his lonely pit once again.

Ahmose carefully used the edge of his cloak to scoop up the venom. When I'd removed Asten's armor to locate the puncture wound left by the snake, he rubbed in the white liquid. The wound healed before our eyes, and color returned to his face.

The lioness in me thrilled at seeing Asten blink his eyes. He reached out and wrapped his arms around me. Ahmose clapped him on the back, and the three of us moved over to Amon. The venom did its work quickly, but Amon didn't wake the same way Asten did. He bucked and moaned as if fighting off a nightmare. When he finally did open his eyes, he grabbed hold of my shoulders and shouted a name, but it wasn't mine.

"Lily!"

The human side of me lurched violently. The pieces that made me what I was split apart at the seams, ripping me asunder. I screamed, and the cosmos heard it. A great storm brewed over the Isle of the Lost just as my eyes rolled back and I collapsed into Amon's arms.

Necromancing the Stone

"Lily? Lily!" Voices cried out to me, but my mind felt dark and fuzzy. I couldn't open my eyes, and my head pounded with the beat of a thousand jungle drums. "Come back to me, Nehabet, *please,*" the voice implored.

I groaned. "Amon?" I managed to wrap my lips around the word, but my tongue felt thick and wrong in my mouth. It was like I'd drowned and been wrenched violently ashore, hands pounding my chest, willing me to live again.

"Wait," another voice said, and I felt the cool touch of a hand on my forehead. "They are wounded."

"Where?" a man asked. "How? I don't see any injuries."

"Their wounds are on the inside. They've been riven apart like the snake. Amon caused this." The accusation had come from Ahmose.

Despite the arms that cradled me close, I felt cold, empty. I shivered and retreated, mentally distancing myself from the others.

Another being came close and touched my hand.

Something stirred. *"Asten?"* the lioness whispered, using my voice.

"Tia," he said, relief evident in his tone. "Will you recover? Are all three of you there?"

"Yes. We are all here, but . . . something's missing."

"Wasret," Ahmose said with a heavy sigh. "She's gone. Bits and pieces of each of them went with her."

I felt a small trickle of energy course through my body. Ahmose was attempting to heal us. *"No,"* Tia said as she opened my eyes. *"You must not. You are too weak to give more."*

Ahmose set his jaw stubbornly, but Tia was adamant, and he finally backed away. Asten took our hand and pressed a quick kiss on our knuckles, concern etching his features. Turning my head, Tia stared into the face of the third man, the one who clutched us in his arms. His features instantly blurred. I turned completely away from everyone then, even Tia and Ashleigh. I curled up in a ball, keening in the background, unable to look out of my own eyes.

Then the man, the one whose voice had penetrated the darkness, the one who held me tenderly, even now, said, "Lily?" His voice was soft. "It's time for you to remember."

There was a pause. *"She doesn't want to, Amon,"* said Tia.

"I know she doesn't. She's afraid. You all are."

"Amon," Asten started. "Maybe we shouldn't push them just yet. Let them rest while you summon our bodies."

Warmth trickled into my skin where the man touched me. It felt familiar and comforting. His body was arched over mine, sheltering, protecting, as he attempted to coax me out. Somehow, using just his voice, he'd created a space where it was just me and him. Despite the others around us, I knew he loathed to leave me just then. But I wasn't ready to see him yet, to talk of the things I knew we needed to.

"I've brought what you need," Ahmose said, and he handed a bag to Asten.

The man holding me shifted and sighed. "All right," he said. "Ashleigh? Will you sit here with Ahmose for a time while I help Asten?"

I felt my lips pull back in a grin as the fairy rose up. *"Aye, I will,"* she said, and Tia joined me in the back of my mind, curling up companionably next to me. If she were still a lioness, she would have been licking our wounds.

The man settled us back against a rock. Ahmose sat beside us and wrapped an arm around our shoulders. Ashleigh nestled into him and sighed softly. *"It's glad I am ta see ya, lad,"* she said.

"I'm happy to be with you again as well."

"Are ya certain o' that? Seems ta me like ya took a shine ta Wasret. Maybe you're regrettin' havin' us back."

Ahmose was quiet for a moment. He pulled a strand of our hair and wrapped it gently around his finger. "No. I don't regret having you here. I'd never regret that. But you must understand, Wasret was all I had of you then. How could I reject her?"

"Pretty words in the moonlight don' sound the same in the day. She is not like any of us."

"No. She's not."

"Do ya think ya will come ta love her, then?"

"I don't know. She's not as . . . as easy. Do you remember everything?"

"No. Jus' bits an' fragments. But it's fadin' away, like a dream. One thing we do remember, though, is how she felt about ya. She wants ta keep ya after all is said and done. Assumin', o' course, that we all survive."

Ahmose nodded solemnly, and Ashleigh threaded her fingers through his. *"Ach, lad, what 'ave we done ta ya?"* She planted a kiss on his forearm. *"Troubled thoughts knit yer brow near as much as they do ours."*

Together we watched as Amon summoned his power. His form gleamed bright as the sun in the dark cavern. Reaching into the bag Ahmose had provided, he uncapped the jars. Four dancing lights orbited around him, one in the shape of a bird. Then he took out something small and placed it in his palm. As he chanted a spell, weaving it in the air, Ashleigh asked Ahmose, *"What did ya bring?"*

"Their canopic jars. Also, Amon needed a piece of their mortal bodies to create new ones for them to inhabit. In the case of Asten, I was able to get a lock of his hair."

"I see."

Power swirled in a vortex, and Amon opened his hand. Wind swept through the cave and lifted the hairs from his palm. There was a small explosion in the center of the vortex. White, brilliant lights, millions of them, filled the whirlwind swirling in front of Amon. They spun faster and faster. They became so bright I had to look away. When the light dimmed, a healthy young body had formed. It gleamed with starlight.

Asten moved toward the body, which could have been his twin. Then, closing his eyes, he stepped into the gleaming form and disappeared, armor and all. The body twitched, the chest rising and falling in its first breath. When it opened its eyes, I saw Asten. His chest and legs were bare. With the white skirt wrapping around his waist, he looked like the ancient Egyptian prince come to life that he was.

Picking up the bag, Asten opened the remaining jars, then pulled out the second object and handed it to Amon. This item was bigger, bulkier.

Ashleigh turned to look at Ahmose, a questioning expression on her face.

"Amon's wrappings were too stubborn for me to get any of his hair, so for him it was easier to simply bring his hand." Ahmose finished with an apologetic grimace.

"His—his hand?" Ashleigh stammered. The sick feeling in her stomach was something all of us felt. We watched a bit horrified as Amon hefted his own mummy-wrapped, dismembered hand and held it out, not shying away at all from his former appendage. Summoning his power again, he wove his spell. The hand lifted into the air, twirling like a macabre Halloween decoration hanging from a tree before exploding into dust. The gleaming powder entered the maelstrom of light.

This time the ball of light was golden bright. It exploded in rays that filled a space roughly the size of a human form, each ray growing more dazzling until Ashleigh had to look away. When the light dissipated, another body had taken shape. The golden man I could not bear to see stepped toward it.

From the deep place where I hid, I looked upon the form of the man and saw a chiseled jaw and molded lips. His strong chest was bare like Asten's and covered with smooth, golden skin. Dark lashes brushed his cheeks, and when he took his first breath, his lips parted. Brilliant hazel eyes fluttered and opened. Immediately, they locked onto mine. I trembled, and the aura around him brightened, casting his form into pure golden light once more.

His shoulders slumped visibly. But after just a moment of hesitation, he approached and held out a hand. "Young Lily?" he asked. "Will you come with me?"

Ashleigh liked Amon and would have readily accepted his help in rising, but I held her back, knowing it wasn't her he was asking.

Let me, I told her quietly.

When my hand grasped his, it was because I'd willed it myself. He lifted me to my feet, nodded to both of his brothers, who watched us with searching eyes. Amon indicated that I should walk with him. He released my hand in what I assumed was an attempt to help me feel more comfortable.

I followed the golden man as he led me farther away from the pit where the snake had curled up to sleep. We walked around stones and rocky arches until we were far enough away from his brothers that we could be alone. Of course, we were never truly alone, not with my inner passengers, but at least we were as alone as we could be given the circumstances.

When he stopped and turned to me, the first words he uttered were not what I expected. "I've missed you," he said, trailing a fingertip along my hairline, brushing the loose strands back. Something inside me cracked. An inner wall that I'd built between us.

I swallowed and tilted my head, reaching for something to say. "But you've seen me," I stammered, "in my dream."

"Yes, but it's not the same. Not like it used to be."

"How was it before?" I asked. My breath caught as I waited for his reply.

He didn't answer right away. Instead, he pressed his palm to his chest and pulled something from it. It gleamed with a different light than his skin.

I gasped. "Is that . . . is that your heart?" I asked, shaken at the idea.

"No," he replied simply. "It's yours—your heart scarab, anyway. If you want to know how we were before, then take it. All you need to do is cup it in your hands and will it to restore all that has been lost."

My fingertips stretched out almost of their own volition, but then I drew back. The other two voices in my mind were quiet and still. They waited expectantly to see what I'd do. "Why?" my voice cracked. "Why do you want me to remember?" I turned my back to him, unguarded and vulnerable.

"Because, Nehabet. What you feared came to pass anyway. Was-ret has been born. I won't have you giving yourself over to her again without you knowing everything." He placed a hand on my shoulder. Warmth and love trickled into me. "That's why I sent her back, though I knew it damaged all of you." My stomach quivered; my limbs shook. "Please, Lily," he said. "I know it hurts. It hurts me, too, when I think of what we might lose."

I turned to face him, and his hand slipped down my shoulder to grasp mine. He pressed on. "Don't you see, Nehabet? I need to know which path you'll choose to walk upon because I am determined to walk it with you. If you are being asked to weigh your own life against the good of the cosmos, then you need to put everything on the scales. Only you can determine which value is greater."

The fear and pain that had sunk deep into my heart, weighing it down like a stone, like something baleful and lifeless, melted at his words. His utter acceptance of me caught hold of my soul and cradled it. Amon was what compassion and unconditional love felt like. It was freeing. Whatever I chose to do, he'd support me.

I took a deep breath, taking the scent of him into my lungs and stepped closer. Running my hand behind his neck, I pulled the golden god down to me and pressed my lips against his. Light filled me as his sunshine lips molded against mine. Stroking my hand down his arm, I opened his fingers, and placed my palm over the heart scarab. Our hands locked together and a rushing wind filled my mind.

Memories flooded me. I saw everything at once—all the pain, all the joy, all the triumph, and all the loss. It culminated in the netherworld, in that last dream we shared together before I left him behind.

We were to be separated again. The gods were content with the fact that I'd saved Amon, brought him back to the afterlife. They saw no reason that we needed to be together, but they'd granted us one last moment. A single opportunity to cram an infinite amount of love into a finite period of time. One last chance to say goodbye.

I'd told Amon that I would never forget him, and I hadn't. I'd just locked up everything I felt for him in my heart, hiding it away, and then placed it into his hands. I knew that by doing that, even if the gods used me for their own purposes and tossed me out when they were finished, even if it meant my demise, Amon would at least have that part of me. I'd hoped we'd find each other again. And I'd also known that our reunion might not happen until the afterlife.

He'd thought the gods were responsible for keeping us apart, for stealing our dreams. We hadn't been able to see each other, not truly, since that last time, despite our bond. But Amon came to realize that the reason it happened wasn't because of the gods, it was because of me. I'd done that to him. To us.

Still, I didn't regret it. He was right that I'd been worried about Wasret. I'd been afraid that losing myself meant losing him. I'd known what could happen, would happen, if he chose to remain by my side through the inevitable trials. I'd thought that forgetting him, moving away from him, would keep him safe, keep our love safe. Or at the very least, that forgetting myself would make the transition easier when Wasret inevitably rose up. How could I willingly, knowingly give up something as amazing as I'd found with Amon? Not knowing was the coward's way, but it was the only way I could see at the time.

The kiss ended, but I moved toward him again to kiss him briefly, softly, once more—an apology for what I'd done. When I opened my eyes, the golden gleam had diminished, and I could finally see the face of the man I loved. "I'm sorry," I said, my eyes filling with tears. "You're right. We should have done this together."

"They didn't give us much time to talk it through," he said reassuringly. "But know, Young Lily, I am with you, whatever you choose," he said, stroking my cheek. "If you want to run from this, from their expectations of us, we'll run."

"No," I answered. "At least, not yet. I need to talk with Tia and Ashleigh first. And then we'll have to consult with Asten and Ahmose as well. It's not just us anymore," I said, touching my forehead to his. I folded his fingers over my heart scarab once more. "Will you keep it?" I asked, unsure if he still wanted to after all we'd been through.

"Always," Amon said, and touched the scarab to his chest. His skin absorbed it, and when it disappeared, he wrapped me in his arms.

"You'll have to teach me that trick," I said, pressing my cheek against the hard planes of his bare chest, listening to his new heartbeat. We stood like that for several moments, until finally I stepped away and held out my hand. He took it and together we made our way back to the others.

Two sets of eyes flickered to my face and then to our clasped hands.

"She remembers," Amon told them.

Asten nodded, an unreadable expression on his face.

Ahmose grunted, turning away and collecting the things we'd brought with us. When he handed me my bow and quiver without making eye contact, it hurt. He was important to me. I loved him. But I loved Amon and Asten, too. Everything was confusing, and I had a hard time sorting out my feelings from Tia's and Ashleigh's, especially now that we'd fully bonded to become Wasret.

Amon refused to let go of my hand and was content to let Ahmose lead the way. He followed our path back toward the open shaft where we'd first entered. Asten passed us by, giving me a small smile that only lifted one corner of his mouth. It was as if the rest of his happiness had deflated and that meager effort was all he could muster. He gave me a nod and then moved alongside his much larger brother.

I studied them as they walked together. Asten attempted to draw Ahmose out with halfhearted jabs at humor while Ahmose strode with a stiff back and a too-quiet demeanor. There was a telltale slump to their shoulders and a tiredness in their gait. Sadness over the state of those two men leached into my heart and burrowed deeply. The happiness I'd felt over my reunion with Amon ebbed.

Seeing Asten and Amon step over the rocky ground with bare feet made me wince. It was within my power to make clothes for them, and yet I shivered at the notion. None of us were too eager to embrace the powers of Wasret again. Personally, my plan was to avoid channeling both her and her power at all cost. If I'd thought my shoes would fit either of them, I would have gladly given them up.

We came to a section of recently fallen rock, and Ahmose paused. "This is the way we came earlier," he said as he crouched down, inspecting the rocks, looking for a path. While he did, a tingling sensation crept up my spine, tightening the skin along my scalp. Something was watching us.

Rubbing my arms, I glanced around. *It smells of anguish*, Tia cautioned.

"It's smelled like that since we came in," I replied.

Yes, but somethin' watches us from the shadows, Ashleigh said. *Can't ya feel it?*

I could. When I alerted the others, they fashioned weapons from the sand and guarded Ahmose's back as he worked. My senses prickled as a sensation of one's hot breath on my neck flared and then melted away. Lifting my head, my cat eyes peering into the darkness, I sniffed and caught a new scent on the air. It smelled of rotting meat, swamp, and corrosion.

From the surrounding corridors a steely fog crept over the ground creating a soupy, fetid cloud. The air became sticky and humid. Amon's and Asten's bare backs and arms soon glistened with sweat.

"What is it?" Asten asked. I wasn't sure if he was asking me or Amon. Before either of us could answer, we froze. A clicking sound, of claws or talons against stone, echoed from the surrounding caves in such a way that we found it impossible to tell where it was coming from.

The sound wedged itself deeply in the place inside me where fear existed. Each scrape of a claw chafed and irritated the already raw unease I felt. It was like prickly clothes against sunburned skin. Of all of us, I knew what hid in the caves. True, we'd passed through them easily enough before, but that was because Wasret knew which ones to avoid. Her abilities frightened off most of the creatures. Now they knew she wasn't with us, and they were coming.

Finally, Ahmose cleared the path. Rocks and debris hurtled all around us. Stalactites with surfaces smoothed over like refrozen ice cream fell, crashing down around us, making the passageway even less traversable. Once the dust settled, he jumped into action.

"Let's go," Ahmose called out, grabbing my hand and pulling me along. He didn't even pause to see if his brothers followed.

"Amon?" I called out, but he and Asten trotted behind us, weapons drawn, as they picked their way across the debris, trying to find the smoothest places to step. "I can't stop them like Wasret did," I warned him. "She hid most of them from you. Some of them were simply horrible, but others were dangerous."

"Yes," he answered. "I knew she kept things from me."

I felt like I should apologize, but we were moving too quickly for me to get a word in. We passed a ghost. He was very bright, considering. His head snapped up at our passage, and his mouth formed a rictus grin as his eyes flashed. His cloak was torn and shabby, and when he moved it aside I saw he held a skull in one hand, à la Hamlet.

He stroked the smooth top of the skull and cackled as he called out to us, "Come back! We have questions." I had twisted to glance at him once more before we turned a corner and was shocked to see it wasn't the ghost speaking, it was the skull.

The three men around me glowed with power, their skin as luminous as if they stood in a spotlight on a stage. "You might want to tone down your light," I warned them. "The two of you aren't wearing enough clothing. Ahmose is like moonlight through a small window, but the two of you are shining like New York City. People in space could see you."

Asten's lips curved upward, his brown eyes glinting as his light dimmed completely. Amon, too, reduced his light, though I could still feel his warmth at my back. It was as if the light had been merely a trick to disguise the true heat that radiated from deep within him. Now the only illumination came from the little light put out by Ahmose. Our rasping breaths and the pounding of our feet drummed out the other noises I heard as we passed through cave after cave.

"We're close," Ahmose said finally.

A brush of fresher air hit my face, and I smiled as we rushed toward the main cavern. We came to a sudden stop at the end of the passageway. The small pools of water that sat stagnantly in rocky hollows had grown. The entire area was now filled with black water that lapped at our feet. In fact, the stony floor had changed.

Amon lifted a leg, and I saw that the once-dusty passageway was now spongy and soft. He shook a foot, and thick clumps of mud dropped to the cave floor. Above us, the lights of the little dead creatures winked slyly as if they had orchestrated the entire thing from their lofty posts.

The fog crept in again from dozens of passageways, and I saw a ripple in the black water. It stirred the dead starry creatures that made it their home. The stench I'd smelled before—swamp and rotting meat—returned, and my nerves prickled as the lioness sensed a completely new predator.

Still, something smacked of the familiar for both of us.

"Let's not wait around here," I said, then pointed up. "The shaft we entered through is up there."

Ahmose put his hand on my arm. "You can't fly without the power of Wasret, can you, Lily?"

I bit my lip. "No."

"Then I'll carry you."

"You can't," I insisted. "You need to conserve your energy."

"Lily, you're hardly—"

Whatever he was going to say didn't matter because not five feet away from us, a monster burst out from under the water. It was the largest crocodile I'd ever seen. It targeted Amon. Fortunately, instead of clamping on to Amon's waist, the giant crocodile slammed against a boulder and the heavy jaws of the creature snapped together mere inches from Amon's belly.

Asten took hold of my arm and wrenched me close. Amon quickly levitated out of the range of the beast, who had slipped back into the water. Asten picked me up in his arms and followed. Ahmose trailed behind, his ascension slower than his brothers. I wrapped my hands around Asten's neck, his soft hair tickling my fingers.

"That's not just any crocodile," I murmured.

Looking down, I gasped as the beast sprang out of the water and snapped at the place where Ahmose's legs had just been. He'd drawn them up just in time.

"It's gotten bigger!" I shouted.

The three of us surged up. Amon entered the shaft first. Just before Asten plunged ahead, I looked down. To my horror, the crocodile had grown three times its original size. It attempted to catch Ahmose one last time, scrambling with claws up the sides of the dome, before it fell back with a splash high enough to get us wet. After we were inside the cool confines of the well, I let myself breathe a little, especially when I saw Ahmose coming up behind us.

Asten set me down on the edge of the well, and Amon took my hand and helped me down. An island breeze stirred the edges of my shirt, along with the leaves in the trees. The full moon had nearly set. It sat low in the sky, cold and hard against the suppleness of the dark jungle as it drenched us in its garish light.

When Ahmose finally touched his feet down on the thick grass next to us, he took hold of my shoulders, his eyes raking over me. "Cherty might be gone," he warned.

"Maybe he waited," I offered. "If we can just make it to the beach before sunrise—" I began.

Ahmose looked disconcerted. He rubbed a hand through his hair as he interrupted. "Lily, it's been three days."

"What?" I demanded. "What do you mean?" My heart dropped as if I'd been tossed back into the well. "That's not possible."

"I can sense the paths," he said. "Not only are the creatures on the island lost, but the island is, too."

"What does that have to do with it?"

"I'm afraid that time works differently in the well. All I know is that the path that led us here has aged longer than we would expect."

"Are you certain?" I asked.

"Unfortunately, I am," Ahmose replied.

Just as he finished those words, the ground shook, and I stumbled against him. "What was that?" I asked. "Has Apep returned?"

"I'm not sure."

The ground heaved again and buckled. This time I stumbled to the jungle floor along with Ahmose. Asten helped me up. Amon had picked himself up from the base of a tree that stopped his roll. Before I could form another question, the well cracked as something boomed beneath it.

"It can't be," I murmured as Ahmose handed me to Asten and took a look down.

"It is," he said gravely as he scrambled backward. "We've got to leave this place. Now!" he declared.

The land beneath our feet surged violently, and all four of us were sent flying. Nearby trees tore away from the jungle floor and crashed around us. The Well of Souls burst explosively, the stones shooting like cannonballs, some of them ripping away branches.

Amon called out my name. "Lily! Lily, where are you?"

"I'm here," I answered, pushing away a heavy branch that had fallen over me.

Once we were together, we looked for Asten and Ahmose. Asten had been grazed on the back of his head with one of the stones. A lump was forming, and he was bleeding profusely, but he was alert enough to follow us. Ahmose had rolled to his feet, but he didn't turn when we called his name. Instead, he stared at what remained of the well.

"Ahmose?" I asked. "Are you al . . ."

My breath left me as the word trailed off. I'd come around Ahmose's side and turned to look at what had transfixed him. The ground rumbled again, and he automatically reached out a hand to steady me. We both watched as the snout and huge jaw of a crocodile emerged from the gaping hole in the ground. Its teeth were now the size of traffic cones. When the eye appeared, I stepped back, pulling Ahmose with me, desperate to leave before the creature freed itself.

"I thought the dead things couldn't escape the well," I said, more to myself than to anyone else.

"That thing's only half-dead," Amon said.

Sharp claws tore the ground on either side of its head, and it wrenched its body side to side to exhume itself.

"What do you mean 'half-dead'?" I questioned.

"Don't you recognize him?" Amon asked.

Just then, the crocodile thrust its head to the side, trying to snap at me. I was too far away, but the giant reptile didn't seem to notice. Its heavy jaw opened, its sharp teeth in vivid detail. The reptile's breath washed over me, stinking of rot and decay.

"No." I shook my head. "It's impossible."

Before my eyes the creature grew even larger. Heavy limbs burst from the earth.

"Can you shift?" Asten asked Ahmose, his face intense.

"I don't think so," Ahmose answered. An expression fraught with meaning transpired between them.

"Then you'll ride my back," Asten said. With that, his body shimmered and the light grew, coalescing into the form of the starlit ibis. Beside me, Amon also changed. He gave me a small smile, and then his features blurred, the golden rays that ruptured from his body forming the shape of a second bird, this one a golden falcon.

Ahmose hurried to my side to help me up as the falcon screeched, his cry echoing across the island. When I was settled on his back, the falcon raced across the grass to a spot where enough trees had toppled so he had clear access to the sky. The great bird flapped his wings and, with me clinging to his neck, soared upward.

A moment later, the ibis followed after us, Ahmose riding on its back. We circled the treetops, and I glanced down at the place where the Well of Souls had once stood. The crocodile had pulled the rest of its body from the ground and sat there, head lifted, looking up at us with beady black eyes.

As we angled away, heading toward the distant beach where Cherty had left us, a voice echoed in my mind, and it was one I recognized.

I'm coming for you, Lilliana Young, it said. *There's no escape.* He then laughed. *We know where you are now. And the Unmaker has promised me vengeance.*

I didn't even try to suppress the shiver that racked my frame. Dr. Hassan's traitorous assistant, Sebak, had returned somehow. It was bad enough knowing that Seth and the Devourer were after me. Now the evil necromancer-slash-Godzilla-crocodile had returned from the dead, too.

Wrapping my arms around Amon, I buried my face in his golden feathered neck just as the sun burst over the horizon. It bathed the Island of the Lost in its yellow light. Despite the cheerful way the light filled the air, there was a chill inside me that not even the sun, not even Amon, could take away.

The Belly of the Beast

We found the beach quickly enough. The two great birds scanned the shores for any sign of *Mesektet*, but Cherty was gone. After a brief debate, Asten and Amon decided they had no choice but to fly in search of him. Only Cherty had the ability to navigate the Cosmic River. If we tried to do it, find Heliopolis or even Earth on our own, we'd inevitably go astray. The only other choice was to stay on the Island of the Lost with a very hungry spider and a vengeful crocodile big enough to eat all four of us and still feel hungry.

I told them all of Cherty's warning not to look back on the island when leaving it, and then, with pounding wings, we left the beach. Amon rose higher in the air, keeping the sun at his back as we flew. The Cosmic River flowed beneath us, stretching as far as the eye could see. Soon we entered the mist that surrounded the island. Long after we passed through it, we kept our eyes forward, hoping the island and the sun that shone upon it had disappeared. I knew that once it was out of sight, even if we wanted to find it again, odds were we couldn't.

My sense of equilibrium vanished, a concerning thing, especially for the cat within me. In fact, it quickly became difficult to discern between the space above us and the river below. Twice we almost flew into it accidentally. It was like being in a house of mirrors. In space.

Gravity worked differently now that we didn't have the timbers of Cherty's ship solidly beneath our feet. My hair rose off my shoulders, and my body felt weightless. Clinging tightly to Amon was the only thing that grounded me. Amon was worried. So were my inner passengers.

Getting lost on the river was easy enough when we were on the boat, but at least the boat provided some sense of balance, of normalcy, in the shifting cosmic terrain. One slip, and we'd plunge headlong into the river, becoming dinner for whatever hunted the dark waters. I knew Apep was still out there, and I also knew the only way to stop him from devouring us was Wasret.

None of us were too eager to give ourselves over to her again. At least, not until we had no other choice. Amon had brought us back. I wasn't sure he'd be able to do it a second time. It was too big a risk.

We flew for hours and hours. The vigilance necessary to keep us airborne above the river was taking a toll, especially on the birds. I knew Amon and Asten needed food. Their new bodies hungered when they woke, but neither I nor Ahmose had anything to give them. The two newly raised mummies were doing all the work, and I could see that their energy was beginning to wane.

Ahmose did his best to find a path, but now that we'd located his brothers, the trail he sought had become unclear. The Sons of Egypt always had an inner sense of where they were in relation to everything else in the cosmos, but the Cosmic River was different. It was wild and untamed. Pesky rules like gravity and direction didn't apply to it so much. Now that the brothers were strengthened by their reunion, Ahmose should have rebounded. Instead, he had no sense of direction. It was that, coupled with the fact that we traveled along the river, that left us flying blind.

"Take my energy," I begged Amon when he banked unexpectedly and then struggled to right himself.

Our continued bond still allowed the possibility of an energy exchange, but Amon was very stubborn and seemed determined to place extreme limitations on my offer. He acquiesced, but only took enough to sustain his flight.

As I stroked his feathered neck with my hands, I willed energy into him. It trickled from my fingertips into his body at a frustratingly slow rate. It drained me, but not nearly as much as when I'd been fully human. I realized then that Tia and Ashleigh were also sharing their energy.

We continued in that manner for quite some time. Ashleigh and Tia despaired that we couldn't aid Asten and Ahmose in a similar fashion. The two of them debated over how we might accomplish it. I couldn't tell how much our combined strength was actually aiding Amon, but we started to feel depleted of energy. I soon slumped over against his neck, exhausted, but I kept my hands pressed tightly against him. After another hour, he cut off the siphon altogether, insisting that he'd taken enough.

No more, Nehabet, he said.

I stirred, not realizing how close I'd been to falling asleep. Rubbing my eyes, I said, "But you're the one flying. I'm just sitting here, and I've eaten within the last day." Ahmose and Asten turned their heads to look at us. My voice had carried in space, and I winced, hoping I hadn't spoken loudly enough to draw the attention of Apep.

No, Amon countered patiently, *you were in the Well of Souls more than one day, remember? Besides, I won't have you weakened to the point of falling off. To lose you in the river is unthinkable. You know what lives in those waters.*

I shivered. He was right about that. I absolutely did not want to fall in. Looking to my left, I saw Asten was gliding, preserving as much energy as he was able to.

"How are they?" I asked, my voice more restrained.

Since I had direct contact with Amon while he was in his bird form, he could speak to me mentally, much the same as Tia and Ashleigh.

He could also hear his brothers that way as long as they were close enough, but I couldn't speak with the two of them. I knew Ahmose was weak. He'd done something for me, something Wasret knew, but he'd hidden it from us and, try as we might, we could not bring it to our recollection.

They are . . . endeavoring not to give up.

My eyes filled with tears at his words. It was quite obvious to us that whatever Ahmose had done had taken a huge toll, and not just on him. The Sons of Egypt were connected, and if they were struggling to sustain him, then it must be very bad indeed. That Amon wasn't saying anything either alarmed me. Perhaps I was reading too much into it, but I knew Asten's and Ahmose's hearts. It wasn't just the arduous journey we were on that made them consider giving up. It was more than that. And it had everything to do with me, or at least with all three of us.

The starlit ibis cocked his head, peering at me with a sparkling eye as he drew his wings up. Fatigue had set in long ago. Each time he beat his wings I winced, seeing how difficult it was for him. I wondered how long we could continue on this path until his exhausted limbs would work no more and I lost both him and Ahmose. It broke my heart to even think about it, so instead I reflected on the first time I met him.

To the casual observer, Asten came across as one of those men with an ego big enough to irritate any woman to the point of storming off, but he was also charming enough to reel them back in. He was devastatingly handsome in the way that the most wickedly desirable boys are. He was a temptation that beckoned a girl to dangerous places. That was only his surface persona, though. At least that was my perspective.

Interestingly enough, Tia's view of Asten was entirely different. A lioness sought out a powerful mate. In that way, she admired all three of the Sons of Egypt, but Asten held a special place in her heart. When she looked at him, she didn't see the cheeky man with a roguish gleam in his eye. She saw an equal. One who didn't quite belong with the others, but had made his home with and fought with them and for them anyway. Tia liked that he saw her, knew her, and counseled with her.

The ibis glided behind us, resting a bit as he trailed behind Amon, taking advantage of his draft. I bit my lip and closed my eyes. Tia mourned. As much as I loved Amon, I knew as she did that Asten needed us. He flourished when we were with him. We reminded him that he was good and strong and worthy of being a Son of Egypt despite his mortal origins. He was free around us and relaxed his guard. There was no need for him to put on a show.

Loving Asten was easy. It made sense. We knew that Asten had been watching our dreams for a long time. Had seen himself a part of them, and yet denied himself his own dream to show loyalty to his brother. This made Asten truly special. He was tenderhearted. He saw every dream, both the good and the bad, and he cared for us anyway.

Then there was Ahmose. There was no denying that what I felt for the big man was more than friendship. I'd fallen for him before I remembered Amon. My heart still ached from seeing him with Ashleigh, knowing that he loved her more than he did me. I allowed this hurt to linger, even knowing I'd done the same to him.

In my defense, Ahmose knew of my connection to Amon even as he wooed me—well, us. In his mind, he saw our paths merge. He felt it was inevitable. His experience wasn't that different from Asten in that regard. But where Asten had dreamed of our being together and then denied it, Ahmose had embraced the possibility and pursued me. True, he'd stepped aside easily enough, when I'd asked him to. He deferred to Amon when I'd regained my memory. But I knew it hurt him. He felt betrayed by me, by all three of us.

He'd been so sure his future path rested with Wasret. Perhaps he was the brother all three of us most related to. We didn't like thinking about Wasret's point of view, though it still lingered in our minds.

As for Amon . . . When I thought about the golden god who carried me on his back, my mouth curved in an involuntary smile. Amon was mine. It was simple. It was . . . well, perfect. Though he treated Tia and Ashleigh deferentially, he did not love them, not in the way he did me. For him there was no confusion. Wasret held no sway for him. Though Ahmose believed it, Amon did not hold that our becoming Wasret meant I was still in there somewhere.

I tended to agree with him. It was unclear to us where Wasret went when she did not inhabit our body, but it was quite obvious to us that she was not in residence. And though we had no clear memory of what our lot had been when she was in control, we did know that the beings we were had been suppressed. In fact, they had begun to diminish.

It's the heart scarab, Amon said, interrupting my thoughts.

"What do you mean?" I stammered.

I didn't want to intrude, but I thought you should know that your heart scarab was the way I brought you back. It protected you from disappearing completely. Though I should warn you that I am uncertain if this will be the case from now on. I fear that now that you have your full memories back, there is nothing anchoring you. When she possesses you, she takes it all.

"You anchor me, Amon. If it is at all possible to bring me back, you will."

I hope you are right, Young Lily. There was a pause for a long moment, and then Amon said, *You should be aware that harboring your heart scarab also allows me not only to communicate with you but to read your thoughts.*

"Oh. Well, that's . . . awkward. Just how much did you hear?" I asked as I quickly tried to figure out where all my thoughts had taken me. I'd learned that nothing between me, Ashleigh, and Tia was a secret. I guessed I'd have to add Amon to that list. The idea was slightly disconcerting.

Amon was quiet for a moment. *Possessing your heart means I have access to all your wishes, hopes, thoughts, and desires. This sustained me during our time apart, when I was prevented from communicating with you, though there were instances when this proved difficult. You should know, though, that possessing your heart scarab does not give me access to Tia's or Ashleigh's thoughts. I only hear your response to them.*

"So this has only been since I got my memory back?"

No.

I swallowed. "Do you mean you felt my . . . desires, heard my thoughts, even when I couldn't remember you?"

Yes, he answered softly. *The only exception to that was when Wasret took over. The powers of Wasret blur my connection to you.*

"Do you mean I disappear?"

Not exactly. You're not gone—it's like you're hiding behind a wall of sand, and I can't see you clearly. Each moment she is here, she roots herself more deeply, and you wander farther and farther from my reach.

"That's what I'm afraid of."

I am frightened of this as well, Amon said. Then he asked, *Are you angry with me, Young Lily, for seeing the things I have?*

"Angry? No. Not angry. I guess I just didn't understand all the ramifications of giving you my heart scarab."

Do you . . . do you wish for me to return it?

"No," I answered automatically, but then I thought further upon my answer. Did I?

If the idea that I can read your thoughts makes you feel uncomfortable, then I can refrain from doing so.

"You mean you can turn it off or on?"

In a way. It is similar in fashion to how you shield your thoughts from Tia or Ashleigh.

"Can I read your thoughts, too? I wasn't aware that reading your thoughts was a gift with purchase."

He didn't ask me what my modern phrasing meant and just answered the question. *You can, but to do so would require you to absorb my scarab.*

" 'Absorb' as in put it inside my chest like you did?"

Yes.

"Does it hurt?"

No. At least it doesn't for me. I'm not sure how it would feel to a mortal, though you're hardly what I would call a mortal now.

I sensed his hesitation. "What aren't you telling me?" I asked.

Placing my heart scarab inside your body might be . . . confusing for Tia and Ashleigh.

"How so?"

Because they reside in you, they are susceptible to your feelings, just as you are to theirs.

"Yes?" I pressed.

With our heart scarabs exchanged in so complete a way, our feelings for one another will cloud their minds. They will not be able to ignore our bond.

"You mean it will make them forget the others?"

They will not forget, but they will likely come to eschew the ones they care for.

"It would take away their freedom, then."

Yes, he answered.

"Then we'll hold off on that for the time being."

As you wish.

"So . . . it would seem there are a few things we need to talk about, then . . . ," I began.

There is nothing you need to explain. Just as I hear your thoughts and sense your desires, I also feel what motivated them. I do not blame you for anything. The time and attention you paid to my brothers does not invoke jealousy in me like it does for them.

This is not because I don't mind seeing you in the arms of another man— believe me when I say it does cause me anguish, just as it does them. But it is because I know your mind and heart perfectly. Had you been fully yourself, you would not have been tempted. Even now, it is your compassion and kindness that drive you. It is not the desire to have a prince on each arm and one kneeling at your feet.

In truth my intimate knowledge of your heart assures me more than it alarms me. It is my brothers I am more concerned about. I do not wish for them to feel the pain and sorrow of loss, but I will not give you up to them, Lily, especially not when I know your true feelings.

They may need the three of you, but as for me, I just need you. You're all I want. All I think of. If the cosmos fashioned me a perfect companion, one I could share my life with, it would be you.

My eyes welled up and I blinked rapidly but a few tears trickled down. "I'd choose to be with you, too," I said, wiping my eyes. "I mean, I do. I do choose to be with you." It was the truth, and it felt right in my heart, though I couldn't ignore the other two girls in the back of my mind. My heart was bound to Amon in more ways than one, and there was no changing it.

The rocking of his body soothed me, and soon I drifted to sleep.

I woke to the sound of a hearty voice ringing through the cosmos. "Ahoy, guardians!"

The birds turned as one and flew headlong toward Cherty's ship, which bounced on the waves of the river, stirring up a swirling of stars. When we passed over the ship, I laughed gleefully, seeing the red-faced captain bracing an arm on the tiller, steadying *Mesektet* for our approach. He squinted and hollered up at us to hurry up already, a big smile lighting his face.

Asten drew close to the ship, his wings beating wildly as he hovered over it. Ahmose dropped down lightly to the deck and then caught me when I slid off Amon's back. Just as he set me down, the starlit ibis drew in his wings, his great body shimmering, and then he fell. Ahmose leapt and caught his brother just as he took human form, preventing him from crashing to the deck. Asten was so drained he couldn't move.

"Here, Dreamer," Cherty said, bringing him a skein of water and yanking open his bag of supplies.

Amon landed on his own two feet, but he quickly sat, his back against the ship railing as he closed his eyes and panted. I brought him water and food, and after eating a bit, Amon slumped down, pillowed his head on my lap, and promptly fell asleep.

When I looked up at Ahmose and nodded toward Asten, Ahmose said, "He'll be fine. They both just need rest."

Cherty crouched down next to me. "The sailin' is smooth for the time bein'. My passengers have been left at the dock of the afterlife." He grunted. "What remains of it, anyway."

"What about them?" I asked, pointing to two remaining ghosts who hovered in the corner of the ship watching us with dark eyes and stony expressions.

"Those two took a look and decided to head toward greener pastures. They asked if they could stay on board and if I might drop 'em off at my next port. I was feelin' more amenable than I usually do, so I agreed. Between us, I wouldn'a wanted ta stay there either. Still better'n the Island of the Lost. You'll hafta tell me all about yer adventure when ya've a mind to. But for now, go ahead and catch some sleep yerself, girlie. I'll wake ya when we reach Heliopolis."

"Thank you," I said. I managed to give Cherty a small smile, and with one hand in Amon's hair and the other clutched in his, pressed against his chest, I rested my head against the railing and slept, too.

I wasn't sure how many hours we slumbered. For all I knew, it could have been days, but when we awoke, we were all ravenous. Cherty not only spread out his typical rations but managed to produce an abundance of juicy grilled fish (I didn't allow myself to consider what species), jars of preserved fruits that we spread on dried biscuits, salted pork (at least I thought it was pork), pickled vegetables, and a bowlful of beans and rice.

We ate until we were sated, and now that we'd slept and our bellies were full, my mind turned to other things, like bathing and clothes. After tugging the hem of my own filthy shirt, I looked up at Amon and Asten, expecting them to still be wearing their white skirts. Instead, I found them dressed in ragged, loose-fitting sailor clothes.

Amon wore baggy breeches tied with a rope at the waist and an open-necked shirt that had seen better days, but his feet were still bare. He looked every inch the pirate king as he stood atop the railing holding on to a rope for a balance. I itched to join him there and feel the spray of the river on my face as I stood in the warmth of his arms.

Asten wore a similar set of pants, but they were cut off just above the knee. His cloak was threadbare and tattered, and he obviously hadn't found a shirt. Asten's muscular frame was ripcord thin even after he'd consumed a large portion of our meal, a sign of just how much energy he'd expended on our flight. Even so, a part of me rather enjoyed seeing the wide expanse of exposed skin. A pair of scuffed boots adorned his feet, but he strode across the deck as confident as if he'd been born sailing.

I headed over to Cherty. "Thank you for loaning your spare clothes."

"Weren't nothin'," he said, and turned his gaze away. Red patches crept up his neck.

Peering at his face, my eyes narrowed. "Ahmose told you."

Cherty shrugged. "Told me enough. Wasret took you over. Nobody wants ta lose ya just so's they can have nicer clothes."

"Well, thank you again."

"Welcome. It's nice ta have ya back, girlie. I . . . I'll have ya know, I stayed as long as my ship allowed."

"I understand," I said, quieting him by placing my hand on his arm. "I don't blame you for leaving. You warned us."

He grunted and spat over the side of the ship. "Stayed two days. The groanin' of the ghosties was so bad, I couldn't hear myself think. When *Mesektet* started shaking, itchin' ta leave, I held her back as long as possible."

"I know," I said, surprised to see a telltale glistening in his eyes. Not wanting the big captain, the ferryman, to be caught in such an emotional state, I changed the subject. "How close are we to Heliopolis?" I asked.

"Not far now. The shore is just over the horizon. You four slept a

good deal of the way. Surprised ya found me. The gods must be smilin'
on ya, for ya ta get that far on yer own."

"I think if the gods were truly smiling on us, we'd be a bit better off
than we are now."

"Maybe," he replied. "The gods have been a bit busy as of late."

"Yes. I imagine they have."

Just then, the boat shook as something hit it from below. Cherty
drew his river sticks from the side, raising the weapons. "Take the rudder, girlie, while I check to see what beastie hunts us."

Another shudder rocked the ship. Asten and Ahmose leaned over
the side, pointing at something. I glanced over myself and saw a spiny,
armored tail disappearing into the river. The two ghosts had moved
closer to me in the meantime. I wasn't sure if they wanted my protection or if they were merely curious. Amon strode over to me quickly, a
wicked set of swords materializing in his hands.

"Never seen that beastie before," Cherty called out.

"We have," Amon replied. To me he added, "It's the necromancer."

Alarm coursed through me. "Are you sure?"

"I'm sure."

"How did he find us?"

"I don't know, but we're going to have to end him once and for all."

"But how?" I hissed. "He's so big!"

"We'll give him a second death."

"But you said he was only half-dead. So we must not have killed him
completely before."

"You're right. The spell Hassan used banished him from the mortal
realm. He came here instead." Amon held me steady as the boat was
wrenched to the side in danger of capsizing. "We've got to end him for
good now. Stay here. And don't use your power." When I nodded hesitantly, he ducked his head to look in my eyes. "Please," he added, waiting for me to answer after he'd read my thoughts. When he was satisfied
with my response, he went to help his brothers.

Ahmose called the same meteor rocks that had held Apep at bay and pummeled the river with them. His wicked-looking cudgel, silvery with a sharp edge, and his lethal ax sat at his feet, waiting to be used. Asten had his bow and arrows and he shot them into the water as the beast passed beneath the boat. The projectiles moved more like torpedoes than arrows once they hit the water, but they still glanced off the crocodile's rough hide.

Amon summoned the power of the sun and giant balls of fire appeared in his hands. He lobbed them at the beast, but it ducked under the surface of the river. The giant reptile moved under us, lifting the ship on his back. It fell with a crash back into the water. I was relieved to see Ahmose still at the bow of the ship, but Asten and Amon were missing.

"Where are they?" I screamed, but then I looked out over the water, and I knew.

Both Asten and Amon were moving quickly through the starlit river, riding the back of the beast and stabbing the crocodile with their weapons. In retaliation, the beast dove, leaving them stranded, treading water on the surface. The river became still, and as Amon and Asten swam back toward the boat, I scanned the horizon, looking for the monster that I knew lurked beneath the surface.

Then I saw the creature surface. His powerful tail thrust back and forth, and his enormous jaws opened wide to swallow the swimming men. In my mind, Sebak reached out to me. *I told you I'd be back for you. This meal will be most satisfying indeed.*

Ahmose used his power to rain down fiery boulders upon the beast, but many of them missed. He was obviously concerned about hitting Amon and Asten. The two men reached the ship and were scrambling aboard. Still the monster came at us, mouth open, with sharp teeth gleaming in the starlight. He was going to ram the ship and bite them in half in the process.

"No!" I screamed, hauling myself up on the railing as Ahmose helped them up. "You won't take them!"

Just as I was about to channel my power, there was a pounding of feet on the deck. "Come on, beastie!" Cherty shouted as he ran. "Show me what you got!"

He leapt over the side of the ship with a terrible war cry, his river sticks with sharpened points raised over his head. My breath caught in my lungs as I watched him fall down, down, his weapons positioned to thrust into the head of the crocodile. The monster angled his head upward at the last minute and caught Cherty around the waist. The monster's body slammed into the ship, creating a wide hole that sucked in water. I knew the ship would heal itself, but I couldn't say the same for its captain.

With a terrible crunch, the jaws of the beast snapped together again and again. Cherty's cry turned into a gurgle as the crocodile shook him hard and swallowed down the lower half of the captain's body as it thrashed in the water. The captain rallied and managed to stab the beast in the eye with one of his sticks, but it wasn't enough. I leaned over the side, my hand against my mouth, watching in shock and terror as Cherty disappeared, moving down the crocodile's pale throat swallow by sickening swallow, until he was gone.

"No!" I screamed, my whole body shaking with rage and grief as I pounded the railing with my clenched fists. Tears blurred my vision, and I became a beast myself. Hurriedly, I dashed the wetness from my eyes, relishing the hot, burning trails coursing down my cheeks. *I will destroy him.*

A pair of arms wrapped around me. I wrenched back and forth. "Let me go, Asten!" I demanded.

"There's no helping him now."

"But I can—"

"*No.*" There was no hesitation in Asten's voice. He would brook no argument. Horror and anguish tore through me like a living thing. I twisted and bucked, but Asten held firm. Just then, the giant crocodile leapt from the water, breaching the river entirely and gliding over the boat as if he were simply a giant, reptilian bird looking for a fish.

Amon and Ahmose made their move. The two men ran and leapt, lifting their weapons to the crocodile's exposed underbelly. As it passed over them, their blades found their marks and sank deep into the soft underbelly of the creature. Thick sheets of black blood coursed down from its deep slashes. By the time it passed over the boat completely, we knew it was mortally wounded.

It fell with a heavy splash into the water on the other side, and we waited, breath held, watching the heaving water until it stilled. There was no sign of the beast. Not a flicker of movement in the water. Then something stirred. At first, I wasn't sure it was the giant crocodile, the upside-down body looked so pale in the water, but it was. He had finally died.

Amon and Ahmose came over to me, black smears of blood on their faces and arms. The river turned oily, its surface peeled back like torn skin, exposing the ruined beast that had lived within it. Quickly, the water began to churn anew as unseen creatures, attracted to the smell of the crocodile's blood, began to feast. Feeling sick and brokenhearted, I turned away and pressed my face against Asten's shoulder, sobbing with all I had.

I only lifted my head when I heard a strange sound. The two ghosts who had cowered the entire time were whispering as they stared up at the stars. "What . . . what are they saying?" I asked. They were speaking a language I didn't understand.

Asten furrowed his brow. "They're saying . . . Master, the necromancer is dead. They are coming!"

"What? I don't under—"

With a violent expression, Amon sliced the heads off of both ghosts. "They were shabtis sent to spy for Seth," he said. "Now he knows."

Ahmose shuffled behind me to take the tiller, and the ship moved jerkily forward, only partially repaired. Soon we left behind the half-eaten corpse of the necromancer as well as the remains of our dear friend. I was inconsolable. Amon tried to get me to eat or drink, but I refused all their attempts to comfort me. When the shore of Heliopolis came into view on the distant horizon, I felt nothing. Not joy or happiness or a need to help the gods. All I felt was sorrow over what had been lost.

I didn't even register the fact that we were slowly sinking.

Heliapocalypse

Amon figured it out first.

"The boat's dying," he said.

Something about that prompted a giddy, wrong internal response, and a crazy-sounding chortle, one of half amazement, half insanity, burst from my mouth. *Mesektet* was dying? I guessed it made sense. She was connected to her captain. Without him, she either couldn't heal herself or didn't want to. Asten and Ahmose scrambled to keep us afloat for as long as possible, but it soon became obvious that we were going to have to leave her behind.

I cringed, wondering if we might be going down with the ship. There were evil things that lived in the water. Monstrous wormy creatures that wove nets to capture prey, malicious cousins of mermaids called serin. Then there was a myriad of venomous and aggressive fish that were just waiting for their next meal. I'd had an up-close-and-personal experience with a few of those monsters before. In my mourning, I regarded them with very little fear. After battling with the necromancer, anything else seemed easy.

"Can you just transition and fly us to shore?" I asked Asten. It would seem a more logical solution. But he nervously explained, "The moment *Mesektet* sinks, Heliopolis will disappear from view, just like the Isle of the Lost. We'd likely become disoriented again on the Cosmic River. The best we can do is swim to shore while holding on to a piece of her."

It looked like a piece was all we were going to end up with, and that was only if we were lucky. *Mesektet* was not only sinking but shrinking. The bow and the stern were much closer together than they'd originally been, and the sides were narrowing gradually as well. The mast cracked, fell into the river, and was swarmed by creatures that chewed through the sails and gouged the wood into tiny pieces as if the boat had been a living thing. I watched the process, feeling a cold ache in my heart.

Sitting in the back, water lapping over my toes as we limped along, I ran my hand over the slick deck and whispered my sorrow to the ship. I told her how much I'd admired her captain and how beautiful I thought she was the first time I boarded her. I wasn't sure if the boat was still alive in her way or if she understood me, but the ship seemed to respond, at least from my perspective. The rudder shifted, angling us toward the distant shore.

The boys all scrambled around the deck tossing anything they could overboard to give us more time to narrow the distance, and they bailed river water as fast as they could. Ahmose used his power to draw it up and out, sending it away from the ship, but it filled again almost instantly. Water hissed around the sides as it sloshed over the boards near me, and then finally it swamped over the front. We knew we had no choice then but to leave the ship.

Just as the brothers began making their way toward me, there was a splash as a large creature bit into the bow. The stern lifted out of the water, and I dug my claws in to hold on. Whatever it was tore away a chunk of decking. When the creature dropped back, the river surged over in an angry, hissing wave. The ship settled with a splash, and then *Mesektet* finally let go.

I could almost sense her leave. It was as tangible as the loss of Cherty.

Water surged up around my waist, and I could no longer feel the deck with my feet. I treaded water on my own as I resisted the pull of the sinking ship beneath me. Bubbles erupted around my body, and something grabbed my arm and tugged. I hit a solid chest.

"Here," Amon said, pressing a small piece of the ship into my arms. "We've got to swim away from her as quickly as possible. We're hoping she'll attract all the predators for now."

I felt sick using Cherty's broken ship in that way. It was like throwing your friend to a pack of zombies so you could escape. But my legs automatically kicked when Amon started pulling me. Asten and Ahmose drew near, each of them taking a position around me as if to draw attention away.

Asten held on to a piece of railing and Ahmose a section of the mast. When I glanced down at what I gripped in my hands, I saw it was the rudder. Though the shore seemed close, the river pushed against us, and we struggled for more than an hour before the waves finally assisted and pushed us toward shore.

"Do you know where we are?" I asked Ahmose. Sand coated my skin, but I was so grateful to be on shore that I didn't care. The healing stela began working on the cuts and scrapes on my skin. When I was whole, I'd make sure we used it on each of them as well.

"The far side of Duat. We'll make our way to Heliopolis on foot. Amun-Ra forbids anyone to move across his lands via sandstorm."

I nodded. "Then let's go. We'll feast in Cherty's memory when we get there."

We moved quickly over the hilly terrain until the sun set over the mountains. While Ahmose and Amon built a fire, I pulled my bow from behind my back. "Come, Asten," I said. "Let's hunt."

Amon looked up with a questioning expression, but he said nothing. Ahmose wouldn't look at us at all. Asten, however, gave me the kind of smile I hadn't seen from him since the dream. "Yes, my devotee."

"Cut the 'devotee' stuff or Tia will hunt you herself."

"That might prove interesting." He summoned the sand, and it formed his bow and a quiver of diamond-tipped arrows.

The night was dark. Very few stars graced the sky, but with my cat eyes, the landscape was easily visible though it was cast in varied shades of green. I found a game trail and followed it for several minutes, tuning my ears to the night sounds, until I came across a tantalizing scent, one I was already familiar with. Feeling more lioness than human, I stalked forward, pausing to wait for long minutes at a time.

I drew my bow, but then I paused, staring at the images on the shaft. They'd been foreign to me before. Mysterious. Written in a language not even Dr. Hassan knew. Even in the weak starlight, the carvings gleamed as if lit from within.

Tracing my finger along the edge, I suddenly understood its meaning. I now knew what the bow was truly for. Immediately, I thrust it away. It dropped into the grass at my feet as I stared at it in horror.

"What is it?" Asten asked as he came around the tree to face me.

He'd brought down an animal. The scent of blood was on his hands, warm and metallic. It was the smell of life and death. Normally, the lioness in me would think nothing of that. Tia appreciated that Asten was a bold hunter like she was. But the human part of me recoiled as blood from an entirely different being filled my mind.

I pointed to the shaft of the bow. "It's hers," I murmured softly, my voice drifting away in the breeze that lifted my hair from my shoulders.

"What's hers?" Asten pressed.

"The bow. It's not for a sphinx. It's not mine or Tia's. It was fashioned for Wasret. She's to carry it into battle."

I looked up into Asten's handsome face—now shadowed, his mouth tight. "I see," he said.

But he didn't see. Not really. Beginning to pace, I wrung my hands as I tried to explain. "I read it. The carvings. And then it . . . it spoke to me. I will have to sacrifice one I love in order to slay the beast."

"Are you sure?" he asked quietly.

"Yes."

"Lily," he said, moving in front of me to halt my pacing. "It will be okay."

"No. It won't, Asten. Don't you get it? Wasret has a thing for Ahmose. She thinks he's going to be her companion when all this is over. That leaves only . . . only Amon and . . . and you."

"Maybe there's more to it than meets the eye."

"That's not how Wasret works. We've retained fragments of her thoughts. She's very matter-of-fact. If she's banking on Ahmose, that means you or Amon might end up out of the picture, and she knows it."

I waited for him to say something, but apparently he had other ideas. He studied me for a brief moment and then headed back to the stream and methodically washed his hands.

"We won't sacrifice you, Asten," I said, following him.

He rose, picked up the carcass of the animal he'd killed and slung it across his shoulders, then gave me a tight smile. "I know I'm not the first choice, Lily. In fact, I rather expected something like this. It was only a matter of time until the cosmos brought things back into balance."

"What are you saying? That you want to die?"

"No. No, I don't want to die. But I'm . . . I'm different from my brothers. More expendable."

"Not to me, you're not."

"Be that as it may, little sphinx, now isn't the time for us to dwell on such things. In fact, I think now is the time to eat. I'm famished. What do you say we forget this little revelation for now and head back to get some dinner cooking?"

My fellow passengers and I were irritated at the way Asten handled the news. It also bothered us that deep down that we thought he might be right. I picked up the bow, though I now hated the thing, and thrust it angrily onto my back.

Amon rose to help Asten prepare our kill when we entered the campsite. I sat down next to Ahmose with a scowl on my face. Amon and Ahmose probably thought it was Asten I was irritated with, but I was mad at myself. If it were up to me, Tia, and Ashleigh, there would be no question. We would not sacrifice any of them. And though we knew that Wasret was not us, not really, we all wondered what we had contributed to make her what she was. We felt like traitors.

How could the cosmos give us these three wonderful men as companions and then expect us to sacrifice one of them? It didn't seem fair. Not that anything that had happened so far had been fair.

Was it fair that we'd lost Cherty? Was it fair that Tia and Ashleigh didn't have bodies of their own and were stuck being passengers in mine? Was it fair that we three were somehow supposed to save the cosmos? No. We didn't want any of it.

While we ate, I pulled out the hated bow and studied the markings, hoping I'd gotten it wrong. Asten didn't feel the need to bring up my revelation to his brothers, and I figured I needed to mull it over a bit more before I told them. The beams of their eyeshine haunted me in the dark—silver, gold, and green. Which of those lights would I snuff out?

I traced my fingertips over the bow. It wasn't a language, at least not like any on Earth, but I discerned the meaning of it, and the longer I stared, the clearer the message became. The bow had been fashioned long, long ago. Millennia ago, in fact. It had a very specific purpose, and its purpose was outlined. The bow had been created to destroy the Unmaker. The catch, and the part I couldn't accept, was that the bow would only find its true target, accomplish the goal it was created for, after the sacrifice of one loved by its wielder, me.

Clutching the bow to the point of breaking it, I vowed that we would rather lose the battle of the cosmos than lose one of our young men. If we had to die to ensure that would happen, then so be it.

When I'd finished the promise, a tiny tickle of energy coursed through my veins. An idea came to me then, and I worked it in my mind, committing it to memory. Even if Wasret should rise again, she would remember. We hoped it would be enough.

I must have fallen asleep, because I woke with the morning sun slanting across my face, my hands clasping the bow tightly.

"Good morning," Amon said as he crouched down and handed me a cold piece of meat. "Ahmose is seeking a path. Asten accompanied him."

I nodded and shifted my bow to my back, only to find Amon holding my harness. "You took it off me?"

"I thought you might sleep better without your knives poking into your back."

"I must have really been out of it not to wake up," I said as I thrust my hands through the leather straps.

"You were," he replied. "You didn't even stir when I repositioned you. It was . . . disconcerting."

I gripped his arm. "I'm okay. I promise."

"Do you want to talk about it?" he asked as he placed the bow across my back. Amon had always been able to read me easily, even before possessing my heart scarab. I peered at him, trying to discern if he was linked into my thoughts, but he'd apparently turned off the ability when he'd seen how it had made me uncomfortable. Still, it was obvious he knew something was wrong.

"No," I answered with a heavy sigh. "At least not right now."

He began to move away, but I put a hand on his arm to stop him. "Amon?" I asked. "Will you . . ." I caught my lip in my teeth and went on, "Will you teach me how to put your heart scarab in a safer place?"

Amon cocked his head, studying me. "Do you mean to keep it as I do?"

"Yes." I gestured with my hands. "Not right now, I just want to know how to do it when I'm ready."

"I see." He paused for a moment and then placed his hand over his heart and withdrew my gem. The sparkling jewel twinkled in his palm.

I itched to examine it further. I'd not even had a chance to study the differences between his and mine, but I knew it would only be a few moments until Ahmose and Asten returned.

"To place it within you," Amon explained, "you simply think of the person you love as you hold their heart. And what you would sacrifice to keep them safe." Amon put the jewel next to his chest and closed his eyes. "Your body automatically absorbs the gem to protect it." Slowly, the scarab melted into his skin. "But, Lily," he said, once the scarab had disappeared, "after you do this, your heart will only yearn for that one other person from that time forward. This is a commitment that cannot be broken."

I placed my hand over his heart. "And you have done this for me?" I murmured softly.

"I have. And I do not regret it."

More than anything, I wished I could return his sweet gesture in that exact moment. To show Amon how I felt. That I was as committed to him as he was to me. But I couldn't do it. Not yet. Instead, I offered him a sweet smile and a soft kiss. "I promise you," I said, "that your scarab will rest next to my heart very soon."

Amon took me in his arms and tucked my head beneath his chin as he stroked my hair.

"We've found a path!" Ahmose cried out as he came into camp.

I stepped away from Amon, regretting not moving away sooner when I saw the pained looks on Ahmose's and Asten's faces. Still, I managed to give them an encouraging smile. "Let's head out, then," I said. "We have much to do."

By the afternoon, we scaled a tall peak. A terrible, familiar scent of rot and decay carried on the wind. When we reached the summit, we looked down and my breath caught. We'd been traveling through dense forests full of game. Now, seeing what lay before us, I understood why the woods had been so crowded with animals.

"It's scorched," I said. "What could have done this?"

The great trees and hills were blackened, and the remaining stumps stood like row upon row of marked graves. Holes pockmarked the ground where burrowing animals had tried to hide, but I could smell their burned, rotting carcasses. A dark mound shifted and moved. Then a cry rang out as a mass of writhing, winged, bat-like birds lifted from a downed creature and rose into the air.

I hissed when I recognized them. "They shouldn't be in Heliopolis," I said quietly, horror filling me.

"No," Ahmose agreed. "They only appear when their mistress is close."

"The Devourer is here," Amon said, his voice catching.

We hadn't enough time to talk about what she'd done to him, but I had a pretty good idea. If she was in Heliopolis, dreadful things were happening.

"But surely the gods—" I began.

"If she is here," Asten said, "then it's possible they've abandoned the city."

We crouched behind a large stone waiting for the flapping, bat-like creatures to leave the valley. If they spotted us, they'd surely alert their mistress.

"They're heading toward Heliopolis," Ahmose said. "I am certain of it."

After a brief discussion, we decided to stay on the path to Heliopolis. We'd enter the city at dark and try to discern what was going on before we made our next move. Asten used his ability to cloak us in a fog of shadows, and Ahmose hid the sun behind clouds as we made our way down the mountainside.

The closer we got to the city, the bleaker the situation appeared to be. Where there had once been gleaming buildings, green plants hanging like veils down their sides, and bridges attaching each to the other, we now saw ruined husks. It looked like bombs had been dropped all over the city. Large craters were littered with debris and stones. The great stable and the gardens of Osiris were completely leveled. Even the river, normally bright purple where it touched the shore, was nearly black, and flotsam was pushed back and forth in the wake by the beach.

There was no sign of the citizens who made the city their home. I wasn't sure if that was a good thing or a bad thing. I knew the Devourer liked to round up people to feed on. Perhaps she'd already eaten everyone. More likely, she had them all locked up for easy amusement. Where was Amun-Ra, I wondered. How could he abandon his great city?

I looked up at the tall tower, the one Amun-Ra lived in and ruled from. It was still intact. Perhaps he was still there. Maybe he'd managed to keep the Devourer out, and he and his people had holed up inside. When I pointed up to it, they all agreed that we needed to know one way or another, so we sought out a spot we could take cover in until nightfall.

They found a half-destroyed home that must have been owned by a cobbler at one time, for there were bits and pieces of half-made shoes everywhere, as well as a pattern of different-sized soles. Asten and Amon dug around through the rubble until they each found a pair of shoes that fit. Ahmose used his waning energy to heal their bruised and sore feet, and when he was done, he sat back, panting. We'd discovered, to my dismay, that the healing Stela of Horus only worked on me.

I eyed Ahmose from where I sat and said, "Don't you think you should tell me what you did?"

"You don't know?" Amon asked, surprise evident on his face.

"No. He won't say anything. All I know is that he did something to save me, and he drained himself enough that even Wasret couldn't fix it. At least not without some thought and some serious channeling of her power."

"It's nothing," Ahmose said. "Any of us would have done it. Besides, it doesn't matter *now*." His simple words spoke volumes. I knew he was no longer talking about his body's weakness.

"It matters to me."

Ahmose raised his eyebrow, his jaw set stubbornly, giving me a look that I understood well.

I narrowed my eyes. "Hey. Despite what you think, I didn't betray you. If anyone was leading anyone else on, it was more you than me. At least I have the excuse of memory loss. You knew. You knew how I felt and chose to act anyway."

"Perhaps your memory isn't as intact as you believe it to be, love. I didn't push you to do anything you didn't want to do."

"Be that as it may—"

"Lily?" Amon touched my arm, and I immediately clapped my mouth shut, feeling my face go hot. We had an audience—a very awkward one, in fact. "Perhaps you should return to your original question. Ahmose has always been skilled at distracting both me and Asten from anything he doesn't want to tell us."

Asten snickered softly in the other corner.

I folded my arms across my chest and gave Ahmose a very stern look.

Sighing, Ahmose lifted a knee and cupped his hands around it. "I gave up part of myself to save your life when you died from the snake bite."

My mouth fell open, and then somehow I started speaking. "I . . . ," I sputtered, "I . . . *died*?"

"You were nearly dead when you hit the water. Almost every bone in your body was shattered upon impact. With the poison of Apep running in your veins, your powers were diminished to the point of being nonexistent. When the water entered your lungs, you drowned. Cherty discovered all three of your shaking souls huddled together in a corner of the ship. We had to work together to heal you and put you all back where you belonged."

Do you have any memory of this? I asked Tia and Ashleigh. When they responded that they did not, I asked, "What did you do?"

"I fished your body out of the water, used my power to clear the liquid from your lungs, and then told Cherty to put all three of you into your body. He, of course, said he couldn't do that. At least not without a hefty price."

I swallowed. "What did you pay?"

"You must understand that Cherty would have done it if he could, even without the price, but the cosmos required a balance, an exchange."

"How much?" I asked again, trembling as I waited for his answer.

Ahmose fell silent.

When Ahmose wouldn't speak, Amon volunteered, "He had to give up something for each of you. Do you remember the canopic jars? How they contain enough energy to sustain us when we are alive?"

I nodded.

Amon continued, "Ahmose gave up three of the four. For Tia, he gave up his mastery over animals. For Lily, he gave up his ability to pull energy from the moon. And for Ashleigh, he gave up his wings."

I could hear Ashleigh sobbing in the back of my mind. Hot tears burned behind my eyes, too. "That's why he can't become the crane," I murmured.

"Yes. It's also why he's so drained. He dared not give up his calling as pathfinder or his ability to heal others. And obviously, he still needed his skill in commanding the weather. But without drawing from the moon, he can barely sustain himself. All of the powers he did keep have grown weak without renewal, especially when he uses them too frequently."

I looked up at Ahmose, who was studying his clasped hands.

After squeezing Amon's hand, I scooted closer to Ahmose and picked up his heavy arm, draping it around my shoulders. "Thank you," I said and kissed his cheek softly.

Ahmose sighed heavily and drew me closer so I could rest my head on his chest. "Like I said"—his chest rumbled beneath my cheek as he spoke—"any of us would have done the same thing."

The room grew still and quiet. We must have slept, because the

entire encounter felt like a dream—that is, until I woke wrapped in
Ahmose's burly arms. He blinked his eyes open and rubbed my back.
Moonlight poured down on us from a broken window, and I despaired
thinking of how he could no longer gather strength from its silvery
beams. With an apologetic smile, I left him and went over to the gaping
doorway loosely hanging from its hinges where Amon stood.

He brushed his lips against my forehead and gave me a poignant
look, one that told me he understood and didn't need any further reas-
surance from me. I held out a hand and he took it, clasping mine warmly
in his. "Do you think it's safe to try to sneak in now?" I asked him.

"If we're going to try, now would be the right time," he replied.

Wind pushed through the gaps between the homes and shops, whistling
eerily and moaning like the ghosts who were planted in the Mires of
Despair, as we made our way to the tower.

We pushed on, finally spying a dark entrance to the tower that lay
open. I was about to step into the moonlight to head toward it when
Asten pulled me back and pointed up. On top of the tower, almost
hidden in the turrets of the building, were large creatures with thick
wings.

"What are they?" I whispered. "They're much larger than the
Devourer's bats."

"I've heard of them, but I've never seen one before, even in the
netherworld. They're called sky demons. You would think of them as
gargoyles, but these are much, much worse than anything the mortal
world could have imagined. They are a cross between the Devourer's
flying minions and her wolves."

"How do we get past them?" I asked.

In answer, Asten created one of his magic firefly clouds. All of us
stepped inside, and we slowly began making our way across the moonlit ground toward the door. A screech was heard overhead, followed by

another. I would have run, but Amon held me back. "They know we are here. They can smell us, but they can't see us," he whispered.

Winged creatures took to the air, filling the sky in a swarm of dark bodies. They moved over the land like disco ball lights cast in negative exposure. When we were finally through the door, Asten let his magic fade, and we continued through the tower.

The hallways were dark, the sconces unlit. Gorgeous golden mirrors had been shattered, and sheer draperies had been torn, the rods broken. Even the once-gleaming tile floor had been smashed, the beautiful patterns ruined.

We went up level after level, finding nothing but destruction. Finally, we reached the uppermost floor, the one where Amun-Ra made his home. When we arrived at the grand atrium where I'd first come upon Horus, I held up a hand. We heard something. The panting of a man or a beast and the all-too-familiar clink of chains.

I edged behind a curtain and peered out at the tableau before me. The golden fountain had been knocked down, and the trees were burned stumps. On the chaise where Horus had first attempted to seduce me, a figure reclined. He appeared to be all alone and, what's more, his limbs were chained to the floor.

Quietly, I stole around to get a better look, the Sons of Egypt following behind me. We paused often, the lioness in me patient and watchful. Together we waited and listened for any alertness on the part of the man, but he appeared to be asleep. My nostrils flared as I smelled sweat and blood. We moved closer.

Shifting the curtain for a better look, I took in the purple bruise on the side of the man's face. All at once, he shifted, eyes locking on to mine. "Lily," the man choked out in a hiss, his swollen mouth barely able to form the words.

I stepped out from my hiding place. "Osiris?" I asked. When I saw what had been done to him, I recoiled. His entire leg was missing below the knee. The stump was loosely bandaged and still bleeding. A double-bit ax rested against the wall, crimson stains bright on the edges. I knelt at his side, putting a hand on his trembling arm. "What happened to you?" I asked, a catch in my voice.

"There's no time," he mumbled. "You must regroup with the others. They are hiding in the great adder stone. It's at the peak of Mt. Babel." He coughed, and blood trickled from his mouth. "She must not find you here!"

Amon and Asten came up behind me. Osiris looked up at them with beseeching eyes. "Please," he said with a gurgle, "take her away. Now!"

"But we can help you," I began.

"You must not. She will know you're here. Do not worry about me," he said, when he saw the hesitancy in my face. "All she can do is harm my body. My soul belongs to Isis. As long as she is alive, I will survive."

There was a clatter in the adjoining passageway. "Go! Hurry!"

Not a moment after we'd ducked behind the curtain, we heard the clicking of heels as someone entered the room.

"Are we talking to ourselves now, Osiris? Any little birdies been by to visit you? No? Ah well. One can still hope. Now then, my handsome pet, where were we?" She laughed seductively. "That's right. We were discussing where your wife might be hiding." When there was no response, she continued, "Don't despair. I've a mind to keep you for myself once my master takes her as his bride. After all, I'll need someone to distract me. At least for a while. It will be such a pleasure to watch the flame of love between you flicker and die as he unmakes your bond."

My fists clenched at hearing the voice of the woman I'd grown to hate. Only Amon's hands on my arms stopped me from attacking her. Green light crept beneath the curtain. I knew it meant the Devourer was feeding from Osiris. While the Devourer busied herself with Osiris, we quietly backed away, staying behind the curtain. Asten cloaked us in his cosmic cloud just in case anyone should notice.

It felt so very wrong to turn our backs to the captured god, but unless I was willing to give myself over to Wasret again, I knew we were no match for the Devourer. Closing my eyes, I let the tears flow silently as we crept from the room. Once clear, we moved quickly down the stairs, knowing we needed to find the other immortals to figure out a plan.

I pressed my hand against my mouth as Osiris began to scream.

The Vision of Nephthys

We moved through Amun-Ra's palace quickly. Ahmose led us out through the back of the building hoping to avoid the living gargoyles that protected the evil queen's newly conquered lair. It swiftly became apparent that the screeching sentinels surrounded the decimated city on every side. Asten summoned his firefly cloud and covered our escape, and though the sky demons circled overhead, searching for us, we were soon able to leave them behind.

When the sun topped the horizon, painting the landscape a ghoulish red, Asten's power waned while Amon's grew stronger. Ahmose knelt to try to discover a path to Mt. Babel, only to find there was no such thing.

"I don't understand," I said as Asten finally let his cloud dissipate after deciding we were far enough away even though we were still in the scorched lands. He leaned over, panting from the exertion of maintaining it for so long. "How can there be no such place?"

"Perhaps Osiris meant a site outside of Heliopolis," Amon suggested.

I put my hands on my hips and frowned. "It didn't sound like it. We need to figure out where it is. The more time we waste, the more suffering the Devourer causes Osiris," I said. A sick feeling of guilt at having left the god in her clutches tore at my insides.

"What if we trace the path of Isis instead?" Amon suggested.

Ahmose shook his head. "It won't work. I don't have the ability to trace the paths of the gods, especially not here. The impressions I get here are vague at best. My ability works most accurately when I focus on the two of you and on Lily. In giving up my power to draw from the moon, all the gifts I've kept have diminished. The paths are simply not as clear as they once were."

"So how do we find the gods, then?" Amon asked.

"Wasret could find them," I said softly.

"We can figure this out without her," Amon replied instantly.

"Can we?" I turned to him. "I'm not so sure."

Amon set his jaw stubbornly and refused to broach the subject.

It was easy to think of running away when I didn't see what was happening. But then we'd be abandoning everyone else. The Devourer would surely suck the rest dry and torture them just because she could. Then, when she'd had her fill, Seth would come around to clean everything up. He'd unmake Earth. Maybe even the entire cosmos. What would I do then? If even the gods were hiding from Seth and the Devourer, then it was bad. Really bad.

As the three men argued about where we should look next, I had an inner conversation with the girls in my head. *Can we do it and remain in control?* I asked as I chewed on my bottom lip.

There's no way to know, not truly, Tia said.

We can't let the Devourer 'ave 'em, Ashleigh added. *Look what she's done to Osiris! She's a wicked enchantress, she is. I'd rather give meself up than give our men over ta the likes o' her.*

Are you sure you want to risk it, Lily? Tia asked.

No. I'm not sure of anything at this point. Pacing a few steps away, I shook out my hands trying to draw upon my courage. *We need to try,* I said. *Just don't . . . don't merge fully. At least, try not to. Combine only enough to figure out where we need to go.*

Ashleigh and Tia gave their silent consent and our consciousnesses drifted closer. We didn't realize how powerful the pull of Wasret actually was until we moved toward her again. She was a powerful magnet, and we'd just flipped a switch, turning her on. Desperately, we bucked against the bright light threatening to engulf us. It was like fighting against a riptide. Our energy waned quickly as we circled the chasm at the drop-off. If we slipped in, we knew we'd lose ourselves. That's when we heard the voice.

Hello, again, the female voice said.

H . . . hello? I called out mentally. *Am I—are we talking to ourselves?*

Not precisely, the woman's voice quickly replied. *You are yourselves and I am myself. I have to say, it wasn't kind of your man Amon to cast me away so abruptly. I wouldn't have been so cruel to him.*

Choosing to ignore her comment about Amon, I focused on the other revelation. *Do you mean to say that you are not wholly made up of the three of us?*

No. I am not.

My thoughts were a chaotic jumble. *Impossible!* Tia and Ashleigh were as astonished as I was. *Then what are you?* I asked her.

What am I? It's rather rude of you to assume that I am a what instead of a who. Though, technically, you are right. The who I get from the three of you; the what comes from a different place.

Why are you speaking to us now? Tia demanded. *You've never done so before. You could push us over the edge at any time and take over. We feel your power. Do you play with us as if we are vermin you can bat from one paw to the other?*

Not at all, she replied. *You are a part of me. As precious as my eyes, my hands, and my mind. I do not consider you three to be vermin.*

Then what are we ta ya? Ashleigh said. *Why do ya seek our destruction?*

I do not wish you harm—at least, not in the way you think. It's simply a fact that if I am to inhabit your body, make use of your talents and abilities, I must re-create you. It is a perfectly natural process. Every old thing must make way for what's new. Can a fish survive without consuming his fellows?

Can a building be constructed without depleting the mountain of its ore and stone? Can a farmer grow a crop without first clearing the forest? Creation and destruction are yin and yang. When it happens correctly, they are in absolute balance. For me to exist, you three must, unfortunately, cease to exist.

Then why can we be here . . . in this place together?

Because we are in an in-between space—the infinite darkness that lies between memory and future potential. This is where I was born. It is a place of watching. Where time stretches out in an eternal round before and behind. You've been here before, though you have no memory of it. Unfortunately, your limited scopes mean you can only exist here for a finite amount of time.

What do you mean to do now? Tia asked bluntly.

Ah, the ever-practical side of me. I don't think I've told you how much I appreciate you and your raw, honest view of the world, Tia. It's quite refreshing. It keeps me grounded in reality. The answer to your question is that I plan to do nothing. I will simply wait here until you summon me. I do not worry about it overmuch. It is inevitable.

You won't try to take us over? I asked suspiciously.

I never did. You invited me each time. The difference between us is that I don't invite you back.

And why don' ya? Ashleigh asked.

And there's my passionate, impulsive side. Let me ask you, fairy, is it wrong to want to experience life and love? Do I not have a right to reap the rewards of my efforts? What gives the three of you a more powerful claim to exist than me?

That's just it, I said. *There are three of us and only one of you. The needs of many overshadow the needs of one.*

Wasret turned her attention to me. *The ever-philosophical human. Let me ask you, then, Lily: Would you give up your body so Tia could possess it, or Ashleigh? Their mortal forms are long dead. You allow them to share yours, but you remain rigidly in control, don't you?*

How does it feel to sit in the background? To be a silent observer? Could you tolerate that? You ask them to. Then again, humans always play the domi-

nant role, don't they? Just because the fairy and the lioness are other does not mean they are lesser.

My existence means perfect harmony for the three of you. There's no winner or loser. If you truly loved them like sisters, as you profess you do, you would choose to make this sacrifice. You would bring about this balance. The needs of the many indeed. What you really mean when you argue in this manner is that the needs of the human should take precedence.

I didn't have any words to counter her argument. I felt ashamed and angry at the same time. Was I truly that narrow in my thinking? She wasn't wrong. And that was the problem.

She went on. *Did I not pick a man all three of you could love? How could you all be so selfish when the cosmos is at stake? When the lives of your other two men are endangered? The preservation of your individual identities, though understandable, comes at a cost. Ashleigh, you have already given yourself up once. Your mortality, your humanity was sacrificed simply to protect yourself from an unfortunate trial.*

Her voice trailed off as Wasret turned her attention to Tia. *And you, lioness. You were desperate for a sister to replace the one you'd lost. Tell me, is it better for Lily to live the dual existence that came when you made her a sphinx? I don't think that it is. In fact, it would have been a kindness if you had simply consumed her on the plains. Because you forced Lily to become your sister, she has given up a piece of herself.*

I was about to protest when Wasret cornered me. *And last, we come to you, Lilliana Young. You longed for a life of meaning, of purpose, of freedom from your parents. But this is a falsehood you have told yourself time and again. You believe your parents held you back, forced you to attend a certain school, act in a certain manner, or date a certain boy, but this is not your parents' doing. It is yours.*

Only you decide your fate. You were weak because you allowed yourself to be. You chose the path you are on. You embraced it, in fact. Even now, you would like to imagine that I am the one forcing your hand. That I will rip away your existence to save the cosmos. But I will not.

When the time comes for you to make a decision, I would hope you are strong enough to choose the right path. The one uncluttered by self-doubt and self-preservation. But know that whatever you choose, it is and has always been your choice. Just because you don't like the options before you, does not mean you have none. Make peace with that, Lily.

The three of us had fallen silent. How strange that we all felt schooled by ourselves. It had to be the most bizarre experience of my life. And that was saying a lot.

We floated in the darkness, feeling the pull of Wasret, but it no longer felt like a vortex. Now that we knew we had the ability to resist it, we could. The three of us hovered there, unwilling to look each other in the eye either literally or mentally.

As each of us tried to piece ourselves back together, she said, *For now, I will help you, give you what you seek without asserting control over our body. But know that the next time you come for me, I will not be so generous. I cannot afford to be. Not in the face of the battle to come. You know now, and with the knowing comes choice. When you return, I will assume that you three have made one.*

To find the gods you seek, head toward the rising sun until you come upon a mountain so tall, its peak brushes the clouds. You will know it is the right one when you hear the buzz of voices in the trees. At the top lies the place you seek. But be warned. The way to the top is difficult. You must stay close to your men. Do not separate under any circumstances.

I was going to say thank you but then stopped. Why should I thank someone who had just thoroughly dressed me down? Then the three of us were suddenly thrust away from the vortex. We spun and, for a time, lost ourselves, but slowly we returned. Blinking, I saw Amon staring at my face with an intent expression, the bright sky above him, the sun haloing his head. Hours must have passed for the sun to be at its zenith in the sky.

"They've returned," Amon said.

"You're sure it's not Wasret?" Ahmose asked.

"No. It's me—I mean, us," I said with a slight shake of my head.

"What happened, Lily?" Asten wrapped a hand around my elbow to help me up.

I got to my feet, stamping them to bring the feeling back. "We . . . we spoke with Wasret."

All three boys lowered their eyebrows in a nearly identical expression of concern. It would have been funny, if the situation weren't so serious.

"What did she say?" Amon asked.

"She was . . . she was upset you sent her away so quickly. She said . . ." I hesitated.

Go ahead, Lily, Tia encouraged. *We have no secrets from one another, and they will not think the less of us for it.*

"She said we were selfish and weak and that we should want to do what's best for the cosmos and best for each other."

"You aren't weak," Asten said with a clenched jaw.

"Or selfish," Ahmose said, folding his arms.

"She obviously doesn't know you well at all," Amon added.

"That's just the thing," I said. "She does. Wasret is us, or at least a part of us, whether we like it or not. That is to say, she knows us better than we even know ourselves. But there's something else. Wasret isn't *just* us. She's something other. There's an extra piece that makes her different." I looked into each of their faces and saw a new expression, a closing off. "You knew. All of you knew," I accused.

Ahmose spoke first. "I could tell there was something about her that was not coming from the three of you. It was the way she viewed the world."

"When I looked at her with the Eye of Horus," Amon began, "I could easily discern the three of you, even though you'd faded. It was how I brought you back. I focused all my energy on seeing only the three of you, and you were strengthened enough to return. But there was another part that retreated, that stayed behind. I thought we'd have time to talk about it further, but so much has happened. . . ."

His words trailed off. I put my hand on his arm. "We've been a little busy since then," I said.

"I cannot see her dreams," Asten murmured, and I turned to face him. "I should be able to. I can access the dreams of every creature in the cosmos—even Apep, should I choose—but not hers."

I was pondering this when another thought occurred to me. "Asten?" I asked. "You can see anyone's dreams? Even the gods?"

"Yes. As long as they aren't blocking my access. But since they aren't technically dead, it doesn't just happen when we meet, like those who arrive on the docks. Believe it or not, I don't actually try to invade the dreams of others. Why do you ask?"

"Can you see Seth's dreams?"

He grimaced. "I've never made an attempt. Even if I somehow could, we might not like what we see."

"Something tells me it's time. I mean, after we find Mt. Babel."

"But we still don't know where it is," Asten said.

"We do now. Wasret offered the info up free of charge. Well, at least free of body swapping. But she did warn us that next time all bets are off."

"Then let's hope there isn't a next time," Amon said gravely.

I gave him a weak smile. It wasn't that I didn't want to divulge everything, I just wasn't sure the Sons of Egypt would truly understand, not to mention accept, the experience we'd had with Wasret. She'd said *when* we came calling for her again, not *if*.

My gut told me she was right. We'd be back for her. And the next time would be the last time. A sorrowful pain twisted my gut, and I reached for Amon's hand. There was more pain on the way. Wasret said I'd have to come to accept it. That we'd all have to. The best thing for me to do at the moment, however, was to focus on the task at hand.

After checking the position of the sun, we headed off in the general direction Wasret had given us. It took the rest of the day to find the mountain. We had hiked into the thickest, blackest part of the forest at the very edge of Duat. Even Tia felt nervous and uncomfortable.

There are ancient things here, she said. *Things best left undiscovered.*

I tended to agree. The top of Mt. Babel was covered in gray clouds, though Ahmose said he sensed no moisture in them. The sides were dark with large trees that covered the land from the bottom to as far up as the eye could see. There was no discernible path.

The sun was now low in the sky. I knew climbing in the dark would be dangerous, even if the mountain didn't have a frightening, supernatural element about it. After warning them to stay close, we entered side by side and immediately felt the stirring of the trees. They came to life, slapping at us with thin branches and tripping us with roots. They didn't want us there.

Then they began to whisper. Quietly at first, and then their murmurings became louder. There was a definite sense that turning back was the smartest move. Once, when I stopped and backed up a step, the voices lessened, they became almost encouraging and soothing. But the moment I set my sights ahead again, they recoiled, hammering at us with increased intensity. Ahmose was the first to react with more than just a disturbed expression.

About halfway up he froze in place, the corded muscles of his back bunched as if he were preparing for an attack. When we came up alongside him to take a look at what had halted his progress, we saw nothing. Ahmose simply stared at the trunk of a massive tree, jaw working and eyes brimming with tears.

"Ahmose?" I wrapped my hand around his arm. When he didn't respond, I pushed up the sleeve of his loose shirt and pressed my fingers gently to his wrist, seeking his pulse. It raced wildly, but my touch seemed to break the trance. "What did you see?" I asked him.

Blinking rapidly, he grunted, "It's . . . it's not important. Let's keep going."

Asten, too, began showing signs of emotional trauma. He kept trying to wander off, saying he'd lost her and he had to find her. He'd look up in the trees and peer into every large bush he came across. He even crouched down by each stream, tracing the ground, looking for tracks.

"Find who?" I asked. Again, it wasn't until I pressed my hands against his cheeks and made him look at me that his eyes cleared.

Amon was able to focus a bit better. When I asked him why, he just shook his head as if he didn't understand the question. We assumed it was the Eye of Horus that kept him grounded. It was Amon who suggested that I hold Asten's and Ahmose's hands as we continued. It made climbing a bit more ponderous for us, but the two men were able to hold themselves together much better when I did. The climb was strenuous enough by itself, but the mental focus it took to keep going quickly exhausted us.

We stopped once and learned that staying in one place was a bad idea. I leaned back against a tree, closing my eyes. It only took a moment for my mind to be swept away in the visions sent by the trees. Lowering my guard must have given them a way in, and they took advantage.

I dreamed I was spinning away in a whirlwind and nothing, not even Amon, could pull me back. For a short time, I was with Tia and Ashleigh, but soon not even they could remain with me. Rising higher and higher, I soared through clouds and then into space.

Planets passed me and then galaxies and stars as I was pulled backward. No matter what I did, I could not halt my ascension. Then, when I'd risen above it all, hovering over the cosmos in the nothingness that surrounded it, I watched a shadow smother it as I let out a silent scream. Life and love and everything I cherished was there one minute and gone the next. I began to fade, and I didn't care. Nothing mattered anymore. All I knew was I didn't want to be alone.

A light slap on my face brought me back and I realized that Amon's palm still rested against my cheek and both Asten and Ahmose clutched my hands. Apparently, while we'd rested, the trees had actually made a sort of trap or barrier around us, almost as if the land were trying to cage us in. Amon refused to even think about me using my power, so we hacked our way out with weapons and my claws.

By the time we hit the stony peak, we sank to our knees, panting. To say the journey had been arduous would be an understatement.

Thick mist enveloped us to the point where I couldn't even make out the features of the boy next to me.

"Hello?" I called out, not really expecting an answer. My voice echoed over the mountaintop and seemed to slide away into space itself. The effect was eerie. A shape appeared in the fog. It grew larger, and when it was close enough that we should have been able to make out the form, it paused. I knew it studied us, watched us. Then, whoever it was must have felt satisfied, because a hand lifted and the mist parted, revealing a goddess I'd seen before.

Long blond hair hung down her back in a silken wave, and silver still adorned her body. But instead of thin, pounded bracelets and hair ornaments, she wore armor. The softness of her face and form was gone. In its place, a steely determination, and something else—a sorrow so heavy it nearly crushed her.

"Lily," she said with a slight nod of her head. "Tia, Ashleigh. We've been waiting for you. Come."

She offered a hand, and I took it. Instantly, the riotous voices from the trees disappeared. I stepped forward and turned to see Asten, Ahmose, and Amon still kneeling. All three of them were pressed down by the weight of the same voices I had been. I lifted my eyes to the goddess, the unasked question floating between us.

"You must welcome the Sons of Egypt yourself," she said. "They cannot cross the threshold without you. Once they do, the stars will recognize them as your companions, and the madness they cause will dissipate. Then you may traverse the mountain and even fly from its peak without harm."

I wasn't sure if there was some ceremony to the welcoming, but I touched each of their shoulders. This seemed to be enough. The relief was evident on their faces. After they stood, Nephthys turned, indicating I should follow. The mist returned, filling the air behind us and making the trees disappear.

The top of the mountain was a series of rocky steps punctured by tall granite pillars. They stretched into the sky like great spears thrust into the ground. I imagined that from the air it must look like the fortress of a dragon.

We wove a path between the spiked pillars until we came upon a stone rotunda. A series of openings disappeared into the mountainside. In the center of the open area was a large fire pit encircled with flat stone benches.

With the snap of her fingers, Nephthys started a bonfire. When she clapped her hands, other gods emerged from the dark caverns, including Amun-Ra, Horus, Isis, Anubis, and Ma'at. There were a few others I didn't recognize, but the numbers were very small considering the decimated city we'd just seen.

I thought it interesting that the shy and demure Nephthys, who'd sat quietly in the background during our judgment, should have the presence to command the others. That they gave her their undivided attention did not go above my notice.

"She has arrived," Nephthys said simply. She moved to the other side of the fire, positioning herself between Amun-Ra and Isis. We stood there for a long, pregnant moment, staring at each other across the flames. I was waiting for the gods to say something, anything. I wanted them to explain why they'd sent me on this crazy journey. Why they were holding back information. I wanted to demand what they expected from me. But they said nothing. It appeared I would have to be the first one to talk.

I looked from one face to another, growing more irritated by their lack of communication with each passing moment. "What happened to everyone else? Are all your citizens dead?" I demanded, letting accusation color my tone. Now that I'd finally broken the silence, I narrowed my gaze on Amun-Ra as I folded my arms. "Are you even aware of what's going on down there, or did you just come up here to bury your heads in the sand as usual?"

"Of course we know," the sun god replied with more patience than I deserved. "We held her off for as long as we could, but we ultimately decided to let her take the city once we got everyone to safety. The citizens of Heliopolis are hidden away for the time being."

It was a relief to hear that most of the population hadn't been devoured.

"I think you forgot someone," I said, still feeling testy.

There was a gasp, and I quickly looked over at Isis. The statuesque goddess had stepped closer to Anubis, who had wrapped an arm around her shoulders. "You've seen him, then?" she asked, her lovely voice wavering with emotion.

"Yes. He told us to come here. He's been . . ." I hesitated. "Badly hurt." Isis trembled but said nothing, her gaze turning stony. I realized then that she already knew. "The Devourer drains him," I added, pressing the goddess. "She seeks your location in order to present you to Seth."

When all she did was nod, I threw my hands up in the air. "I don't understand you. You know he's down there, and yet you let him suffer at her hands. I thought you loved him."

"I do love him," she said, a bit of fire lighting her swirling nebula eyes. "More than you know. It kills me to leave him there."

"Then why do you?" I charged, raking my eyes over each one of them. "You're supposed to be gods. Surely you're an equal match to her."

"They leave him there at my request." Nephthys stepped forward and placed a hand on Isis's shoulder, smiling softly at her before looking at me once more.

"*Your* request," I echoed, puzzled. "Why would you do such a thing?"

"There is more going on here than meets the eye, Lilliana Young."

"Obviously." I sighed heavily. "Look, don't you think it's time you all clued me in? I have to say, I'm growing tired of being your pawn."

Nephthys came around the fire to our side. "You misunderstand. You are not our pawn. You're our queen. We've been playing this game for a long time. Now that all the pieces are assembled, it's time we make our final moves. And hope the stars planned everything out as carefully as we'd hoped."

I took a step back, realization slamming into me. "You've been after Wasret this whole time."

"Yes. Each journey we sent you on prepared you for what we needed you to become."

My body shook at her words. Warm hands cupped my shoulders, and I was soon pressed against a hard chest.

Nephthys continued, "A long time ago, I had a vision. In it I saw a girl, a very special mortal who would accomplish great things. Things not even the gods could do."

The goddess raised her hands in supplication, but I stood ramrod stiff in Amon's arms. She sighed and dropped her hands, placing them behind her back as she began speaking again.

"Amon was placed purposely in New York City, and he rose at the precise time you were nearby." She dipped her head toward Amon, indicating the man standing behind me. "When he escaped the afterlife, heading to the netherworld, we saw that as an opportunity to test you, to determine if you had the strength to pass through the Rite of Wasret. When you did so successfully, we knew you were the one we'd sought."

"I could have just as easily been killed."

"You could have," she admitted, "but you met your destiny." She smiled. "As well as your inner lioness. With Tia, you gained the powers of the sphinx, which allowed you to enter the netherworld. This was a place not even the gods could access. But with the help of the Sons of Egypt, you not only entered, but survived, and brought home Amon to us as well.

"But there was another piece missing. We knew that for you to truly channel the power of Wasret, you'd need to become the host to a third girl. For only a triple goddess, a binding where each girl was yoked to the other in absolute harmony, would form a true syzygy that would grant Wasret entrance to our realm."

Isis stepped forward. "For a number of reasons, neither I nor

Nephthys could take on the role of the third goddess, so Ma'at volunteered. She was planning to give up her physical form and merge with you upon your return to the afterlife." She smiled wanly. "We did not expect Ashleigh. In fact, we were not even aware that she was in the netherworld."

I looked over at Ma'at, who stood stiffly and proudly. I shuddered. All things considered, Tia and I preferred our inner fairy.

Isis said, "When the fairy tree sacrificed herself and gave her charge up, she knew what she was doing. Ashleigh complements the two of you perfectly. Ma'at would have added more power to your trio, but Ashleigh brings her own talents and personality. It worked, and that was the most important thing. We did not expect you to need to use your power so soon. The Devourer was an unexpected complication. Then Seth broke out, and we had to accelerate our plans."

"So when Dr. Hassan asked you if the stars knew about me, you lied?" I asked Isis icily.

"Not precisely," Isis said. "We knew Wasret was coming, and we hoped it was you. You had great potential. No other girl had formed a connection with a Son of Egypt before. The fact that you have relationships with all three—"

Nephthys quickly cut her off. "The point, Lily, is that we've now come to this. Suffice it to say, we've been waiting for you. Yes, we've kept back information. Yes, we made you suffer through trials. Yes, we are putting all our hopes in you. Despite everything you've endured, comfort yourself in knowing that we are here now. We are ready to help, ready to answer questions, and ready to fight alongside you. What we need to know right now is . . . will you help us?"

A Change of Hearts

Every person on the mountaintop looked at me expectantly, hope lighting their faces. That is, all but the three men behind me whose opinions I cared most about. Buoyed by their commitment to me, I steeled myself to answer.

With a heavy heart, I answered softly, "Yes. I'll help you."

Almost as one, the Sons of Egypt straightened their shoulders as if preparing themselves for the inevitable fight I'd just pledged myself to. "*We'll* help you," Amon said, voicing the sentiment of all three brothers.

I put my hand on top of Amon's where it still pressed into my shoulder. "Tell us what we need to know," I said.

Nephthys was about to speak, but Isis came forward first. Her words spilled from her so quickly, I wondered how she'd been able to hold them back for so long. It was such a different version of the icy, quiet goddess I'd met before. Perhaps her worry over her husband was causing the change in her demeanor. "We must protect you from the Devourer first. I will weave a spell, a powerful one," she said, "so that she cannot find the rest of you if she just so happens to capture one. Keep in mind that we will try to avoid this at all costs, but we must be prepared for anything, regardless."

I tilted my head. "You mean to do the same thing to us that you did to Osiris? That's why she's torturing him instead of seeking you out, isn't it?"

"Yes," she answered, eyes dropping. "The mountain hides us from her, but once we leave here, she can find us. Then not even our mother, Nut, could shelter us from her view. And no cavern our father, Geb, could fashion would be deep enough. We are prepared for the consequences of this, but the four of you are too important to risk losing in a battle with the Devourer. In the end, she will be of no importance. We must reserve most of your energy for Seth."

"Then why don't we just leave her alone and seek out Seth?" I asked. "You know, cut off the head of the snake and the rest dies."

"Unless it causes two heads to spring forth instead," Asten mumbled, almost under his breath.

Isis winced at my analogy, but Nephthys proceeded to answer my question. "Seth has invested much of his energy in the Devourer, just like he did with Sebak. In defeating the necromancer once and for all, you weakened Seth's hold. It will be nearly impossible to overwhelm him even with all of our strength combined, but if we sever the ties between him and the Devourer, it will make him that much more vulnerable."

"Wait a minute." Something I'd learned about Seth long ago surfaced. "Dr. Hassan once told me that Seth could create but that he only did it in order to unmake the thing he'd created. Won't we inadvertently give him more power by getting rid of the Devourer?"

"Your Dr. Hassan, though he possessed the Eye for a short time, and though he is very knowledgeable for a mortal, does not understand everything," the blond goddess answered. "The Devourer has already freely shared her energies and her powers with Seth. He cannot take more than he already has, even if he should choose to unmake her. He can only gain back that which he loaned her to do his bidding.

"When Dr. Hassan talked of creation and of unmaking, he was speaking about the Sons of Egypt. Since understanding this is important, we will tell you what we can. Let me begin by saying that what we do know of his ultimate plans regarding them is very little, but our best guess is that Seth, in fostering the Sons of Egypt, was trying to re-create the spell that Isis wove. From what we discerned, Seth was channeling a great deal of his power into the three young men. The way in which he accomplished this is still a mystery to us. It would be impossible for him to re-create her spell."

"Why impossible? Didn't he have the power?"

"It's not the power that he didn't have," Isis said. "Spell making requires a certain talent, surely, but this particular spell requires even more. The key ingredient for it is love. Love and a willing heart. Love is not something Seth can understand."

When the two goddesses fell quiet, Anubis added, "Seth dabbling with necromancy is likely a key to understanding his motives. What we do know is that cosmic energy can only be harnessed and bound in certain ways. Death, both a first and a second death, appears to be a catalyst in breaking and creating bonds; cosmic energy flows through those connections."

"That would explain his connection to the Devourer, then," I mused. "Those two are like birds of a feather. She gains energy through the eating of hearts, which isn't altogether different from unmaking. Since death is a catalyst, it makes sense that's how she kept herself fed, so to speak."

"Yes," Anubis considered, as he rubbed his rugged jaw. "It's no wonder they were drawn to one another, even through the walls of his prison."

"Yeah," I added with a scornful laugh. "I guess they were a regular Pyramus and Thisbe, talking through the chinks in the wall." The gods all stared at me blankly. "What . . . you guys don't study ancient Roman poetry in Heliopolis? Well, I guess it's not that ancient to you." Still nothing. "Shakespeare?" I raised my eyebrows, then sighed. "Never mind. Please, go on."

Anubis raised an eyebrow as he considered me and then continued, "Where Seth was thwarted with the Sons of Egypt, he found willing participants with Sebak and the Devourer. Though he could not truly cast the same spell that Isis did, there is an undeniable connection between the three of them all the same. It's why he reabsorbed Sebak just at the point of his death in the mortal realm."

"Hold on," I said, lifting a hand. "You're saying he unmade Sebak? But that was, if not instantaneous, then surely quick. Dr. Hassan said unmaking takes a long time."

Anubis cast a glance over at Isis, who explained, "The unmaking happens very quickly, at least for the creature Seth is focusing on. Unfortunately, when he unmakes a certain tree or an animal, it would appear that he has the ability to unmake the entire species. It is not inevitable, as we've seen him unmake several individuals and humanity still exists, but it's possible. This unmaking is likely the thing Hassan was referring to. If Seth was trying to unmake all of humanity by destroying the Sons of Egypt, then, yes, that would take some time. Happily, we stopped him before that occurred."

Anubis added, "You should also be aware, Lily, that when he unmakes an entire species, he gains the skills and advantages of that creature."

"Like Tia's claws," I murmured.

Isis replied, "Yes. But he not only gets the claws, he can become that creature entirely. It masks his presence. Not even we can detect him when he roams as a beast," she said. "Though some of his favorites have become very familiar to me."

Nephthys took her sister's hand and squeezed. Again I got the creeps and decided not to press for further information regarding that. "Okay," I said, "Seth's connection to the Devourer makes sense, but what about Sebak? Why did he choose him, fill him with power, and then abandon him?"

"After his death was certain," began Anubis, "Seth reabsorbed the energy he'd bestowed upon the necromancer. Then he cast what was left of Sebak into the Well of Souls for safekeeping should he ever need him again. Though Sebak was mortal, he was a powerful spell master. This was likely what interested Seth originally. But once you caused his first death, Sebak was trapped in the shape of the crocodile god and could no longer use his spells. Seth largely ignored him after that, losing interest."

"Sebak said he wanted to prove himself to his master. That's how Seth knew where we were," I said. "Also, there were shabti minions on the boat who were trying to communicate with Seth. Should we be worried?" I asked.

Nephthys and Anubis made eye contact. "There's something we haven't told you, Lily," the goddess said.

I snorted in a very unladylike fashion. "No kidding. Well, bring it on. I can't imagine it could be much worse."

The goddess winced. "The answer to your question is 'no.' Seth can't exactly . . . see you. It's part of what makes you special. Dr. Hassan taught you about an adder stone, did he not?" she asked.

Lowering my eyebrows in puzzlement, I answered, "Yes."

"Well, this place where we've been hiding is a giant adder stone. It's why Seth can't find us. And you . . . *you* are an adder stone as well."

"How can I be an adder stone?" I asked. "Are you saying I'm made up of snake bones?"

The way her face screwed up made me feel very uncomfortable. "There's just something about you, Lilliana, something that cloaks you from his view and ours. It could be Wasret, but I don't think so. You possessed this quality even before you became a sphinx. This is why not even your sisters knew about your hidden memories that you stored in your scarab. It's a good thing to be an adder stone. I promise."

I bit my thumb, thinking. "So then Sebak and the shabti spies were supposed to report our location to Seth, since he couldn't see us."

The goddess nodded. "As long as Sebak had you in his sights, so did Seth."

"Then why didn't Seth attack while we were on the river? We were weak. Vulnerable."

"He could see you, but he didn't know where you were exactly," Anubis explained. "The river is vast. It covers the entire cosmos. It would be like looking for a grain of sand in the desert, and, as you know, it's very easy to get lost there."

"Yeah," I said, remembering the close call. I'd almost lost Asten and Ahmose on the river. It was just dumb luck that we'd found Cherty. I choked down the sob that threatened to escape when I thought of the lost ferryman.

Anubis interrupted my dark thoughts. "As for the shabtis, they were probably assigned to watch Cherty. If he dropped you off in a place Seth recognized, then he could come after you. The exception being the Island of the Lost. It's why Ma'at hid the Sons of Egypt there."

"But you said you didn't know where you hid them," I said to the stern goddess.

"I did not lie, if that is what you are implying," Ma'at countered. "I truly didn't know where they were. Cherty told me of your where-abouts. The Isle of the Lost is a place only you and pathfinder could have discovered. It was safe. Seth could not follow you there, and since it constantly shifts, it is virtually undiscoverable."

"When you escaped the island," said Anubis, "you inadvertently attracted the attention of Sebak. Then, later, when you caused the nec-romancer his second death, it wounded Seth. We saw it in the faltering of the Devourer. He hadn't expected it, and as a result, he pulled back from her and left her virtually alone here. It's given us an opening."

"Not that she's ever truly alone," Nephthys said. "Still, we believe that if we can destroy the Devourer before he reabsorbs the energy he bestowed upon her, it will break whatever bond exists between them. Once she, too, experiences a final death, the energy linking them will drain away completely, and he will have to make his stand alone."

"Well, what's to stop him from unmaking her the moment we've got her cornered like he did with Sebak?" I asked.

"We'll distract him," Nephthys said, her eyes flitting to the goddess standing next to her.

I sputtered, "But . . . but isn't that exactly what he wants?"

"Seth cannot have what he wants," Isis said darkly, a dangerous edge to her voice. "It is out of his reach forever."

"But you will make him think it's still a possibility, sister," Nephthys said. "It will buy us time." A look passed between the two goddesses.

I shivered, an uneasy chill racing through my veins. There was a part of me that wanted to ask what it was Seth wanted from the beautiful goddess, who also happened to be his sister-in-law. But then again, I could guess. "This daytime drama of the gods, notwithstanding," I said, indicating Nephthys. "I thought *you* were his wife. Wouldn't it be better if you were the one to, you know, distract him?"

"No," Amun-Ra said, speaking up for the first time. His body gleamed for just an instant with a power so bright, it hid his handsome features. "He's already damaged her enough."

"Right." I bit my lip. "There's still something I don't get. If Seth is free and he can unmake anything he chooses and he's powerful enough to send all of you into cowering on this mountain, why hasn't he simply unmade everything already? He could destroy Duat or Earth and all its inhabitants without a thought. What's holding him back?"

Amun-Ra answered this time. "First, he's convinced himself he's in love with Isis. He wants to possess both her and Nephthys and have them rule beside him as his queens. If he tried to unmake Duat, or any other refuge we fled to, he'd risk losing them."

"That's disturbing, but okay."

"Second, though Seth is technically freed from the prison we fashioned for him, he is still contained."

"What does that mean, exactly?"

Nephthys answered, "Our grandparents Tefnut and Shu gave up their corporeal forms to trap him. To explain it in terms you might understand, Seth is still shackled, even though he isn't confined behind the walls of his cage."

"I see." I said this though I didn't really mean it. There were so many unanswered questions. What did shackling a god mean? Could he still come after us? Unmake things? Take animal form? "So, this spell—" I began.

"Can wait for the time being," Nephthys said. "All of you must be tired. Your journey here was surely arduous. Come. We will provide refreshment, and then you will rest until tonight. While you do, we will prepare."

Amun-Ra clapped his hands. The surface of a large cut stone shimmered before platters of food appeared. Ahmose immediately began filling a plate, which he then handed to me. I gave him a grateful smile, and he went to pick up another one.

While the three men piled their plates with thick slices of meat, roasted vegetables, stewed fruits, and flatbread, I skirted around the various gods and goddesses, who conferred quietly together, to find an empty bench. I'd just taken my first drink of the golden liquid brimming my goblet when someone sat down next to me.

"I see you are still wearing my gift," a man said. I choked on my ambrosia and leaned forward to cough. After setting down my goblet, I said, "What are you doing here, Horus?"

"Is it not obvious? I am hiding with the others."

"No. I mean, *here,* here. Sitting on my bench pestering me."

"I am hardly pestering you. In fact, I resent the notion. How unkind you are to me when all I have done is miss you."

"Have you, now?" I answered with a smirk.

"Is that so difficult to believe?"

I glanced around us. "I guess not. I can't help but notice that there aren't too many females around to keep you distracted. None that aren't relatives, anyway."

"That is true. Though"—he picked up my hand and pressed my fingertips to his mouth, then kissed them in a very deliberate fashion—"you know no other woman holds a candle to you."

I sighed. The fairy in my head giggled. And Tia's inner voice rumbled throatily.

A plate hit the stone bench with a clatter, and Amon stepped into view. He looked from my hand to the god holding it. "I believe you have usurped my spot," Amon said, barely restrained tension tightening his arms.

Horus laughed. "Have I, young godling? I was just telling Lily how the halls of Heliopolis have been dull since her departure."

"How interesting," Amon said. "I would imagine that if there was anything dim about Heliopolis, it would be attributed to you."

Horus narrowed his eyes on Amon. "Tread carefully, youngster," he said. "I have already generously allowed you to borrow my golden falcon. Do not seek to make me regret that precious gift."

"That is the difference between us," Amon said, leaning closer, towering over the seated god. "I would never give up something so precious."

Rising to his feet, fists tightened, Horus spat, "You ungrateful whelp. It would seem you need to learn a lesson."

Before he could even make a move, Ahmose and Asten appeared behind Amon. "Was he bothering Lily?" Ahmose asked.

"Isn't it obvious?" Asten remarked.

I stepped between them, pressing my hand against Amon's muscled chest and Horus's. "Horus didn't mean anything by it."

"Oh, I think he did," Amon said, his eyes fixed on the god.

Seeing he wasn't going to back down, I cupped his cheeks with my hands. Amon's eyes were lit up bright green. He was close to channeling his power. "Hey," I said gently, and he finally looked away from Horus to me. "This fight isn't worth it. Let's focus on the one we really need to think about. Besides," I said, flashing the god behind me a pointed look, "I can handle anything he throws at me."

Horus laughed. "I think that is an encounter I would rather enjoy."

This time it was Asten who stepped forward challenging the god. "Lily is not yours. If you know what's best, you'll back away from her."

The god snickered. "Is she yours, then, Dreamer? Or yours, Path-finder?" Pained looks crossed both of their faces, but they said nothing. "What exactly are you three going to do with one woman?" he asked.

"Tell me. Will you tear her in half?" He glanced at Amon, whose eyes glimmered with crystalline shards sharp enough to kill. "I'm sorry," Horus said in mock apology. "I mean, thirds?"

"Horus!" Isis intervened and slapped a hand down on her son's shoulder. "Your conduct is unbecoming."

The god sobered instantly. He bowed to Isis. "I apologize, Mother. My intention was merely to check on the gift I bestowed Lily. As far as these three prickly groundhogs," he said, indicating the Sons of Egypt, "I was just having a bit of fun riling them up. They looked like they were itching for a fight to release some of their pent-up frustration."

"Be that as it may," Isis said, "there will be plenty of fight for all of us later. Come, son. I wish to confer with you before I leave."

"No, Mother," Horus said. "Please reconsider this. Father wouldn't want—"

"It is for your father that I do this," she said softly. "Do not make it harder than it is, son," she said. I would have thought being reprimanded by his mother in front of a girl would have been embarrassing for Horus, but actually he seemed much more worried about his mother's well-being than he was concerned over appearances. It made me like him more. There was definitely much more to Horus than met the eye.

After he departed and we began eating, Amon, who was uncharacteristically not enjoying his feasting, said quietly, "I know what you intend to do."

"It must be nice to get an inside peek into anything you want to."

"It is not . . . nice. There are many times I wished I did not have the Eye, especially in instances such as this one."

"I know," I answered softly. "But we need it. You know it's not something we can set aside, as much as we want to."

One of the citizens of Heliopolis that hovered around Nephthys came over and asked if we were finished with our meal. When I indicated that we were, noting that none of the brothers had eaten as heartily as they typically did, she bade us follow her.

She led us to a wide canopy that sheltered the opening of a cave in the mountainside. It was large enough that not even Ahmose had to duck and wide enough that two of us could enter side by side. Carved stone sconces made the torchlight dance over the walls. Inside, the air was cool and a little damp.

We went down a series of stone steps until we came into a wide cavern. A few caves had been arranged for us. In one there were three beds, a stone basin for washing, and fresh clothing. The other had one much larger bed covered with silken fabrics of gold, gunmetal, and bronze. A mirror adorned the wall, and the stone floor was carpeted with a thick woven rug. It looked so inviting.

When the woman left, I checked my appearance in the mirror. Smoothing my brown hair, I paused, fingering a blond highlight. Twisting, I noticed others, some more subtle, some older and faded, and some brand-new. Each man had left a visible reminder. Sweeping back my hair, I tied it in a knot at the nape of my neck. *Are we really going to do this?*

We will give them a choice, Tia said.

And what if they say no? Ashleigh asked.

They won't, Tia replied confidently.

It's a risk either way, I said. *But it's the only solution I can come up with. If you have any other ideas, now's the time.*

Tia and Ashleigh said nothing, so I steeled myself and headed out of my room to find the men. Standing outside the cave, the entrance draped with a cloth, I was about to clear my throat when I heard them talking.

"We cannot let her do this," Amon said.

Asten answered, "I'm not sure how we'd stop it."

"I'd rather see them with you than have them disappear," Ahmose said.

"Come in, Nehabet," Amon called.

Embarrassed to be caught eavesdropping, I stumbled forward, kicking loose pebbles and catching myself on the stone entryway. Ducking beneath the fabric cover, I entered their much smaller room and placed my hands behind my back, clutching the gemstone I'd retrieved from the hidden pocket in my quiver.

Asten spoke first. "We don't want you to do it," he said.

I stammered as I placed Amon's scarab in my pocket. "Do what?"

"Give yourself over to Wasret."

Blinking, I said, "Oh. That's what you all were talking about."

"Isn't that why you're here?" Ahmose asked. "To break the bad news?" His sooty lashes lowered, casting shadows on his cheeks. It bothered me that my Ahmose could no longer look me in the eye.

"No." I bit my lip. "I'm not planning to make any kind of announcement like that. In fact, my hope is still to avoid channeling Wasret, if it's at all possible."

Amon pursed his lips. "Then, what is it?"

"I . . ." I wrung my hands. "I have an idea. I mean, we have an idea. We think it's a way to stay connected with you. Like I am with Amon. We want to form a bond."

"A bond?" Amon said. "Do you mean like the one I used on you in New York?"

I nodded my head. "I mean like the permanent one. The one you cast before you died at the pyramid."

"You remember what I told you about this?" Amon asked softly.

"Yes."

"And the others know?"

"Yes."

"It might not work," he said.

Amon stood up and took my hands in his. "You know how I feel about you, Young Lily. And I do not wish for you to mistake my hesitancy for reticence, but I need to understand what you hope to accomplish before I attempt to help you wield this spell."

"Okay," I said, wetting my lips. "First, you said that having my heart scarab helped you find me, that I didn't disappear completely from your vision, right?"

"Yes. That is correct."

"You also said that you could read my thoughts if you wanted to but not Tia's or Ashleigh's."

Amon nodded.

"Well, we think there's a reason for that." I sucked in a breath, glancing over at the closed-off expressions of Asten and Ahmose. "We think the heart scarab you have belongs only to me."

"I am afraid I do not understand."

Asten stepped forward and took one of my hands. "Is it possible?" he said. His eyes lighting.

"Is what possible?" Ahmose asked, thick arms folded across his chest.

Cupping my hand in his and rubbing his thumb across my fingers, Asten murmured, "It makes sense. Their dreamworlds are different."

"Of course they are different," Ahmose said. "Get to the point."

"Ah," Amon said. "I see."

"Someone had better explain what all of you are talking about," Ahmose threatened.

"Ahmose," I said. "We think that Tia and Ashleigh have heart scarabs of their own. If we're wrong, we've lost nothing, but if we're right—"

Amon held up a hand. "We will hold back our hopes until we verify with certainty our first premise. Come, then, Lily. Let's find out."

Taking my hands, Amon drew me close. Looking into my eyes, he said, "Tia? If you will come forward . . ."

The lioness uncurled from the back of my mind and switched places with me. My muscles tightened with her strength, and she blinked. Turning to Asten, she twitched up a corner of her mouth and then squeezed Amon's hands. "Do I have a heart to share?" Tia asked softly. "I am uncertain if I ever did have one."

"You have one," Asten said quietly.

"Place your hand over your heart," Amon instructed. When she did, he cupped his hand over hers. "Now concentrate. Ashleigh and Lily, try to quiet your thoughts. Be as still as possible. Tia, close your eyes and see yourself in your mind. Find your true nature. Think of what makes you strong. What is solely you. Think of your talents. The things you love. Now . . . concentrate all of those things into one place. Listen to your heart as it beats. Imagine that each beat is freedom. It's your foot hitting the ground as you run. That's it. One . . . two . . . three . . . Wrap your fingers around it and pull."

Amon stepped back, and Tia opened her eyes. Lying in her hand was a gleaming golden scarab. The bright yellow gemstone had a band of light that traced a straight vertical line down the center. At the base were not the spindly legs of a bug, but the claws of a lion, and powerful golden wings shot out on either side. Over the top was a golden lioness with hollowed-out eyes that gleamed with the light of the gem behind them.

"It's a cat's eye," Amon said. "How fitting."

Tia ran her fingertips across the stone. Asten held out his hands, asking, "May I hold on to it for you?" She nodded distractedly.

"And now for Ashleigh," Amon said.

Tia retreated to the place where I hovered in the dark, and Ashleigh surged up. Amon repeated the process with her and soon, in her palm rested a green scarab with delicate butterfly legs and fairy wings. With a twinkle in her eye, she handed it to Ahmose for safekeeping.

When that was done, Amon said, "You were right. They each have a scarab. Now, ladies, what are your intentions, exactly?"

"Well, it's a bit obvious, then, isn't it, lad?" Ashleigh said, using my voice. "I'd like ta ask the 'andsome bloke standin' there all sulky-like if he'll take care o' my heart."

Ahmose replied by lowering his eyebrows and taking hold of my elbow, steering me out of the cave so his brothers couldn't listen.

"Ash," he began. "This thing you ask—"

"Aye, it's important, I know. It's how ya'll find us in case we lose ourselves again."

"It means much more than that."

"Ach, lad," Ashleigh said, making a clucking noise with her tongue and stepping closer. "After everythin' we've been through together, do ya not desire ta be with me?"

"You know I do."

"Then what maligned beastie torments ya so?"

He rubbed a hand across his jaw, the stubble scratching against his palm. "I just don't think you fully realize the implications—"

Placing my hand over his, I wrapped his fingers around the green gemstone. *"All three o' us understand the implications. Don'tcha see? It's a wee match we're givin' ya—a tiny light we can follow ta find our way home in the dark. An' make no mistake, lad, you are my home. If ya keep it close, I'll come back ta ya. Have no doubt."*

I took hold of his shirt and pulled him down, capturing his lips with mine. His arms roped around my waist, tugging me closer as he made a low sound in the back of his throat. Ahmose pressed me so tightly against him, I could hardly breathe. Yet breathing seemed to matter very little. I didn't realize he'd picked me up until he broke away and set me down, steadying my trembling limbs.

"Now, that's how a girl should be prop'rly kissed," I said with a mischievous grin and a wicked glint in my eye.

Ahmose brushed a loose strand of hair from my cheek as he gazed deeply into my eyes. There was nothing teasing about the way he looked at me. "I want you to know, I know what this means," he said. "I accept your token, Ash. From this moment on, my heart will desire only you."

He began chanting a familiar spell. The one that would bind us together permanently. After it was done, he stepped back, placing the green scarab over his heart, and before I could say anything, it sank into his chest. When it was gone, a soft smile lifted the corners of his mouth. "It's as it should be," he said with a sigh. Lifting his other hand, he touched his chest, and a shimmering light appeared between his fingers. A scarab materialized. It was a moonstone.

With only a slight hesitation, he handed me the gem and folded my fingers over it. "I know you cannot keep it in the same way," he said. "But it is yours all the same."

"My lovely Ahmose," Ashleigh said. *"I'll treasure it always."*

I put his precious scarab into my wide pocket next to Amon's. He kissed my hand and tucked it on his arm as he guided me back to the others. When we ducked inside the cave, he said, "It's done."

Ahmose stepped aside, and I turned to Asten, who held the golden scarab in his hand, thoughtfully staring at it as he sat on the bed. He glanced up at me and bit his lip, his handsome face troubled. After a tension-filled moment, he said, "I don't think I'll be keeping this scarab in exactly the same way Amon and Ahmose are," he said.

In the blink of an eye, Tia rose to the surface. Our claws emerged, and she stalked toward Asten and lifted her palm to his throat. As she squeezed, his eyes widened. The lioness narrowed her eyes and hissed, *"I'll give you exactly five seconds to explain your actions before I rip you into tiny little pieces and toss your shredded, deceitful carcass to the four winds for the scavengers to choke down."*

A Wing and a Prayer

"Now, wait just a moment, Tia," Asten managed to cough out.

Amon and Ahmose stepped forward as if to intervene, but Tia's low growl gave them pause. When we were satisfied that they weren't going to press, she retracted her claws and moved her hand to Asten's shoulder, gripping his shirt tightly but keeping her eyes narrowed on him.

As Asten rubbed his throat, a handprint standing out on it, Tia accused, *"Do you fear the lioness, Asten? Perhaps you are an unworthy consort and I have chosen my mate unwisely."*

Angrily, she thrust Asten aside and turned her back on him. *"Ahmose?"* she began, but Asten rose suddenly from the bed, grabbed her arm, and spun her around. He tugged my body against his form and held it in an inescapable grip. With a tight expression that brooked no argument, he said without glancing at his brothers, "A little privacy?"

Amon and Ahmose gave us a long look and then left. Tia was done being manhandled. She broke away from him, but Asten grunted. He grabbed her shoulders and pushed her up against a wall, barring our escape with his body. Heat radiated from him, and his skin gleamed in the dimness of the cavern room.

"You will do me the courtesy of listening, lady lioness."

Tia bristled at the threat she recognized in his voice. Something inside her wanted to rise to his challenge. My breaths came in pants as my chest rose and fell. The anger she felt—no, we felt—was a heady and almost tangible thing. Yet I sensed the rage was draining, slowly changing into something equally powerful and perhaps even more dangerous. Through Tia, I became aware of the press of his body against mine and the way his eyes darted to my lips.

Bucking against him only resulted in him locking my hands against the wall. Tia shot him a cutting glare as my whole body bristled with fire. I could see he wasn't frightened of the ferocious cat inside me. Still, Tia taunted him, needing to provoke a response. "You are a coward," she spat. "Admit it."

Asten tilted his head, a frown marring his features. His grip on my hands lessened, but I didn't lower my arms because he pinned us in place with his eyes. We were transfixed by his gaze. We were like two predators, staring each other down, seeing who would flinch first. Slowly, he moved his hands lower until his fingertips grazed my palms. Then he came closer, so close his hair brushed my face with a featherlight touch.

Tia's cat instincts were a jumble. Part of her screamed that she should protect my vulnerable neck, the source of my lifeblood. But another part of her wanted to feel Asten's lips on my throat. Asten's warm breath lifted the fine hairs on my neck as he murmured in a low, dangerous voice, "Just because I am cautious does not make me a coward, Tia. Do not mistake my hesitancy with a lack of . . . desire."

My body shivered as his lips brushed my earlobe and trailed along my jaw. My eyes closed, the human side convincing the cat side that even though it was dangerous, it was the kind of danger we liked. When his lips found the corner of my mouth, Tia let out a little moan of pleasure. We gave ourselves over to sensation.

As he nibbled the corner of my mouth and kissed my cheeks and jaw, his hands trailed down my bare arms, slowly, tantalizing my skin, lighting each nerve on fire. When he got to my shoulders, he swept his hands up over them and caught hold of my neck. Sinking his fingers into my hair, he tilted my head and kissed me.

Tia wanted furious, blazing heat. To grab hold of him and race through the tall grasses at breakneck speed. But he held her back, teasing and stroking as he kissed her in a slow burn that seemed never to end. He lifted his head and traced his thumbs over my cheekbones. All he'd done was kiss Tia, and yet my heart beat as rapidly as if I'd been chasing down a gazelle.

Asten's brown eyes were round, glistening pools that mesmerized me. Tia licked her lips, wanting to taste him again. This time he was the one who groaned. "There will be more of that later." Pressing his forehead to mine, he wrapped his arms around my waist and pulled me closer. "I promise," he said.

It was hard for me to separate Tia's feelings from my own. Ashleigh was less affected. She didn't know Asten the way we did, but even she felt the emotional stirrings. The pronouns were confusing. He touched me, my body, and yet I knew it was Tia he longed for.

I didn't think I was in love with Asten, and yet, in that moment, I could have sworn I was. It was the ultimate 4-D experience. Willing my heartbeat to still, I heard Tia whisper with my voice, *"Then why, Asten?"* I could feel the muscles of his back stiffen, but she had to know—we had to know. *"If you feel for me in this way, why will you not protect my heart?"*

"You misunderstand me," he said, drawing back and taking my hands. He touched his lips to the back of each one, kissing them in a way that left Tia breathless. "I will cherish it," he said. He looked at us with complete sincerity in his eyes. "I consider it a gift beyond measure, and I vow that I will protect it until I am no longer capable."

"But you will not keep it inside you," my voice said flatly. The lioness was confused and heartbroken. She felt like any human would after the first sting of rejection. The idea that she was now more human than lioness bothered her.

"No." Asten stepped away and turned his back to me. I was about to walk away from him when he shifted. "But I will offer you mine."

He held out his hands and Tia looked from his earnest face down to what lay nestled inside them. A chocolate diamond scarab with bronze legs and wings rested in his palms. She touched the surface of the scarab, marveling at the smooth, almost-cold gem. A faint pulse shot into my fingertips, and we knew it was his heartbeat.

"But I thought . . . ," Tia began.

"You thought what?" he asked. "That I didn't care for you? That a fairy and a human deserved love, but a lioness didn't?"

She froze. That was exactly what she'd been thinking.

Asten took my hand and placed the scarab into it. "You thought Lily was the one," he added quietly.

She glanced up quickly, but his lashes were lowered, shielding his eyes. "Isn't she?" Tia asked.

He paused for a long moment, his mouth twisting before he answered. "I'll admit, loving a human would be easier in many ways. But"—Asten tucked his finger beneath my chin, lifting my face so he could look us directly in the eye—"I've gotten to know both of you pretty well by now. I like Lily. But it's you I'm interested in, Tia."

His words were what Tia wanted to hear, and yet she'd been a witness to the sweet and tender exchange between Ahmose and Ashleigh. Tia knew how Amon and I felt about one another, too. There was something wrong. Something Asten wasn't telling her, and it chafed. She didn't like human deception.

"What are you hiding from me?" she asked. "Are you ashamed to tell me your true reasons? Are you ashamed of your feelings?"

His mouth fell open. "No, Tia. How could you even think that?"

She turned away from him and gazed at his heart scarab. A wet drop splashed on its surface, and she smoothed a thumb over it. Tia was crying? Tia was crying! Lionesses do not cry. Her shock over the emotional response reverberated in my mind. Irritated, she wiped the tears away and shrugged off his hand.

Asten came around and took hold of my shoulders. "This has nothing to do with you. I'm not ashamed. It's just . . ." He ran a hand through his hair and paced the small room. ". . . it's just that my heart isn't . . . built the same."

"What do you mean?" Tia asked, cocking my head.

"I mean I . . ." He swallowed and sighed. Heavily, he sank down on the bed and rested his head in his hands. "I already tried, Tia."

"What?" she asked, not sure if she understood the words he'd mumbled.

He looked up, shame coloring his cheeks and neck. "It wouldn't work. When you were out there with Ahmose, I tried to absorb your heart. I thought I'd save us time. I already knew how I felt, but I . . . I couldn't. Amon knows," he added dejectedly. "He thinks it might have something to do with my judgment in the netherworld. Truthfully, it could also be because I'm not the prince born to this calling. It could be a number of things."

Tia sat down next to him, so stunned she didn't know what to say at first. *"But,"* she began, *"but you gave me your scarab."*

"Yes. Apparently, I do still have one of those. If you don't want it, I'll understand."

Not want it? Not want the heart of the fierce and fiery god of the stars? How could he think such a thing?

Tia clenched my hand reflexively, enclosing the scarab. Carefully, she put it in my lap and turned to the man at her side. Cupping his face, she stared hard into his eyes. *"Now, you listen to me, Asten. There is nothing wrong with your heart. There is nothing wrong with you. When this is all over, we will seek an answer to this issue. But for the time being, it matters not."*

"What if it means you are lost to Wasret? Perhaps you should find another who can summon you from the darkness," he said almost wearily.

"Asten," Tia said, *"there is no one else that I would heed."*

He nodded and then asked almost tentatively, "Do you still want to be bound to me?"

"Can you enact the spell without taking my heart inside yourself?"

"Yes."

"Then you may proceed."

Lifting his hands, Asten wove a starry cloud and chanted the spell that would bind Tia to him forever. When it was done, he pulled Tia into his arms and they sat there for several minutes, just simply holding on to one another. We then heard a slight cough on the other side of the curtain.

"You should sleep now," Asten said. "We're leaving at sundown."

Tia nodded. *"Good night, then."*

"Good night."

As she slid from his arms, Tia retreated, and I came forward once more. Opening the curtain, I saw Ahmose and Amon standing there. Taking each of their hands, I squeezed them and then headed back to my cave room. Though I got into bed, I tossed and turned as my mind ran through the various reasons why Asten couldn't absorb Tia's heart.

Unable to be separated from them, I put all three scarabs beneath my pillow and buried my hand under it, too, so that my arm touched each one. The little pulses of three separate heartbeats soothed us. Tia and Ashleigh spoke with me long into the night. When we'd all agreed upon a course of action, I finally closed my eyes and slept.

It seemed like only minutes later when a hand touched my shoulder.

"They are gathering above, Lily," Amon said. "Come when you are ready."

Groggily, I rose from the bed and splashed cold water on my face. The fresh clothes that lay in a nicely folded stack nearly brought tears to my eyes. After I was dressed in a loose shirt tucked into soft breeches, I made a halfhearted attempt to work my fingers through the tangled mass of my hair but soon gave up.

Carefully, I placed each heart scarab in the quiver where the few precious arrows of Isis lay and examined the leather harness. It had neither stretched nor loosened from the wetness of the Cosmic River.

Comfortable boots completed my ensemble. When I was ready, with
my bow, quiver, and harness with knives strapped on, I exited my cave
and found all three men waiting for me. Nodding to each of them, I said,
"Let's go."

The servant of Nephthys waited for us at the bottom of the stairs. I followed her up with the Sons of Egypt trailing behind me. After a few
steps, my neck felt prickly and hot as if someone held a burning candle
too close to it. The heat stole around my neck like a tight collar and
crept slowly up to my cheeks.

When I looked back, wondering if anyone else was having the same
problem, three pairs of eyes locked on to me. My steps grew heavier.
My clothes suddenly irritated my skin. I pulled at my shirt, fanning my
skin with the fabric. The blood in my veins became roiling lava. Liquid
hunger pooled in my belly.

The fire ebbed when a hand cupped the small of my back. It was like
ice touching a fevered brow. Amon murmured quietly in my ear as he
lifted the hem of my shirt to rub soothing little circles on my bare skin,
"It is a side effect of the bond, intensified by the sphinx side of you."

"What's happening to me?" I asked, limbs trembling.

His hazel eyes gleamed in the dark cavern. "The blood of a sphinx
is volatile. Especially when she takes a mate."

I gulped. "But we haven't . . ." My words trailed off as I realized
how awkward a turn the conversation had headed. "Mated," I finally
managed to spit out.

Amon's lips twisted. "The fire burned in you before, despite our
lack of a—what would you call it—a honeymoon?"

I nodded, grimacing at the same time. I vaguely recalled Dr. Hassan
saying something about a sphinx's blood before. Now I wished I'd paid
more attention.

"Do you remember how our bond led you to find me in the nether-world?"

"Yes."

"Imagine that times fifty." When I raised an eyebrow, giving him a you-can't-be-serious look, Amon further explained, "Once a sphinx selects a life companion, they are bound in such a way that only he can cool her fiery blood. When you gave me your heart scarab before we left the netherworld, the first sphinx bond was cemented."

"But I thought we were bound together permanently in the pyramid," I said, rubbing my arms, my cooling skin itchy.

Amon shook his head. "That was just you, the human, Lilliana Young. The sphinx bond couldn't occur until Tia accepted me, too. That didn't happen until you gave me your heart. If she had been against it, you wouldn't have been able to draw it out. That Tia and Ashleigh were able to bring forth their heart scarabs as well means that you were all in agreement with the bonds created."

"Okay, but this fire thing is new. We didn't burn up at Nana's farm," I said. "Does it only happen every so often? Can I turn it on and off?"

"No. Not exactly. The mind is powerful. Without your memories of me, your body didn't prickle with heat. Since your memories awoke, I've been with you enough to keep the fire banked. You won't normally experience it while you're close to your bond mate anyway. But when a sphinx heads into battle, which we are about to do, the embers become a wildfire. It is a means of preserving you. The fire fuels your skills in battle. In your case," he said, "the reaction is amplified even more since you are now bound to three different men. Your blood burns for each of us, and we feel it. It's a message to us that you are headed into danger. If it happens when we are apart, we can follow it directly to you and, hopefully, assist you in vanquishing whatever foe threatens your life."

"Wait a minute. You said it normally won't happen when I'm near you. So what does it mean if we are together when it happens?"

"When we are together, it means . . . it means you desire to be close." Amon took hold of my hand, threading his fingers through mine. "When your blood calls," he said, "we cannot deny the pull. It sings us a siren song. For me, this has always been the case, even before you became a sphinx, but the strength of it is irresistible now. Any separation from this time forward would be almost unbearable for us. Any of us," he added so the others could hear.

"So as long as you, Asten, or Ahmose are nearby, I won't burn up like a rocket entering the atmosphere?"

"We must touch you to bank the flame once it begins. But the fire will not harm you, Young Lily, though it may be overwhelming at times. I should have anticipated such a response when enacting three bonds. You are a sphinx and are, therefore, subject to the instincts that govern such a creature. Binding oneself to a sphinx is not something to be taken lightly."

Seeing my concerned expression, Amon added, "We do not regret it. Not one of us. Do not think to entertain the idea in your mind that we are not as committed to you as you are to us. We take our vows seriously."

Vows? Does our bond mean we're . . . we're married? Wow. I was so not in the place I ever thought I'd be at this age. I didn't think I was going to get married until . . . well, I supposed I'd never really thought about marriage, at least not seriously. *But still—*I gave my new bond-mates sidelong glances, admiring the stubbly jaws and the strong shoulders, felt the hand entwined with mine, and let out a sigh—*a girl could do worse.*

When we reached the top of the stairs, we were immediately surrounded by the gods. Nephthys gave me a long, discerning look—the kind that said she knew all the things we'd been up to. "Isis," she announced, "it's time."

The beautiful winged goddess approached and walked around us in a circle, murmuring soft words I couldn't make out. The sun had just set, and the sky was the fleeting shade between purple and black. In a moment it was gone. Then something brushed across my consciousness. I could have sworn I heard the whispering of voices in my mind. They were nothing like Tia or Ashleigh. They felt . . . foreign.

"This spell," Isis said distracting me from the voices, "will channel the energies of the cosmos. We will bind you in such a way that you are cloaked from the Devourer. If she captures Amon again, your bound hearts will not lead her to you and vice versa."

"This is how you and Osiris are connected?" I asked.

"Not exactly." Isis cocked her head. Her mouth puckered, then wrapped around a word. "Wait," she said. The goddess closed her eyes and raised her nose as if seeking a scent. When she opened them, she narrowed her gaze on me and said, "Well, well, you have been busy. We knew about Amon, of course, but this . . . ," she said, indicating Asten and Ahmose. "This is new, is it not?"

Flushing, I nodded.

"I see," Isis said. "It . . . complicates things." Turning to Amon, she asked, "I understand the reasons for using my spell for your own benefit, but why did you give it to your brothers?"

Amon, as tall as the statuesque goddess, stood before her boldly as he answered, "They have as much right to happiness as I do, I should think."

"Interesting." A corner of Isis's mouth lifted, and there was a telltale sparkle in her eye. "And very generous, I might add, considering you've bound the woman you love to your brothers. I'll have to make a few changes because of it."

He didn't bother to clarify that the spell enacted had been for Tia and Ashleigh and not for me, but perhaps to her it didn't matter. *Or . . .* I bit my lip, considering. *Is it possible Amon didn't tell me all the details of the spell?* Whatever the case, it was too late to do anything about it now. I'd have to confront him about it later.

Isis turned, pacing. Her lustrous wings quivered slightly. I remembered the feel of her feather-tipped arrows brushing my cheek when I drew the string and wondered if it hurt when her feathers fell out.

When Isis came to a decision, she asked me to stand in the middle and for the Sons of Egypt to form a triangle around me. Amon was to place a hand over my heart and his other on the shoulder of Asten. Asten and Ahmose were to also put one hand on the shoulder of the brother standing next to them and then the other one on my shoulder.

"Since you have already chosen to bind your hearts," Isis said, "I will finish the portion of the spell that Amon started, but know that you will still have the power to walk away should you choose."

"Hold on," I said. "I thought our bonds were unbreakable. That nothing could ever come between us."

"And nothing can," Isis said, "except yourselves."

"I don't understand," I said.

"You have bound your hearts, but as you know, a heart can be broken." Isis glanced over at her sister, Nephthys, who lowered her head to stare at her hands. "There is a deeper bond, though, than just the exchange of hearts. It is a union that is shared by two beings who cling to one another so tightly, they become one. This is the spell I have created that connects me with Osiris. It is a bond of souls, of the cosmic power that makes up the both of us.

"To enact it, I had to give up a part of myself. Now we share our energy, feel one another's pain. If one dies, so does the other. This is a hidden spell. An invocation not even Amon can discern, for it was enacted here on this mountain, where not even the stars could be witness.

"I will not coerce your affections or take your agency from you to create such a lasting bond at this time. But I will link the six of you. From this point on you will be yoked together. The only way to separate you after this will be to break the yoke. When this happens—if it happens—it will devastate you. You may recover from this break, but you may not. Do you understand?"

We all voiced that we did.

"Again, know that I will not touch the bonds you created yourselves; instead, I will create a syzygy, a powerful spell that will serve to strengthen the ties between the Sons of Egypt as well as those of the

Progenitors of Wasret." She touched a hand to Amon's shoulder, her face full of sympathy. "Amon, if you had come to me, I could have guided your path, strengthened the bond you attempted so that truly nothing could sever it. Such a tie would have prevented all that has befallen your loved one. It is unfortunate that the one you chose to love is the one my sister was waiting for."

Amon stiffened his shoulders, and his eyes met mine. They were full of sorrow and apology. I wanted to reassure him, to tell him I understood and I had no regrets. Maybe he was able to read my mind, but I suspected he had turned off that ability. He chose to respond to Isis with only with a nod.

"Sister," Isis said, "it is time to begin."

An icy rush of air swept over the mountain. My skin prickled and turned as cold as if my arms were frostbitten. When the wind died, I stood there, eyes closed, feeling the beating of not one, not three, but six hearts. Swallowing, I opened my eyes and found I was looking straight into Amon's. He gave me a brief smile and raised his eyebrows in a silent question.

A slight nod told him that, yes, I was okay. I was, in fact, more than okay. After the spell, I felt an even deeper connection to the others. It had nothing to do with love, though—at least not romantic love. It was more like we were a unit, a team of warriors heading into battle. If we were asked to put ourselves in harm's way to protect each other, then that's what we would do.

Amon raised his hands in the air, murmuring a spell, and sand gathered around him, swirling in heavy gusts. When it settled, he was dressed in gleaming battle armor, his deadly scimitars strapped onto his back. Sand swirled around Asten and Ahmose as they also prepped for battle.

I stood, uncomfortably wringing my hands. Nephthys approached. "Why do you not use your power to create your own armor?" she asked.

How could I share my fears with the goddess who'd been seeking Wasret since, pretty much, the dawn of time?

Isis touched her sister's arm. "She is worried that calling forth her power summons the other," she explained.

"Ah," Nephthys said. She compressed her lips, studying me for a moment, her eyes brighter than an Iowa sky. Then she said, "I understand your hesitation. You wish to remain yourself for as long as possible." When I only nodded miserably, she went on, "Your ability to clothe yourself was present before you added Ashleigh to your circle, was it not?"

"Y . . . yes," I stammered, remembering how Nebu taught me how to use my newfound power in Heliopolis. "And Amon's scarab clothed me in armor when I faced the Devourer in the netherworld."

Nephthys smiled. "You may continue to draw upon this. It comes from within you. It is a part of being a sphinx and therefore not exclusive to Wasret. The protection that comes from your heart scarabs is a visible result of the love your young men have for you."

I swallowed. "Are you certain?"

Isis laughed. "If my sister says it, then it must be true."

Nephthys's expression tightened, but then she took hold of my hand. "Trust me in this."

"Okay," I said, blowing out a breath. "Here goes."

Carefully, almost hesitantly, Tia and I worked together to draw upon the power of the sphinx. Particles of sand blew over our feet and encased our legs. Becoming more confident, we summoned more sand. The wind blew harder, creating a shifting wall between us and the others. My clothing battered my body, and my hair whipped back and forth like frenzied Medusa snakes.

When it settled, I wore a boned leather vest that cinched my waist. It was plated with thin-pounded armor. My blouse was dark and made of thickly woven gray material, as were the leggings I wore. Armor-plated boots and gauntlets protected my lower legs and wrists. A metal collar and shoulder plates finished out my attire. The clothing was heavy, but it would offer protection. Especially if we had to go after those sky-demon things.

The harness had shifted from my shoulders to a leather belt that slung low on my hips. My spear-knives were now easily accessible, one on each hip. I practiced drawing them out, and when I returned them, they snapped back into place almost of their own volition.

The quiver and bow were still in their usual positions across my back. For a brief moment, I panicked, unable to find the heart scarabs in the quiver. Then Isis pointed to my midsection, and I saw the twinkling scarabs were now embedded in my belt. Amon's was in the center, and the other two on either side. When I touched them, the sparkling gem-stones spread out in overlapping scales that wrapped around my body like armor. They were hard as diamonds, but they weighed nothing.

Isis walked around me, inspecting my attire. She frowned and shook her head.

"What's wrong?" I asked, patting the wound braids that created a chignon at the nape of my neck. "Did I forget something?"

"I think you did," she said.

I checked my quiver, tugged on my shirt, and looked over at Asten, who just shrugged.

Sighing, Isis said, "It pains me to see such a gift wasted."

"What gift? The bow and arrows? I've used them as little as pos-sible, but—"

The goddess hissed and waved her hands. "No, I do not mean the arrows."

"Then what . . . ?" I began. The goddess lifted her wings pointedly and rustled them.

At seeing the still-clueless expression on my face, Nephthys came to my aid. "What my sister is wondering," she said, "is why you aren't using your wings."

24

Waiting in the Wings

"My . . . my what?" I asked, wondering how I had found my voice.

"Your wings," Isis said. "I was sure Hassan understood," she mumbled.

I put my hands on my hips. "Apparently, you played things a little too close to the chest." I pointed a finger at the goddess, waggling it in the air, and then swept it in a big arc. "That goes for all of you."

Isis sighed and gave me a long-suffering look, like I was a child asking her to explain the most basic of things. "Do you not remember that the symbol you found on the temple was that of the Greek version of the sphinx?"

"Yes, vaguely," I answered.

"And what is the difference between the Egyptian and the Greek depiction of a sphinx?" she asked.

"Hold on. He told me this." I paced away a few steps and then returned. "The Greek version is female."

"Yes, and what else?"

"It has wings?"

"Very good. The day I left you to your fate on the African plains, I gave you not two but three weapons." She paused, waiting like an impatient teacher for me to answer her unasked question.

"The spear-knives," I said, "and the bow and the arrows that make creatures answer my questions and bend to my will, and then there was the . . ."

Isis lifted a hand. "That isn't what my arrows do."

"They don't? Then why did the reapers—"

She interrupted, "My arrows have healing powers. In the netherworld, the arrows healed the mystical wounds caused by true evil. The reapers were not true minions of the Devourer, so the arrow freed them from her control. In the case of the hellhounds, they must bow to the arrow's power, but they are dark in nature in and of themselves. So the arrow did not heal or transform them."

"It didn't kill him either," I said drily.

"No. Hellhounds are not living, nor have they ever been. They are simply shadows that are born in the netherworld. Their sole purpose was to chase the dead toward paths of healing, so that those assigned there might leave it one day. The Devourer has used and corrupted them."

"Fine. Whatever. Let's get back then to the third weapon you mentioned. It is . . . ?"

"Your wings, of course."

"Okay, even assuming I have them, which all indications show that I don't, how would I use them as a weapon?"

"When my feather entered your back, it hurt, did it not?"

"Of course it hurt. Still does on occasion."

"It hurts because you keep your wings locked away. Close your eyes." When she saw me obey, she went on. "Focus on that nub between your shoulder blades. The place the feather entered. Now allow that irritation to expand."

I twitched uncomfortably and stretched my back, rolling my neck back and forth. The tiny itch turned into something burning. Hissing, I said, "It stings."

"It will the first time they emerge. Think of the hurt like a splinter. It will feel better once your wings are out."

My skin tore open, pain exploding along my spine, and I cried out and sank down to one knee, placing my hands on the ground as I gasped. I bit the inside of my cheek and tasted blood. My claws emerged and drew furrows in the dust as I panted. With a last heaving push, the agony escaped, leaving behind a relief so palpable I laughed.

Retracting my claws, I shifted to my feet but almost fell backward from the weight. Then something picked me up and steadied me. The moon had risen, and though we stood in its direct light, shadows moved across my face. I turned my head slowly and saw a wing hovering near my shoulder. It definitely didn't belong to Isis.

"They're yours," she said. "Quite a lovely pair, too."

I took two quick steps back and had the overbalance issue again, but this time my body actually rose into the air. The wings above me flapped once, twice, and then set me down. Apparently, gravity worked differently now. I curled my right wing around myself until I could press my hand against the soft feathers.

"You control them with your mind," Isis said. "They will not be as difficult to navigate as you might think. You can send them away again with a mere thought." I shivered, thinking about the suffering they caused when they first emerged. The goddess must have read my mind, because she added, "It will not hurt any longer. Not now that they've been released."

Testing out her statement, I bit my lip and willed them away. The wings tucked up behind my back and shrank down, disappearing. I reached my hands over my shoulders, patting my shoulder blades as best I could, but the wings were completely gone.

"Before you summon them back," Isis said, "may I suggest a slight change in your wardrobe?"

I nodded dumbly, realizing just then that my wings had effectively torn the back of my shirt in two. Moving behind me, the goddess murmured something and sand shifted, rising up behind me. "There," she said after the sand stilled. "I have modeled your clothing after my own.

Your wings will emerge from a long slit in the back of your shirt above your vest if you're careful enough. If not, they might damage your clothing too much for it to continue covering your body."

Licking my lips and glancing over at the boys, I said, "I'll be sure to watch out for that."

Closing my eyes, bracing for the pain, I called to my wings again. This time I felt nothing but a comfortable relief. It was like kicking off high heels at the end of the day. Experimentally, I flapped them, and my body lifted from the ground several feet before I sank back down.

With my cat eyes wide, I gulped. *Holy Egyptian heaven,* I thought. *I have wings. If only Nana and Dr. Hassan could see me now.* I missed them.

Up close, I noticed that the feathers were variegated, much like my hair, the colors a palette of rich metallics—including silver, platinum, and gold. Finding a tiny, downy feather, I plucked it out and yowled. It was like wrenching out a handful of hair. I rubbed out the sting on the injured wing, and the pain slowly ebbed.

Amon came closer and lifted a hand, pausing as if asking for permission. When I nodded, he ran his hand down the inside of the wing, marveling at it the way I had. The sensation was heady, almost sensual. I could feel it in the wing, but I could also feel it in my back. It was like the ultimate back massage from the hottest guy in the world, which wasn't too far from the truth.

A shiver ran down my spine. Taking hold of Amon's muscled arm, I tucked my wings back like a bird, shaking my head slightly in apology. Willingly, he stepped aside, lowering his head, his hair falling in his eyes. Any other time, I'd be over the moon to have him close, exploring them with me, but I couldn't afford the distraction right then.

With my wings folded neatly behind me, I could no longer see them, but there was still no way on earth I could forget they were there. The entire distribution of my weight had changed. I felt not unlike when I first became a sphinx. I was a new animal.

Ashleigh was thrilled, and I mean absolutely thrilled, at the idea of trying them out. It was hard to talk her down from her excited ready-to-leap-off-the-mountainside enthusiasm.

"Tell us how our wings are a weapon," I said to Isis. Then I winced and added, "Please. And thank you"—I raised a hand indicating our wings—"for this, by the way. It must have killed you to pull out a feather of that size."

"I'll admit it was painful but I hope worth it, in the end. Now you see why I did not wish to see my gift squandered."

"I do."

"The wings of a sphinx," Isis explained, "have the power to draw great winds. She can bend them to her will, creating cyclones, sandstorms, and tempests. You do this with your mind, though it can be a natural response to danger as well, much like your claws."

"I see. Well, all of that would have been nice to know before."

"Unfortunately, I do not have the leisure to teach you all the things I know about the power of the sphinx. I wish I did," she said sadly. Straightening, Isis turned to her sister. "It is time for me to go," she announced.

Nephthys nodded, and the two women embraced. Isis stroked the long white-blond waves of her sister's hair. When they separated, Isis plastered a smile to her face, though all of us could see right through it to the fear and doubt that lay beneath. Horus came forward and wrapped his arms around his mother. Tears rolled down his cheeks, and his eyes were bloodshot.

The dark mountain was quiet. When Isis pulled away, she took hold of Horus's arm and whispered something in his ear. He nodded, his chin wavering. Unfurling her wings, Isis blew a kiss to her loved ones, looked up at the shining moon, and with a mighty flap, soared into the sky.

When the darkness swallowed her, my gaze drifted down to Nephthys and Horus. They stood leaning against one another, supporting each other's sorrow.

"He'll unmake her," Horus said as he wiped his eyes.

"It won't come to that," Nephthys replied. "Remember, he's still shackled."

Horus sneered in open contempt. "There is much a man can do to cause pain even without the powers of a god."

"Seth believes he loves her, nephew."

"He was supposed to love you." Horus's face was a thundercloud. For the moment, the storm inside him was far off, but we would be wise to prepare for the onslaught.

"In his own twisted way, he does," Nephthys replied quietly.

"That snake in the grass does not know what love means," Horus said and stalked away, leaving us with his aunt.

Nephthys turned to us, her lower lip trembling. "Come, let us get you on your way, then, shall we? But first we must tell you of our plans."

She spent the next hour explaining her proposal in detail. The gods were going to head out in three groups in an attempt to distract the Devourer. Two groups would attack the Devourer's first wave of minions. Their job was to destroy as many of the sky-demons as they could. The third group would sneak into Amun-Ra's palace and save Osiris, taking him back to the mountaintop so he could recover. We were to wait until they were clear and then take out the Devourer when she inevitably chased him. Hopefully, we would catch her by surprise.

Two groups of gods left, Anubis leading one and Amun-Ra the other. They headed down the mountainside as nimbly as deer. The third, led by Ma'at, would leave when we did. We had just enough time left in the night to return to Heliopolis and find a place to hide. Nephthys shooed us away, indicating that I should take to the sky.

I unfurled my wings just as Amon and Asten were about to change into bird form, when Nephthys stopped us. "I nearly forgot," she said. "Horus has to see you all before you leave. I must go now and confer with the last group."

With Asten, Amon and Ahmose trailing me, we sought out Horus and found him sitting on a stone bench beneath the trees, his head in his hands.

When he glanced up at our approach, his mouth twisted, the ghost of a cheeky grin. "Come to give me a goodbye kiss?" he asked, taunting the men behind me.

"No. Nephthys said you needed to see us."

"Ah yes. It's regarding your clipped bird."

"My what?"

Horus waved a hand, indicating the brothers. "You know, the one who can no longer fly."

Glancing at Ahmose, I could almost sense his longing to cuff Horus right in the chin.

The god, either not noticing or not caring about Ahmose's reaction, stood up and headed over to the stump of a tree, purposely bumping Ahmose's shoulder as he did so. He knelt down and brushed at the roots.

Leaving the brothers behind, I trailed after Horus. "For what it's worth, I'm sorry," I said to him. "About your mother, I mean."

"I am, too," he replied quietly.

Satisfied with his efforts, Horus stood and chanted a spell—one that sounded slightly familiar. "Stand back now," he said when he was finished, taking hold of my arm. "He wanted to help. I have to admit, I was surprised. You must have had an effect on him. Then again, beautiful young virgins usually do," the god finished with a halfhearted snicker.

The ground rumbled, and I staggered against Horus, my wings lifting to help steady me. At that moment, a hole opened in the ground and a glimmering, golden shape burst from it.

"Nebu!" I cried, happy to see my old friend again.

Hello, goddess. It is good to see you.

"And you. Thank you for coming."

You are welcome.

"I thought you didn't want to join the fight," I said, stepping forward to stroke his back.

I did not. But after we left you, I was racked with terrible guilt at the thought of what you would face alone. My purpose is to shield you from Seth to the point of my own demise. Though my preference, of course, would be not to find my end in such a way. The unicorn lifted his head so I could scratch his neck. *Do you think me a noble beast?* Nebu asked with a stamping of a hoof.

Laughing and backing away as he shook out his mane, I said, "Extremely noble."

Circling me, his head bobbing up and down, Nebu exclaimed, *Your new wings are lovely! With gifts such as those, you are a befitting companion for a unicorn.*

"Getting ideas in your head, old man?" Horus provoked with a chuckle. "You'd have to stomp on the competition first." He tilted his head, considering. "I can't say that I'd mind that too much. Could possibly free up a spot for a lonely god. What do you say, unicorn? Want to work together to trim the ranks?"

Snorting, Nebu said, *When a unicorn throws his horn in the ring, there are none who dare interfere, not even a god.*

I rolled my eyes but then sniggered as Nebu whinnied and quickly went off to greet the others.

When he was gone, Horus took my arm and turned us so my back was to the brothers. "Thank you," he said.

"For what?"

"For distracting me from my sorrow. You are very good at that, you know."

"You're welcome," I said and offered him a smile. "You're not so bad. In fact, you're a pretty good guy, all things considered."

Horus took a step closer and trailed a fingertip down a gleaming feather. "So generous," he murmured. "And so beautiful."

"Thank you," I said, giving him a pointed look as I lifted my wing away from his hand.

He lowered it and smiled. "Now, about that goodbye kiss?"

"Young Lily is not yours to kiss, Horus."

"Amon," Horus said, disappointment coloring the tone of his voice. "Never far enough away, are you?"

"I was about to say the same about you."

Bending over my hand, Horus kissed it, a wicked twinkle in his eye. "Until we meet again, Lily," he said. "May fortunate winds blow in your direction."

"And in yours," I answered.

Horus left us, and I twined my arm through Amon's, heading over to Nebu. Ahmose was settled on Nebu's back, and Asten had already transformed into the starlit ibis. Amon kissed my cheek and asked, "Are you ready?"

"As I'll ever be."

Once I was in the air, the golden falcon on one side, the starlit ibis on the other, and Nebu with Ahmose on his back behind us, I whooped, arcing in a big circle. I let Ashleigh take over, since she was a natural and was practically dying to do so. We sped quickly over the landscape, Ashleigh tutoring me along the way. Tia had zero interest, telling both of us that flying was unnatural for cats, but to me flying was so, so much better than hiking. I was amazed at how easily I'd taken to it. Though I didn't have a fear of heights and had long been used to skyscrapers, roller coasters made me slightly queasy. I'd thought flying would be the same, but being in control of the swoops and dives was not only exhilarating, it served to stave off any motion sickness.

Ashleigh gave back control, content to enjoy the ride as I practiced. I swept over the tall trees, reaching out to brush the needled tips with my hands. The dark landscape was punctured by icy veins of sparkling blue and purple with shimmering rocks that moved. Curious, I drifted down closer and saw the glimmering purple-blue light was coming from a river. The rocks were winged fish, gleaming with color. They leapt from the river, flapping wildly to reach the top of a waterfall.

They are spawning, a voice in my mind said. *Their scales light up during this time.*

I gasped. It was Ahmose's voice, not Amon's like I'd expected. I realized then that Ahmose could hear my thoughts now, too. The night breeze was swollen with moonlight. I could almost taste the cool freshness of its beams. The moonlight made me think of Ahmose and the long hours we'd traveled together. I found I'd missed how close we used to be.

I miss being with you, too, his familiar voice echoed in my mind.

Why can you hear my thoughts? I asked him. *Amon couldn't hear Ashleigh's or Tia's voices, and you have Ashleigh's heart. You shouldn't be able to hear mine.*

If it bothers you, I apologize, Ahmose said.

It doesn't bother me, exactly, I replied. *It's just a bit shocking.*

Interesting, a new voice added. It was Amon. *It could be due to the spell enacted by Isis.*

My wings flapped quickly, causing me to drop and my heart to race. Slowing the beat, I steadied myself.

You heard all that? I asked.

Yes, Amon answered. *Though I do not wish to eavesdrop.*

Too late now.

It is not something we can help, Amon said. *At least, not anymore.*

Could it be because of my connection to all three through Wasret? Ahmose asked.

There is one way to find out, Amon answered.

How? I asked.

Call to Asten. If he can hear you, then we know this ability comes from Isis, Amon instructed.

Asten? I asked mentally. *Can you hear me?*

There was no response.

Tia? Can you try?

Tia made an effort to communicate with Asten, but the ibis coasted silently alongside us, starlight winking off his feathers. He showed no signs of hearing us.

Perhaps it is because he could not absorb my heart, she suggested sorrowfully.

Maybe, I replied.

We flew on until we came to the edge of the forest and then descended, Asten and Amon transforming back into their human forms. A signal lit the night sky on the far horizon. It was only a matter of minutes until we heard the screeches of the sky-demons. Backing into the dark shadows of the trees, Asten immediately wove his cloaking spell over us just in case. We watched them pass overhead by the hundreds.

Another signal came, and a horde just as large as the first soon headed in that direction. It was time to move. Ahmose threw me up on Nebu's back, and we made our way swiftly to the outskirts of Heliopolis. The dark, crumbled buildings rose above the purple-dark sea, the still-gleaming tower of Amun-Ra standing out among the heaps of destruction like a precious gem.

We headed toward a ruined garden and hid beneath a gazebo. The overhanging vines and broken tree branches cloaked us well enough. I slid from Nebu's back and saw my reflection in the murky waters of a round reflecting pool. My wings twitched. I definitely didn't look like the girl I'd once been.

Wings aside, my hair, usually long, straight, and glossy with product, was wild and unkempt. I couldn't even begin to determine its color. It curled in a similar way to Ashleigh's. Even the shade of my skin had changed. I'd once been as pale as moonlight, but now I was as tan as if I'd spent the summer in Florida.

My frame had always been svelte, but now my limbs were lean and strong, more like Tia's. Even my temperature had changed. My new normal was somewhere between hot tub and a recently blown-out match. I wondered then if my body was still truly mine or if I was morphing into someone new.

Amon came up behind me and wrapped his arms around me awkwardly, trying to encompass my wings as well. I pulled them back into my body, and he turned me around, taking in my frowning mouth and wrinkled nose.

"What is wrong?" he asked his eyes shining with an iridescent green light.

"Pretty much everything." I sighed. "I don't feel like myself. Everything is wrong. The wings are just another thing on top of all the others. I'm a stranger in my own skin. As out of place as a pair of flip-flops at a fashion show. I'm not the girl you met in New York, Amon. Not anymore."

"No, Nehabet," he replied. "You are not." I raised my eyebrows, surprised that he wasn't trying to placate me. "You no longer walk the path of yesterday. Whether that is a good or a bad thing in your mind is for you to choose. All I know is that your soul is an unquenchable flame. It crackles like a storm cloud full of lightning. The changes to your body mean nothing. I would know you no matter what your form."

The corner of my mouth quirked up. "Are you trying to say you'll love me when I'm old and gray?"

"No," Amon said. "I mean to tell you that I will still love you when your physical form becomes dust and nothing is left of either of us except our wills. Whatever becomes of us, wherever death leads, I will find a way to be with you. Do you believe this?" he asked.

I pressed my forehead against his. "I think I do," I said.

Nebu stamped a hoof, pawing nervously at the ground.

"Something is wrong," Ahmose said, approaching from the place he'd been standing guard. His silver eyes burned in the night. "A lot of paths just abruptly ended. Something has happened to the contingent sent to rescue Osiris."

"I thought you couldn't sense them," I said.

"Remember when I said the paths here were difficult to discern?"

Nodding, I said, "Yes. You couldn't follow the paths of the gods."

"Right. Well, the group led by Ma'at to Amun-Ra's home was large enough that I could make it out. They entered, several paths converging on the same place, but then they just . . . just disappeared."

"We've got to help them, then. So, what's it going to be?" I asked. "Sneak in or fly up to the top?"

"Both," Amon said. "Give me and Asten a head start, and then you three fly up. Hopefully, we can provide enough of a distraction that you can get in, get Osiris out, and get to safety."

I was about to protest when Amon took my hand. "Asten will provide cover for us," he said, knowing how I would respond to separating. "Remember that because of our connection we are now cloaked the same way you are. She won't sense us."

Swallowing the lump in my throat, I nodded in agreement. Asten and Amon crept through the darkness and disappeared into the shadows between the remaining buildings.

About twenty minutes later, Ahmose decided it was time. He climbed on Nebu's back, and I spread my wings. We flew up and up, circling the dark city. When a sky-demon screeched, Nebu flew close, his wings brushing the building where it crouched. Ahmose quickly bashed it over the head with his cudgel. It crumpled, falling from its perch, and its thick body hit the ground below with a heavy thump.

If there were other sky-demons around, they were quiet. We landed on a damaged balcony. Stone broke away as Nebu's hooves touched the surface and we tucked in our wings. Quietly, we made our way inside. I pulled my spear-knives from their sheaths. We were now on the opposite of the large room where we'd first seen Osiris, but there was no sign of the god. There were, however, some very discernible bloodstains where he'd once been.

Treading farther, we came upon the fallen warriors who had accompanied Ma'at. Ahmose crouched down and turned over one of the bodies. "Their hearts have been eaten," he said. Grimly, we inspected room after room, but we found nothing except broken furniture and shattered glass. There was no sign of Asten or Amon. Dread built in my chest.

"I don't understand," I said. "Where is everybody?"

At that moment, a boom shook the building, and I stumbled against

Ahmose. After helping me regain my feet, he took my hand. "Come on," he said. "That happened in the courtyard."

We peered down off the balcony. The air was full of sky-demons—many more than we'd seen leave. They were being joined by their returning brothers, who carried captives in their talons.

One of the captives broke away from the sky-demons. He was joined by a snarling hound. "Anubis," I hissed to Ahmose. When he was cornered and captured once more, I watched in horror as the Devourer exploded in a flurry of bat-winged creatures and then materialized before him.

Her throaty laugh caught on the wind. "Ah, now, here is one I can take my time with."

The dawn sun stretched its light over the scene below, bathing the courtyard in blood-red rays. Before Ahmose could stop me, I leapt over the side, snapping open my wings and screaming a battle cry. Sky-demons veered to attack, and I eviscerated one with my knife and tore the wing of another. Nebu and Ahmose soon joined me. The unicorn's hooves barely missed my head as Ahmose sank his cudgel into the shoulder of a flying demon before it could grab my wing.

We fought our way to the ground slowly, dispatching demon after demon. They dropped one by one to the courtyard below. The Devourer looked up to watch our progress, a confident, glee-filled smile on her bright face, but it took much longer to reach her than I'd anticipated.

Once we got to the ground, I headed directly over to a still-alive sky-demon and sank an arrow of Isis into its back. It writhed and squirmed, but it didn't answer me when I demanded its obeisance.

The Devourer's laugh carried to me from across the bloody field. "Did you think I wouldn't learn from my past mistakes?" she said.

"These are loyal to none but me. And," she added as she strode closer, "they don't have enough of a mind to manipulate."

Yanking out the arrow and seeing it disintegrate in my hand, I quickly plunged my spear-knife into the beast's head. It slumped over, a black tongue lolling out its mouth. Up close I saw the immediate change in its skin as it turned from a dark bronze to an unhealthy green to an ashy gray. Chunks of it broke off and turned to dust as the creature melted. It was like watching corroded metal disintegrate. One. There was only one arrow of Isis left. With a shiver, I turned to face my enemy.

Nebu landed lightly beside me, and Ahmose leapt down. Dozens of sky-demons still swarmed above us, but they seemed to have a healthy appreciation for our skills, because they didn't attack again.

The Devourer glanced up at them, her mouth downturned in a sour expression. She raised a hand, crooking her finger at Ahmose. "Hello again, handsome," she said. "Back for another kiss?"

When Ahmose said nothing, she pouted prettily. "No? And here I was willing to set aside this luscious one just for you," she said, indicating Anubis. "If you'll excuse me. I'll have to get to you next. I'll save you all for my dessert." Ignoring us, she turned back to the god.

"Something is wrong," I hissed to Ahmose. "She's not even concerned that we're here. Considering the fact that I almost did her in last time we met, I'd think she'd show at least a tiny bit of worry."

"I feel you are right. She has set a trap for us. But until we can discern it, we must attempt to free her captives."

Abutiu, Anubis's loyal dog, lay next to him. He had been struck with a lance. It impaled him, fixing him to the ground where he kicked limply, struggling to get to his feet again to protect his master. Ahmose and I stalked closer, determined to stop her before she even began to think about draining the god.

"There, there," she said to the handsome god who wrenched himself back and forth, trying to escape the demons who held him prisoner. "It won't hurt. Much," she added with a devilish laugh. Placing her hand on his chest, she trailed her palm down to his stomach. "Oh, my," she said, biting her lip, "I do like a man who keeps himself fit. By the time they get to me, all the men are so starved. It's almost doing them a service to consume their hearts." The Devourer clucked her tongue in appreciation. "It's so rare to find such a . . . vigorous specimen. I'd rather like to savor you awhile."

Placing her palms against Anubis's tight stomach, she pulled him closer, opening her mouth to let her green light leak out.

"I don't think so," I said and pressed a button, elongating my spear. Taking aim, I threw it. Spinning like a javelin, it headed straight toward the Devourer's heart. But before it struck, a man dropped from the sky, grabbing it in midair. He touched lightly down on the ground and dropped my weapon. It landed in the grass with a heavy thump.

My heart broke as Ahmose said the name I couldn't bear to utter.

"Amon?"

Ding Dong, the Witch Is Dead

"Amon?" I echoed, after I regained my ability to speak. "What are you doing?"

The Devourer turned to us. "How nice. I was wondering when you were going to make an appearance. I should have known that whenever the girl arrives, you won't be far behind." The woman put her hands on her hips and strode boldly across the grass, but as she did the entire area shimmered and faded.

The Devourer disappeared for a moment and then came back into view. She must have been distracted by the incident as well. She halted and laughed, spinning in a circle, her arms in the air. "Soon, my minions," she cried out to what I assumed were her sky-demons. "Very soon now."

That doesn't bode well, I thought. *What's she up to?* Something was wrong. The Devourer was entirely too confident. I hoped it didn't mean she had Amon under her thrall again. We'd only been separated a short time, but where she was concerned, anything was possible.

Amon had vanished at the same time she did. When he reappeared, he headed in our direction. I braced myself for an attack. But as he drew closer, I relaxed, seeing the warmth in his eyes, rather than the blank nonexpression he'd worn in Heliopolis. He was still my Amon. "We cannot kill her yet," he said as he ran up to us and returned my weapon.

I took it, relieved that he was still on our side. "Why not?" I asked.

"We must close the barrier to the mortal realm first. Seth has given the Devourer the power to breach it." He held out a hand, circling the area. "Do you see where it's starting to bleed together? It should be visible to you now. With the Eye, I noticed faint traces when we entered the building."

When I indicated I couldn't see anything, he scanned the grounds and then pointed up to the broken towers of Heliopolis. There was a shimmer in the air, and when I squinted, I could just make out Times Square. "Oh no," I said. "It can't be."

I ran forward, spinning as building after building took form. They phased in and out as if trying to gain purchase in Heliopolis. A moment later, sidewalks and streets appeared, along with ghostly images of mortals from my world. Soon they became aware of our presence and walked around us with irritated glances and raised eyebrows.

All at once, I was in New York City, and I could see what was happening from their perspective. A group of passersby stopped cold and looked up, staring in confusion at the ruins of Heliopolis that began to replace buildings in the city. A famous theater became a crumbled building of marble. The Devourer, who'd disappeared again, materialized nearby and tried to latch onto a passing mortal. He screamed and threw up his arms to defend himself, but her hair swept right through him. Quickly, he ran down the street.

A cop made a beeline toward us. I can't imagine what he thought we were—a winged girl standing next to a golden unicorn and a villainess with needle-sharp hair. Next to us were Ahmose and Amon, two men that could have stepped out of a video game, one with a large cudgel and the other with gleaming gold scimitars. Maybe they'd think we were an elaborate advertising ploy for a new show on Broadway.

A large broken fountain with a statue of a benu bird taking flight appeared in the middle of the street, causing the cars to veer abruptly. A cab slammed right into a minivan, and the cop lifted his radio, gesturing wildly as he tried to control the screaming crowd. But as quickly as the fountain materialized, it disappeared again, and we went with it. I was back in Heliopolis, but the tall tower of Amun-Ra still flashed with rippling pixels announcing an upcoming movie, then it too faded into stone.

An oncoming taxi suddenly burst from the air. It zoomed straight in our direction. The driver didn't seem to see us. Amon shouted and grabbed my arm, but we were trapped between the fountain and a building. The familiar sounds of the city came back at us all at once. The driver finally saw us and braked, but he didn't react quickly enough. He was going to run us down. I raised my arms instinctively, my wings shooting out on either side, but the taxi barreled through us like a ghost and faded into the mist along with the noise of the city streets.

"It's getting worse!" I exclaimed when I saw the shifting between the two worlds increasing. "We've got to stop it! Are you sure killing her won't work?" For the moment, the Devourer was distracted by a panhandler.

Amon shouted, "If we kill her first, the celestial barriers will burn. The crossover will happen abruptly instead of in stages, and the two realms will implode. All the creations living in either realm will be instantly unmade. Either way, Seth wins."

"How much time do we have?" I shouted as I waved our party over to a space where a sidewalk became visible. In New York we appeared to be standing in an alley between buildings. A fire escape shimmered above our heads, merging with our reality and then vanishing again.

"Until the breach is irreversible?" Amon asked, thumbing his bottom lip with his fingertips. "I would think it would happen fairly quickly. Her sky-demons are hovering, waiting until they can enter the mortal realm and sweep up the living victims, gathering them for her to consume. Once she begins feeding . . ."

Amon trailed off, and I shuddered. "Where's Asten?" I asked, suddenly realizing he wasn't nearby.

"He . . ." Amon's face fell. "He was taken by the sky-demons. He'd been scouting one building while I checked out another. By the time I heard his shout and found him, he'd been engulfed by an entire contingent. From all appearances, he came upon a nest of them sleeping. I would have attempted a rescue, but by the time I fought off the stragglers, Asten was gone."

My claws emerged as Tia yowled in my mind. *We must save him!* she screamed.

We will, I comforted her. *But first we have to stop the Devourer.*

"How do we close the breach?" I demanded, taking hold of Amon's shirt and yanking him away from a delivery truck that came out of nowhere driving up our alley. I didn't let out a breath until it passed us by.

"Only celestial energy will seal the breach," said Amon. My vision blurred. *Where are we going to get celestial energy?*

Amon glanced up at the unicorn, who peered back at him and blew a soft breath from his nostrils.

Resignation filling my soul, I closed my eyes and prepared myself to call forth Wasret. We were out of options. Nebu nudged my shoulder.

I can close the breach, he said. *Unicorns have such power. You already know we can cross through the barriers. We can seal them as well. But a yawning opening such as this will require help from many of my kind.*

"Will they come?" I asked him, laying my hand on the unicorn's back.

He seemed to hesitate, then answered, *They will if I ask.*

Amon stepped closer. "Are you certain you wish to do this, Nebu?"

I cannot think of a nobler cause than this, Revealer. Thank you for helping me see the possibilities. Nebu pressed his cheek against me, resting his head on my shoulder. *Farewell, young sphinx. Perhaps, if the gods are willing, I will see you again.*

"See me again?" I said, but Nebu moved away, stepping out into the street. He rose up, his front legs pawing the air, and when he came down, hitting the ground, a wave of electric power shot out in every direction. The entire area shook, and we stumbled as if we'd been caught in the epicenter of an earthquake. Nebu's golden body flickered, and a bluish light trickled down his mane and over his heaving form, turning him as white as a pulsing star. Golden sand particles lifted from his skin and hovered where his alicorn should be.

The Devourer rose from where she was leaning over a baby in a stroller and scanned the ghostly crowd suspiciously. When she saw Nebu, she took in his new appearance and screamed. She ran toward us, abandoning her search for human hearts, but her efforts were too little, too late.

The land trembled and split in two, cutting the Devourer off from us as dozens and dozens of unicorns emerged. Their whinnies and pounding hooves were loud enough to distract even the sky-demons. They quickly vacated the area, taking refuge as best as they could in the transitioning buildings.

Nebu nickered loudly, and the animals surrounding him responded in a wild cacophony of noise. He touched his head to one after another. When he did, the unicorns danced and shook their bodies. Golden sand exploded from their forms until they were as pure white as their leader.

When Nebu was done, his long-lashed eyes met mine, and though no words echoed in my mind, a heartfelt sentiment passed between us. Then he turned and galloped. As one, the unicorns stampeded. The ground shook anew, and if it weren't for Amon, I would have fallen.

They snapped open their wings and rose in the air, Nebu leading the way. A part of me wanted to stretch out my wings and join them. Seeing their gleaming forms take to the sky was a sight I'd never forget. They were beautiful, magical, almost frightening in their glory.

The glint of the golden sun shining on the tips of their wings stung my eyes. I shielded them but recognized Nebu's body as it surged forward toward Amun-Ra's tower. It was currently flashing an ad for an upcoming runway show. When he hit the screen, Nebu burst into pure energy and light exploded all around Times Square. Sparkling bits rained down in a crackling shower.

The Devourer, enraged, opened her mouth, and green light shot toward the herd of unicorns. But her light never reached them. One by one, they flew to the wall of light that grew brighter as each unicorn disappeared inside. When the last one leapt into the breach, a sonic boom resonated. Then the visual light show seemed to collapse in on itself.

Cars disappeared first, then stoplights. The noise of New York faded into the quiet of the ruined city of Heliopolis. The buildings shimmered and then returned to normal. The ghostly people blinked and went on about their business as if it had all been a strange illusion. Then they, too, disappeared.

The shimmering wall of light grew smaller and smaller until all became still as the breach finally closed. I blinked once, twice. "Where . . . where's Nebu?" I asked Amon, turning around to see where he'd rematerialize. "When will he come back?"

"He . . . the unicorns . . . will not be returning," he said quietly.

"What do you mean they won't be returning?" I stammered, a cold kind of horror filling my veins.

"Their paths end here," Ahmose offered.

Amon explained, "They have given over their lives, Nehabet."

"You mean . . . they're dead?" I cried, my voice trembling. "All of them?" I asked, looking back and forth at each of them.

"Yes. They sacrificed themselves to close the breach," Ahmose said gently.

"But . . . but . . . ," I stammered, tears blazing a path down my face, "but unicorns are immortal."

"Young Lily," Amon said softly, "many are given the gift of immortality, but as you know, a gift can be returned."

"No," I whispered, shaking my head. "No." The tears came freely as I thought of the dozens of beautiful creatures who had just sacrificed their lives. "They can't even enter the afterlife."

I collapsed in a heap at Amon's feet. He wrapped his arms around me and pulled me up, cradling me in his arms and pressing soft kisses on my fevered cheeks.

"He never even asked for his boon," I said through quivering lips.

A scream of rage distracted me, and I pulled away from Amon to see a furious Devourer. "If you think this will stop me, stop us, you are woefully mistaken," she spat. "I'll make you regret what you have done." Her hair writhed in the air like snakes as she pointed toward us. "Bring them to me!" she cried in fury. "But remember, the master wants them intact!"

A hundred sky-demons erupted from the ruined buildings. They descended on us as she turned to Anubis. "But he said nothing about you," she said, teasing the god. "I was going to draw this out, but I am famished, and your friends have rudely sent my dinner back before I could partake. Shall we get on with it?"

"You help Anubis," Amon said quickly to Ahmose, taking his brother by the arm. "Distract her, but beware her poison. Do not allow her to get her hooks into you. We will take care of the sky-demons and come to your aid as soon as we can."

Ahmose nodded gravely, touched his fingertips briefly to my cheek, and headed off, cudgel raised. I swallowed, knowing we stood little chance of staving off even half the demons in the sky, let alone to help Ahmose and Anubis.

Amon seemed to read my mind, because he took my arm. "Do not summon her, Young Lily. Not yet. Give us a chance to succeed first." After a moment, I nodded, doubt still filling me. "Please," he added. Amon captured my lips in a brief kiss, then he stepped back and switched to his golden falcon form.

With a cry, he soared into the air, and I snapped open my wings to follow. He flew straight into the crush of demons who sped by us like clawed meteors on every side. With his talons, he tore apart a demon, ripping him in two, and slapped another one off course with his wings. The severed creature dropped to the ground and crumbled to pieces on impact. *One down, ninety-nine to go.*

Ashleigh took over our flight. She was brilliant, flying through the horde and always staying just out of reach. Tia's cat eyes spotted holes where my human eyes would only see masses of flying bodies. I nocked an arrow, a regular one this time, and let it fly. It struck true, sinking into the shoulder of a demon, but it still came at me. The sky-demon snarled and sunk its claws into my arms. I wrenched back, but a trio of deep scratches bled freely on my forearm.

Our wings thrashed as we spiraled in the air. Thrusting my own claws out, I sank them into the place in its chest where the heart should be and twisted. The beast yowled and shoved me away. Its nose wrinkled as it pulled its hand from the wound in its chest. It stared at the black blood in confusion. The wound changed color, turning green, and the creature's body fragmented in the air. Its scream cut off when its mouth dissolved.

Another creature burst through the remains of its brother, coming at me with arms open and wings pounding the air. Folding my wings, I dropped down and then snapped them open just before I hit the ground. Lifting my head, I squinted at the rising sun as I rocketed up, a mass of sky-demons hot on my tail. I took out a few using the power of the sphinx to strangle them, but I had to concentrate and do it one by one. It was too difficult a power to manage in an air fight.

I heard the golden falcon but couldn't see him. Ashleigh used her skill to navigate between buildings. Brushing purposely against the remains of a tower, I turned to see it fall behind us, collapsing and taking down a half dozen demons with it. But as many as were felled, even more rose up to take their places.

The sky darkened and storm clouds gathered overhead. I knew it was Ahmose helping us as best he could. Lightning struck and hit a number of sky-demons in quick succession. Giant balls of hail began to pummel the backs of the beasts, driving them down. I alit on a rocky overhang with a shallow alcove where my head would be protected and drew my knives. Letting the hail do its work, I took out those who flew around me, thrusting my spear-knives into their chests. They cried out and dropped limply, spiraling to the ground like unmindful birds that had hit a window.

When the hail stopped, they swarmed, climbing the rocks and flapping their wings wildly as they tried to reach me in my little cave. I knew it was just a matter of time before they cornered me. With a battle cry, I lunged, claws out, and dove through them, tearing their leathery wings. When I cleared the flock, I thrust out my wings and soared toward the place I'd last seen the Devourer, dozens of sky-demons on my heels. There were just too many of them. We were never going to stop them.

I managed to spot Ahmose far below, struggling against the Devourer. He'd actually brought a thundercloud down upon her and lightning struck her body repeatedly, but Ahmose was on his knees, struggling to remain upright. A dangerous green fog swirled around his legs while Anubis continued to lie bound behind him. I knew Ahmose was no match for her, not in his current condition.

Scanning the sky, I searched for Amon. Catching sight of his golden wings, I beat mine to chase after him. When Amon was still a distance away, his form suddenly switched to human in midair. I screamed his name and rushed upward, trying to reach him before he crashed, but dozens of sky-demons clouded the air between us. Furiously, I took out demon after demon, but still he plummeted.

Amon summoned his weapons. The golden scimitars gleamed in the sunlight and, as he fell, he slashed, cutting the heads off several demons, then he turned, rotating in the air so his back was to the ground and threw his swords, impaling two of them from above. Both the weapons and the demons dissolved in the air, and when I blinked, Amon was a golden falcon again. He twisted, beating his wings rapidly and headed up again, an angry horde in his wake.

Something hit my back and ripped into my wings. I screamed and, following Amon's example, called them back into my body. The demon fell, but I followed, plunging right along with him. Turning in midair,

I shoved my spear-knife through him, then I summoned my wings again, beating them furiously to regain my previous position. As the stela healed me, I switched from defense to offense, turning head-on into the group tailing me. I pinned two to a building with one spear while impaling another.

The need to help both Amon and Ahmose was weighing on my mind. They were both formidable warriors, but if something was to happen to either of them, I knew I'd blame myself.

My body was covered in oozing scratches, and there was a puncture wound in one shoulder and a stinging bite in the other. One of my wings was ripped and ached terribly. The stela just couldn't keep up. Desperately, I sought out Ahmose again, hoping to see the Devourer still thwarted. She wasn't. In fact, Ahmose was now tied up and held by demons like Anubis. We'd run out of time.

I was about to tuck my wings and head down to help him when I heard a bellow from above. Amon stood in human form on top of a building. A mass of sky-demons circled him. With each pass, their sharp claws ripped his body. He slashed at one and overbalanced, falling to one knee. He cried out as he slipped from the top of the building and disappeared over the side.

"Amon!" I cried. I felt pulled in two different directions. A part of me desperately wanted to head down to Ahmose, but another insisted that Amon's current situation was more desperate. I turned toward the tower.

Determined to get to Amon, and seeing the demons closing on me again, I beat my wings in giant thrusts, ignoring the sting of pain. I grit my teeth and surged forward, quickly outdistancing the sky-demons. Channeling all my waning energy and power into each beat, I willed my wings to take me to Amon. If I could just reach him before he hit the ground, I knew he'd survive. But then I'd have to turn right around and save Ahmose. I needed to be in two places at once.

My hair streamed behind me, the wind rushing past my face.

Adrenaline fueled me, diminishing the pain of my injuries. I lifted my wings and felt the sun's rays touch the feathers. Then something happened.

The air that stirred in my wings became electrified. Swirls of golden light snapped and popped in the air around me. When the enemy came close, the light surged toward him, enveloping him in a funnel. The sky-demon's body shook as it struggled, and then the creature disintegrated in a burst of dust.

I beat my wings harder, the stream of energy spreading in curling squalls, shooting from one to another to another, capturing them in an electric funnel cloud. I snapped my wings sharply, and a wave of light sped toward the demons holding Ahmose and Anubis. They, too, disappeared.

The remaining ones surrounding me veered away, and I let them flee. Turning, I raced toward Amon once more and found him hanging on to the rooftop by his fingertips. His shirt had been slashed to ribbons. The sky-demons pecked at him with sharp beaks and raked their claws down his trembling form.

I clapped my wings together, and a burst of light shot toward the flock surrounding him. They scattered, all but a few disappearing in a cloud of dust that rained down. My newly discovered power filled me, invigorating my tired body. A great howling wind erupted from my wings and chased the rest away.

Hovering in the air, I waited for the dust to clear, hoping I hadn't injured Amon in the process. For a minute, I was alarmed. I couldn't see him. Flying around the building, I searched for his form on the stone and then on the ground. That's when I heard the cry of the golden falcon and found him banking toward me. Together, we headed back to Ahmose. I just hoped we weren't too late.

My eyes went round when I saw the Devourer. She clutched Ahmose's large body in her arms, her mouth upon his. He was limp, his limbs dangling like slack ropes, and still she clung to him, drinking him in deeply. From a distance it looked as if she was cradling someone she loved, but as we neared I could see her hair wrapped around him, squeezing him like a mass of constrictors, the sharp barbs impaling his skin. He kicked feebly as green light leaked from the seal of their lips.

I landed near them, touching down nimbly. Rage filled my frame. *"Let 'im go, ya treacherous witch. Ah'll no' bear ya touchin' ma Ahmose. Drop 'im now, else ah'll cut out yer heart an' feed it ta yer demons meself."*

Slowly, the Devourer lifted her head, green tendrils dangling from her ruby-red, glistening mouth. Green light glowed in her eyes, and they twinkled as they took in my ragged form. Automatically, we attempted to strangle her, but it was like trying to swallow a watermelon whole—the Devourer was just too powerful. With a too-casual sigh, she dropped Ahmose as if he were a sack of potatoes and stood up straight and tall, a knowing smile on her face. Delicately, she tucked the strings of remaining energy into her mouth and licked her lips.

"Mmm," she said. "As delicious as I remember."

Clenching my fists, I was about to attack when Amon grabbed my arm, instantly chilling my boiling blood. "He's still alive, Ashleigh. Let's do this together."

"Yes, pet," the Devourer said, addressing Amon with a wink. "Unfortunately, he is still among the living, so to speak. He wouldn't be if you hadn't interrupted my meal," she said. Though her mouth pouted prettily, her eyes shot daggers.

She leaned close to his cheek and wrapped an arm possessively around his chest. "I think I'm ready for seconds, handsome," she said, pressing her mouth to his ear.

"Now, Ashleigh!" Amon cried as he sprang into action, whipping out his scimitars to attack. The Devourer simply disappeared again in a flurry of creatures and his sword slashed through the fluttering mass. They melted away, unaffected. Slowly, he turned in a circle waiting for her. We heard her taunting giggle and caught sight of her sparkling green light, but she didn't rematerialize.

As much as I wanted to help Amon, Ashleigh was in total control and would not relinquish it. She knelt down next to Ahmose and tried desperately to rouse him. My eyes were flooded with tears. With Asten gone and Ahmose poisoned by the Devourer, I felt as if the pieces holding me together were fading. All it would take was a sharp tug and my whole world would unravel.

"Ach, my bonny lad. What has she done ta ya?"

Amon hacked at the ropes binding Anubis, and the god fell into his arms. "She's killed most of the others," Anubis said. "Ma'at's gone."

"Osiris?" Amon asked.

Anubis shook his head. "Not yet. He's still locked in the tower. She knew we'd come for him."

Nodding his head grimly, Amon said, "It's time to go. Can you move?"

Anubis trembled. "She's drained me, son. I've very little left."

Amon threw Anubis's arm over his shoulders. "Then let's get you out of here."

"There's no time," Anubis said, his brows knitted. "She's toying with the lot of you. Keeping you busy until Seth breaks free of his shackles."

"Then we'll make sure we finish her before he does. You'll have to hold on to Ahmose. Ashleigh," Amon called, "help position them on my back."

Amon changed into his bird form, and Ashleigh stepped aside so I could take over again. Anubis, weak as he was, helped me get Ahmose on his brother's back. I was just about to help Anubis, too, when the Devourer reappeared behind him.

"Leaving so soon? We can't have that, can we?" She sank her writhing hair into Anubis and actually lifted him in the air. He cried out in pain. Desperately, I turned to Amon. "Go. Get him to safety. I'll keep her busy until you get back."

Amon took off, barely keeping a groaning Ahmose on his back. His golden form disappeared over the buildings. The Devourer watched him depart with an expression of amusement. "You think to thwart my master?" Her eyes had lit up just thinking about him.

"Your master?" I spat. "I would think a woman as powerful as you are would chafe at the very idea of having a master."

She tossed Anubis aside easily and he crumbled to the ground in a heap. "Says the girl who has not one but three masters."

"The Sons of Egypt aren't my masters," I replied. "They are my companions. Warriors who stand alongside me."

"Are they?" she asked, sizing me up. "I think perhaps they are much more than that. I must admit you've impressed me. To wrap the three Sons of Egypt around your little finger so quickly is something to be admired. Tell me," she said, stalking closer, "what have you done with their hearts?"

"I'm sure I don't know what you mean."

"I think you do. That one you just spirited away had barely any energy left to give, and his heart was missing. A telltale sign that they are much more than just your . . . warriors." The Devourer screwed up her face as she studied me. "Why are you so . . . unreadable? You are still mortal. I can smell the rank odor of humanity on you, and yet I do not sense your heart. It's powerful. I know that much."

The Devourer circled around me slowly; my nerves prickled at her proximity. Closing the gap between us, she wrapped a hand around my arm, her long nails scraping my skin. Her hot breath wafted over me as she said, "I know you have one. I've tasted it through Amon." I could feel her eyes boring into me. "My master says you need to be taken alive, but surely he wouldn't mind me having just a little taste." Her eyes closed. "The bond of true love is so rare a delicacy. To consume a heart engorged by it is something one such as I could never resist."

"Is that because you've never experienced it for yourself?" I asked quietly.

Her face turned scarlet. "My master loves me."

"Seth loves Isis. Nephthys told me all about it."

"Nephthys lies," the Devourer snarled. "She cannot appreciate a man such as Seth."

I rolled my eyes. "What's to appreciate? One who hurts others can't love. He's a bond breaker, not a bond maker. Even you, with your limited experience, should be able to recognize that."

Her forehead creased as she laughed bitterly. "And what do you, as young as you are, know of love?"

"I know it means sacrifice. Being willing to give up anything to protect the person that you love. The Sons of Egypt would do so for me, and I would do the same for them. Tell me, would Seth give up his ambitions for you? Would he rush to your side to save your life?"

"Your naïveté is laughable. I do not need to answer your childish questions. I am the Devourer. I have taken in all the suffering, all the sin, all the hate and bitterness that has ever been a part of the world. It lives in me. For me, it is enough to know that Seth has helped me break free of the netherworld. Perhaps he does not love me according to your definition, but he valued me enough to give me my deepest, darkest desire."

"Then I feel sorry for you."

She gave me a half smile. "Oh? Why is that, my succulent tidbit?"

"Because you deserved more. It's not too late, you know. You can change. Give up this ambition and try to become something different."

Her forehead creased but then smoothed out. "You think you know everything. But unfortunately, you'll find," she said as her glinting eyes drifted down to my chest, "that you sorely underestimate me."

With a snap, her hand pierced my chest, penetrating right through my armor, and I yowled in pain. The Devourer threw back her head in a triumphant shout as she delved deeper, seeking my heart. I breathed heavily, tears running down my cheeks as she probed. Gritting my teeth, I took hold of her arm and wrapped my hands around her wrist.

Her smile faded as I clenched my jaw and lifted my wings. Beating them heavily, I lifted off the ground, pulling her with me. She paled when her feet could no longer find purchase. "Where is it?" she hissed. "Where is your heart?"

I ignored her and soared higher. She glanced around with concern then turned her gaze back to me. Tendrils of her hair shot out and dug into my arms and back, the fiery darts latching on to me beneath my skin. Her pupils were huge, and her nostrils flared. It was obvious she was frightened, and yet still she dug. Letting out a gasp, I warned her, "If you stop, I will let you live."

Her face twisted into a mask of hatred. "Do your worst," she taunted. "Your power is nothing next to mine. I am the Devourer. I am—"

"Yeah, yeah," I interrupted and then peered down at her with a raised eyebrow. "But I'm a New Yorker," I hissed. "And you messed with my hometown."

Channeling my power, I beat my wings, letting the feathers gather in the sunlight. An electric current sizzled and popped. The Devourer wrenched her body back and forth, beating on me with her free hand. I looked down at rivulets of blood streaming down my torso and felt a tug on my waist. She'd discovered my belt with the heart scarabs. She yanked my belt free, and I gasped and let go.

The Devourer fell through the air, her barbed hair ripping out of my skin as her hand slipped out of my chest. Mouth open in awe, she stroked the scarabs, completely oblivious to her precarious position. The power I'd channeled had reached its zenith, and I clapped my wings together. A sizzling stream of light shot out toward her, and when it hit, she threw her arms and head back, electricity streaming from her mouth and out the ends of her hair.

The belt slipped from her fingers, and she grasped for it feebly even as she screamed. Her skin turned white and then brightened. I could have sworn I saw her lashes flutter closed and a smile of peace spread across her face before her entire body exploded.

I sank down to the ground, my wings barely keeping me aloft, and crumpled next to Anubis. Nearby, I spied the fallen belt and stretched as far as I could. Clasping it between two fingers, I pulled it close and crushed it to the gaping wound in my chest. Blood soaked the ground around me. I heard the cry of a falcon and felt a shadow pass over my face before I closed my eyes.

26

The Waters of Chaos

When I woke, it was to the crackling, popping sound of a fire. I tried to move, but every part of me ached in a way I'd never felt before. Letting out a moan, I shifted my elbow to the ground to lift up my body, but I fell back heavily. A pair of arms caught me before I hit the ground.

"Shh. Lie still," Amon's voice murmured in my ear. "We are safe for now."

"Ahmose?" I managed to say.

"He is here. Ahmose is resting now. It took nearly all his remaining power to save you. If it weren't for him and the emblem of Horus, one of you would surely have perished. Even if Anubis had been able to properly tend to one of your bodies, Cherty is gone. There would be no safe passage to the afterlife. Your souls would have been lost at best, food for Apep at worst."

Good to know, I thought. I reached up to my neck and found the necklace Horus had given me. The healing stela had come in very handy. Amon gestured to the other side of the fire, where Anubis sat next to a sleeping Ahmose. Anubis appeared to be resting, too. He sat back against a dirt wall, knee raised, his arm propped on it, his hand pressed against his forehead.

"How is he?" I asked.

"Anubis will survive."

"Ashleigh wants to see Ahmose," I whispered to Amon. He nodded and lifted me up.

I retreated, letting Ashleigh take over. She picked up his hand and held it gently. Tears blurred my vision, making the firelight dance in shimmering patterns as we looked at his face. She leaned closer, pressing her hand against his heart. Light bloomed beneath his shirt as she channeled the power imbued in her by the fairy tree.

Finished, Ashleigh sat back and asked Anubis, "Will you tell us what happened to the others?"

"The group Ma'at led was captured and destroyed. The Devourer made me"—he paused and swiped his eyes—"made me watch. It took a long time. Ma'at was powerful. She said . . ." Anubis stopped as a shudder ran through him. "She said Ma'at harbored a secret love for me. I told her she was mistaken. That Ma'at argued with me at every turn. That she hated my way of circumventing her rules and the way I mocked her rigid nature." Anubis sniffed sadly and ground his jaw. "But then Ma'at turned to me, horror filling her eyes, and I knew the Devourer spoke the truth."

"Oh, Anubis. I'm sorry," Ashleigh said.

Sadness clouded his features. "Now I suppose we'll never know what could have been."

"There was no way ta save her, then?" Ashleigh asked.

"No. I have to capture the life essence before it departs the body. The Devourer sucks down every last bit until there is no chance to recover anything. Ma'at is gone."

Ashleigh took his hand, squeezed his fingers and settled next to Ahmose. With our energy funneling into him, we slept again.

We rested until the dawn and felt recovered enough to head back to the mountain to regroup. Once there, we found only a third of the people remained. Amun-Ra had made it back and Nephthys had never left. They mourned when Anubis told them about losing Ma'at. They shared the good news that Osiris had been found and brought back, and we told them of killing the Devourer. Our victory was marred with loss.

Leaving Amun-Ra, Anubis, and Nephthys to form plans, I sought out Horus and found him kneeling next to his father's side. Osiris was pale and feverish, and in his sleep he thrashed and called out over and over for Isis.

Without acknowledging my presence, Horus said, "He feels her suffering. It hurts him worse than the pains in his own body."

"We'll save her," I said.

"I hope we will. Thank you, by the way. Thank you for killing the Devourer."

"I should be the one thanking you," I said. "Your stela healed me. I would have died without it." Reaching behind my neck, I loosened the clasp and held it out to him.

"You should keep it," he said, turning as his wet eyes met mine.

"Will it heal your father?" I asked. "It didn't heal the Sons of Egypt."

"The stela only heals those who are part of my family."

I cocked my head. "Then why did you gift it to me?"

"It . . . it felt right. The fact that it heals you means something. We are connected, you and I, in our own way."

I didn't know how to feel about that, but I couldn't deny it either. Kneeling down next to him, I pressed it into his palm, folding his fingers over it. "Your father has more need of it now than I do. Thank you for sacrificing such a gift for me."

Horus gave me a long, penetrating look, then, nodding, he placed the necklace between his father's hands. I took in Osiris's slack jaw and clammy skin. Horus leaned over his father's missing leg, bathing it gently. As he did so, he murmured a quiet spell, finishing with, "Water unmakes and makes anew." After squeezing Horus's shoulder, I left him with his father and headed back to the others.

"What's the plan?" I asked Amon and Ahmose, who stood on the out-skirts of the group as the gods talked.

"It would seem they are unwilling to wait for Seth to break free and find them. They will seek him out instead," Amon said.

"Is that wise when we are so few?" I asked.

Amun-Ra looked up suddenly. "We are not as few as Seth might believe," he said, his brows drawn together. "Prepare yourselves, citi-zens," Amun-Ra announced. "We head into battle within the hour."

Anubis approached, his expression hardened. Already he'd changed. He was clean and dressed in black battle armor, but his eyes were tired and there was a grim determination in the set of his shoulders. He wore a sword on his hip and carried a black plumed helm beneath an arm. I heard a whine behind him, and my jaw dropped when I saw a limping Abutiu trailing his master.

"He made it!" I exclaimed.

"Yes." Anubis's sad eyes crinkled at the corners, and his downturned mouth twitched into a lopsided smile as he knelt and scratched his dog behind the ears. "At least I still have him. They brought him back to me when they discovered Osiris. I gave a bit of myself to heal him. I'm sure my sacrifice will be well worth it. Won't it, you mangy beast?"

The dog butted his head against his master's hand and licked his fingers. After a moment, he stood and said, "Abutiu will stay here with Osiris and some of Amun-Ra's elder servants who are not able to fight. The rest of us will head into battle. I've been instructed to stay with you and protect you for as long as I am able." He nodded to Ahmose and Amon. "Are the two of you recovered sufficiently?"

They gave a stiff nod of their heads, indicating that they were.

"Good. You will not be traveling in your bird forms. You're too big of a target, and we'd like to keep your identity hidden for as long as pos-sible." Amon and Ahmose seemed surprised by this.

"Where will we be going?" I asked, interrupting. "Is Seth in Heliop-olis?"

Anubis shook his head. "Seth is still shackled to his prison, though he has breached the walls. Our goal is to finish him before he loosens his chains and while he is still weak from the loss of the Devourer. It is probable that he'd been counting on her to provide him with enough energy to break free. That is why she sought the mortal realm. Feasting on the hearts of the living would have given her enough power to release him. If Seth had been loosed, we doubt that even we would have been able to contain him."

"Okay, so where is his prison?" I asked.

"It lies in the only place with a strong enough gravity to hold him—the Waters of Chaos. The obelisk where we trapped him orbits the rim. We should find him there, and hopefully we will finish this fight with our brother once and for all."

I was about to ask, "How are we going to get there?" "How can I breathe in space?" and "What about Isis?" when the air around us shook.

The fabric of the sky rippled, and dozens of golden forms burst through. My eyes stung as I fought back tears. "How?" I managed to say, which was pretty much the lamest of all my questions.

"They were inspired by the sacrifice of their brothers and decided to come to our aid. They will carry us into battle."

Unicorns flew overhead, kicking out their legs in a gallop, and whinnying to announce that they'd arrived. I took in the sight of them and swallowed a painful lump. In my mind, I knew Nebu was gone, but I scanned the sky for his familiar form anyway. Losing both him and Cherty along with Ma'at was something I wasn't going to get over any time soon.

A hand took my arm. "Are you okay?" Amon asked.

"I'll be fine," I said and turned to him, hoping to step into his arms for a hug. I stopped when I saw he was already dressed in his golden armor. His eyes sparkled at seeing my consternation. Leaning down, he took hold of my shoulders and brought his lips to my ear. "Someday, I promise, there will be no armor between us."

I flushed. "I hope so," I said.

Amon backed away, holding me at arm's length, and gave me the once-over. "I would prefer to see you better protected, Nehabet."

I glanced down at my ruined clothing, crinkling my nose. "Me too. I'll be back. Don't head off to battle without me."

His forehead puckered. "I will never leave your side again, Young Lily."

"Good. I'll hold you to that."

Heading off to one of the empty tents dotting the top of the mountain, I summoned the sand and let it cleanse my form. My arms rose, and the ripped, bloody clothes melted away until I wore nothing at all. The wind buffeted and scraped my skin until it gleamed. It tore through my hair, whipping it back and forth until I felt it slapping my bare back, smooth and silky.

When I was clean, the sand coalesced, forming clothing. I closed my eyes and envisioned not exactly what I wanted to wear but how I wanted to be protected. Fabric, soft and supple, wrapped around my limbs. Lightweight plates covered my chest, legs, and arms in a variegated pattern that mimicked my wings. A special harness formed with a pouch between my shoulder blades, and there were rimmed openings in my armor large enough for my wings to emerge.

On my feet, thick boots formed. They were cushioned on the inside and laced tightly up to my knees. Plates grew over the tops of the boots and stretched over my legs, creating shin guards. The toes of the boots were sharpened to shiny points. The heart scarabs now rested in a thick armor plate that stretched from one shoulder to the other.

My gleaming hair was swept away from my face and hung down my back in a straight line. It didn't even move in the wind. I twirled my spear-knives and slid them over my head and into the harness, then placed the quiver and bow in the spot I'd created. My weapons settled securely against my body. When I emerged from the tent, bending my arms and testing my boots, I didn't even hear Ahmose or Amon approach.

Ahmose took my hand and kissed my fingers. Though I had gloves, they were fingerless so I could use my bow and grip my spear-knives. The corners of his eyes crinkled as he said, "I am honored to fight at your side. My cudgel, my ax, and the rest of me are yours to do with as you wish."

"Thank you," I said, heat stinging my cheeks. "My biggest wish is that we all come out of this alive."

"I will endeavor to make that happen," Ahmose said.

Next I turned to Amon, who was leaning against the tent pole with one hip, his hand on the hilt of his blade as he took in my attire. I blushed even harder beneath his gaze and drew my lower lip between my teeth before asking, "Did I forget something?"

His eyes opened wide. "No, Nehabet. I was just thinking that I have never in my long years seen a woman, or a warrior, as beautiful and awe-inspiring as you. I pity the one who finds the pointed end of your spear at his throat, and yet I understand how he feels."

"Why do you say that?" I asked, cocking my head.

"I say this because I know you have the power to dispatch any and all who oppose you. Thus, I pity them. But I understand because since I met you that first time in New York, I have felt a pressing need to surrender myself, body and soul, to your will. Young Lily, I want you to know before we go into battle that I henceforth renounce all the gods and proclaim you are the only object of my worship."

He knelt before me, took my hand, and kissed it.

If a boy in New York had said something like that to me, I would have laughed my head off enough to bring tears to my eyes, and then would have repeated the story to the cabdriver on the way home. But I couldn't laugh at Amon. He was utterly serious, and a twinge of worry entered my mind, effectively killing any tendency toward a mirthful reaction.

I narrowed my eyes and looked down my nose at him suspiciously. Yanking him up to his feet, I placed my hands on the broad armored plates of his chest. "You're not thinking of doing something crazy and noble like you did when you ditched me and headed off to the pyramids by yourself, are you? 'Cause if you are, you should know that I'm a different girl now than I was then."

Though I didn't think it was possible, he wrapped his arms around me and pulled me into a tight embrace, our armor and weapons crunching together. "You are my Lily," he said. "The same Lily that I feasted with, even if our first feast was warmed-over dogs. You may be more powerful. You may be clothed in battle armor. You may have faced demons and slain a great enemy. But the girl I fell in love with, the one who saved me on the pyramid, the one who carried my heart even then, is the same girl who stands before me now. And I would not change her for all the worlds in all the cosmos."

He kissed me. And it was sweet and soft and full of every wish and promise that I wasn't sure either of us could keep. But I knew we desperately hoped we'd get the chance to make it possible.

"I love you," I said when we broke apart. "But I can't help noticing you didn't exactly answer my question."

"Then take this as your answer. I love you as the flowers love the rain. They open their mouths to drink it in, and it sustains them. You give me sustenance, Young Lily. I will not—I cannot leave your side again."

My heart felt tight and full and warm in my chest. I touched the tip of my finger to his soft lips and stroked the light stubble on his jaw. "I think I've heard that sustenance thing somewhere before," I said with a smile. "But this time you don't have to coerce me."

I kissed him again and touched my forehead to his, unwilling to let him go, but it was time. Backing up, I spread my wings, and two unicorns touched down. Their hooves stomped, and bursts of lightning shot out from beneath them, disappearing into the ground and making it quake. Their tails flicked nervously, lashing the air as if they fought an invisible enemy. They twitched and danced as they waited for Ahmose and Amon to mount.

When they were ready, I summoned my wings and we followed Amun-Ra into the sky. He waved his hand and a portal opened. Horus and Anubis closed in next to me on one side while Amon and Ahmose protected the other. Together, we were a storm cloud of power, a maelstrom of fury. And we were headed to war.

I heard the cry of a unicorn below me and looked down. It was Zahra. I gasped.

Come, Lily, she said. *I would be honored to carry you into battle. You need not expend your energy so soon.*

I . . . I thought you followed Nebu when the breach was sealed.

My father would not allow me to go with him, though I was willing. He wanted you to have a familiar mount to carry you into battle.

Thank you, I said. *I'm glad you're here.*

Flapping my wings once, twice, I dropped down, landing solidly on her back. For a moment I imagined we looked like a giant, double-winged dragonfly. She was right that I needed to preserve my energy, and I was grateful to have her close. Though she kept her thoughts from me, I heard the gnashing of her teeth. She, too, was angry at the loss of Nebu.

We entered the greedy mouth of the vortex and were sucked in one by one. Thick, viscous oil coated us, but then we were through and aloft in a vastness of empty space. I lost all sense of gravity as I gaped at the limitlessness of the cosmos around us. My pulse raced and my breaths came in short, tremulous pants as my pupils dilated to take in as much light as I could.

I wasn't the only one shocked by our surroundings. A prominent vein popped out in Amon's neck, and even Anubis looked uncomfortable, his mouth pressed in a thin line and his expression hard and determined. Amun-Ra pushed onward, and we followed—the breaths of my fellow warriors, the thumping of unicorn wings, and the seesaw bellows of hot steam shooting from their nostrils were the only sounds I could hear.

When we cleared a dark void, there was a sense of space pressing down on us, and then light pierced the darkness. It popped and sizzled like a firecracker before fading away. Another one came, this time pink.

Then I saw yellow and green, each shape different, each color amazing. Soon more and more bursts of light filled my vision, each one creating its own special place in the immeasurable emptiness.

"What . . . what are they?" I asked Anubis as a burst of turquoise filled my vision.

"They are galaxies being born." His face turned crimson and gold, the colors dancing across the rugged planes.

Soon after, metallic threads became visible. They tied one light to another like swaying bridges that crossed back and forth, over and under. "It's . . . it's a web," I mumbled, marveling.

"Yes," Horus said. "What you see is the remnant of the Cosmic Web. Its lines fade now."

"Because there's no one left to weave," I said.

Horus shot me a sharp look. "How do you know of this?" he asked.

I swallowed. "Wasret and . . . I sort of had a run-in with a cosmic spider."

Anubis raised his eyebrows but said nothing.

Studying the pattern of lines that crisscrossed the darkness of the cosmos, I said, "It's like a giant map. It reminds me of what Earth looks like from space at night. All the lights linked together. New York was always the brightest."

"Yes. But since this is actually a web, the brightest spot is at the center. And the center is where we will find the one we seek."

As we flew closer, we began to turn, and what looked like a thin line sparkling and crackling on the horizon widened and curved until I could see what we were really looking at. It was like something right out of a sci-fi movie. *Holy Egyptian heaven,* I thought. No. In this case it was just *holy heaven.* I wasn't schooled enough in astrology to understand what it was exactly, but to my non–science person eyes, it looked a bit like a black hole.

What is it? I asked Zahra.

It is the edge of the cosmos was the unicorn's reply.

The unicorn's natural light winked out as the cosmic phenomenon came into view. At the center there was indeed a spiraling funnel, but the rest of it was brimming with vibrating color. It looked like a churning oil-slicked pond, and just on the outer edge, lashed to it like a balloon on a fiery string, was a dark, indiscernible mass.

"Is that it?" I asked. "Is that him?"

"Yes," Anubis said. "Seth is shackled to the event horizon. What you see is the remnant of his prison."

"So it is a black hole, then?"

"No. Not in the sense you understand. The Waters of Chaos hold all the lifeblood of the cosmos. The galaxies that are born originate here. The building blocks of life, the energy that courses through all things, comes from this place. What you perceive as a hole is the unmaking. We have shackled Seth to the place where creation is the strongest. It cancels out his power and has contained him within his prison since the Sons of Egypt were born into their second lives."

Now what I was seeing made more sense. The phenomenon known as the Waters of Chaos was shaped like a ring, but it wasn't rotating like a hula hoop—instead, the uppermost layer was constantly being swept over the rimmed edge, colors flowing over like water dropping off the edge of the world.

The closer we got to it, the more the matter seemed to move in certain patterns. Bits rose up out of the liquid, coalesced, and then shot off to distant galaxies.

"What was that?" I asked Anubis.

"A tree. A whale. A newborn kitten. A new world. A star. It could be anything."

"But I thought the Waters of Chaos had been drained," I said.

I heard a soft exhalation before Anubis said, "The Waters of Chaos used to fill this entire area of the cosmos. The dark place we entered is now a void where there used to be life and color. Seth is not entirely wrong. What you see now is a result of his handiwork. But his motives are flawed and autocratic. We could not allow him to use this mighty power unchecked."

We flew closer, the silence pressing upon me as I considered everything Anubis had said. Zahra shook her head as we angled sharply. The edge of the colorful matter ahead dropped off the curved edge, falling into space like a giant galactic waterfall. It was an awesome sight. I could easily envision Cherty with his lost boat, *Mesektet,* riding the waves of color and then screaming aloud his defiance at the universe as he went over the edge and sank into oblivion.

Wiping a tear from my eye, I studied the Waters of Chaos in wonder. "Here, there be dragons," I whispered.

I didn't know how right I was.

St. George and the Dragon

"They are coming," Anubis said as dark shapes swarmed before us.

"Sky-demons!" Amon warned, and his unicorn veered down as a demon flew right between me and Ahmose, his leathery wings scraping my leg.

"Try to keep them from Lily!" Anubis warned as he drew a shimmering sword. Amon's golden scimitars flashed in the darkness. Now that we'd worn out our surprise, the unicorns allowed their natural light to shine, and we saw what we were really facing. The sky was full of shadowy creatures who came at us with claws extended and mouths open, ready to tear into us.

Pulling out my spears, I pressed the button to elongate them and jabbed one deep into the chest of an approaching demon. He crumbled to dust in the open space. On my right, Amon took out two at once, severing the head off one and the wing off another. Without its second wing, the creature spun wildly, unable to direct its course. It spiraled off and disappeared among the swirling galaxies.

Out of the depths of space, sizzling asteroids appeared. I glanced over my shoulder and saw Ahmose sinking his cudgel into the neck of a demon passing nearby, then he lifted his arms and directed the path of fiery rocks straight into the mass of demons. Horus fought with his sword, and he also wove spells of some kind that seemed to confuse the demons. They'd veer off and end up attacking each other instead of us.

The space around me echoed with the shrieking of both unicorns and demons, and the refrain of steel striking bone was something I didn't think I'd ever forget. A nearby unicorn lost its rider, and the horde descended, slashing into the animal's tender flesh. Glittering blood pumped from the great beast's neck and, with a mournful cry, it folded its wings and fell away into space.

My pupils flared as I felt red wrath crawl up my neck. I summoned my wings, took to the air, and gathered light. But this was no ordinary light, like that of the Heliopolis sun. This was the light of the cosmos itself. The light of billions of stars. It coalesced, beams hurtling toward me. Wings pumping, I slowly turned in a circle, arms lifted.

Power coursed through me, and my skin turned bright enough that I cast my own glow. In that moment, I was a true sphinx—a creature born of the cosmos—full of as much fire and gold as if I'd been fashioned from the yellow sun under which I was born. My speed increased until everything around me became a blur of color and light.

When my wings clapped together, the whole area around me lit up like an atomic bomb. The unicorns carrying my protectors veered away, uncertain of the power I channeled. With a stiletto smile, I pointed, sending my wave of energy out to the nearest demon. The lightning vortex struck with deadly accuracy. In an instant, every demon in our immediate area vanished in a dusty puff of glitter.

When the immediate danger was over, Zahra returned and I sank down onto her back, noticing only then that she trembled beneath me. I scrunched up my face. "Did I hurt you?" I asked.

No, but you should know the power you drew upon did not just come from the distant stars. You took energy from the unicorns and the gods themselves.

"What?" Her revelation was shocking. Quickly, I glanced over at

Anubis, who'd soundlessly glided up next to me again, resuming his place at my side. He wore a poker-faced expression, but I could see, even in the darkness, that the hand holding his weapon shook.

Do not worry overmuch, she said. *We unicorns are a hardy breed. We would have expended energy fighting them regardless. At least this way we won't need to recover from wounds as well.*

Despite her reassurances, I snapped my mouth shut, pressing it into a thin line. I determined to use only my own power from then on and not take it from my companions again. I couldn't afford another error in judgment. The fact was that I really didn't know as much about my newfound power as I would have liked.

Another wave of demons approached, but they were much more cautious than their brothers. They fought us in tight groups, ten demons charging each unicorn and rider, taking out those on our outermost edges and slowly working their way to the middle. After each victory, they'd slink off, and we could never tell which direction they would be coming from since they melted into the darkness so well.

There were so many sky-demons. I'd thought the ones we fought before were vast in number, but clearly Seth had been holding them back. Keeping them at his side. Even without the Devourer, it seemed Seth still retained great power.

We fought valiantly but lost several of our warriors. Still, it appeared as if we were making progress. We drew nearer to the Waters of Chaos. Up close it was larger than I'd first thought. It was almost the size of a vast city. *The size of Manhattan*, I thought with a start. Beating back our enemy, we reached the edge, only to be assaulted by a new, invisible enemy. One that seemed very familiar.

I heard a hissing noise, and Anubis cried out as rivulets of red appeared on his forearm. He dropped his sword, but it vanished and rematerialized in his hand. A nearby warrior was yanked from his mount, and his arm completely disappeared, blood streaming from his severed stump as he screamed. Zahra shrieked, and a row of bite marks appeared on her foreleg. As I watched, keeping my eyes peeled for her attacker, I slashed the empty air with my knives. Her unicorn blood swelled on her puncture wounds.

"*Biloko!*" Amon cried.

The very word caused me to balk. I remembered my all-too-frail, human form being attacked by the invisible crocodile demons that Sebak sent to attack us while we were recovering at Dr. Hassan's home. Amon held out his bare hands in space, stretched-out fingertips wiggling and palms flat as if he were hand-fishing in a river. Then he grabbed on to something I couldn't see. It was large, though. Large enough that he could wrap his arms around its body and his fingers still didn't meet.

His unicorn bucked beneath him, and Amon's face contorted as if he was in pain. He gyrated in the air as the thing he held wrenched wildly back and forth. Amon's legs shot from one side to another, and he spun in a circle before accelerating upward at breakneck speed. He then tunneled back down and seemed to stop in midair. I edged closer, waiting for the right moment, and struck out with my spear-knives, sinking them into the space between Amon's hands.

He stilled, floating in space, and then let go. Zahra moved closer to him, and Amon reached for me. I grasped on to his hand, pulling him closer until his face came up just a bit lower than my own. He levitated easily enough and moved with us as long as I held on to him. I allowed myself the briefest of moments to revel in the strength of his hands, the way they wrapped around my own smaller ones. Amon's face was blanched whiter than moonlight, but I couldn't see any obvious wounds. His eyes gleamed green, as green as a northern sea.

"Stay close to me," he said. "Remember they have a taste for females." I only had time to nod before he let go and fell down, landing perfectly on his unicorn, who surged up from below. The fight became bloody as demons both visible and invisible tore into our ranks. Amun-Ra and Nephthys came closer. The sun god told us to ride around the far rim of the Waters of Chaos while he and Nephthys would take the rest of the warriors and unicorns in the other direction. He instructed us to dim our light and head off when he gave the signal.

We fought mightily for the space of several minutes when I heard the sharp cry of a bird. It was the benu bird. I knew that was the signal we'd waited for. I gave the command to Zahra and she turned off her light and banked sharply. Amon, Ahmose, Anubis, and Horus followed. The space surrounding us became quiet as the battle moved off.

When the unicorn's hooves met the Waters of Chaos, I was shocked to learn that the nebulous colored matter had a solid enough base that we could walk on it. The mist still roiled and moved like water, but it spilled past the unicorn's legs as if we were wading through a shallow river. With the light reflecting up, I could clearly make out the faces of my companions. It cast shimmering patterns on our limbs and faces, giving us enough light to see as we made our way forward.

"Where do we go from here?" I asked.

Horus answered, "We go to confront Seth once and for all."

I turned to Amon, searching for the reassuring upward twist of his lips that he so often gave me when he glanced my way, but his expression was closed up. Zahra moved alongside his mount, keeping pace with the large male unicorn that looked so much like Nebu. "What is it?" I asked him.

"I am not sure. It feels like something is wrong. My chest burns. I do not understand it."

"So does mine," Ahmose said.

"That's strange," I said rubbing my own chest. All at once, my own heart began to burn. Zahra stopped, and I kicked a leg over her back, landing hard on top of the slick surface beneath the shimmering Waters of Chaos. I suddenly felt suffocated by my own clothing. I tugged at the neckline, feeling like my armor was acting more like a burial shroud.

Amon and Ahmose seemed to be experiencing the same thing. I reached my palm up to cup Ahmose's face, only to pull it back with a hiss. "What's happening to us?" I asked Anubis, who got off his own unicorn.

He closed his eyes, chanting a spell. His face scrunched up as if he were in pain. Terror overtook his expression, and he quickly dropped to my side. "No! It can't be!" he cried as he took hold of my arm. He quickly withdrew his hand. His palm had turned bright red.

I tugged on my hair and rocked from my heels to my knees, desperate to end the pain. Clenching and unclenching my fists, I pulled and pushed on my temples, groaning. I wanted to ask Anubis what was happening, but I couldn't form the words. Instead, I gestured wildly with my hands, trying to show him that something was very wrong. All of a sudden, my back shot ramrod straight, and I screamed. Tilting my face to the swirling stars above me, I felt power lift from my body. It hovered over me in a cloud.

In my mind's eye, I saw a man, one whose ebony hair framed a face so handsome, it rivaled the very stars. I beamed as he made elusive promises that appealed to me more than lounging in sweet-smelling grasses on a savannah night. *"Tene, my love,"* I whispered as I kissed the edge of his mouth, just where his lips curled in a familiar smirk. I smoothed the silky hair away from his forehead so I could gaze into the depths of his eyes.

He slid his hands from my waist down over my hips and splayed his fingers, then pulled, tugging me close. Grinning at me, he said, "Are you in the mood to play tonight? Come and find me, then, my lovely minx."

Then he winked and stepped back. I was about to chase him when the smile ebbed slowly from his face until it disappeared altogether. Darkness shrouded him. I observed a change in his eyes. Before, they were open to me. I could see my reflection in them, love pooling in the centers and spilling out. But now the depths of his eyes were closed, cold. They held nothing now but secrets.

Secrets.

Secrets.

My body collapsed, and when I opened my eyes, I felt hollow and dead inside. Light from the Waters of Chaos spilled over me in a colorful fog. The heat was ebbing as the foamy clouds bathed my fevered skin. I winced as strong arms lifted me. "What happened?" I asked as I got to my feet.

"The yoke," Anubis said grimly. "The yoke has been severed."

"How . . . how is that possible?" I asked.

"It is Asten," Amon said, a bleak, hopeless expression transforming his face. "Can you not feel it, Lily?"

"Asten?" I stood there, mouth parted in shock, as I tried to understand what he meant.

Anubis took hold of my shoulders and turned me toward him. "Lily, you must know that this is not irreversible. Asten can still be saved. You mustn't give up on him."

I raised my eyebrows. *Give up on him? Of course I wouldn't give up on him.* "So he's not dead, then? Are you certain?"

"He is still living," Horus said as he ran a finger along a blade. "For the moment."

A dozen scenarios ran through my mind at his words, and I wanted to grab Horus up by the collar and make him spill everything he knew.

Horus continued. "Asten is just no longer . . ." He waved a hand in the air with a flourish, as if seeking the right word. "He's no longer protected by your bond. Your collective power is now cut off from his."

"What aren't you telling me?" I accused, hands on my hips as I cornered Horus, giving him my best don't-mess-with-me look.

The god actually took a step back.

"Lily," Anubis said. "We don't have time for this. Fortunately, you recovered after being severed from him. There was a chance you wouldn't, that breaking the yoke would destroy you all. The fact that you regained your strength so swiftly bodes well. It means there is still hope. Hope for Asten and hope for us. But regardless, we must find him. Quickly."

"You mean he's here?" I asked as I flew up to Zahra's back and settled astride her once more. Ahmose was bent over her leg, healing the bite from the Biloko demon.

"I fear the severing of the yoke means Asten is very close. Come," he said. "We must make haste."

Tia mourned anew, and it was all Ashleigh and I could do to comfort her as we continued on. Now that we understood what had happened, I recognized the vision for what it was. The scene we'd witnessed had been a small glimpse into the mind of Asten. Tia confirmed that the particular dream we'd seen had never occurred in real life or in one of his dreamscapes. She hoped it was a sign that he was near. That he wanted us to find him. I dreaded the notion that she was right. I'd much prefer that he was back in Heliopolis, safe. That somehow he'd escaped the sky-demons and was even now pacing atop the mountain, wondering where we'd all gone.

Finally, we saw the black box coming into view. Approaching closer, we saw it was as large as football field and appeared to be torn open; sections of it had been completely dissolved, but it was so dark inside and still so far away, we couldn't make out anything from where we were.

The box, or obelisk, as Horus referred to it, was tethered to the edge of the glimmering ring where we stood. When we reached the border where the crackling and popping link had been affixed, I gazed up at the box, which shifted slightly back and forth hundreds of meters above us. It looked as if it were a giant square balloon or a kite, and the tether was a lightning bridge stretching into the dark heavens above.

I gulped, looking across the great chasm of space between us and the object we sought. Lucky for us, we had unicorns. The idea of climbing the spitting, snapping chain hand over hand was terrible and nightmarish.

"Are you sure Seth is still up there?" I asked, narrowing my eyes as I scanned the dark object in space.

"If he weren't, the chain would have broken and dissolved back into pure energy," Anubis answered.

"Okay, so what's the game plan?" I asked.

"We were supposed to meet Amun-Ra and Nephthys here. They

should have arrived before us, since we went around the long way. The fact that they are not here makes me nervous."

"Do you think the sky-demons or the Biloko got them first?"

Anubis scanned the sky around us. "I do not believe so. Amun-Ra is powerful enough that any demon who dared bite him would immediately perish. As far as Nephthys is concerned, she is something of a prophetess. She sees enough into the future to know when and how to alter her course. There is no reason they should not have reached us by now." Anubis rubbed his jaw as he turned, considering the heavens above us.

A burst of sparks erupted from atop the obelisk. The entire structure shifted, and the long chain swayed back and forth wildly across the expanse. We heard the unmistakable sound of a woman screaming.

"Mother!" Horus leapt onto his unicorn's back and galloped right off the edge. He plummeted below the falling waters, and then he burst back into view as he soared upward, heading for the obelisk.

Anubis threw his hands up in disgust as he glared at the god. "Reckless youth," he quietly hissed. "There he goes, running off all cocked and loaded, forgetting the whole point of his mother's sacrifice." He furrowed his eyebrows at us. "You lot better not be getting any ideas to follow in Horus's footsteps. Think before you act. Do you understand? Seth already knows we're here. Let's not give him more of an advantage than he already has."

"We understand, Anubis," Amon said.

"Good. You've never met Seth. Not in person. But I'll warn you, he's like a far-off storm. You think you have time to prepare for his onslaught, but—boom—he's upon you before you can take shelter. He circles beneath you, waits you out like the most patient of hunters. He studies you and finds your weak spots. And then snap." He clapped his hands together. "You're caught in the teeth of the crocodile."

I shivered.

"And keep in mind," Anubis continued. "He's much more dangerous than he looks. To see him as a scrawny powerless boy, unworthy of notice, was a mistake. He took advantage of our blindness." Anubis stared overhead and added softly, his jaw tight, "Seth's become a cruel man, prone to torture. Destruction is his ultimate goal. He's devious and smart. Give him an inch of sympathy and he'll fill you with his poison. Don't believe what you see either. Seth can change his shape into creatures you've never seen before. He harnesses their abilities, too. Bottom line—don't underestimate him. It will be your undoing."

"Then how do we stop one such as him?" Ahmose asked.

"You can stop him because he underestimates you, too. Or, perhaps more accurately, he overestimates himself. His goal will be to try to break you. Because he created the Sons of Egypt, he will attempt to use you, to harness your power. But you can resist him. We've given you that ability. Still, your own determination and courage is the only thing standing between him and his ultimate goals. Seth won't try to kill one of Egypt's Sons—at least I can't imagine he would attempt such a thing. If he did, the outcome would be . . . well, let's just say it would be very unpleasant for him. It would mean his downfall.

"Lily is the weapon he won't see coming. Between all of you and us, I think we can win. We have to. Any other outcome is unthinkable. Good luck, my sons," Anubis said, taking hold of both Ahmose's and Amon's shoulders." He stroked a finger down my cheek and sniffled, giving me a weak smile. "Good luck to us all," he finished, muttering his words into the empty sky. "May the stars bless our efforts this night."

We'd just climbed on the backs of our unicorns when we heard a terrible screech above. An object hurtled toward us at breakneck speed. It rotated in the air, and our unicorns danced nervously as they recognized what it was.

It is Horus and his unicorn! Zahra cried. The spinning ball of legs and wings came closer and then hit the Waters of Chaos with a resounding crash. Waves of color splashed high in the air as our fallen comrades created a wide furrow of matter. They slid across the slick surface quite a distance before stopping. Waves lapped wildly, splashing against the breastbones of our unicorns, spilling over my legs. Finally, they came to a broken-limbed stop, and matter quickly rushed in to fill the space they'd carved out.

We raced, hooves pounding and slapping the water, until we reached the side of the fallen god and his mount. The unicorn kicked weakly. A leg was broken, and an object pierced his side. When I pulled it out, I saw it was Horus's own sword. Horus was pinned beneath the male unicorn and appeared to be unconscious. Foam dripped from the mouth of the heaving beast. As it dug its hooves into the misty waters, struggling to find purchase despite his broken leg, I could see the unicorn was terrified. Its ears were laid back as it whinnied in alarm, not for himself but for us.

My blood went cold. Quickly scanning the heavens and seeing nothing, I dismounted and knelt by the unicorn, running my hand down the bridge of its long nose and stopping at its flaring nostrils. Quick, hot breaths puffed out over my palm. Zahra touched her nose to his, and I could feel her mourning as she took in the injuries of the animal. He was dying.

I was about to ask Ahmose to help, but he was kneeling by Horus using his power to save the god's life. Instead, I turned to Anubis. "Can you do anything?" I asked.

He shook his head. "The curse that has fallen upon the unicorns prevents me from preparing his soul for the afterlife." Zahra stomped a foot and gave a mournful cry as the struggling unicorn laid down its head. After a moment the body of the great animal shimmered and became insubstantial. It melted away from Horus and was carried by the Waters of Chaos to the rim, where it slipped over the edge and disappeared from view.

I held on to Zahra, stroking her soft neck as she grieved and watched Ahmose work. When Horus finally took a breath and his eyes fluttered open, I let out the one I'd been holding. But the feeling of relief I had at seeing Horus rise slowly to his feet was soon snuffed out when I heard a roar come from above.

A long, sinuous shape—no, two long sinuous shapes erupted from the obelisk and headed toward us. When they came closer, they circled above us lazily. One, a dragon, had a golden chain of lightning attached to its leg. It landed on the surface of the Waters of Chaos and crouched down, eyes taking us in as if assessing which one of us would make the tastiest appetizer. Its tail thrashed back and forth, causing the surface beneath our feet to quake.

The other shape hovered in the dark. When the dragon lifted its head and bellowed, it came closer and landed nearby. Its shifting coils were all too familiar.

Hello again, goddess, Apep said with a slap of his tail. *Fancy meeting you here.*

"Apep?" I cried, deliberately turning my head to as to avoid his hypnotic stare. "I thought you didn't care about the gods or their little war!"

I didn't, the giant snake responded as he twisted around us, effectively trapping us in the circle of his coils. *But this one,* he said, turning to eye the dragon, *promised to fill my belly with as many souls as I could eat. And as you know,* he added, lowering his head to peer directly at me, *I'm always so hungry.*

He jerked suddenly, opening his mouth to show us his glistening fangs. Foamy waters lapped his scales, and like before, I thought them beautiful. In fact, they seemed to reflect the very waters at our feet. So pretty. I took a few steps closer to the snake, mesmerized by his exquisiteness.

Amon yanked me back, and I shook my head. I pulled out my blades and lengthened them into spears, but before I could call out a battle cry, the dragon addressed us directly.

"Not just yet," the dragon said, his tongue forming around the words as if they were foreign to him in that form. "We are still missing a few players, I think."

A number of dark, shrouded objects drifted down from the obelisk. They landed softly on the colored surface of the Waters of Chaos near the mouth of the snake and immediately they collapsed. The dark hood of one was swept back, and I gasped. "Nephthys?" I cried.

Darting around the snake, I rushed to the fallen form and gently pulled back the hood. The dragon looked on and laughed as golden hair tumbled over my hands. Two puncture wounds oozed black venom. *Apep.* I wasn't sure if the snake's venom would affect them as badly as it had me, but we'd need to help her, and soon.

Anubis and Ahmose kept their weapons trained on the snake as Horus limped as quickly as he could to the next victim and stumbled, going down right next to the body. He pulled off the hood. It was Amun-Ra. Snarling, he looked up and screamed, "What have you done with my mother, you vile beast?" Even across the distance, Horus's eyes were dangerous switchblades, open and ready to cut.

The dragon simpered, "Oh, Isis is here, I assure you, whelp."

I moved to the next person, and the next, hoping to find Asten but instead I found a few of Amun-Ra's fallen warriors. When I'd checked them all, I stood and brandished my blades, rejoining my fellows. "You take the snake," Amon murmured. "I'll take the dragon."

"I heard that, little princeling," the dragon sneered. "How fun it will be for you to playact the part of the armored knight slaying the dragon. All to impress your princess, isn't it? How romantic," the dragon spat. "Well, I assure you, I will not be easily bested, and I have absolutely no fear of you or any other knight in shining armor."

The dragon snorted, and puffs of smoke blew out its nostrils. Then it sneezed, a very undragonly thing to do. I grinned, seeing the small little man behind the great beast. My confidence rose, but then I considered the warning from Anubis and tightened my resolve. Seth was indeed tricky, and I had a feeling he was going to fight dirty.

"I think your ego is telling you you're a fifty-foot billboard with your name in lights," I called out across the expanse. "Unfortunately, you aren't even important enough for a byline. You're overrated and underbaked. Why don't you pull up a chair and learn from your elders, you spoiled little half god?"

Perhaps I'd gone too far in provoking him, but I wanted to test him for weaknesses in the same way Anubis said he'd be testing us. The dragon gave me a slick smile and narrowed his eyes. "I have to admit. I look forward to swallowing you down whole. How refreshing you will be after I consume your too-handsome-for-his-own-good champion."

That was it. The chink in his character. Jealousy raged in him like a beast. All I'd have to do was wave a red flag before his eyes, and he'd charge right onto my sword. I'd have to be careful with him, but I thought defeating him was doable.

"But before I do that," the dragon said, "I'd like to tell you the tale of the dragon and the self-righteous St. George. Have you heard it?" Seth asked almost politely. "No?" He didn't wait for our answer. "Then let me give you the true version. Once upon a time, a city of spoiled mortals asked a dragon for aid. 'We're dying of plague,' they said. 'Please help us!' The dragon knew that plagues were nature's way of creating balance. The citizens were packed together like rats. They were filthy and vile. The land would be better off if they were cleansed from its surface. But the dragon, too kind for his own good, agreed to help and asked only a boon in return. A small token of gratitude.

"He wanted the king's lovely daughter to be his companion. To keep him company and offer him the kindness he deserved. But the king's daughter thought the dragon too ugly to love. His horns were too sharp, his breath was too hot, and his clumsy claws would tear her pretty dresses.

"So instead, the king held a lottery, and a girl was sacrificed once a year and given over to the dragon's keeping. Inevitably, the girl angered the dragon by attempting to escape. Sometimes, he grew tired of her sobs and woe-is-me attitude as she mourned, begging him to return her to her family. Either way, he lashed out, destroying the girl in the process. Soon the city ran out of young women, and the unfortunate king at last sent his daughter.

"The dragon was thrilled, but the king secretly sent a knight along with her—one especially trained to hunt dragons. Seeing the handsome knight coming to her rescue, the princess immediately fell for his simpering beauty and would no more consider the sincere offer of the dragon. Forced to fight, the dragon battled the knight and would have beaten him if not for the scream of the girl. She distracted the dragon, and the knight killed him.

"Now, before you get any ideas, this little play fight we're about to engage in is going to have an entirely different outcome."

"Oh?" I called out. "And why do you believe that?"

"Because this time I'm not fighting alone. Underlings, I'd like all of you to meet my son." The dragon twisted his neck, peering at something behind him. "Son?" he continued. "Why don't you come on over here and make yourself known to our enemies?"

A shrouded figure stepped from the shadows cast by the dragon. The man lifted his hands and touched the rim of his hood, and as he did so, my heart beat so wildly, I thought it would explode out of my chest.

I hadn't intended to show any weakness to my enemy, but a name escaped my lips as he drew back his hood. It echoed softly into space, a whisper barely recognized; it came back to my ears as if it had been whispered by the mouth of an angel.

Asten.

Son of a Dragon

Tia rose up inside me. *"He is not your son, Unmaker!"* she spat.

"Oh, I assure you, he is. Aren't you, Asten?"

Asten lowered his gaze. "Seth speaks the truth," he said. "Without the barrier of the obelisk, I have finally seen Seth's dreams and those of my true mortal mother."

"I don't understand," I said, turning to Anubis. "I thought Asten was a full mortal, in which case Ahmose and Amon would be more Seth's sons than Asten. Seth facilitated the pregnancies of their mothers."

Anubis wore a pained expression. His eyes combed over Asten.

"How is this possible?" Amon asked Anubis with a hiss, while keeping his eyes trained on Apep.

"It's possible," Anubis answered loudly, his voice carrying across the expanse, "because the bricklayer father identified by a so-called uncle was not Asten's true father. Seth kept a mortal concubine, Asten's real mother, one that he abused even while she carried his child."

"So then his father and sisters? The mother who died?" I asked.

"Were no relation to him whatsoever," Anubis said.

"But he tried to have his own son killed!" I argued. "Why would he do that?"

"He didn't know that Asten was his son."

Seth said, "I beg to differ, you overstuffed ostrich. I did know. In the end it made no difference. I knew that once my little princes died, their energy would fill and sustain me. A son of my own body would fuel me even more so than the energy from Amon and Ahmose. But access to their energy was cut off from me before I could absorb it. Anubis and the others tricked me and trapped their life energies in canopic jars, turning the three boys into the Sons of Egypt.

"They then proceeded to lie to them, of course. The ceremony to align the sun, the moon, and the stars was never about keeping me imprisoned. It was about trapping their energy again and again before I could wrench it away. For this to happen, their deaths had to occur every one thousand years. This is why the boys live as mortals for a time, but only long enough, only long enough."

"Is this true?" Ahmose asked.

Anubis ground his teeth. "It is," he said. "But you must understand we had no choice. Deceiving you was the only way to prevent Seth from reaping the rewards of his efforts. If he had absorbed the power of your life energy, he would have become unstoppable."

"You could have told us," Amon said. "You could have hidden us, let us live. Love. Have lives."

"Yes"—Anubis nodded wildly—"and then what would happen when Seth discovered you? Which he would have. With the snap of his fingers he could have raised a minion or an army to destroy you, and without me nearby to lock away your power, he would have seized it. This was the only way to control it. We limited the time of your exposure, keeping you alive only long enough to set back the clock for another millennium."

"What about our powers, then?" Amon asked. "The birds? Why did you bestow gifts? Lend us your strength?"

"We had no choice," Horus said. "You needed the gifts to recognize and battle Seth's followers. And the birds?" he sighed. "The birds were a tether between your mortal frames and the heavens. They cloaked you, and they were a way for us to keep tabs on your whereabouts. You were protected by the glory of Amun-Ra. This is why Ahmose's sacrifice of his crane was so grave. It made him weak, vulnerable to attack. Did you never wonder why you could not transform in the afterlife?"

"I . . . ," Amon began. "I assumed it was because the birds were locked away in the jars of death."

"Yes. The birds were locked away along with your energy. Trapped for thousands of years," Horus said sadly.

"I almost caught your bird, too," Seth said. "The necromancer had it in his grasp. If it wasn't for your lovely companion, all of this would have been over with a while ago. So now you know the truth. The gods turned my creations against me, deceived them and me, and locked me away in a prison. But here you are. Here you all are. It couldn't be better if I had imagined it. Now all I have to do is sit back and let my sky-demons destroy you once and for all. Then I will absorb your energy and break free from these chains.

"Of course it would have been nicer if this had happened when I intended it to, but I am a patient man. And do you see what patience has brought me? There at my feet lie my traitorous wife and our pathetic leader, Amun-Ra. Osiris has been maimed beyond repair. Isis is at my side, and my little chicks have come back to the nest. Everything is as it should be. And I got a bonus, too. A lovely, most interesting kitty that I can chain to my throne. I'll pet her and feed her if she's a good girl, and I'll kick her across the cosmos if she's not. Either way, I'm sure to be entertained."

I put my clenched fists on my waist. "I don't think so," I said. "First of all, we are no more a kitten than you are a dragonfly. Second, keep in mind that we took out the Devourer and the Sebak. To my way of thinking, the score is two to zero. Looks more to me like you're a desperate man looking to run out the clock. I wouldn't be celebrating victory so soon if I were you."

"You are a foolish child," Seth said. "And so very fragile. I'll enjoy teaching you the art of respect." Seth addressed Anubis. "This is a pathetic showing, Anubis. Did you actually think a mere sphinx could stop me? I am a god!" he declared. "The most powerful of you all. All I have to do is have your precious Sons of Egypt killed. You cannot prevent my rise to power. You've only delayed it by trapping me in a prison of my own design. You used the very power I gave them to build the walls. Seeing through Asten's eyes was the only thing that kept me sane."

"What is he talking about?" I asked.

Anubis explained, "Seth has spied on us, using Asten's power to see into dreams. It's why Asten has difficulty wielding the ability from time to time. Seth causes a sort of interference."

"It's how I was able to communicate with you in your dreams," Seth said to me, "boring as they are. It gave me insight into a potential weakness of one of Egypt's Sons." The dragon laughed, clouds of smoke billowing and rising up from his mouth as he sidled closer.

"Enough of this!" Horus spat. "Where is my mother?"

"Are you still here, Horus? I would have assumed that you'd tucked your trembling self beneath the wing of your golden falcon. Oh, wait, that's right. He's not yours any longer, is he? You've given him up. Oh well, a creature such as that was bound to leave a sniveling child like you at one time or another. If you must know, your mother isn't feeling too well right now. I'm sure she'll be right along directly. Being near me has"—the dragon chuckled—"given her a slight fever. Just between us, my friends, I'm a bit of a handful, even for Isis."

"You wish," I mumbled under my breath. I didn't think I'd ever hated anything in my life more than I hated Seth at that moment. The Devourer was an irritating pageant contestant compared to him. The necromancer, a spoiled, name-dropping, out-of-work-and-money theater producer. But this guy—Seth—was more than I imagined. Seth was sick. He was twisted in such a wrong way that he'd convinced himself he was right.

"I must say, I enjoy this form," Seth said, waving his wings. "Unmaking dragons was the best decision I ever made." Seth suddenly took to the air and landed with a crash next to the crumbled figures covered with hooded robes. Smoke streamed from his nostrils. "Back away from Amun-Ra, healer. I'd hate to have Apep bite him again. Strong as he is, even the great god of us all is unlikely to recover from a double dose of venom."

Ahmose straightened and moved back, hands in the air, until he was next to us again.

"What do you say we move on to the third act?" the dragon said. "Asten, I'd like you to unshackle me now. Please proceed immediately. And don't forget what will happen if you should prove difficult."

Asten swallowed and glanced briefly in my direction, then he turned to the dragon.

"No!" I shouted. "Asten, what are you doing?"

"Think carefully about this, son," Anubis said, holding out his hand in warning. "I think you know what you should do."

Asten paused, shifting his eyes from Anubis to me. His mouth was tight with both resolve and regret. "I know who I am now," he said. "I'm so sorry, Tia. Sorry that I couldn't be the person you wanted, the mate you deserved. Sorry that my heritage makes me incapable of holding your heart. Trust me when I say that this is for the best. Everything makes sense now. My dreams. My ambitions. My very nature. It all came from him. This is my purpose. My destiny. I cannot deny what I am or where I go from here."

Tia raged and keened inside me as Asten summoned his bow and nocked a brilliant arrow. "Father?" he said. "If you will grant me a bit of the energy leaking from Amun-Ra, I will remove your shackles."

The dragon opened his mouth and sucked in energy. It lifted from Amun-Ra and traveled through the air, spinning and weaving in a variety of colors. Then the dragon turned and blew light from his nose. It wrapped around Asten's arrow until the entire shaft gleamed.

"Now don't forget," the dragon said, "you have to aim for the chain at the point of attachment, then the entire shackle will fall away. If you attempt to injure me in any way, even a mistaken scratch, there will be irrevocable consequences. Consequences you are well aware of. Do you understand?"

"I understand, Father. You forget that I cannot miss."

"Very good."

Stretching back his arm, Asten loosed the arrow. "Stop!" I shouted, but it was too late. The dragon looked on with a greedy expression of delight as the arrow flew toward the center of the Waters of Chaos, right to the point where the chain attached. But instead of hitting the link, the arrow skirted it and turned in a wide arc, heading right back to the dragon. Seth bellowed and scrambled, folding his wings around his body and tucking his head to protect his neck. "Traitorous offspring!" he screamed.

Asten ignored the thrashing dragon. Opening his arms wide, he lifted his face to the stars. "No," I whispered as a small voice in the back of my mind told me something very, very wrong was happening. Despite Seth's efforts, the arrow's aim was true. But Seth phased his shape at the last moment. The arrow blew right through his form, bursting out with a spray of blood and streaking right toward Asten. Recognition of what Asten had done dawned on me. "No!" I screamed more loudly and set off at a run.

My feet pounded over the smooth surface, and I slid the last few meters on my knees in a vain attempt to catch Asten. But the arrow had done its work too quickly. It sank directly into his heart. The power of the blow rocked his body into the air. His legs scissored as he flew through the air and fell with a crash to the glittering surface. When I reached him, I pulled his body toward me, lifting his head and cradling it in my arms, totally unconcerned with the dragon who bucked and screamed nearby.

Rivulets of color streamed over Asten's body, cascading down his heaving chest. I pressed my hands against the hard plane to stem the tide of blood. I pressed my hands on either side of the arrow to staunch the blood. The feathers tickled my cheek, and I froze. "Impossible," I whispered. The bobbing shaft was tipped with a feather of Isis. Reaching behind me, I clutched empty space where the last feather should be.

"I magicked it away from you a few moments ago," Asten whispered. "I knew you'd never use it on me yourself, and this way, my brothers will be safe, too."

Rage and fear and panic roiled through my frame, but Asten touched me, banking the fire until all I could feel was a sorrow so deep it was shattering me in two. Blood pooled from the injury despite Isis's claims that her arrows healed, and we knew then there was no saving him. The warnings on my bow had come to pass.

At that moment, all three of us grieved, we were one, suffering with the man we loved. *"Tene,"* I whispered, tears clouding my eyes. *"How has it come to this?"* Smoothing his hair away from his face, I kissed Asten's forehead and sobbed. I didn't realize he was trying to speak. *"What did you say?"* I asked, leaning closer to hear him.

He swallowed. "Did . . . did it work?" he asked. "Is he gone?"

"Is who gone?"

"S . . . Seth?" he finished. His skin had lost its warmth, and my trembling hand was coated in his blood.

I looked up. The dragon had fallen. His great sides heaved, and sparkling liquid poured from his mouth. "Were you trying to aim for him?" I asked, confused. "I thought you never missed your mark."

He shook his head slightly then started to cough. More blood gushed with each hack. Finally, when his body settled a bit, he flashed a sad smile and said, "I don't."

"Why, Asten?" I asked, pleading to understand. "Why did you choose this? Tell me it wasn't just the writing on the bow."

He shook his head. "Do you remember the woman who demanded a terrible price from me as payment to help make a potion for my mother, the queen?" I nodded and Asten took a few shallow breaths and continued. "Her demand was that when the time was right I should kill my father."

"What?" I mumbled.

"I gave her my oath, but she"—he coughed again—"never collected payment. Last night, she visited my dreams and said the time had come. But to kill my father, I'd have to aim for my own heart." Asten's face turned white. He lifted his palm to my face and cupped my cheek. "I know now, Tia, that this is the reason I could not harbor your heart. But know that mine always has been and always will be yours. I love you, my ferocious lioness." He pressed something into my hand. My vision blurred anew as I felt the familiar shape of Tia's heart scarab.

I closed my fist over it and nodded, tears leaking over my lips as a faraway look stole across Asten's eyes, and then he was gone. A roar of pain unlike anything I'd ever heard before burst from my mouth. When I was finished, I slumped over his body, clinging to it while I sobbed. Gradually, I became aware of light filling the area around me. Turning, I saw Anubis, a determined expression on his face and arms in the air, directing Asten's life energy into four canopic jars that he'd created.

After the energy was safely locked away, I bent over Asten and gently pressed a kiss on his soft lips. Extending one claw, I cut a lock of his hair. Then I stroked his face, my eyes and heart stinging with pain, and folded his arms across his chest. The Waters of Chaos began tugging at his body, and soon the foaming waters shifted him away from me. I stood shakily, watching as the man I loved was swept to the edge. Tia's voice echoed in my mind.

Lie back on the green grass, my love, and gaze up at the stars. I will come and find you, Tene. I promise you won't have to wait long, for my only desire is to live in any manner of happiness with you that the cosmos offers us. But before that, I vow to finish what you have started.

When his body was swept over the side, my claws emerged. A primal rage filled me, and I stalked toward the still-breathing dragon. Before I could sink my sharp claws into his form, he shifted, becoming a small animal. He sprinted away across the slick surface of the churn-ing waters. I stood there gawking, wondering what had happened. The quickly moving creature changed form again, becoming something so minuscule I could no longer see it, even with my enhanced vision.

I raced back to Anubis. "What happened?" I demanded. "Where's the chain?"

Tracks of tears ran down Anubis's face. I took hold of his shoulders and shook him. "Anubis! What happened?"

"Asten must have misunderstood," he said, darting a hand across his cheeks. "Killing himself couldn't destroy Seth. Instead, it somehow released him."

"But why?" I demanded, fury and grief spilling out in my tone. "Why didn't it destroy him?"

"Because, Lily, Asten wasn't Seth's son." Anubis's shoulders drooped like he was a man too old to stand upright any longer. "He was mine," he said softly, his thick, dark brows lowering in sorrow.

I took a step back, shock freezing the blood in my veins. "H . . . how?" I asked.

"I found him as a small child," Anubis said. "He *was* the biological son of Seth, that much is true, but the mortal that was his mother was so distraught at the idea of having had Seth's child that she smothered her baby at birth. Then she took her own life.

"Since an immortal child was near death, his little soul called out to me. I didn't realize then that he was the immortal who'd summoned me and not his mother. Her soul still hovered nearby, and she entreated me for aid. When his little finger clutched mine, I made the decision then to give him a piece of myself, much as I did with Abutiu.

"It changed Asten enough that he became more my own son there-after than he was Seth's. I raised him from a babe. Abutiu took quite a liking to him, in fact, preferring to sleep next to his cradle. When Asten's real mother came to me as a ghost and warned me that Seth had blessed the barren queens with children, I took notice.

"When the young prince of Asyut died, I was drawn to his side and told the nurse that the child could be switched. I disguised myself as a beggar woman and took the coins the nurse offered, then handed her Asten. Before I left, I cast a spell over the child so that his powers would be blocked until the time came when I could train him properly in their use. Unfortunately, I never got that chance.

"I watched over Asten through the years, and my love and admiration for him grew. When Seth had him and his brothers murdered, I . . . I did what I could to restore what was taken from all three of them. And unbeknownst to Asten, I released the binding I'd set on his power so many years before. His ability, we discovered, always rested in his dreams."

My eyes traced Anubis's face, lingering on his features, as he told his story. I'd always thought him handsome, and now that I looked closer, I could see the similarities between him and Asten. Though Anubis's hair was shorn to below the ears, it was the same texture and color. As Anubis pursed his lips, I saw there was a tiny cleft in his chin. I sucked in a breath. "You are his father!" I exclaimed.

"Yes." Anubis nodded sadly.

"Why didn't you tell him?" I asked.

"I wanted to, but it seemed safer to keep the knowledge to myself. Not even Ma'at knew. If I had told him, she would have read the truth of it in his heart. And Seth would have discovered his true identity and use it to further his own plans."

Ashleigh rose to the surface and patted Anubis's arm. *"My mother always said, 'You've got to do your own growin', no matter who your father is.' Asten was a good man an' woulda been proud ta claim you as his papa."*

"Thank you, Ashleigh," Anubis said.

Amon said, "None of this explains why the mystery woman told Asten to kill his father by destroying himself."

"Ah, I believe I can answer that," a voice above us said.

Seth materialized into his human form, his arm wrapped around a familiar figure. Her face was mottled and bruised, and one of her wings hung limply. The dress she wore was ripped at the sleeve. With a violent shove, Seth commanded, "On your knees, second wife."

Isis obeyed, but she looked up and locked eyes with her son, Horus, shaking her head slightly.

"Now then," Seth said with a warped smile on his face, "where were we?"

Secrets of the Stars

"Ah yes," Seth said. "The mystery woman."

My inner New York socialite noticed that Seth's hands dangled several inches below his sleeves. Apparently, he'd been growing while in the obelisk. Either that, or he just had no sense of style or didn't care about his attire. I studied his face and observed that there was something off, something almost gangly about him. Like he was a late-blooming teen that still hadn't quite reached adulthood. Or perhaps he just had one of those faces that always made him look younger than he actually was. Like one of those actors who could still take on roles as high school students far into his twenties and thirties.

Hadn't Seth been alive for centuries? Was that how immortal puberty worked? Wow, that sucked. The idea that I'd be stuck wearing braces and battling acne for centuries was horrifying. I'd probably want to lash out at everyone around me, too. Seth had not one but two cowlicks, and as Isis cowered before him, he made repeated attempts to smooth down his hair. He didn't seem to be aware that he was doing it. His fingers twitched, and his pale blue eyes frequently shifted to the woman at his feet.

His body seemed strong enough, but his too-long limbs didn't seem to be coordinated at all. To Tia he resembled a gangly male cub, all roar and posturing with nothing to back it up. Ashleigh wondered if his appearance was a result of his imprisonment. She reminded me that her form had changed while she was hidden inside the fairy tree. He'd probably been starving while trapped inside the obelisk.

Seth narrowed his hard-as-flint eyes and attempted a condescending laugh, but instead snorted and froze as if shocked that such a sound had come from his body. My lips twitched. He immediately noticed my reaction and gnashed his teeth. Red embarrassment crept up his face, and I could see the moment when his embarrassment changed to anger.

Without consciously moving, I took a step back until I could feel Amon's steady presence behind me. The rage roiling through Seth's form was something powerful. He was like a terrible thundercloud preparing to unleash his fury. A wise man would take notice, board up his windows, and seek shelter.

Now I understood why Seth preferred to take on the forms of animals instead of his immortal body. As an animal, he felt powerful, comfortable, and proud, but as a man he felt awkward and self-conscious. The animals' faces were masks that he wore to hide his imperfections. It made a sick kind of sense when considering the all-too-perfect family he'd grown up with.

Asten looked nothing like Seth. In fact, Asten carried himself more like Anubis and his brothers than he did the man who'd actually brought him into the world. It was a relief in many ways to see how different they were. They weren't just different in looks. With the right skin care regimen, a good haircut, and tailored clothes, Seth wouldn't be too hard on the eyes. But, to me, attractiveness was centered on the inside. When considering that, Seth was repulsive.

The problem was, Seth was powerful. And worse, he was cruel. Maybe the reasons he'd become that way weren't entirely his own fault. Seth had a nervous tic and a need to be adored and appreciated whether he deserved it or not. A lot of teen boys were the same way. They'd abuse their girlfriends or bully those they considered weak because it made them feel powerful. I'd just never imagined a god would be like that.

"Did you think," Seth began, interrupting my assessment, "that I would simply forget about my offspring?" He reached down and stroked Isis's broken wing. She winced in pain. "I found Asten's birth mother and tortured her wandering spirit enough to learn what I needed to know. She was much more useful in death than she was in life, for she'd been spying on her godling son. It came as no surprise to me that Anubis had saved the child. He does have a weakness for puppies, lost kittens, and abandoned infants.

"After gleaning the information I needed, I enacted my plan to have the three princes killed, and yes, even knowing one of them was my son. I used the priest Runihura to whisper in her ear that the only way for me to be killed was if a son of my blood wielded the knife. I knew she'd then do her best to steer him in my direction if my plans went awry and he lived. Of course, there was never any danger of him actually killing me, but it would be easy enough then to motivate him when the time was right.

"He didn't, of course—live, that is. Runihura killed him as instructed. Unfortunately, the gods intervened and trapped the life energy before it could return to the Waters of Chaos. Shortly after that, I was imprisoned in the obelisk and have been whiling away the years plotting my revenge. And, well, here you are."

He offered a smile that seemed almost genuine, and I realized it was. He was happy to be the center of attention. This was his big moment. His final curtain call. Seth was soaking up every second of limelight he could. I managed to slap an interested expression on my face and asked, "So why did you send his mother in a dream? It seems like everything was going your way. What changed?"

"The scheming of the gods is what changed. It was a good thing I'd taken the precaution with Asten's mother. You see, I knew there was a chance, albeit a slim one, that you lot could have actually stopped me."

Now, this I wanted to hear. "Oh?" I said simply, knowing he

wouldn't be able to resist the opportunity to expound upon his own achievements and wisdom.

"Once I realized what Isis had done, yoking the three boys together, I knew I had to cancel out her spell." He wrapped his hand around Isis's neck and squeezed. "You know, darling, that your spells are meant to work for me, not against me."

"Yes, Seth," she mumbled wearily.

"What was that?" Seth asked, tightening his fingers.

"I mean, yes, husband," she said and offered him a thin smile.

"That's better," he said. He lifted his hands from her neck to stroke her long hair absentmindedly. "Now then, where was I? Oh yes. When my sky-demons brought Asten to me, I held him prisoner for a time, not revealing myself to him so I could decide what steps to take. I couldn't break the yoke myself. Isis's spell was too powerful. Only a Son of Egypt could break it. I couldn't risk open confrontation when all of you were bound together in such a way. There was too big of a risk for me.

"But then my lovely wife appeared—my first wife, Nephthys, that is. It didn't take much threatening on my part to convince her that helping me was in her best interest. In fact, now that I think on it, she seemed very willing to make amends for all the trouble she'd caused me. I suppose it's only right that a woman should miss her estranged husband." He turned to look at Nephthys, who lay on the ground, her ethereal face framed by the waters flowing past. "Perhaps I shall reconsider killing her. It might be nice to pit my two wives against each other.

"So as I was saying," he said, turning back to us, "I imprisoned Nephthys with Asten and, in very dramatic fashion, she confessed to him that I was his true father and that to kill me, he'd have to kill himself."

Seth chuckled. "She also warned him that severing the yoke was paramount. That if he killed himself while yoked to his brothers, they would share the same fate. Asten, noble creature that he is, believed wholeheartedly that killing himself would save all of you and would weaken me to the point of death."

I glanced at the form of Nephthys. She'd betrayed us. I couldn't believe she would do that to us, to her own family. Did she really have that much loyalty toward her husband? Perhaps she was jealous of Isis, but Nephthys more than anyone seemed to lead the way in taking the battle to Seth. His story made sense, but it just didn't feel right. Something was off.

"But why go through with it?" I asked. "Why let him kill himself? Once Asten was unyoked, there was no need to destroy him. You weren't able to absorb his life energy anyway. Anubis captured it in the canopic jars. Why would you even suggest he lift the bow?" I sneered in disgust. "Only a monster would do such a thing."

"You are a simple girl, young sphinx; therefore I don't expect you to fully understand the game of the gods. You're just a player, a pawn, tossed onto the board to distract me as the other pieces play out their parts. I'd thought you would amount to much more than what I see, but I have to say, I'm fairly disappointed. Anubis knows why Asten had to die. Don't you, Anubis?"

Anubis glanced at the god. "Because he was my son?"

Seth laughed so hard a tear formed at the corner of his eye. "Do you think I really care about Asten's parentage? His death gives me even more pleasure knowing it hurts you. That's why I sent one of my followers to lead him to a manufactured family that was terrible enough to break the most stalwart of souls. But no, my too-large, dumb friend. That is not the reason. Surely you know the real one."

Seth paused for a moment, waiting, and then his mouth stretched into a wide smile. "Or perhaps you don't. Between us," Seth said to me in a stage whisper, "Anubis wasn't granted the biggest brain in the cosmos."

Anubis took a menacing step forward, but Seth held up a hand. "Now, now. There's no need to get brutish. You might want to check your jars, though. I'm not sure even you, the mighty god of the dead, are aware of everything that's happened."

Anubis wouldn't break eye contact with Seth. Instead of doing

Seth's bidding, his black sword materialized in his hand. "I've grown weary listening to you boast," Anubis said. "I believe I'll cut out your tongue first."

In a mocking answer, Seth clucked his tongue and wagged a finger then pointed to the canopic jars near my feet. Since Anubis wouldn't move, I did. Kneeling down, I lifted the jar with the head of an ibis and broke the seal. The inside of the jar was dark and empty. I stared into it for a full minute, waiting for a white light to appear, then raised my head in alarm and locked eyes with Amon. "Nothing's inside," I said.

Amon shifted nervously. "That's not possible, Lily. We saw the energy go inside." Since Apep seemed content to wait upon Seth's command. Amon knelt next to me. He opened the second jar, the third, and the fourth.

"Do you see?" Seth said. "Asten's energy *is* mine. It made me powerful enough to break the shackles chaining me. Now I can draw upon the power of unmaking, taking it in as never before!" Seth clucked, mocking our despair. "There, there. You should take heart in knowing he saw his own demise in the Dreams That Could Have Been. I guess that makes my son more powerful than the lot of you. Of course, that doesn't do much for him, now, does it?"

"No. It's not possible. I . . . I saved his hair so you could remake him!" I said to Amon. Reaching for Amon's hand, I dropped Asten's hair into it and closed his fingers over the strands. "Try," I begged. "Try to fashion him a new body."

"Yes," Seth said, glee written all over his face. "Let's see you try."

Anubis's mouth was set in a grim line, the thick muscles of his neck were bunched as if he was readying himself to leap. Isis wouldn't even look at us, and Horus just stared blankly at his mother. He looked like a man who'd just lost everything, which is exactly how I felt.

Amon closed his eyes and lifted his hands, murmuring a spell. The hair lifted in the air as magic gathered around him, but then the light dimmed and dispersed. The hair scattered in the winds stirred by the Waters of Chaos.

"No!" I cried as I desperately grasped for the hair, but it flew away and melted into the churning fog before I could snatch it back.

Amon caught me, pulling me into his chest, and I collapsed against him, sobbing. "There is nothing I can do," he murmured against my ear. "Asten is gone."

Seth grinned. "Why do you think I had you all brought here? This is a place of creation, but it is also a place of unmaking. Canopic jars, no matter how magical, cannot prevent the natural process of birth and death that occurs here. The Waters of Chaos drained the jars, just as it drained the energy from every creature who died in your tiny unicorn war. I was able to absorb all of that energy, including Asten's. Now all I have to do is finish off the rest of you."

Furious, I turned to him. My fingers became talons, the extra knuckle growing immediately as my claws emerged. Their sharp tips glistened in the reflected light of the Waters of Chaos. Vaguely, I heard a cry. "Lily, no!"

But I wasn't Lily anymore. I was sphinx, and the creature standing before me had killed my mate, causing a second and final death. My only purpose in life now was to cause his murderer the same. With a vicious snarl, I sprang, my cat eyes narrowing on the pulse at his throat. I sunk my claws deeply into his shoulders and opened my mouth.

Seth screamed and bucked as I lowered my lips to the vulnerable spot at his neck, preparing to rip him open with my teeth, fangs or not, but he threw me off. I slid many meters backward, claws digging into the surface but finding no purchase. My other companions sprang. The snake attacked. Horus ran to his mother, pulling her away from a distracted Seth, who was being cornered on all sides.

I summoned my wings to brake myself on the slick surface and then ran a few steps before soaring into the air. While I gathered the energy from the cosmos, I watched helplessly as my companions faltered. Seth was attempting to unmake Horus, but Horus's mother kept her hand on his shoulder, chanting a spell that seemed to slow the process. So far only his forearm had turned to dust.

Meanwhile, Apep had managed to bite Anubis on the shoulder. When he scrambled from the slick surface to rejoin the fight, he was knocked aside again. The poison began to work, and the powerful god staggered to his knees. This time, he didn't get up. Apep's coils wrapped around Ahmose, suffocating him while Amon hacked viciously at the monster's neck. Black blood dripped on the surface of the waters and disappeared with a hiss. The unmaking of Horus was progressing, and Seth summoned his remaining sky-demons. Having no other choice, I clapped my wings. The flying gargoyles burst into flame, the ashes raining down on the warriors below.

I opened my wings, hovering, cursing the fact that I'd had to expend my energy on the flying army instead of blasting Seth. While energy gathered, I sensed a stirring in the air around me. Something tore at my arm and another wound opened on my leg. The Biloko were back as well. I pulled my knives from their harnesses and slashed wildly. But they continued coming.

Horus had collapsed against his mother. His leg was missing to the knee. Ahmose had either passed out or he'd been bitten, too. I screamed in pain as claws tore into one of my wings, and I dropped my knives. Slowly, I drifted down, my wings unable to hold me up any longer. Instinctively, I raised my hands upward, and a burst of light shot into the air turning the dark space green, then silver, then bronze. I heard the screams of hundreds of Biloko as they were destroyed by the light from the heart scarabs I carried. As quickly as it came, the energy left me. I was drained, my power exhausted.

Tears filled my eyes as I dropped and saw Apep toss aside Ahmose and butt against Amon, throwing him up in the air. He spun wildly, and before he could right himself, Apep bit down into his chest. Amon screamed, and I did, too, as I saw the fang emerge out of Amon's back.

The snake shook his head vigorously and Amon detached, falling with a heavy thump onto the shimmering Waters of Chaos. My whole body was numb when my feet touched down. Even Horus's screams didn't register in my mind. I looked across the expanse to see a gleeful

Seth hovering over Isis and Horus. Apep was opening his jaws, preparing to strike again, but I could no longer hear them. Even Tia's and Ashleigh's voices were lost to me. Or perhaps they had become as senseless as I was.

As my mind and body floated away, I began to make out the smallest of whispers. I looked up and realized it was the stars themselves. They were speaking to me. Telling me someone's name.

But naming was something Wasret did. Not me. Still the whispers pressed against my mind. *Liberator,* they said. *It is time for the Liberator to rise.*

"Liberator," I echoed. My lips forming the word. "The Liberator is the key." Suddenly, I remembered Dr. Hassan's words: *The person for whom this rite remained on Earth is a person who hadn't even been born at the time the name was inscribed on the wall. It is the name the stars have whispered to us over the eons.*

The stars were whispering a name now. *Liberator,* they said again and again.

There is an ancient prophecy regarding chaos, Ma'at's voice spoke in my mind. *It says that there will come a time when chaos reigns the cosmos. Harmony will be lost. Order will fragment. The power of the gods will be trapped in a spider's web. That is the time when the Liberator will appear.*

I knew then who the Liberator was. It was she and she alone who could defeat Seth.

Tilting back my head, I closed my eyes and wrapped my arms around Tia and Ashleigh, drawing them in close to me. All my life I'd lived trapped in a cage of my own making, too afraid to disappoint others and be the person I wished to be, but I was no longer that girl. More than anything I wanted to be with the one I loved, to explore the life just beyond my grasp, but it wasn't meant to be. I'd never know what I could have been, what Amon and I could have been, but at least I'd gotten a taste of it.

I reassured my two sisters, *Sometimes sacrifices must be made, and we must give up the thing we want most in the world so that others might live contented and happy.* "Wasret," I said, murmuring the words to the stars above. "We are ready. We summon you by the name whispered across the cosmos. We summon the Liberator."

A burst of bright light enveloped us. *"Thank you, Lily, Tia, Ashleigh. Your sacrifice will be woven among the stars,"* said a voice we all recognized. A cold wind passed me, and I rose from the place I'd been drifting. For a moment I was aware of Tia and Ashleigh clinging to me tightly, and then I was aware of nothing.

Joined

I inhaled, breathing in the scents of blood, life, energy, loss, death, pain, and ambition. They were tangy and sharp, spicy and sweet. Centering myself in my new form, I opened my eyes and took in the scene before me. Ahmose lay nearby, barely breathing. His lungs were crushed, and one of his organs had ruptured. His right leg was broken in two places.

Anubis was slowly dying from Apep's venom, as were the other gods lying prostrate on the surface of the waters, including Lily's Amon. Asten was nowhere to be found, but I sensed his energy drifting somewhere around me, spinning and nearly unrecoverable.

Hovering around were terrible beasts born of darkness. They suffered in a way no creature born of the physical world should. Their bodies phased between life and death. Every movement was agony for them. They had no freedom, no choice but to obey the one who'd fashioned them from bits and pieces of both planes of existence.

Pursing my lips, I took in a deep, steadying breath and blew gently. A brisk wind rose from my mouth, sending all the half creatures back to the unseen dimension they belonged to. What was left of their physical forms changed into pure energy and drifted down like snow onto the Waters of Chaos. I knew this act would strengthen the one I'd been summoned to fight, but there was no helping that now.

When they were gone, I took a step forward and grunted, finally becoming aware of the injuries to my own body. One wing dragged the ground—the bone had snapped in two, and a jagged piece was visible just over my shoulder. Dark infection pulsed in my leg and arm where the creatures had bitten and scratched.

Raising my arms, I closed my eyes and pulled energy from the Waters of Chaos. It licked at my feet and rose up my legs. Soon my whole body pulsed with it and I could feel each cut, each bruise, and each wound stitching itself back together with power and health. "That's better," I murmured.

With my body healed, I could tend to my duties, the first of which was to take care of Apep, who even now glided toward me, mouth wide-open. "Stop," I said, lifting a hand. Knowing I didn't want to be distracted from my work, I used the energy from the water to form a bubble around Seth, Isis, and Horus. Seth was busy trying to unmake Horus, and the god seemed resilient enough to withstand a few more moments. Isis looked up and cocked her head in my direction, but she just gave me a slight nod. She continued speaking to Seth, distracting him further.

Apep didn't notice this. He surged forward even faster. Now that we wouldn't be disturbed, I closed my eyes, reached for his true name, and found it. It was almost too easy. Smiling, I said, "Thoho, you will hear me and obey."

The snake immediately stopped. Coiling into a large ring with his head resting on his body, he stared at me with glittering eyes filled with hate. *Who are you?* he said. *How do you know my true name?*

"How is it that you do not?" I asked. "You have forgotten yourself. You have been told that you are the creation of Seth. This is incorrect. Seth lied to you. Took advantage of your fragmented mind and made promises to you he could not keep." The snake stared, but I could see he didn't understand. "Perhaps you will remember when I reunite you with your twin."

It is not possible, the snake said. *He is lost to me.*

"Tshamut!" I cried. "I grant you escape from your prison. Come to me from the Isle of the Lost and be reunited with your brother!" There was a rumbling like an earthquake, and the surface of the waters tilted sharply one way and then righted itself. Out of the dark hole in the center of the waters, a head emerged. The snake's body glided toward us then it reared up as if preparing to attack its brother.

"Tshamut, settle yourself." When the snake came closer, angling so that it could keep one eye on its brother and the other on me, he stopped moving. His long body stretched across the waters. His scales were a light gray and his eyes yellow. A startling contrast to his dark brother. "Tshamut," I began. "When I met you in your cave, you agreed to release the Sons of Egypt in exchange for revenge upon the one who trapped you. The time has come to fulfill my promise."

Throwing back my head, I shouted into the dark skies above, "Abject Anthropophagus! The end of your days is nigh. Come to me and accept your punishment!"

A moment later, an object flew up from the dark center of the Waters of Chaos and drifted overhead in an arc. I spotted a thin filament of a web trailing across the sky. A giant spider landed softly on the surface of the waters, its long legs finding purchase despite the slick plane.

"Have you woven your tapestry?" I asked quietly.

I have, mistress, the spider replied.

"Then look around you. This is what your actions have shaped."

This is not all my doing, said the spider. *You cannot blame me for the choices others have made.*

"Ah, that is where you are mistaken." I turned to the two snakes watching me with interest. "This is the being responsible for your separation. Once you were Nommo, the twin creator gods that guarded the poles. Your duty was to protect the Waters of Chaos. Your long bodies wrapped around it in an eternal circle. The hunger was balanced because Thoho's head bit down on Tshamut's tail and vice versa. As you moved, you kept the cosmos in alignment.

"Because of this cosmic spider's greed, the web connecting all things was weakened. But she couldn't consume you. Instead, she uprooted you, tore you apart, leaving the waters unprotected. Then a storm came and a mighty stone plunged into the waters. This was the birth of Amun-Ra. The Waters of Chaos attempted to correct the shift by granting one of the gods the power of unmaking, but the two gods could not come to terms on how to balance the great powers of creation and obliteration. The chaos worsened."

Can this be repaired? Tshamut asked.

"Some things can be repaired. Just as the Akh locks the Ka and Ba together to create something new, I can bind the two of you again. But to do so, I will need to give you a new name, a ren, by which you will henceforth be known."

I turned to the spider. "Abject Anthropophagus, as your penance for the terrible deeds you have wrought, you will be transformed. You will join these two and trail in their wake as a *shuwt*—a shadow, a mere reflection of the being you once were. It will serve as a reminder that greedy ambition is a seed sown in the blackest of mires and only evil fruits can grow from such a planting.

"It will be said of you, 'When the shadow of the spider haunts the moon's light, it is a dark omen of chaos.' Mortals will look up and know that to continue along such a path is a folly most dangerous, for it would mean the destruction of all things."

Raising my arms, I chanted a spell, and the trembling spider screamed as her body transformed. Its depth and substance melted away. When nothing was left but a shadow, the creature slunk into the darkness beneath Thoho's coils.

"It is done," I said. "Now let us deal with the others."

I turned my back to the snakes, who followed closely behind me and knelt briefly by Ahmose. Passing my hand over him, I willed enough energy into his body to heal him. "Tshamut?" I asked. "Will you give of your venom to heal the ones injured by your brother?"

I will, the snake said. As gently as a cosmic snake could, he carefully bit Anubis and then moved on to Amon. The venom he injected hissed and bubbled where it met the dark venom of his twin. The two canceled each other out, and victims began to heal.

When Tshamut finished Amun-Ra and Nephthys, I raised my arms and lowered the bubble. Horus's eyes were glazed over. He was missing an arm, a leg, and half of his other leg. Seth was bent over him, sweat pouring down his face, his breaths coming in great, gasping pants as he struggled. Isis chanted feverishly over her son, her lovely hair tumbling across her face.

"Seth," I said. "You will stop."

Seth looked up, his brow lowering in confusion, taking in both me and the addition of the second snake. "What is going on here?" he asked impatiently.

"I am the Liberator," I said quietly. "I have been summoned by the stars to bring the cosmos back into alignment. A grave mistake brought you into being, and my duty is to correct it."

Seth spat angrily, "I am not a mistake! I am the most powerful of the gods. The only mistake is that I've had to take the honor that should have rightfully been given. There is no one who can defeat me!" He gestured wildly to the gods around him. "Not even Amun-Ra is as powerful. All creation must bend to my will."

"No," I said. "You will bend to mine."

I said it so softly that Seth cocked his head unsure of what he'd heard. He studied me, and I saw the moment his anger turned into unmitigated delight. "It's you!" he said. "The one meant to be my true queen! I've sensed your absolute power in my dreams, and I thought the sphinx was the one that wielded it, but it was never her. It was always you. You've come to me at last."

"How woefully wrong you are. You insult me with your assumptions. I am the Liberator! You think I have come to liberate *you*, when, in fact, I have come to liberate the cosmos *from* you!"

With a roar, Seth turned his power on me. I could see the force of unmaking filling the air. It rippled in the space between us, transforming the matter it touched into pure energy that drained down into the Waters of Chaos. Holding out my hand, I cupped the energy and held it in my palm. It was beautiful. As glorious as the waters. I let it trickle through my fingers and glanced up at the young god.

"Who are you?" he asked, taking a step back in shock at seeing how easily I countered his power.

"This body once belonged to Lilliana Young. She was the adder stone. The light that pierced the darkness. I was drawn to her and saw the world through her eyes. Her gift gave me the ability to enter your realm. Your Nephthys glimpsed me through the veil of the stars, and I was able to guide her over the eons. It was your first wife who helped bring me forth.

"I have many names. I am known as Wasret, the Liberator. Some have called me Qetesh, or Hecate. Others have referred to me as the three furies, the Moirai, or as the Siren Who Sings to Men and They Must Obey. All of these are true. I am the mistress of the cosmos. Its caretaker. And I have come to make an accounting of your works."

Licking his lips, Seth narrowed his eyes shrewdly. "If you truly watch over the cosmos, then you know that I've been unfairly treated," he said. "My own family locked me away for centuries. Surely you cannot discredit me for reaching out for what I fairly deserve."

"You are not wrong, Seth. Your ambition was fueled by hurt and misunderstanding, but you had the opportunity to rise above it and chose to steal from others rather than working in earnest to build up yourself.

"You have seen the choices you've made, but you shut out your son's true power. Now you will see it. Behold the Dreams That Could Have Been!"

I drew from the energies that swirled around the Waters of Chaos and showed Seth his most cherished dream. The outpouring of love he would have received from his brother and sister gods made him tremble, but it wasn't in self-reproach, it was in fury. He was angry that his dream hadn't been realized in the way he wished, and he blamed others for his own failures.

Channeling Ahmose's power, I showed him each forked path he'd walked and how each would have led to a more pleasing end. When it was time to show him the revealer's power, I sighed, knowing it would change nothing. But Seth needed to see it. To help him understand all that he'd lost, the happiness he'd let slip through his fingers, would do more than any punishment I could mete out. When it was done, I said, "Now you know. Your sons, dreamer, pathfinder, and revealer, were given to you to guide your footsteps. To make you take stock in your choices.

"Every thousand years, the exile you suffered could have been alleviated if you had taken heed to their warnings. Instead, you pushed away the very beings you'd once longed to embrace. You attempted to create your own impossible triangle, thinking to draw its power into yourself, but instead, it acted as a gateway, giving me access to your realm so I could fix what has been broken. There is no balance in this, Seth. I hold you in reproach for your actions."

I sensed the awakening of those who had fallen. Amun-Ra took Nephthys's hand, lifting her to her feet, and the two of them approached. The goddess smiled and knelt at my feet. Anubis crouched down by Isis, taking the dying Horus from her trembling arms. Then Ahmose and Amon came forward and stood alongside me.

"Lily Young was the key that finally woke me," I said and was very aware of Amon's sharp inhale. "She locked the Sons of Egypt, your creations, together. The fairy gave me wings to fly from my place of rest to your realm." This time it was Ahmose who stiffened at the mention of the one he loved. I paused only a moment. "And the lioness gave me her strength, that I might do what I must."

Seth's hands clenched into fists, and he ground his jaw. His stubbornness was irritating me. "You talk of what's fair. Of what's owed to you. I will tell you now that these six beings deserve more respect than you. They have used their powers selflessly out of love for one another and love for the beings that inhabit the cosmos."

Turning to Ahmose and Amon, I said, "I am sorry for your loss. But the time has come for you to make your final sacrifice. You have given over your hearts already," I said, indicating the three scarabs that ran shoulder to shoulder. "Now I would ask for the hearts you hide within you.

"Before you do this, you must know that once I possess these hearts, I will steal from you your lives one final time. Your physical forms will dissolve, joining the Waters of Chaos. You will be no more. This energy will align in me in a perfect syzygy so that I might have the power to restore balance. I will not force this decision upon you, though I could if I wished it. I would rather have it freely. Ahmose, Amon, will you do this?"

Ahmose was the first to respond. Placing his hand over his heart, he brought forth Ashleigh's heart scarab. He pressed his lips against the green gem and then quietly handed it to me.

"Thank you," I said. With the snap of my fingers, a tiny piece of Ahmose's hair lifted away and dropped onto my palm. "I have chosen you to be my companion, Ahmose. Your body will die, but I will fashion a new one for you when my work is complete."

Ahmose looked like he wanted to say something, but paused. He looked at his brother for a long moment and then turned back to me and nodded. It pained me to know that he wasn't as enthusiastic about the idea as I had imagined he would be. I tried to comfort him by saying, "It is a great honor to serve alongside me. There is much of the cosmos we could explore."

"Yes," Ahmose said. "It *is* an honor." He bowed his head deferentially, but something about his demeanor felt out of harmony. It struck a sour note that, try as I might, I couldn't dismiss. Still, there were other matters to attend to.

Amon drew out Lily's scarab, but instead of looking at it, he looked at me, scrutinizing my face as if searching for his lost love.

"She is not here," I said gently. "I am sorry, but I have not chosen you. My selection was based upon which brother would live most amicably with me."

Ignoring my last statement, Amon asked, "Will I see her again?" He took my hand and cupped it in his warm ones. "Will she be in the place I will go?"

I offered him a sad smile. "Even I do not know all things, Amon. But the two of you are joined. If I succeed in bringing back balance, then your energies will be drawn together whatever you become and wherever you go."

Amon nodded and handed me Lily's heart. I pulled Tia's heart from inside my belt and opened both hands. The heart scarabs belonging to Tia, Ashleigh, and Lily, lifted into the air, spinning faster and faster, each gemstone glowing, the light streaking until the three balls of light became pure energy that shot toward my chest and disappeared.

I took off the strip of leather that hung tied to each shoulder. Embedded in the material were the three heart scarabs belonging to the Sons of Egypt. Anubis nodded to both young men, his eyes brimming with emotion. Amun-Ra was tight-lipped while Isis looked grave and Nephthys smiled tearfully. With the hearts of the three girls inside me, my emotions roiled. I attempted to tamp them down, knowing this was what I must do.

Before I could begin the process, Seth threw out a burst of power and transformed himself into a dragon. *You will not take what belongs to me!* he cried. I stood calmly as the dragon beat his mighty wings, rising into the air. He circled once while I looked on. Amun-Ra and Nephthys leapt back with cries as Seth blasted the air with fire. On his next pass, he opened his mighty jaws, the flames igniting within as he angled himself directly at me.

Then you have made your choice, I said. *Prepare yourself for the conse-*

quences. I sucked in a breath and whispered Seth's true name directly to his dragon mind. *Ascalon.*

At that moment, the dragon screamed, not only because I'd used its true name but also because Amon had taken one of my spear-knives, extended it, and leapt into the air, piercing the dragon's hide in the vulnerable spot beneath its wing. The dragon fell in a heap, its powerful chest heaving, my spear still imbedded in its side.

I crouched down, looking the creature in the eye. "Your young men were the key to your defeat. You gave them your own power, thinking to take it back, but Amon has unmade you as surely as you were going to do to him. The cosmos had gifted you with so much that only one of your own making truly had the power to harm you in this way. It is unfortunate that it has come to this. But I will finish the task he began." Lifting my arms, the three remaining heart scarabs rose in the air.

"Wait!" Nephthys said. "Amon must return the Eye of Horus first."

"And the . . . the golden falcon," Horus added, barely getting the words out. "She is more than just a symbol."

I nodded. "Very well. Amon, will you come forward?"

When he did, Horus, panting with pain, wove a spell. Light rose from Amon's body and took the shape of a winged bird. I heard a screech as the light transformed into an actual falcon made of gold. It flew to Horus, who caught it on his remaining outstretched arm. He brought his lips to the top of the bird's plumed head and kissed it. "I have missed you terribly, old friend," he said.

"Now the Eye," Nephthys said. "Amon cannot excise it himself. Horus will have to draw it back on his own."

Closing his eyes, Horus murmured softly, and a golden light gleamed from his broken body. Amon screamed, and from the center of his forehead burst a brilliant white orb. It hung in midair, rotating. As Horus finished his spell, the orb sped toward him and sank into his forehead. Wearily, he opened his eyes and they glowed gold. Light filled his body, and as it did, there was a discernible change in his expression.

Horus held himself differently. Peering down at his body, he held up an arm and studied it as if seeing it for the first time. Then he gave me a long, thoughtful look. Finally, he glanced at Nephthys and nodded. "It is done."

"Very well," I said. "Then I shall proceed."

Amon crashed to his knees. He seemed broken. Ahmose knelt beside him, wrapping his arm around his brother. The spell began, the heart scarabs spun in the air, and then they, too, entered my frame. The hearts locked together—three hearts, aligned with three hearts. Each of them bound to the other, never to move again. Lifting my bow, I summoned an arrow and whispered Amon's true name to the shaft. It shot out with a twang and circled, then plunged into Amon's chest. I repeated the process with Ahmose. My eyes closed of their own accord as I felt the pang of loss. When I opened them, Amon and Ahmose had already slumped to the surface of the Waters of Chaos, their bodies melting before my eyes.

Seth glared at me as I approached. "Let me die by Amon's strike," he said as his life-blood leaked into the Waters of Chaos and disappeared. His form was slowly changing to pure energy. "Lay my death upon his head. I will not perish by the hand of a woman."

Cocking my head, I studied him. "It is not a woman slaying you this day," I said, then smiled, "but a goddess. In fact, it was a trio of goddesses that have brought you so low. Remember their names—Isis, Nephthys, Wasret. But also know that you have brought this fate upon yourself. When mortals speak of Seth, they will only recall how the mighty one fell. It would serve you well to reflect upon this. Perhaps in your last moments you will strive to appreciate the wise women who agreed to be a part of your life, however misguided. Apply this lesson in the future."

"Apply this lesson?" Seth spat. "What do you mean?"

"You will see, Ascalon. Nephthys, Amun-Ra, come forth."

The two gods stepped forward.

"Do you know what I intend?" I asked softly.

Tears came to Nephthys's eyes, and she nodded, then turned to Amun-Ra. "Are you certain?" she asked.

Tenderly, he stroked her face. "I would be with you in any way I can," Amun-Ra said. "I feel in my heart that this is the right choice. This is the day we've long prepared for."

Nephthys reached her arms tightly around his neck and brought his lips to hers. Isis gasped and Anubis's mouth opened in shock, but they said nothing.

After they broke apart, Amun-Ra took Nephthys's hand, and they both turned to me. He pressed her fingertips to his lips briefly and said, "We are ready."

"Very well." Raising my voice to the cosmos, I pulled power into my frame, lifted my bow, nocking not a feather but one of my spear-knives, and cried. "Ascalon, I strike your name from the cosmos. I take your life energy and fashion you into something new." Drawing the string, I let the projectile fly and it sank deeply into the chest of the dragon. The beast roiled and screamed as his body began to dissolve faster.

Turning to the couple standing nearby, I said, "Amun-Ra, I strike your name from the cosmos. I take your life energy and fashion you into something new."

Amun-Ra cried out as his body transformed into white energy. Nephthys screamed and stepped back, her cheeks wet with tears. At the same time the dragon's body turned into energy. I drew my hands together, and the two energies combined. For a time, it looked like the two beings would tear each other apart, but then the chaos stilled and the energy merged into one being made of light.

"Now I will name you, and as I do, you will take on a new form. Your powers will be balanced, for you will harness the ability to create and to unmake. I have taken the best of both of you. Nephthys is now your true wife and will be your companion through the ages. The name I give you will not be a secret to these who love you. For if you should become derelict in your duties, they will have the power to check you. Henceforth, you will be called Aten."

Aten's body took on form. The light diminished until our eyes could look fully upon him. He was handsome, tall, and straight. His eyes sparkled with awe and wonder as he gazed upon his family for the first time. His hair was dark like Amun-Ra's, but there was a small cowlick in the back. In his features I found a bit of both Seth and Amun-Ra, but Aten was also utterly unique—a being fashioned from the qualities of both men.

He turned and smiled at Isis and Anubis and then frowned when he saw Horus. Waving his hand, he murmured a spell, and Horus's body stiffened as energy returned to him, re-creating his lost limbs. Isis hugged her restored son to her fiercely, tears of joy streaming down her cheeks.

When Aten looked at me, he nodded slightly, and last, he turned to Nephthys and dropped to one knee, holding up his hand. "Will you accept me, my queen?" he asked, raising hope-filled eyes to Nephthys.

She titled her head formally. "I will, my husband."

"And I will endeavor to win your heart and earn your loyalty."

"My heart is already yours."

Aten stood and took her hands as he searched her eyes. Understanding came to him quickly. "You gave Amun-Ra your heart scarab."

Nephthys nodded. "I did."

"Then I will offer you mine."

He drew forth his heart scarab, a beautiful stone swirled with gold and onyx. Nephthys took it and laid it against her breast. Within a moment, it was gone. Her eyes widened. "I . . . I feel you," she said.

"And I you, my love."

While the god of the cosmos and his wife learned of one another, I beat my wings, rising into the air to prepare for my next task.

31

Farewells

Hovering over the others, I cried out with the voice of the stars themselves, "Now it is time to heal the Waters of Chaos! Thoho. Tshamut. Come to me!"

The two snakes lifted their heads off the surface and rose into the air. Their long bodies stretched out, undulating on the waves of energy cast by the Waters of Chaos. "Thoho," I said. "I strike your name from the cosmos. I take your life energy and fashion you into something new. Tshamut! I strike your name from the cosmos. I take your life energy and fashion you into something new."

The bodies of the two snakes, like Amun-Ra's and Seth's, changed into pure energy. They wrapped around each other, biting and twisting until they settled.

"Now you will be called Tharu. Tharu, protector of the Waters of Chaos, embrace your new form and take your proper place long since abandoned."

A new snake materialized before me. This one was thicker of body. His scales winked blue, and his gleaming eyes were yellow. Opening his mouth, he hissed and then quickly sped to the edge of the Waters of Chaos. He circumnavigated the rim until he'd gone all the way around.

He then bit down on his own tail, completing the circle that would protect the waters. I caught a glimpse of the spider's shadow trailing in his wake.

Touching down on the surface of the waters, I said to the watching gods, "My work is complete. As a reward for my efforts on your behalf, I will create a new body for Ahmose, and he will become my companion as I traverse the cosmos exploring all of creation in my new form."

I placed the hairs I'd saved from Ahmose onto my palm, preparing to summon him and create his new body. "Wait," Horus said, rising to his feet, gingerly testing out his new limbs.

Pausing, I considered the expectant looks the gods were giving me. "What is it you desire of me further?" I asked them. "The Dark One is dead. I have restored order to the cosmos, as was my duty."

"We would ask you to return to us the ones who were lost," Horus answered, which surprised me. He'd been the least involved in the events of the day.

"Of whom do you speak?" I asked.

"The Sons of Egypt and the Daughters of Wasret."

"You know that I cannot save all of those that were lost. Some have been remade. This cannot be undone. Content yourself in knowing that, concerning the ones you speak of, their hearts are forever united in me."

"Then I would ask," Horus said, stepping forward, "how it is that you can take as your companion one whose heart is permanently bound to another?"

"He will have no choice but to love me, for I carry her heart within."

"It is a poor gift you take for yourself, then," he said. "It is but a shadow of love. I would offer, instead, for you to consider a companion you have been long separated from. One you have forgotten."

I sucked in a breath, my heart raced at his words. Pursing my lips, I asked, "Who is this you speak of?"

"Like Lilliana Young, the son of Isis and Osiris was born an adder stone. But the body of their young child was weak, for there was not enough energy in the Waters of Chaos to fashion another powerful god.

So Isis wove a spell. She gave a bit of herself and her husband to sustain the child. When she realized he would still perish despite her efforts, I reached out to her."

Nephthys moved closer to her sister and threaded her arm around Isis's waist.

"I made a proposition. One that was accepted. With the help of Isis, Osiris, and Nephthys, a spell was woven that allowed me to coexist with their son, inhabiting the same body. Through Horus I came into the light from the darkness. Like you, I came into being at a time when the cosmos needed me.

"It was I who distracted Seth for centuries so we could have time to prepare for the rise of the second adder stone, but he began to suspect more was at work than just his family being united against him. To protect me further, the knowledge of my true identity was purposely removed from my mind. It was hidden in the Eye and, for a time, Amun-Ra himself carried it.

"To distract Seth, Amun-Ra wove a complicated story where he promised the Eye to the winner of a great contest that lasted for years. When I won, Amun-Ra gave me a trinket, a token. But Seth became suspicious. He desired power and sought ways to steal our secrets. To protect it, the true Eye was hidden inside a Son of Egypt. Amon was imbued with enough power to carry the Eye, but its true nature was veiled from him.

"I've hidden in plain sight all this time, awaiting the hour of your arrival. So you see, Wasret, like you, I came into being with a borrowed body of flesh. But unlike you, I am now fully aware of who I am, for I've had a chance to study out my origins using the Eye of Horus, a power you might know better as the Eye of Re or the All-Seeing Eye."

I sucked in a breath. Horus's body took on a glow as he spoke. It was warm and familiar to me. He drew nearer and captured my hand. Our fingers locked together, and I stared at them, awestruck.

He continued, "The reason I felt bound to Lilliana Young, the reason I pursued her, was because a part of me could sense my life mate when she was near. What I am, the Eye that defines me, does not exist alone. There is a second Eye. Together, the two who wield them see all things. Can you name this Eye, Wasret? Can you name me? Look into my heart and see what I am. See *who* I am. Open your mind to me and know the good and the bad, the selfish and the selfless, and understand me."

Horus now held both of my hands in his. He brought them to his mouth and kissed both in succession. I looked deeply into his eyes, sinking beyond them, seeking the truth. There was something about him that was at once comforting and enticing. With my hands in his, I opened my thoughts, and a name rose to the surface. "You are . . . you are Nekheny."

Nodding, Horus smiled and pressed, "And who is Nekheny?"

"Nekheny is the consort of the one who wields the Wadjet Eye."

He squeezed my hands. "And who wields that power?"

"The one who wields that power is . . ." Suddenly, the energy coursing through me froze. "It is me," I said, marveling at the revelation that burst into my consciousness. "Wasret is the name mortals have given me, but my true name is Wadjet. The source of my power is the Wadjet Eye."

The knowledge of who I truly was gave me a ferocious strength, and I trembled at finally understanding my own origins.

Nekheny stroked my face, soothing the tremors coursing through my limbs.

"Come, my longtime companion," he said. "We must reacquaint ourselves with one another. I have much to teach you. But before we take our leave of the gods, they ask our help in restoring the others."

Thrilled with the revelation that I had a true companion of my own, I nodded. "I will do what I can."

I healed Anubis, who had given away much of himself while my companion healed his parents.

I took the hair I'd saved from Ahmose and summoned his life energy. It rose up before me, and together Nekheny and I fashioned him a new body and worked until all that he'd given away when he healed Lily's body was restored.

Anubis stepped forward then and bowed to the both of us, offering up hair in each of his hands. "These belonged to Asten and Amon," he said. "Hassan left a token for me from each boy just in case we lost one of their bodies again."

Raising my hand, I wove the spell for Amon while my companion did the same for Asten. When the young men took in their first breaths and their wandering shadows had merged with their true frames, I said, "I can fashion a new body identical to this one for Lily, but I cannot create bodies for Ashleigh or Tia since their mortal forms are long since gone. I will give you a choice. I can summon the energies of all three girls into one body once more, or I can summon only Lily. What do you wish me to do?"

Amon stepped forward. With no hesitation, he said, "Lily would want them with her."

"Then let it be as you say."

I pulled a hair from my own head and fashioned a new body, then called upon the life energies of Tia, Ashleigh, and Lily. Three bands of light rose from the Waters of Chaos and entered my twin. Lily blinked and staggered. Amon took her arm, and she nodded in gratitude. "What . . . what happened?" Lily said.

Interrupting her, eager to explore my new reality with my companion, I said, "We have done what we could." I drew out the six bound hearts and handed them to Lily, then offered her a smile. Nekheny kissed the cheeks of his mother and his aunt. "Mother?" he said and held out a hand to the woman who had given him life. "The price has been paid for the spell you cast in reviving your husband. There will be no more barriers between you and Osiris. Thank you for giving me a home and for gifting me with your love. But the time has come for me to leave you."

Isis wiped away a tear and hugged her son. "Go with my blessing and that of your father. No matter your origin, you will always be our son."

"And you will always be my mother."

With a final smile, we turned and together looked to the stars.

Latching on to a beam of light, we rose up into the cosmos to begin our new adventure.

"What? What just happened?" I asked.

Amon was about to speak when a man approached. One I'd never met. "Lily Young," he said. "I am Aten the sun god, the husband of Nephthys. If you will return to Heliopolis with us, we will explain all that has happened."

Soon the Waters of Chaos were far behind us, a bright place in a dark, starry field. I pressed myself against Amon's back and held on to him tightly. My wings were gone, my other powers along with them. Even my weapons had disappeared. Wadjet, who was now my—my what? Clone? Identical twin?—had taken them with her.

I attempted to engage Tia and Ashleigh in conversation, but the two of them were strangely quiet on the journey home. My body felt tight and uncomfortable. It was like I wasn't exactly me. It could have been the goddess gown I wore, I suppose. Strappy gold sandals aside, gauzy fabric wasn't really my thing. My hair had even been done up with curls hanging over each shoulder. I felt naked without my harness.

When we touched down, Aten, the new head god, ordered a feast, and while it was being prepared, he told me everything that had transpired. To say I was shocked was an understatement. I was glad I hadn't seen Amon and Ahmose die. It had been hard enough to see Asten's death. When Aten had told us all he could, he took Nephthys's hand and they left to see to the repairs of their city.

I slumped on a golden chaise, twisting my hands, unsure of what was going to happen to me now. Would Amon, Asten, and Ahmose go back to guarding the way of the afterlife? Could I visit them? The power of the sphinx had left me. Did that mean I could no longer see them?

Would I still be connected to Amon in dreams? Our hearts were knit together, that much I could feel, but there were so many unanswered questions.

The Sons of Egypt were called away in a conference with Aten and Nephthys. At the feast, Amon took my hand under the table, stroking little circles with his thumb that shot electric tingles through my body. Isis, Osiris, and Anubis were missing, but I figured Isis was mourning the loss of her son and tending to her husband. Apparently, Horus had seen to it that Osiris was healed completely, but it made sense that they wanted time to be alone together. They'd been apart for a long time. I had no idea where Anubis was. If I was going to be sent home, I would have preferred saying my farewells to him before I left.

When the feasting was over, the few remaining unicorns were summoned. Aten bent down to me and said, "I thought you'd like to do the honors before you journeyed home."

Furrowing my brow in puzzlement, I glanced at Amon, who just shrugged. He was as confused as I was. Aten praised the unicorns for their boldness in battle, their courage in the face of death, and the weighty sacrifice of their elders. He then declared that the curse on all unicorns was hereby lifted and they would be granted access to the afterlife. In his hands, sand swirled. It gleamed golden and sparkling and formed a perfect alicorn.

"Lily," he said, "if you would."

A beautiful unicorn stepped forward, her coat gleaming like bits of diamond were embedded within, approached me, head bowed. She knelt on one foreleg, her long mane shifting over one of her eyes.

My vision became watery as I thought of Nebu. I dashed my finger beneath my eyes. Approaching the unicorn, I carefully placed the horn in the center of her forehead while Aten chanted a spell. Light bloomed around the edges of the horn, and then it attached. At once, sparkling sand formed around the heads of each unicorn in the room and when it solidified, each one had a new horn. As one, they rose up, legs pawing the air, and whinnied in happiness.

The one before me lifted her head and smiled. *Thank you, Lily Young.*

"Zahra?" I gasped. "I didn't recognize you with your white coat."

All unicorns who sacrificed in the battle have earned this honor.

"It . . . it's beautiful," I said.

I smiled, but it was a sad one. She turned to leave, and Amon took my hand. I knew how much Nebu had wanted the curse lifted, and I was glad for his children that it had been. It was decided then that as a reward for their efforts, the Sons of Egypt would be given the gift of mortality if they wished it. I bit my lip as they spoke quietly among themselves. It was selfish of me to wish they would all return with me to the mortal world, but I couldn't imagine never seeing them again. Tia and Ashleigh were again very quiet, neither of them saying more than "Let us wait and see."

When they made their decision, they announced that Amon would take the gift of mortality and return with me to New York. Asten and Ahmose would remain as guardians of the afterlife to the new goddess they would soon be appointing to act in Ma'at's stead. My heart broke knowing I'd have to leave them behind, and I was keenly aware of the soft weeping in the back of my mind.

Aten placed his hands on Amon's shoulders, and I saw the moment when he took on mortality. He seemed to almost stagger beneath the weight of it, but he offered me a sweet smile. I knew that despite the fact that he no longer had powers, he was pleased with the gift. I was withholding judgment until everything was said and done.

Amon and I were given permission to accompany them to the afterlife. Since we were no longer immortal and weren't dead, there was no way for us to get there except to be taken by one of the gods. Nephthys volunteered. She placed one hand on my shoulder and another on Amon's. Ahmose and Asten were able to return to the afterlife on their own. I closed my eyes, and the five of us spun into sand.

I could feel every inch of me unraveling. When we were put back together, I stood in a familiar place, the Hall of Judgment. Running a hand across an arm of Ma'at's throne, I took in deep breaths, trying to temper the wild emotions I felt. A sob escaped as I turned to the three men behind me. My lip trembled, and it took me a moment to hear the soft voice speaking in my mind.

Ya hafta let us go, Ashleigh said.

"What?" I gasped out loud. "I don't understand what you're saying."

We have made our decision, Lily, Tia explained gently.

We don' belong in the mortal world, Ashleigh said. *Not anymore.*

Our wish is that you live your life unfettered, Tia added. *To stay would only cause confusion for you and sadness for us. It would be a kindness to let us depart on our own terms.*

"But . . . but where will you go?" I asked, tears leaking down my face.

Maybe we'll end up here in the afterlife, Ashleigh said.

But we are prepared if we do not, Tia said. *The outcome will not affect our decision.*

"They . . . ," I mumbled, stumbling over my words. "Ashleigh and Tia want to leave. Is this possible?" I asked Nephthys.

"Yes," she answered plainly. "If they wish to go, they simply relinquish their hold on you. Their minds will drift away from yours."

"Will they end up here?"

She hesitated. "I do not believe so. Since they were summoned directly from the Waters of Chaos, it is likely they will return to the same place."

My arms shook. "No," I said decisively. Disturbed by my quivering limbs, I folded them across my chest. "I won't allow it."

Sister, Tia said. When I didn't answer, she called my name softly. *Lily. We love you. You are family to us. But we must do what we feel is right. This is not your choice to make.*

"Please," I begged. "Don't do this."

Before we go, Ashleigh said, *will ya allow us ta say goodbye?*

I pressed a trembling hand to my mouth. Tears pooled at the corners of my eyes and dripped across my cheeks, creating wet, sticky trails. I could only nod in answer. Ashleigh understood and came forward as I stepped back and held on to Tia.

"Ahmose?" she said, holding out her hand.

"Ash?" he answered, then immediately wrapped her in his arms. "Are you sure?" he asked as he stroked her hair.

She nodded and smiled against his chest. *"It's for the best, love. Keep my heart with ya."* Ashleigh took her heart scarab, still linked to Ahmose's, and pressed them into his hands.

After they were secured in his chest, he put his hands on her face, cupping her cheeks. "I love you, Ash. Find your fairy tree and wait for me on the grassy hillside. If it's at all possible, I'll join you there."

"I'll wait for ya, my Ahmose. I'll look for your smile in the face o' the moon an' feel your touch in its beams."

Ahmose kissed her fiercely, desperately, and then collapsed to his knees, quiet sobs wrenching his large frame as he held on to her legs. *"Ah, my bonny lad,"* she said. *"Hush, now."* Ashleigh stroked the hair from his face. He lifted stormy gray eyes to hers. *"Give me one last brave smile."*

Ahmose nodded and attempted to do as she asked but managed only a sad twitch of his lips.

"Farewell, my lovely moon god," she said. There was a slight stirring of the air, and then Ashleigh was gone. I burst into torrential sobs and clung to Tia, but she shushed me and rose to the surface.

"Ashleigh has gone," she said. *"I would speak with Asten before I depart."*

Amon and Ahmose moved off to give Asten and Tia some privacy.

"Tia," Asten started, but she held up a hand, stopping him.

"I am not one for flowery words like my sisters," Tia said, *"but there is much I wished I'd said to you before I watched you die."* She lifted a fingertip and slowly stroked the length of one of his dark brows. *"Asten, you are more beautiful than the sunrise to me. You know who and what I am, and you have managed to love me. I did not regret giving up my form to embrace Lily,*

and if you will embrace me now"—she swallowed—*"I will not regret leaving you."*

Asten stepped close and draped his arms loosely around her waist. Pressing his forehead against hers, he said, "You might have no regrets about your leaving, but I will. I will think of you every day of my long life. Every time I look at the sun, I will see your golden eyes. In my dreams I will look for you and remember the time you asked me to kiss you. You may take your leave of me, but I will never take leave of you."

Tia lifted her head, her veins filling with heat, her heart throbbing. *"Of all men, you are my chosen mate. I will never have another. With all the energy I have left, I will long for you, Asten. Find me among the stars."*

Like Ashleigh, Tia broke apart the two hearts belonging to her and the man who held her and pressed them into his chest. *"Remember me, Tene,"* she said and pressed her lips to his.

Asten slanted his mouth against hers, gently at first, and then the kiss deepened, becoming sweeter and more heartfelt. When they broke apart, Asten said against her lips, "Always, Tiaret."

Then she was gone, and it was just me. Sobs continue to wrack my frame. I was vaguely aware of Asten passing me to Amon. He held me gently, stroking my neck as I watered his sleeve with my tears. When I was finally under control, Nephthys said, "Come, Lily, meet the new goddess of the afterlife before you depart."

She took me to a room where a woman was being fitted with new robes. Nephthys cleared her throat, and the woman turned. My mouth gaped open. "N . . . Nana?" I said, running to her and wrapping my arms around her waist.

"Lilypad," she said soothingly. "I'm glad to see you."

I lifted my head. "But . . . I don't understand. How can you be here?" I asked. "Only the dead or the immortal are allowed. And what does Nephthys mean by a goddess?"

"Well, I was brought here by the new ferryman." She looked up and smiled at someone behind me. "Here he is now."

I turned in her arms and saw a smiling Dr. Hassan. He was dressed the same way he'd always been with the exception of a new belt that housed the river sticks. "Docking was a bit tricky," he said. "I see you've met my new wife," he added with a twinkle in his eye.

"Wife?" I gaped at him and turned back to my grandmother.

She smiled serenely and cupped my chin. "Now, Lilypad, I expect you'll take care of Bossy and bake the twins their cakes on their birthdays. And from time to time, will you visit your granddaddy's grave and tend to his flowers?"

"Yes, but—"

She interrupted me and kissed my forehead, putting her hands on my shoulders. "There's a lot of work to be done. I imagine the two of us will be busy," she said, offering her new husband a smile. "By the way," she added, "I like your Amon. He's got a very strong chin." Tilting her head in Amon's direction, she gave me a wink.

"I, I," I stammered, "I guess Dr. Hassan does, too."

"That he does," Nana said with a soft laugh.

"It's taken care of," a new voice said from behind me.

"Anubis?" I whirled around. He nodded to me deferentially, a surprising gesture from the surly god I'd once known. "The remains of your grandmother and Dr. Hassan are entombed in the place they guarded," he said, "should you wish to visit them. Their sarcophagi lie next to those of Asten's, Ahmose's, and Amon's former bodies."

"Re . . . remains?" I said, horror creeping into my voice.

"Now, Lilypad," my grandmother said, "Aten and Nephthys need more help. They offered us a chance to do just that. You know that neither of us had many years left. Now we'll have centuries to be together and learn everything we can about each other. As the ferryman, Oscar will be able to visit me frequently. What better person can you think of to help the dead transition?"

"He . . . he's a good choice," I admitted. "But what about . . ."

"You'll have your Amon. I've left you the farm. You can sell it or give it to the twins. Do what you want with it."

My lip quivered. "But . . . Nana . . ."

She tugged me close. "Ah, Lily," she said. "I know your heart's hurting. Mine stings a bit, too. But I'll see you again. Maybe there's even a chance that crafty Anubis will let you hitch a ride from time to time to visit." She wiped away my tears with her thumbs. "Now you head off and have a happy life. I'll see you again."

"But how?"

"That Asten of yours promised to let me visit you in dreams. I imagine I can take the young man at his word. Now you get going, I've apparently got a lot of work that needs doing."

She kissed me softly on the cheek, and then Nana was rushed away, being trailed by a large group of servants. Apparently, the line for judgment was very, very long.

"Are you ready, then?" Dr. Hassan asked, placing his beloved fedora on his head. "I'm to take you back to the mortal realm."

I nodded brokenly and tried to offer him a smile. I felt as out of place as a chicken in an eagle's nest. Ahmose and Asten each hugged me, the former lifting me off my feet and kissing my forehead and the later cupping my neck and quickly kissing my cheek. They tried to put on brave faces, but I knew they were hurting, deeply. Soberly, they said goodbye to Amon.

He gripped each of their arms. "In death and in life, Asten. In death and in life, Ahmose."

"In death and in life," they repeated.

"We will watch over you," Ahmose said.

"And we will guard your way to the afterlife," Asten echoed.

Before I knew what was happening, we were following Hassan to the pristine deck of a brand-new ship.

"It's lovely," I said, a twinge of sadness tempering my enthusiasm as I thought of Cherty and *Mesektet*. "What do you call her?" I asked.

"I call her *Hatshepsut*," he said with a grin. "Anubis said that upon my next return he will try to arrange a visit with Hatshepsut—the pharaoh herself! Imagine. Me being able to meet the one I spent a lifetime researching! Oh, I'll have to start making a list of questions."

I smiled at him softly. He was clearly pleased with his lot. As much as I would miss him—both him and Nana—I couldn't deny them this happiness.

"Cast off!" Oscar cried out, and we were soon adrift on the Waters of Chaos. Amon and I stood off to the side, waving to Nephthys, Anubis, Asten, and Ahmose until we could no longer see them. Then I slid down to the deck, Amon right next to me. He cupped my hand in his and traced the lines. "Palm to palm, we risk together, we live together, and, now we will die together." Amon wrapped his arm around my body and held me close as we sailed into a rising sun.

EPILOGUE

Matriarch

I must have slept on the boat for a long time, because when I woke, it was in the bed at my grandmother's farm. Amon sat in a wicker chair nearby, his feet crossed where he'd propped them up next to me, his head nodding in sleep. He stirred when I threw back the covers.

"Lily?" he asked. "How do you feel?"

"Wrung out and hung on Nana's line to dry."

"Me too," he said, scratching the side of his neck.

"How long have we been here?" I asked.

"Hassan dropped us off last night. I carried you inside. Before he left, he gave me this bag full of papers and pictures."

"Can I see it?" I asked.

He handed me the bag, and inside I found a birth certificate, a passport, a driver's license, school records, and citizenship papers to several countries, including Egypt. Along with this was a list of accounts from banks around the world. I gasped when his beloved archaeology tools fell onto the bed as well.

We'd been on the farm for a week, figuring out a way to tell my parents how I'd met a handsome Egyptian boy in Iowa, when I had the dream. The moon was casting its light over the bed, and I breathed rapidly and sat up. Amon's voice steadied me. "What is it?" he asked.

"Asten, I think. He showed me a dream."

I spent the next hour describing what I'd seen. Isis and Nephthys summoned the great gods who'd brought the cosmos into alignment, and Wasret and Nekheny appeared with contented smiles. Nekheny greeted his mother warmly. "What may we do for you?" he'd asked.

"Osiris and I have searched the netherworld. With the Devourer gone, we were able to compel the hellhounds to aid us. The reapers offered their help as well."

"Yes?" Wasret said patiently.

"We've found her hair," she said excitedly. "A few strands of it were caught in the bark of the burned fairy tree." Isis gave the red strands to Nekheny.

"And I have brought you the remains of a stillborn Egyptian girl," Osiris said, placing a tiny wrapped figure on the ground. "I have searched the afterlife and have not found her. I thought, perhaps, you could refashion her."

Wasret and Nekheny looked at one another and then came to an agreement. "We will do as you ask," they said in unison.

They took the offerings and reappeared on the surface of the Waters of Chaos. Then they wove a spell and said, "Tiaret, we summon your life force and fashion a new form for you from the body of one that never lived. Ashleigh, we summon your life force and bid you enter your new form."

Light coalesced and rose from the newly expanded Waters of Chaos. The snake Tharu looked on curiously as they worked. When the two women opened their eyes, they looked upon one another and smiled widely, falling into each other's arms and laughing. The gods escorted them to the afterlife and secreted them in the Hall of Judgment. When the guardians were summoned, Wasret asked them if they still held the heart scarabs they'd been entrusted with. Nodding, they pulled them from their chests and were astonished to feel the beating hearts of the ones they loved. The newly fashioned girls were then reunited with the men who held their hearts.

Ahmose wrapped his arms around a lovely woman with curly red hair that hung down to her waist. Her nose had a dusting of freckles, and her green dress brought out the sparkle of green in her laughing eyes. Behind her, two diaphanous wings quivered with excitement.

After their embrace, Ahmose and Ashleigh turned to the goddess.

Wasret said, "Ashleigh, you have been fashioned anew. You will henceforth be called Luna, the wife of the moon god. Let your new name be engraved upon your heart. Together you will be unified in your desire to serve the cosmos. Your role will be the cultivator of new realms and the guardian of the eastern horizon. You will be granted the power with your companion to walk the Path of Yesterdays and Tomorrows. As this is your desire, the bond between you is now unbreakable, like that of Isis and Osiris. Nothing will part you from this moment on."

Asten came forward then with a gorgeous princess. She walked with confident steps on long legs that stretched for miles and held her head high and proud. Her skin was smooth and dark. The lines of her cheekbones and jaw were prominent, and her mouth and figure were curvy and lush. Around her slim neck hung a thick necklace of burnished bronze. She was a true goddess. When she looked at Asten she gave him a sly smile, her golden eyes twinkling as she tilted her head toward him. A corner of her mouth lifted as he whispered something in her ear.

"Tiaret," Nekheny said, "henceforth you will be called Naledi, the wife of the god of the stars."

Asten murmured softly, "My little star."

"Hush, Asten," the woman said low but with a happy smile.

The voice was slightly different from the one I remembered, but looking at the woman, I could easily see the lioness staring back at me.

Even if it weren't for the mass of tawny curls that framed her lovely face like a golden halo, I'd know it was Tia. The only thing missing was the twitching tail.

"Let your new name be engraved upon your heart. Your role will be huntress of the sky. Guardian of the western horizon. You, with your companion, will be granted the ability to walk the Path of Yesterdays and Tomorrows. As this is your desire, the bond between you is now unbreakable, like that of Isis and Osiris. Nothing will part you from this moment on."

"I'm not much of a huntress without claws," the lioness goddess said boldly.

Wasret smiled. "Then perhaps you will have more use of these than I." She pulled the spear-knives from over her back and handed them to Tia. The lioness-turned-goddess ran her hand over them, practically purring her contentment.

"We have done for you what we could," Wasret said, "and hope that you will find happiness. Just one thing remains before we take our leave of you."

The four gods looked at one another in confusion.

Nekheny smiled at them. "Though you have no further need to align the sun, the moon, and the stars, your new powers grant you the ability to leave your duties in the afterlife when there is a lull in your work. Should you choose to visit the mortal realm, or any other realm in the cosmos you desire, you may do so, but you might on occasion have need for the aid of a mortal to serve as your guide during your sojourns on Earth.

"There is a precedent to call a chief vizier to serve. We have selected one." Nekheny turned in my dream and looked right at me. "Amon, you are henceforth called to serve the gods as the chief vizier of a new order called the Priests of Aten. We grant you the knowledge required to do so, and you will be known to us by your true name, Amset. You will be granted the powers that come with the office, including the ability to work spells, enhanced insight into the working of the cosmos, a sensitivity toward the supernatural, and long life. Your duties will include tending to the business of the gods and providing mortal nourishment and aid as is fitting to the gods who visit your realm.

"Lily Young," he continued, "you are hereby called to serve as matriarch of the Order of the Sphinx. Henceforth, you will be known as Nebthet the mythical goddess. You will be granted the powers that come with that office, including enhanced physical strength, sight, hearing, and long life. You are entrusted with the arrows of Isis to use as you see fit, and you will serve alongside your husband and companion, the chief vizier. You are the first wife of Amun spoken of.

"As this is your desire, and despite the fact that you are mortal, the bond between the two of you is now unbreakable, like that of Isis and Osiris. Nothing will part you from this moment on. We honor you and gift you with the Jewels of She Who Defeated the Sphinx. You have set eyes upon this treasure before. It is hidden in the temple where you first met Isis. You are also heiress to the golden room hidden in the temple of Hatshepsut. Summon the ferryman, and he will further instruct you in its location." He flipped me a golden coin, one that looked very familiar. I caught it in my hand and turned it over. The only difference was in the hat the boatman wore.

"After he said that, I woke up," I said to Amon. "Do you think it was real?"

"I think it was," he said. Taking my hand, he pressed it to his lips and then dropped a golden coin onto my palm and wrapped my fingers around it. "I found this on your pillow," he said.

"Amset," I said. "Your true name. It's the word you whispered to me in the pyramid when you gave me your heart scarab."

"Yes. The Eye gave me my true name long before the gods bestowed it on me."

"And you trusted me with it? Osiris told me not even Isis knows his true name."

"Osiris lied," Amon said. "Both he and his wife exchanged true names when they traded hearts. It was a requisite part of the spell. I know because I watched it happen through the Eye. Besides, I would trust you with anything, Young Lily," he said, tucking a strand of hair behind my ear. "You know, I had a dream as well."

"And what was that?" I asked, wrapping my arms around his neck and scooting closer to him. I felt the thump of his heart scarab in my chest and knew we were reacting to each other in the same way.

Amon pulled me onto his lap, arms locked around my waist, and bent down, teasing my lips with a soft kiss. When I was breathless, he lifted his head. "In my dream, a unicorn we both know nudged my shoulder."

I gasped. "Nebu?" I asked.

Amon nodded. "He was in the afterlife. A beautiful princess sat on his back, and he shook out his mane proudly as he pranced, showing her off, his alicorn shining as he turned. As he galloped off over the hills, he said, "The secret prayer of your mother has finally been answered, Amon. You found what all of us seek." Then he turned to gallop off and called out behind him, 'You still owe me a boon.'"

We laughed together, and Amon captured my lips again.

When we broke apart, I asked, "What was your mother's secret wish? That you would be mortal again?"

Amon shook his head. "She wanted me to find love. To be happy."

"And are you?" I asked, teasing him.

He tilted his head, as if seriously contemplating the question. "I'd be happier if we had some round pastries filled with sugared fruits." When I punched his arm, he sobered. "Are you happy, Nehabet?"

"Are you kidding? I've been given the sun." He kissed me tenderly, and we were soon so lost in one another, we didn't even hear the cry of the bird calling out to her companion from the roof of the farmhouse.

If we had bothered to look, we would have seen a bird of prey, a kite, rise into the air, where she was met by a benu bird. The two of them flew off toward the horizon, their bodies framed in the light of the setting moon.

ACKNOWLEDGMENTS

I've reached the end of a series. It's a thrilling moment to have an entire story arc come together. My cast of characters can now move on in their unseen lives and have new adventures.

Just like a story, a series can't be produced without a bunch of characters. Each one adds new dimension and expertise, whether that's design, editing, formatting, or marketing.

I wish every member of this cast could step forward and take a bow, because they all did a wonderful job. The people who worked on this series were editor Krista Vitola; copy editors Heather Lockwood Hughes, Carrie Andrews, Janet Rosenberg, and Colleen Fellingham; Angela Carlino; Chris Saunders; Mary McCue; and Hannah Black.

I'd also like to thank my agent, Robert Gottlieb, and everyone else at Trident Media Group who have worked hard to get this series into the hands of my fans worldwide.

Thanks to my family, who help me out on tour, talk to fans on email, manage my website, go with me to conventions, and lend a listening ear. Thanks especially to my mom, Kathy, who stuffs all my swag bags and faithfully attends every event I do. And I'm always grateful for the steady presence of my husband, Brad, who stayed up until three a.m. with me so I could finish this book.

I couldn't do it without all of you!

WANT MORE?

If you enjoyed this and would like to find out about similar books we publish, we'd love you to join our online SF, Fantasy and Horror community, Hodderscape.

Visit our blog site
www.hodderscape.co.uk

Follow us on Twitter
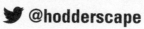 **@hodderscape**

Like our Facebook page
Hodderscape

You'll find exclusive content from our authors, news, competitions and general musings, so feel free to comment, contribute or just keep an eye on what we are up to. See you there!

WANT MORE?